Whenever the Fat Man appeared either in dreams or in my conscious reality, he was usually bringing me a warning.

Artwork by Elizabeth Smily, FFCA, CIPA

The Chef Who Died Sautéing

THE FIRST ARIEL QUIGLEY MYSTERY

To Donna— Happy Sleuthing!
Honora Finkelstein
Susan Smily

HONORA FINKELSTEIN
& SUSAN SMILY

HILLIARD   HARRIS

P.O. Box 275
Boonsboro, Maryland 21713-0275

This novel is a work of fiction. Names, characters, places and incidents either are the product of the author's imagination or are used fictitiously. Any resemblance to actual persons, living or dead, events, or locales is entirely coincidental.

The Chef Who Died Sautéing Copyright © 2006
By Honora Finkelstein & Susan Smily

All rights reserved. No part of this book may be reproduced or transmitted in any form or by any means, electronic or mechanical, including photocopying, recording, or by any information storage and retrieval system, without the written permission of the Publisher, except where permitted by law.

First Edition-June 2006
ISBN 1-59133-160-9

Frontispiece by Elizabeth Smily

Book Design: S. A. Reilly
Cover Illustration © S. A. Reilly
Manufactured/Printed in the United States of America
2006

We dedicate this book to our mothers and fathers, three of whom are friendly ghosts: the late Bea and Stanley Moore and Powell Smily, and to Elizabeth Smily, who is still going strong.

We also dedicate it to Honora's husband, Jay Finkelstein, who has so generously supported us in our work.

Acknowledgements:

We would like to acknowledge the following people, without whose input this book would not be as rich as it is:

The Alexandria Police Department, for their generosity with time and information in assisting us with police procedurals. We would particularly like to thank Lieutenant John Crawford, Public Information Office; Amy Bertsch, Public Information Officer, who not only gave us information but actually copyedited a draft of this book; Sergeant John Gregg, who drove us all over Alexandria; and Charlie Bailey, Commander of the Identification Section, who helped us with what to look for at murder crime scenes. Also, Thomas Durkin, for encouragement.

Rex Tomb, Federal Bureau of Investigation, Fugitive Information Section, for information on the FBI.

Nelson Greene, Greene Funeral Home, and James Klick, Bethel Cemetery, Alexandria, Virginia, for permission to use the funeral home and the cemetery in this novel.

Tom Broyles, Alexandria Alcohol Beverage Control, for information on the legal intricacies of alcohol sales.

Susan (who could not reveal her last name) at the Veterans Administration, for information on the G.I. Bill dating back through the 1990s.

Ernie Jones at the Rock—Allegany County Speedway, Cumberland, Maryland, for information on stock car racing and the race track.

The producers of the 1st Annual Ghost Conference of Tulsa, Oklahoma, October, 2003.

The Monroe Institute for its Lifeline program, which showed us how to make contact with the other side in new and provocative ways.

Steve Doss, whose ghost tours, "Footsteps to the Past," gave us a wealth of information on Alexandria's ghosts.

The late George Camdem, former Shakespeare specialist at Rice University, whose class notes on Shakespeare's ghosts we are still using.

Many shop owners in Old Town Alexandria, and in particular the personnel at the Virginia Shoppe, who gave us information on the damage caused by Hurricane Isabel.

Our generous reviewers and readers, who included Amy Bertsch, Pat Carr, Celinda Reynolds Kaelin, Dianne Eppler Adams, Christine Knight, Donna Welsch, Dar Miller, Jay Finkelstein, Bridget Ingram, Aileen McCulloch, Kathleen and Dave Phillips, Sean Ingram, and Amber Wardwell Finkelstein—special thanks for all your help in making this book better.

Our agent Ming Russell, of Waterside Productions, Inc., who helped us refine the book to fit the genre, and Stephanie and Shawn Reilly, our publisher and editor at Hilliard and Harris Publishers, who have said, "Yes!" to its publication.

Prologue

THURSDAY, SEPTEMBER 5TH
MARTIN LUTHER KING, JR. MEMORIAL LIBRARY, WASHINGTON, D.C.

"YOU DISGUSTING PERVERT!" shouted a woman's voice from behind the vertical files. A piercing scream instantly followed the words.

Dennis Walker and Joel Abrams looked at each other wide-eyed and jumped up from the table in the center of the history section where they had been doing research.

"It's got to be the flasher!" Dennis took off toward the stacks in the direction of the scream, with Joel hot on his heels.

They knew there had been some episodes in that library with an exhibitionist—the guy was jumping out of the stacks and showing his willie to unsuspecting women. But he had always managed to elude the security staff and get out of the building before anyone could catch him.

They followed the scream to its source—an elderly woman being held by a young companion, who pointed down the aisle between tall shelves of books.

"The freak went down there and turned right," she said, as the elderly woman continued to scream like a police siren.

Dennis and Joel ran off in the direction the woman had indicated, following the sound of thudding footsteps on the carpeted floor. They saw the man dart out the exit doors and down the hall to the opposite side of the building. He went right past the elevators and into the literature section of the library. A group of women sitting in a circle of chairs in the foyer reading poetry to each other looked up and turned their heads to watch the chase. They stared openmouthed at the flasher with his raincoat flapping around his skinny, naked legs.

Joel shouted, "You take this door, and I'll take the one over there. He won't get away this time!"

As Dennis ran into the room, the flasher turned between the card catalogue and a row of tall service desks. Dennis moved in behind him, and Joel appeared at the opposite end. The flasher pulled to a stop, realizing he had no place left to run.

He turned to Dennis, laughing and holding his raincoat wide open. "Okay, you caught me! Do you wanna cuff it?"

Joel got out his cell phone and called 9-1-1, while Dennis held his arms outstretched to block the passageway. People began getting up from the tables in the center of the room and gathering to see what the commotion was about, and Dennis turned his head slightly to ask for help.

"Someone see if we can get security up here," he said.

Just at that moment, the flasher lunged at Dennis, slamming him hard in the chest.

Dennis stumbled backward and fell, cracking his head against the corner of one of the tall desks and collapsing onto the floor. The flasher jumped lightly over his body, but two other men grabbed him and held him.

Joel bent over Dennis. Blood was seeping out from the back of his head.

"Ariel," Dennis whispered. Then his head rolled slightly to the side, and his eyes glazed over.

"Oh, my God!" Joel said, turning to look at the flasher. "You've killed him!"

Chapter One

Friday, September 5th, One Year Later

I HAD THE kettle in my hand and was turning toward the counter where a Mikasa teapot and cups sat on a Delft-tile tray.

"Don't step on the cat!" Bernice shouted.

Suddenly there was a squeal and a blur of fur, and I went tush over teakettle and found myself sitting on my keester in the middle of the kitchen floor.

"Too late," I muttered.

MY NAME IS Ariel Quigley, and my life changed the day I tripped over that cat. Bernice Wise, whose cat had just spooked me, is a fifty-five-year-old Jungian psychologist who runs a private practice out of her sprawling eighteenth century Colonial-style home in Alexandria, Virginia. She's also a student in one of my evening poetry classes. In fact, in the past year she'd signed up for the class two sessions in a row. From listening to her poetry in the classroom, I'd been impressed with her sense of humor and her practical wisdom. She was also earthy and gregarious—just fun to be around—and we were beginning to develop a friendship. So she had invited me for tea, to be followed by dinner at a local restaurant where I would be her guest.

And there I sat, my eye position almost exactly level with her knees, and my life about to change in ways I had never imagined.

Bernice laughed and rescued me from my position on the floor. "I should have warned you—Freud the Cat is *always* underfoot. While I refill the kettle, why don't you go into the pantry and grab a box of cookies?"

The cat, a tabby-point Siamese, had skittered away after our encounter, but as I walked into the pantry, I saw her hiding under a shelf, from where she silently glared at me.

"I'm sorry," I said, apologizing to her. "I didn't see you. I mean, how could I have done it on purpose? I don't even know you."

The cat sniffed and backed away, slowly edging her way out of the room, eyeballing me as she went to be sure I didn't make any sudden moves.

"I'm *really* sorry," I called after her.

Bernice answered from the kitchen stove, "If that's about the kettle, don't worry. Hardly anything spilled. If it's to the world in general, I would guess you're either Catholic or Jewish."

"Oh, I just don't want the cat to be mad at me," I called back. "I'm feeling a little bit down today, and having a cat mad at you is kind of like making a teddy bear mad. Pets and stuffed animals are supposed to be supportive."

"Don't worry," Bernice answered. "She'll probably forget it by the time we've finished our tea."

I eyeballed a shelf with about fifteen different varieties of fancy cookies. Somewhat overwhelmed by the choices, I slipped into a sort of daze.

Suddenly, I felt a hand on my shoulder, and I jumped straight up in the air.

"Yikes!" I shouted. I turned to see who had come in behind me, but there was no one there. I felt the hair on my neck bristle. I wondered what Bernice would think of me if I told her she had a ghost in her pantry.

"What was the yell?" I heard Bernice ask.

I snatched a box of cookies off the shelf at random and stepped back into the kitchen just as she was setting the tray on the table. "Did the cat spook you again?"

"No-o-o," I said, "not exactly."

She looked at me with eyebrows raised, but when I didn't elaborate, she sat down and motioned for me to do the same. Then she poured tea into the two cups. "So, why are you feeling down today?"

I handed her the cookies. "Well, I realized when I woke up this morning it's been exactly one year since my fiancé, Dennis, died."

"Oh, my goodness! That certainly could make you feel depressed. Anniversaries are very powerful times." She passed me a cup of tea and pushed the cream and sugar in my direction. "I don't think you ever mentioned having a fiancé before."

"No, I guess I didn't. When Dennis died, I really didn't want to talk to anybody about it, so I sort of buried it. But it's surfaced in the past few days."

"Do you want to talk about it now?" Bernice asked as she piled a large number of cookies on a plate and placed it between us. "His death must have been pretty traumatic."

"It really was because it was so sudden and so stupid. One minute he was in the library doing research, and the next he was lying on the floor with an enormous dent in the back of his head." I described the details of Dennis's experience with the flasher who had killed him.

"Oh, my," said Bernice when I'd finished. "You know, I once had a librarian tell me that libraries are hotbeds of autoerotic sexual activity."

I nodded. "I'm not sure why, exactly, but I can believe that. I mean, didn't Marian the librarian in *The Music Man* have a reputation in town, just because she read Balzac?"

I nibbled a cookie. Then my eyes got hot and I blinked to control the threat of tears. "Dennis's friend Joel told me the last word Dennis said before he died was my name."

Bernice pushed a box of tissues in my direction.

"I felt so guilty," I continued. "I had just that week pretty much decided I wasn't going to marry him. Then I heard he'd died with my name on his lips, and...well, I..." I sniffed.

Bernice looked at me sympathetically. "So you didn't really have closure on the end of the relationship."

I took a deep breath and let it out slowly, looking at Bernice and trying to decide if I should tell her the whole truth. I thought of the hand I'd felt on my shoulder in her pantry. It seemed to me a lot of ghosts were surfacing today.

"Well, in a way, I guess I did," I said softly and sighed again. "You see, Dennis visited me regularly for a couple of weeks after his death."

"What do you mean, he visited you?"

I breathed again, then said, "I'm like the little kid in *The Sixth Sense*. Sometimes I see dead people—or I hear them or feel them or otherwise sense them. It sort of runs in my family, at least among the women. My mom and my sisters have also had a few contacts with paranormal phenomena. Anyway, Dennis came by, usually at about two o'clock in the morning, to assure me that he was all right. And then one night he suddenly said, 'I'm okay, and you're okay. So it's time for me to move on now,'—and he was gone." I blew my nose.

"You see ghosts," Bernice said slowly.

"Yes," I said. Then with trepidation, I added, "And you have one in your pantry."

"Ah." She paused thoughtfully. I wondered if she was about to brand me as a nutcase. "That was the source of your 'Yikes!'" After a couple of beats while she seemed to be considering what to say, she finally confessed, "It keeps knocking spices out of my hands. It's a real food critic! Do you think you might help me with it?"

I laughed in relief. "So you know about your ghost."

"Oh-h-h, yes! It usually appears when I'm preparing meals," Bernice explained. "If you happen to come around some evening when I'm cooking, you might catch it in action."

"Do you know anything about the source of your ghost?" I asked. "Every ghost story is a mystery, waiting to be solved, you know."

"No, I don't. But I can see that," she said, narrowing her eyes and thoughtfully nodding her head. "Now I'm curious. Have you solved many ghost mysteries? And how long have you had the ability to see and hear ghosts? Do they all talk to you?"

I laughed at the barrage of questions. "My mom says I'm fey because I'm Manx. My dad says it's because I'm Irish. In either case, it's Celtic, and it's genetic.

"But with respect to ghosts, I first remember seeing one when I was about five. I was having a bubble bath when a big guy in a tuxedo waltzed into the bathroom—literally. He was heavy but very handsome, with a trim moustache and a walking stick, and he was wearing a little porkpie hat. He looked like an extra out of the 1930s *Thin Man* movies. He paused, shook his head, put a finger to his lips, and held up a sign that said *Sh-h-h*. Then he waltzed out again. I figured the sign meant don't tell anybody, so for a long time I didn't."

"Were you scared?" asked Bernice.

"Not really, because he just seemed like a normal person. He appeared lots of times when I was a kid, usually while I was having my bubble bath. Probably I was susceptible then because I was relaxed. Anyway, the Fat Man would dance in and hold up a sign with some kind of clue or warning, and I realized he was like a guardian.

"When I finally told my Mom about seeing him, she took it in stride. She just said, 'That's nice, dear.' And later she told my dad that I had an invisible friend, although strictly speaking, that wasn't true because he was visible to *me*. But once I'd told my sisters about it, they would burst into the bathroom when I was in the bath and shout, 'Where is he? Where is he? We want to see him, too.' And that was the end of his bath-time visits. I guess that's the reason he'd told me not to tell anyone."

"So you don't see him anymore?"

"Yes, I do, but differently. I started having *dreams* in which he appeared to me, holding up signs. Once when I was in high school, the sign said, *Guard your words*. The next day during a Spanish exam, I realized someone was trying to copy my answers! But the messages are usually cryptic, and I don't always clue in to what they mean until after the fact."

"Do you have any idea who he is? I mean, you said he was a ghost."

"My folks found out that a guy had suffered cardiac arrest during a big party in the house where we were living—hence the tux he was wearing. That's when I first realized every ghost has a *story* attached to it—a history, a puzzle. And I like solving puzzles—I used to be a big Nancy Drew fan when I was a kid.

"Anyway, as I've learned more about the world of ghosts, I've come to understand they don't exist in quite the same timeframe or dimension we do. Some of them interact with people, but others just replay some kind of three-dimensional holographic videotape, recycling the event preceding or including their deaths. We can assist them in moving on if we can connect with them, hear their stories, and help them resolve whatever issues are holding them here."

"You sound like a ghost psychologist!"

"Yeah, maybe I am. Unfortunately, ghosts don't pay in hard currency."

Bernice grinned. "But, tell me, what about your Fat Man ghost? Is he still hanging around? Why haven't you tried to help *him* move on?" Then she added humorously, "Especially if you're not on a weekly retainer."

I laughed. "Well, sometimes ghosts can attach themselves to the people who are currently living in a space, as this ghost seems to have done with me, and act as protectors for the living. I once asked him why he hangs around. He just tipped his porkpie hat and held up a sign that said, *2 cents.* So I figured he hangs around to give me advice.

"Anyway," I said, making a palms-up shrugging motion, "there aren't any rules when it comes to ghosts."

Bernice stirred her tea thoughtfully and shifted gears. "So when and where did you meet Dennis?" she asked. "You said in class once you were in the military. Was he in the service, too?"

"No, I met him later, in school, after I got out of the service."

"When was that?"

"I enlisted in the Army in eighty-nine, right out of high school. When I mustered out in ninety-three, I used my GI bill along with a few scholarships and grants to get my education. My dad, who was also army, was posted to Fort Meade while I was overseas, and my parents were living in Laurel, Maryland. So I decided to go to the University of Maryland. Dennis and I met there in ninety-seven. He was already in graduate school, studying public policy at the Maryland School of Public Affairs. I was in my senior year, but I was two years older than he was.

"We fell for each other—literally—in the school library. I was walking up the stairs with an armload of books, and he was coming down. Just as we both got to the landing, I stubbed my toe on a stair and did a half gainer like the one you saw me do in the kitchen, and I fell at his feet, books flying in all directions. As he bent to help me, I moved to sit up and cracked him on the chin with my head, and he sprawled backwards, too. So there we lay in a puddle of books, both looking sheepish and silly after the multiple pratfalls, and he said, 'This meeting must be fate. You want to go out?'

"He was my first really serious boyfriend. I'd had a few sexual experiments in the army, but nothing that stuck."

"You were together for quite a while, then."

"Yeah, we dated for a year while we finished our respective degrees. Then I found myself with a handful of scholarships and stayed on to get my Ph.D., and he got a job in D.C., so we continued to date, and it just seemed like it was going to turn into a marriage. But then when I completed my degree two years ago and got a part-time teaching job at George Mason, we moved in together in a place in Fairfax, and it was like we couldn't fit in the same space. Just before his fatal accident, I'd been thinking one of us should probably move out."

I got a little misty again and reached for another tissue.

"It just didn't work. And the whole situation seems sad." I blew my nose. "And to add to my confusion over his death, sometimes while I'm thinking about him, I suddenly get a wild visual of the last thing Dennis must have seen as he went down, this guy with his raincoat open, flashing him, and I laugh until I'm hysterical, and then I cry until I have no tears left." I sighed heavily.

"So that's it," I said. "I'm feeling guilty and sorry for myself. I guess I've still got issues. He was such a great guy, so why was I dissatisfied? I was gearing up to talk to him about the relationship, and then he had his fatal accident. And when he came back and visited afterward, I know it was partly to absolve *me* from feeling any guilt."

Bernice nodded and asked, "So why *are* you still feeling guilty?"

I leaned back and sighed, realizing it was confession time. "Because I was wishing there was some way the situation would resolve itself without my having to take action and tell him goodbye. And then suddenly it *was* resolved." This time the tears did start to flow.

Bernice nudged the box of tissues closer to me. "You didn't kill him, my dear. The flasher was *not* an agent of your thoughts."

"I wish I could believe that," I sniffed. "But I couldn't even bring myself to go to his arraignment or sentencing. Joel did, but I just couldn't. I was almost afraid he'd turn and smile and give me a thumbs up."

Bernice leaned toward me and held my eyes with hers. "I'll grant that sometimes not taking action is a form of action. But wishing you could win the lottery and then not buying a ticket just means you aren't ready for the responsibility of having to figure out what to do with the money if you were to win it. When you were in the army, did they train you to just follow orders, or did they also teach you to take responsibility for your choices?"

"Both," I said. "When there were choices to be made, there were protocols to follow, and our training emphasized the protocols were there to help us be sure our actions were responsible and rational, so that if a crisis arose, we'd be able to act quickly, automatically, rationally, *and* responsibly."

Bernice nodded. "But life doesn't always present us with situations where the action—or the responsibility—is ours to take. So could it be that you're fixed on a crisis of responsibility in a situation that isn't rational? I mean, the responsibility isn't yours to claim. You didn't take action to get rid of Dennis—you didn't pray, you didn't write affirmations, you didn't push Dennis against a sharp corner.

"The flasher, on the other hand, was irrational and irresponsible. Clearly, he was over the edge by virtue of the fact that he was flashing people. He was incapable of thinking through any possible consequences of his actions. So what will it take for you to stop trying to make his actions rational and let *him* go?"

Her question brought me up short. "Oh, my God!" I exclaimed. "I think I get it! I've been caught by the irrationality of Dennis's crazy, accidental death at the hands of a crazy, irrational man, and I've been trying to make it rational by taking the blame."

Bernice smiled.

I felt a sense of relief. "You know, I've been so conflicted. Part of me wants to get on with life. I'm thirty-two years old, single, with a loudly ticking biological clock, and a very large chunk of me is ready to start looking for a new romance. I have three younger sisters, and two of them are married. In fact, one of them's already a mother of three preschoolers. And here I am, the old maid in the family. But every time this past year when I've thought about getting romantically involved with someone, I've remembered Dennis and felt disloyal. I haven't been able to shake the sense that it's not okay to want another relationship."

Bernice cocked her head. "There's one other thing you might consider. Maybe Dennis came back to tell you he was okay because he wanted you to be able to keep on living—to experience those things in life that he couldn't. It was a gift he really wanted you to have. So when are you going to accept it?"

I shrugged my shoulders and threw my hands up in the air. "Maybe what I really want is for some authority figure to give me permission to start looking. Where's a top sergeant when you need one?"

Bernice laughed. "All right then. By the power vested in me by the Commonwealth of Virginia and the American Psychological Association, I give you permission. Do you want a hall pass?"

I tilted my head and closed my eyes for a moment, while I considered what that would mean. "Yeah," I replied. "That would be cool."

I opened my eyes and looked at her. "And while you're at it, I'd like a really nice, funny, handsome guy, preferably one who looks like a movie star, to show up and sweep me off my feet. Am I asking too much?"

"Which one of the *Twins* do you want—Schwarzenegger or De Vito?"

I laughed. Bernice carefully tore a piece of paper off her notepad and wrote something, signed it with a flourish, and handed it to me. It read,

HALL PASS
Ariel Quigley has permission to start a romance
with a movie-star quality male of her choice.
Signed: Bernice Wise
Psychotherapist and Universal Wizardess

I read it and felt a great weight being lifted from my shoulders. I smiled and said, "Thanks."

Bernice smiled back. "Anything else?" she asked. "This is *your* life, you know!"

"Well, there's one more thing I need to work on," I answered. "I couldn't afford to stay on in our apartment after Dennis died, so my sister Bibi came and got me and moved me into her farmhouse—she's on the far side of Leesburg—out in horse country. She gave me the guest bedroom and put most of my stuff in storage. Bibi's a very take-charge sort of gal—we used to call her 'Practical Pig,' because she could always come up with a rational approach to any problem. She's kind of like my dad that way. Anyway, I've had two terms of commuting from Leesburg to my teaching job at George Mason, and it's really too far to allow me any time to unwind. Sometimes I have to stay on campus until after seven p.m. to avoid rush hour.

"Living in the country was great for the summer, but now that school is in session again, I'm thinking of moving closer to campus. Plus, as much as I love my nephews, it's pretty difficult for me, trying to handle my mountains of paperwork with a trio of preschool-age boys underfoot. So would you happen to know of any good apartment buildings in the local area that cost less than my monthly salary and that I wouldn't have to be put on a six-month waiting list to get into? Or am I'm just dreaming?"

"No," Bernice responded. "Dreams are the source of what we create in our reality." She paused for just a couple of seconds before saying, "But you *could* move in here."

Then she looked at her watch. "Oops, we need to go," she said. "It's five thirty, and our table is reserved for six o'clock. We'll talk more at the restaurant about your moving in."

She picked up the phone. "It's Bernice Wise," she said. "How long will it be?" She gave a decisive nod at whatever the answer was, said, "Thanks," and hung up.

"I have taxis and pizza delivery on my speed-dial," she said, "and they have me in their computers. We have ten minutes to freshen up—there's a john down the hall, second left." Then she stood up and walked out of the room.

I grabbed my purse and headed for the bathroom, my head reeling from the outrageous changes taking place in my fortune.

Chapter Two

Ten minutes later, we were on our way to the heart of Old Town Alexandria.

From earlier discussions during and after the creative writing classes I had led, I realized Bernice was something of a light-hearted Jewish philosopher. As she had indicated in one of her poems, her frosted blond hair would have been gray-streaked brown hair without the devoted effort of various pharmaceuticals, and her styling efforts were generally lost to the first gust of wind. Her dress was usually more an invention than an ensemble, and today was no exception. Red socks and Birkenstocks vied for attention with a multi-colored shirt and a wrap-around denim skirt.

When she saw me eyeing her shoes, she said, "You know, if Birkenstocks hadn't been invented, I might have had to design them myself. They're no good for line dancing or exercising, but I don't indulge in either of those activities. Did I ever read my poem about 'Jew School' to you?"

I shook my head, so she continued.

"Well, a couple of years ago, I went to a Jewish spiritual retreat in Portland, Oregon, where *everybody* in the class wore Birkenstocks. Furthermore, it was a double whammy for those actually from Portland, because Birkenstocks have been proclaimed the official 'city dress,' and are worn all year round—with socks in winter. I fit right in!"

I looked at her with amusement. "You remind me of Tyne Daly in her role as a social worker—did you ever watch the TV series *Judging Amy*?"

"I take that as a compliment," she said. "You know, psychology and social work aren't that far apart—social workers have to function as therapists a good part of the time. As a matter of fact, I've always had a hard time deciding exactly what brand of psychology I practice."

"I thought you were a Jungian."

"Well, that's how I was trained. But I'm open to new possibilities. It's not that I belong to a Therapy of the Month Club. It's more that I can never be sure I've finally got it right. I've done EST and Gestalt and the training of Carl Rogers. I've been to the Esalen Institute in California, the Omega Institute in New York, and the Findhorn Foundation in Scotland. I have a compulsion to study every approach to mental wellness that gains any popularity. That's my insecurity and my addiction! What if *this* program really is the one that can cure all my clients of all their neuroses? Then instead of charging by the hour, I'll charge by the cure, get rich, and go live on a warm island in the Gulf of Mexico for the rest of my life!

"So, I study them all—you'll have to see the library in my office—and I hope for the best. I guess you could call me a transpersonal Jungian psychologist if you really want to pin me down—and that, my friend, would not be an easy thing to do!"

We continued down King Street toward the waterfront of Old Town Alexandria, where every block boasted the quaint architecture of the late eighteenth and early nineteenth centuries. Art galleries, antique stores, and specialty shops mingled with restaurants of every ethnic type. The sidewalks were full of shoppers enjoying the mild weather and tourists with maps and guidebooks open tracing the paths and gawking at the properties of early American settlers.

I was still musing on the charm of the district when the cab drew up in front of the Riviera Café near the waterfront, one of Alexandria's finest restaurants, and the driver looked around expectantly.

"We're here!" Bernice said, as she handed the driver the fare and a few bills extra. "Thank you, Rajneesh."

She hadn't ever mentioned where we were going that evening, but I knew the Riviera Café by its reputation; it featured a table-d'hôte menu, two seatings a night, a waiting list that might be weeks long, and a final check that could finance some small nations for decades. I gulped, glad Bernice had emphasized when she made the invitation that I was to be *her* guest.

"Thank you very much," the cabbie said as he pocketed the cash. "Enjoy your dinner. I'll pick you up at eight thirty as usual."

Bernice threw open the door and expelled herself from the back seat of the cab. She helped me out, clutched me by the arm, and ushered me toward the restaurant.

"You'll love this place. Best bouillabaisse on the continent! Craziest people! I trade therapy for meals, so I have my own table every Friday night, early sitting, bring a guest if I feel like it. All I have to pay for is any alcohol we consume. About half the seats every night are for regulars, somewhat like box seats at the Redskins games! They pay a premium to be sure of having a table, have to give at least twenty-four hours notice if they aren't going to be here, and need to let the management know if they're giving their table to a friend. For a special occasion, you have to call six months in advance!"

"I've heard of it. I mean, everybody in D.C. has heard of it. I gather it's a step or two above McDonald's."

Bernice laughed. "Two of the owners are Reggie and Penny Whitson. They're an amazing couple. He's an American version of Terry Gilliam, and she's an Australian who looks and acts as if she just walked out of the Royal Perth Yacht Club. And as long as Penelope remains married to Reginald, I think I'll never want for the creations of Chef Daniel's wondrous kitchen!" She pronounced the chef's name with a French inflection. "And while I don't want to be accused of nepotism, I even managed to get my son, Mike, a part-time job here as dishwasher—we'll pop in on him later."

As we stepped into the foyer of the restaurant, a rather handsome Chinese waiter approached. He stood just under six feet tall and looked quite dashing and formal in his outfit, which consisted of black pants, a white shirt, and a short black jacket, with a white towel tucked into the side of the slacks. His shoes had a polish that would put a mirror to shame.

He looked at us for a moment, then hunched forward, furtively glanced from side to side, and reached around behind himself. A second later he was aiming a banana at us as if it were a pistol. In a rasping voice, he said, "Give me your coats, and no one will get hurt."

Bernice laughed. "Ariel, meet John—he's the head waiter here and the third owner of the Riviera. Just do as he says." As we shrugged out of our coats, she looked at my bewildered face and explained, "Surely you've heard that when you step through the doors of the Rivera Café, you enter a Monty Python routine. The rumors are true. Just think of our waiter here as a Chinese-American John Cleese."

John straightened up, and with a formal bow said, "Your coats please, madam, mademoiselle." He hung our coats on a nearby rack and turned to us with a grin. "Do you know how to defend yourself against a man armed with a banana?"

We shook our heads in unison.

"It's really quite simple. First of all you force him to drop the banana, thus disarming him; second, you grab the banana and eat it, thus destroying the weapon. You have now rendered him helpless."

We laughed, and I felt myself relaxing into the moment as he again bowed elaborately.

"John," I said. "It's truly a pleasure to make your acquaintance."

He smiled, said, "Thank you," and made a motion for us to follow him to our table.

He held my chair for me, and as I sat down, I ventured a comment. "A Chinese-American John Cleese is an interesting concept. Did you choose that role because your name is somewhat similar?"

He had picked up my napkin, preparatory to placing it on my lap, but he suddenly stopped, closed his eyes and raised his hand to his face with an expression reminiscent of a grade-B actor trying to express deep sadness.

"It is a sad tale but true," he explained, "My family name is Chan. When

Chinese immigrants come to America, we choose American first names, and since I was a baby at the time, my family chose Charles for me. I was known as Charlie in grade school, but I had to put up with a lot of jokes about being a Chinese detective. So when I got to high school, I changed my name to Chuck. What I didn't know then was that yet another actor was going to cause me grief—because now there was Jackie Chan, so rather than put up with being called Chuckie Chan, which is all too similar to Chuck E. Cheese, I decided to change my name again when I got out of college. Anyway, by this time I had discovered Monty Python and John Cleese, so my next and current incarnation was as John." He wiped away an imaginary tear and straightened up. "What would you like to drink?"

I sat gently shaking my head at his torrent of words, looked at Bernice, and said, "Sherry. Dry Sack?"

John said, "Good choice," and turned to Bernice. "Shall I bring you a virgin?"

She nodded and said, "For the sacrifice." Turning to me, she explained, "I love the taste of a Bloody Mary, but I don't do well with vodka. One of life's little jokes."

When he had walked away and was out of earshot, Bernice bent toward me with a smile. "I think he's taken with you," she whispered. "I've never heard him tell that story before."

On the way to the table, I had noticed a tall, lanky man at the bar, who was holding his thumb up in front of his eye, the way an artist does who is measuring distance. He was also dressed formally, but with a long jacket, rather than the short one John was wearing. He now approached our table, with a towel draped over his arm and carrying a tray with our drinks.

He placed my glass in front of me. In a very proper English accent he said, "Dry Sack for the lady. Pity." He turned to Bernice and put her Virgin Mary in front of her. "Ah. The Virgin Queen. Double pity."

"Hello, Reggie. Meet my friend Ariel. Ariel, this is Reginald Whitson, another one of the owners of this den of iniquity and inane humor."

Reggie took my hand and shook it with a slight bow. He eyed me up and down slowly and carefully, then turned to Bernice and raised an eyebrow. "You told me she was a writer. But she doesn't *look* like a writer," he said. "Where's her tweed cap, the matching cape, the pince-nez, the large, garish ring on the pinky finger?" He leaned forward conspiratorially and in a stage whisper said, "I thought you told me she was a poet..." he paused and glanced around as if to see if anyone was listening, "...and a *journalist*."

I looked at Bernice curiously.

"I wasn't going to tell you this until a bit later," Bernice said to me, "but I'm afraid I've sold you down the Riviera. After I told Penny and Reggie that I'd invited you for dinner tonight, I let it slip that you have a published book of poetry and that you've done a few articles for some of the local newspapers. My extremely creative twins, Mike and Michelle, are developing a business building websites, and they're going to create one for the restaurant, to sort of get themselves started. Penny asked if I could convince you to write a little copy about the Riviera Café, and I said I was sure that as soon as you'd tasted the food here you'd be willing. Everybody is very excited and quite determined to impress you." She paused and glanced at Reggie, "With the possible exception of this lout, who has no manners at all."

Then she turned back to me. "I do apologize for just springing this on you. But believe me, if you say yes, you'll be everybody's new best friend! So—would you be open to doing interviews with Daniel, Penelope, Reggie, and John to give the twins some copy to put up?"

"Oh, sure," I said. "I could do that. No problem."

Bernice bounced up and down in her chair with enthusiasm. "I knew you'd say yes! Reggie, I told you she'd say yes! Bring on the brass band, nothing but the best tonight!"

"My dear," Reggie said to Bernice, "the Riviera is *never* less than the best!" Then to me he added, "Please accept my apologies. But one does associate a lady writer with a tweedy Miss Marple type."

I grinned and shook my head. "Apology accepted."

He bowed humbly, and started to turn away.

"Before you go, I have a question. What was that thing you were doing with your thumb while you were over at the bar?" I asked. "You looked like an artist setting out a canvas."

"Ah, you've caught the truth of it! Setting a table *is* an art, my dear. But my minions sometimes have difficulty with the precise placement of the tableware. It's essential that everything be precise, or The Foot might stomp us all. So it's incumbent upon me to insure accuracy."

"Oh, let up!" Bernice laughed. She turned to me. "Reggie's also an amateur stock car racer, and his language is usually a lot closer to the streets than to the palace."

She looked up at him. "Are you still racing? You do that on Saturdays, don't you?"

Reggie stuck a thumb in his belt and his Brit accent suddenly shifted to a Western twang. "Way-al," he said. "The Rock at the Allegany County Speedway in unda' new management this ye-ah. They call it The Rock on account 'a it's at the foot of a big rock cliff. Ah git ta do a lot more racin' 'cause they run 'em on Sundays now. They're havin' whut they call the 'Big Kahuna' race in a couple 'a weeks, and Ah'll be gone fur four days, sweetheart, so y'all will jist have ta make do without me. Ah wuz in the third row las' time, and Ah may jist finish in the money this nex' one.

"But A'm thinkin' about movin' up ta Nas-cah nex' season, and y'all will have ta come down to the Atlanta Motah Speedway if'n y'all wanna see me race. That is," he added, with a sweeping gesture to the room at large, "if'n Ah kin fin' somebody who can run this place without me fo' a whole weekend."

"Well, Reggie, I know you hate to be away from your precious restaurant," said Bernice.

"You know me well," he said wistfully, shifting out of the Western accent. "It was difficult last year, with the races being on Saturdays. John's superb, but I hate not being here. And, of course, when I *am* here, I want to be racing."

Then he dropped smoothly back into his Western drawl, "Now, you ladies drink up, ya he-a'? An if'n you need anythin', jus' wave yore little pinkie finger at me, and I'll come runnin'." He tipped his imaginary cowboy hat and sauntered back to the bar.

Bernice raised her glass to me for a toast. "Here's to your finding a new romance, as quickly and efficiently as possible." She took a sip. Then she added, "Now, as I said earlier, if you're looking for a place in this area, you can move in with me. I have a large in-law apartment on the second floor at the back of the house that my twins used to claim as their rec room when they were teenagers. When they started college they asserted their independence by moving out of the house to another apartment over our old carriage house, and I've been using this one only for storage ever since. There's a narrow, private rear entrance, but you can use the front door if you'd prefer.

"There's also a phone line you can use—when the twins moved, I had them get a new line installed in the carriage house so the one in the apartment would be available for a contingency such as this. There's a full kitchen, so you can cook your own meals or eat with me. I'll keep the rent reasonable—say six hundred a month—since you're going to help me solve the problem with my ghost."

I was overwhelmed. A rent of merely six hundred dollars was nothing for an apartment in Alexandria, and I was having more fun than I'd had in a long time.

For the past couple of hours, ever since Bernice had given me the "hall pass," I'd felt a subtle shift, as if something as yet undefined had changed for me, or as though someone had stapled a couple of pages of my life together. Maybe I was being sucked down a rabbit hole, but it didn't really feel all that uncomfortable.

"Well..." I murmured.

"Good!" Bernice said. "It's settled. You can move in as soon as you like. No time like the present! Do you teach every day?"

"Monday, Wednesday, and Friday I teach from ten o'clock until three o'clock, but I'm off Tuesdays and Thursdays. I'll need to get a small U-Haul for some of the things I have in storage and out in Leesburg."

"Well then, let's make it Thursday. John, meet my new housemate."

This last was addressed to the waiter who had arrived to take our order. I sighed and gulped down my sherry.

"I'd better have another of these," I said. "Then just feed me whatever they give to the lamb before the slaughter."

Bernice laughed and looked at the menu, which contained two choices for each course. "We'll have the honeydew melon with Prosciutto ham appetizer, the house salad, and the bouillabaisse, of course."

John turned to me. "You do realize that any friend of Bernice is in need of therapy. I'd be happy to be of assistance. Why don't you let me take you to a *really* good restaurant on Monday night, and I'll clue you in on all of this lady's dark secrets. Just write your phone number on a piece of ham and put it in your napkin when you leave." He did a quick pirouette and left the table.

Bernice whistled and said, "I think I'm seeing love at first sight. I've been coming here for over two years, and I've never seen John flirt like that with anyone. You know, he's really very nice. You might consider taking him up on his dinner offer. You could stay over Monday night with me and get the feel of your new place."

"I don't know that I'm ready for that. The move is probably a good idea, but I'm not sure about the date. Let me think about it—maybe I'll have a better sense of everything after dessert!"

THE NEXT TWO hours passed in languid culinary luxury. The ambience of the restaurant was, as Bernice had said, like that of a country club. As well as Reggie and John, there were two other waiters hustling about—taking orders, serving, and cleaning up. There was never any sense of, "That's not *my* table," even though each one seemed to have assigned tables to wait on. I couldn't hear the exchange between the other waiters and their customers, but I did hear the laughter and realized they also played a role in the comedy atmosphere of the restaurant. And the place was a miniature United Nations—in addition to the French chef and Chinese-American headwaiter, the two other waiters were African-American and Arabic.

"Roy lives quite close," said Bernice, "in the apartment blocks referred to as 'The Projects.' He has a family, with two very sweet little girls. Reggie wooed him away from one of the big Crystal City hotels, where he says he was lost in a myriad of serving staff. He does a pretty good Eddie Murphy and can also come across as Peter Cook!

"I don't know much about Jamal—he's relatively new here. Penny tells the story of how he came in one day, asked for Reggie, and did a perfect imitation of Peter Sellers imitating an East Indian actor in the movie *The Party*. Evidently he's an aficionado of *The Goon Show* and old Sellers movies. Reggie hired him on the spot. The two of them really add to the high hilarity of the place."

The food was outstanding. The servings were small but delightful, and I realized quality *was* more important than quantity. And each course was supplemented with healthy helpings of Bernice and the oddball antics of John and Reggie.

The appetizer was just that—it woke my taste buds and left them calling for more. And the Chablis John selected for us to go with it seemed the only possible choice to complement the smoky taste of the ham, the cool tartness of the melon, and the tangy bite of the Calamata olive.

Next, John brought the salad—a blend of spring greens with sun-dried tomato, feta cheese, and pieces of mandarin orange with tarragon vinaigrette dressing. He made a show of checking my napkin to see if there was a piece of ham in it.

"Use a lettuce leaf instead," he murmured. "Remember what Confucius say: Never put off until tomorrow what should have been done in the late seventies!"

"Watch it, John," Bernice cautioned. "This lady is psychic; she just might be able to see right through that polished veneer of yours!"

John smiled enigmatically and moved away again, checking other nearby tables.

I tasted the salad. "Oh, my!" I exclaimed. "How can anyone make so many different tastes blend so perfectly?"

"Wait for the bouillabaisse," Bernice said. "I promise you an experience that might be the closest you'll ever come to the perfect orgasm."

Surprised at her description, I sucked in my breath slightly, and since I had just taken another bite, I started choking. I grabbed my water and gulped down several mouthfuls between gasps. Finally under control, but with tears in my eyes, I said, "You should be on the stage. How did you come to be a psychologist?"

Bernice forked some salad into her mouth. Between swallows she explained, "My story is one for the movies." Then waving over her shoulder, she said, "Soft music please, maestro. A young captain in the Canadian Army during World War II. While he's on medical leave, he marries an English girl. She gets pregnant right away, but after he returns to the front, she has a miscarriage. When the war is over, they stay on in England, and he gets a job writing for the BBC. Finally, a lovely daughter is born to them in 1947—no comments are allowed about my age!

"Heightened dramatic music at this point," she continued with another wave of her hand. "Time marches on. Both of them drink a lot, and the marriage loses the rosy glow it had when they were young and being brave against the threat of Nazi domination. Finally, the inevitable happens, and divorcing his pretty young wife, the captain returns to Canada with his daughter, taking up a quiet life in the suburbs of Toronto, working as a newspaperman to support the two of them."

John arrived in response to Bernice's hand wave and picked up the salad plates. He looked expectantly at a tiny wilted piece of lettuce on my plate.

"Your number must be in code," he said. "I will send this out to be washed and ironed, and then I will spend the night deciphering these tiny wrinkles."

Bernice laughed and shooed him away. "Give the poor girl a break, John. Can't you see she needs a little time to adjust? Let's just feed her and soften

THE CHEF WHO DIED SAUTÉING

her up."

He looked at me with a smile and a shrug and sauntered away.

"Tell me more about this dashing army captain," I said to Bernice.

"Ah, yes. Time goes by and the captain meets a beautiful New York widow in 1961, and they marry. Even though they live in Toronto, they go down every year for American Thanksgiving with her family, and here the next stage of the drama unfolds. Rousing chorus of *Stars and Stripes*."

"So, are you British, Canadian, or American?"

"Oh, I'm an American citizen now," Bernice replied, "but it's not because of my stepmother, or at least not directly.

"But I digress. Ten years of married bliss pass for the bi-national couple, and then the captain dies of a stroke in 1971. His grieving widow moves back to New York, while his lovely daughter stays on in residence in Canada, completing her master's in psychology.

"Thanksgiving comes around, and by force of habit, she flies down to join her family for American Thanksgiving. Enter Alan Wise—suave, debonair, a lawyer, and a ringer for Omar Sharif—whom I'd been in love with ever since I first saw him in *Lawrence of Arabia*."

Bernice wrapped her napkin around her head like a burnoose, as if she were protecting herself from a sandstorm. Then, deepening her voice and slipping into an Arab accent, Bernice said, "'Awrence, you are mad to want to go into the desert, but I will guide you...because it is in the script." Then in her normal voice, she said, "So I married Omar...I mean Alan."

At exactly that moment, Reggie arrived with the bouillabaisse. He looked at Bernice in her head wrap, and as he gently placed the aromatic stew on the table he said, "I'm sorry to inform you of this, my dear, but I have just sold you to a passing caravan driver for forty-two camels. As soon as you're finished with dinner, you'll need to pack your things." Then he turned on his heel and marched back into the kitchen.

Bernice unwrapped her head and primly laid her napkin in her lap. She filled her spoon with soup, looked across at me, and leaning forward she whispered, "Now, my dear, it's time for the orgasm." And she sipped the soup.

I filled my spoon and brought the soup to my lips. Even the aroma was erotic, and as I took the first taste, I closed my eyes. Ecstasy!

Chapter Three

"My God!" I exclaimed reverently as I finished the bouillabaisse. "How does the chef do it?"

Just behind my left shoulder, John said, "Chefs do it with whips and spoons."

Bernice and I laughed, and John leaned over and whispered to me, "I've not yet deciphered the code on the lettuce leaf. But if you need me for anything, just send up a flare."

"You can take my compliments to the chef," I said.

Bernice grabbed my hand and started to pull me out of my chair, saying, "Let's take you to meet the master right now!"

I looked questioningly at John, thinking it would be a bad idea to charge into the kitchen unannounced on a busy Friday night, but John nodded and agreed, "It'll be okay. We're between sittings right now, so the kitchen is relatively quiet. And Daniel loves compliments." And then he added with raised eyebrows, "And pretty women."

So I let myself be dragged behind Bernice as she charged through the swinging doors to the kitchen, where we immediately entered a different world. Unlike the elegance of the restaurant, designed to give the patron the feel of a private club, this was definitely a utilitarian workspace, a combination of white walls and glistening stainless steel, bare of any ornamentation—except for one framed geometric design hanging on the far wall under a clock.

Three men were in the kitchen. One was in jeans and a t-shirt washing dishes at a three-part sink. Another, wearing checkered pants, a white shirt, and an apron, stood at a stove on the far side of the room stirring a pot. The third, closer to us, with knife poised over a cutting board on an island in the center of the space, was wearing all white, from his chef's hat, shirt, pants, and apron, to the elegant little tie around his neck. There was no question who was in charge—the man with the knife had the bearing of royalty.

As we moved toward the island, Bernice called out, "Oh, Dan-ye-el," with the French emphasis and a singsong voice that turned the name into three syllables.

The chef looked our way, and immediately his eyes lit up. He put down his knife and came around the island to greet us, grabbing Bernice's free hand and bowing to smother it with kisses.

"*Ma chérie!*" he enthused. "Have you finally decided to become my mistress?"

Daniel appeared to be in his forties, with a full head of brown hair, slightly gray at the temples, and a neatly trimmed salt-and-pepper beard and moustache. He moved with the grace of a ballroom dancer, and I got the feeling he orchestrated everything, from his meals to his interpersonal relationships.

"After that bouillabaisse, I'm definitely tempted," responded Bernice. "But you'd never be home to cook, so would it be worth it?"

"A mere technicality," he replied, waving away her objection.

At that moment the dishwasher turned around and commented, "Don't you dare marry him, Mom. He's bad enough as a boss, and I can't conceive of him as a step-dad!"

Daniel turned to Mike with his hand over his heart and said jokingly, "*Sacre bleu*, Michael! You cut me to the quick!"

"Never mind, Mike," laughed Bernice, addressing her son. "Daniel wasn't suggesting marriage."

At this Daniel almost had the grace to blush. "Sh-h-h," he cautioned, "We must not corrupt the children."

"Yeah, sure," said Mike, rolling his eyes.

From the banter, I got a real sense of family among this little kitchen staff.

Then turning to me, Daniel raised his brows and cooed, "But who is this exquisite young thing? Such gorgeous copper hair and sparkling green eyes. You have brought me dessert this evening, no, rather than the other way around? An Irish trifle, perhaps?"

I flushed pink at his Gallic profusion and the very idea of being thought "exquisite," but Bernice swatted him on the arm and said, "No trifling with the guests, Daniel. Pay him no mind, Ariel; he's *parisien* and chases anything in a skirt."

"Oh," said Daniel, putting the back of his hand to his forehead dramatically, "you do me a grave injustice. Believe me, please, my taste in women is even more refined than my taste in food." And he grabbed my hand and kissed it with a flourish.

Then Bernice made the formal introductions all around, "Ariel Quigley, meet Daniel Lafayette, chef extraordinaire. And over there at the sink, with soapsuds on his ear, is my son Mike."

Mike, a gangly young man in his early twenties, gave me a mock salute with a dripping-wet, long-handled brush. I got the impression he didn't take anything seriously.

"And..." she paused, "over there by the stove is Daniel's apprentice, Peter. I'm sorry, Peter, I don't know your last name."

The young man at the stove turned around and looked our way, giving a tiny smile at being acknowledged. He was also in his twenties but considerably shorter than the other men, about five feet six or seven, with a head of curly blond hair and a youthful, clear-skinned face. "It's Smith," he said with a shrug. "Sort of boring, but reliable."

Mike waved his dripping brush in the direction of the beautifully painted design I had noticed on the far wall. It was the type one often sees on the sides of buildings in rural Pennsylvania.

"Peter painted that," said Mike. "He gave it to Daniel as a present on his birthday a couple of months ago. If you ask me, there's some serious lobbying going on in this kitchen."

I walked over to the wall to get a closer look at the picture. "Peter, this is magnificent. Are you Amish?"

"No," he replied softly. Then with a little shrug of his shoulders he added, "Actually, my family is Lutheran." He glanced around at Daniel, and it almost seemed to me as if he was looking for permission to continue.

Daniel gave a little nod. "*Mais oui*, your little family joke."

With more assurance, Peter continued, "My mother's German, and my father's English. He likes to joke that we're Pennsylvania Deutsch, not Pennsylvania Dutch."

"Then how did you get into painting these pictures—they're called hex signs, aren't they? I understand they're supposed to give protection."

"Oh," he said softly, "I like the design of this kind of art. The balance. It's like geometry. It looks good. It feels right. You can count on it." He paused, seemingly thinking about what to say next. "Back in high school, some of us kids in my art class worked for an Amish sign maker. He didn't care if we were Amish—as long as we could paint within the lines. And were willing to work cheap!"

This last comment was delivered with a little twist of his mouth that told us all he was making a joke.

"And sometimes," he added, "he paid me extra if I came up with an original design."

"Well, I think you're very talented, Peter. You should be in graphic design, not in a hot kitchen."

Daniel gave a little snort, and Peter smiled in a self-deprecatory way, saying, "I tried that. I mean, I took a two-year degree back home at the local junior college. But ya know, there's no work right now—the need for graphic designers sorta dried up between the time I started school and the time I finished. So I came down to D.C. to look for some other kind of work. Once I started here, I realized cooking is like design—if you put it all together in just the right way, you get something that's...balanced."

Daniel waved his hand at Peter, who turned back to his stirring immediately.

Daniel said, "Tend to your stock, *mon ami*. Not so much pepper in it; it will destroy the delicacy of the mushrooms. And you need a soupçon more of the nutmeg to bring out the flavor, *non*? It is not quite right to the nose yet."

Peter nodded and reached for a shaker. "Okay, boss."

Turning back to us, Daniel remarked, "Peter, he will learn it someday, I think. He is a good listener. He came to us, you know, last year, as dishwasher. Then just a few months ago—March, April—he started to help with salads and *les vegetables*. My sous-chef had just left and is now probably lost in the kitchens at the Watergate. But Peter showed promise as a cook. So, I have given him a chance to apprentice. He could be satisfactory in a hotel in another year...and perhaps someday, chef of a fine restaurant like this. Of course, it is all due to the excellence of my tutelage."

Bernice swatted Daniel again and said, "You are so full of yourself, do you know that?" Then she said in a much louder voice with a big grin on her face, "You're doing a great job, Peter, and don't let your boss give you grief!"

"Thanks," Peter called back over his shoulder.

I thought about what strange bedfellows these three males were. Daniel as the pivot point of the whole kitchen was probably, as Bernice had suggested, quite full to overflowing with his own talent and status. The two young men, one on each side of the kitchen, were like two arms of his compass, but one was a confident quipster, while the other, though higher in rank, seemed shy and reluctant to put himself forward. I expected I would come to know more about both of them as I did the writing for the restaurant website.

Daniel turned to Bernice. "But surely you have not come into my kitchen just to undermine my authority with my staff," he said. "To what do I owe the pleasure of this visit if you are not here to profess your undying love for me?"

"Oh, you are such a smartass," Bernice said to Daniel.

"But, *mais oui*," he agreed. "I am, as you said, *parisien*."

"Well, I don't want to expand your already over-inflated ego too much—it's not good for business for a therapist to work in reverse! However, Ariel here has agreed to write some copy for the website that Mike and Michelle are putting together. And I suppose it would have to include you."

"At last! The world will know the truth about my skills! Of course, there are already thousands who would surely die of grief if they could not come here regularly to sample *genuine* French cuisine."

He turned to me and took my hand. "So lovely," he said with a glint in his eye, "and with writing ability, too! *Ma petite*, the special on Tuesday is duck. You may come and watch me prepare it. The vegetable delivery is at seven a.m., and the fresh little ducklings are delivered by eight. Why don't you come precisely at nine o'clock? Do you have a camera? If so, you will want to bring lots of film. Peter will be here, too—plucking the ducks!"

"Oh, surely you're teasing," interjected Bernice. "Don't the ducks come already plucked?"

"Yes, I am teasing," smiled Daniel. "Peter will be here *stuffing* the ducks."

I jotted some notes in my little day-timer and said, "I have a digital camera, so I won't need film. I hope that will do. I can take about a thousand pictures with it because it has one of those memory sticks."

Mike turned around and gave me a dripping thumbs up. "Digital? You *rule*!"

Just at that moment the back door opened. A woman with platinum hair, designer jeans, and a long, bulky turtleneck sweater hurried in with several grocery bags. She deposited them on one of the counters and turned to Mike.

"Michael, be a love. Take a moment to fetch the rest of the packages, won't you?"

To my ear, her accent was British, but with a subtle difference. I realized this must be Reggie's Australian wife, Penelope. She was gorgeous. She must have been in her early forties, but she looked twenty-five. Even under the bulky sweater, I could see she had a figure like Marilyn Monroe, and she had a face that might launch a thousand ships. She was exquisitely groomed, from her make-up to her gold pendant earrings and her perfectly manicured nails.

Mike set down his brush and took off his rubber gloves. He glanced at Daniel, but without waiting for permission he loped out the back door in three long strides.

There was, however, a definite challenge to Daniel in the set of Penelope's head, and while there seemed to be an electricity between them, it was closer to lightning than sexual attraction.

Peter put his spoon down and mumbled, "I need more mushrooms." Then he ducked into the pantry.

I looked at Penny and Daniel, wondering if I might become an observer at a *Punch and Judy* show.

"What's up, Penny?" Bernice said brightly, in an effort to defuse the charged air in the kitchen.

Penny said, "Hello, Bernice," but then she refocused on Daniel, and her voice hardened. "We have agreed to prepare the luncheon for the guild auction on Sunday. These are the supplies."

"*I* agreed to nothing!" fumed Daniel, fixing Penny with a look of utter disdain. I realized why both Mike and Peter had beaten a hasty retreat.

Bernice decided the better part of valor was to follow their example. "We'll just go have our dessert now," she said with a wave, and pulled me behind her back through the swinging doors.

"I'll hear about how this encounter turns out from both Mike and Penelope," she commented in a whisper. "I have eyes and ears *everywhere*!"

TEN MINUTES LATER we were relaxing at the table, finishing our raspberry glace, which I was sure had been brought directly from heaven, though when I'd said as much to John, he'd assured me it really had come from the kitchen. John had just brought us a cappuccino, and Bernice was giving him an order for Frangelico.

"This will be the crowning touch to a meal from the gods. It's the queen of liqueurs—sheer ambrosia!" Bernice kissed her fingertips and went, "Mwaah!" as she flung her hand into the air. "We still have twenty-five minutes until our cab comes back for us, so relax and enjoy."

As John wandered off again, Bernice asked, "Well, now. Do you plan to accept his offer of a date?"

After a moment's thought, I reached into my handbag, pulled out a folded, bent, and mutilated piece of paper, and handed it over to her. As she unfolded it, I said, "It's confession time. I've been carrying this list around for years."

Bernice read it quickly, and then looked back up at me. "A Jimmy Stewart checklist?"

"Yup. When I was a very little girl, I saw *Harvey* on television. And like you with Omar Sharif in *Lawrence of Arabia*, I fell in love with Jimmy Stewart as Elwood P. Dowd. I think maybe it was because I had an invisible friend and so did he. And he was charming and funny and *gentle*. Anyway, I read a lot about him, how he was such a good family man and father. I think I was about ten years old when I first made a list of all the attributes I wanted in a husband, using him as a model. And I think that's one of the reasons why I became a classic movie aficionado. Lately I've been collecting others of his movies on video—especially those great old Frank Capra films!"

Bernice nodded sagely.

"Anyway, Dennis fulfilled some of the criteria on my list. And maybe John does, too—he certainly has the sense of humor! And he *is* cute in a Jackie Chan sort of way."

Bernice seemed satisfied with that. She folded the list and handed it back to me, and as I stuffed it back into my purse, I said, "So if I'm not being too personal, why aren't you still married to Omar?"

"Ah, yes, the continuing saga," she said. "We married, and I became an American citizen and a career lawyer's wife, which meant being a really good hostess. We put off having children until '82—at thirty-five years of age I reckoned it was then or never! I had the twins, who are now twenty-one and still in school. They both do everything from theater to computer graphics to television production, so things are always pretty lively when they're around.

"I'll tell you, having children is the proverbial mixed blessing! Children often want both to untie the apron strings and to keep a safety net, so there they are, living in the carriage house, but they still raid my fridge and show up regularly for breakfast—mostly to tease me and banter with me. Mike also eats here at the restaurant regularly.

"Anyway, getting back to Alan, he was a litigator with some major companies, but he realized there was a lot of white collar crime, and he wanted to do something about it and all the problems associated with it. So he decided to join the FBI. This was in 1985. We had just moved here to Alexandria, into that wonderful house. But the FBI is a very controlling mistress. Alan's love affair with his job meant we seldom saw each other.

"We divorced in 1995 and have had a great friendship ever since. There was sadness over the separation, but no anger. I still love him, and he's still my best male friend, and I think we actually see more of each other now than we did in the last years of the marriage. We have dinner regularly, sexual encounters occasionally, and we avoid uncomfortable topics of conversation.

"It's strange, you know—a lot of my Jewish mannerisms come from having had a Jewish husband. I picked up some Yiddish, and I've always enjoyed Jewish humor. Then when I was fifty I learned my maternal grandmother was Jewish. Since Judaism is passed on matrilineally, this fact of heritage made me and my children Jewish. My immediate reaction to this news was a desire to run home and make a large pot of mashed potatoes!"

I laughed and said, "Ha! The ultimate Jewish mother!"

"Yes," Bernice continued. "And my daughter, who was fifteen at the time, really jumped on the idea and started studying Kabbalah. Now she's designing a meditative garden for the back of the house, with a thirty- by twenty-foot brick layout that looks like a Tree of Life. We just went shopping last weekend for some of the materials she says she needs. As a matter of fact, I'm expecting the delivery truck tomorrow!"

"I study the Kabbalah," I said. "I don't think I've ever told you this, but I read Tarot cards, and I'm actually pretty good at it. And Tarot and Kabbalah are intertwined."

"I bet you didn't learn that in the army!"

"No," I laughed. "On my fifteenth birthday, my three younger sisters—Bibi, Catherine, and Deirdre, who were ten, eight, and six at the time—pooled their allowance money and bought me a deck as a present. Then they clamored day after day to have me tell their fortunes and guilt-tripped me into actually learning to read the cards.

"There's a lot more to the cards than just fortune telling. I believe they help us make contact with the subconscious. And from a practical standpoint, I often use them when I need to make decisions."

"I've never studied the Tarot cards, but I know Jung worked with them as a body of archetypal images."

"Doesn't surprise me a bit! Anyway, when I discovered how deeply intertwined Tarot and Kabbalah are I decided I needed to learn more about Jewish mysticism."

"Don't tell Michelle," Bernice exclaimed. "She'll monopolize the rest of your life!"

John appeared at the table just then with the Frangelico, and I leaned back and smiled up at him. His eyes were a gorgeous deep brown, and I decided to encourage his earlier attention to me.

"When you brought us that glorious glace, I wrote my phone number in it," I said. "But then I lost control and ate it."

His eyes widened a bit and he said, "Does this mean you'll go out with me?"

"Yes."

"Oh, my gosh," he said excitedly and did a little hop, and his body wiggled. He looked like a puppy wagging his tail and I was immediately smitten. "U-m-m," he said, "how about this Monday—for starters? My mother is a musician, and she's doing a concert at a fundraiser on Monday night. A string quintet sort of thing, I think, combined with a dinner. The Riviera is closed Sundays and Mondays, but I'm helping Penelope with her luncheon and guild auction on Sunday, so Monday is my first night off," he added, as if to explain why he wasn't putting his tray down and carrying me away immediately. "Anyway, how does Monday sound? Would you like to accompany me?"

"I'd be delighted," I said, still holding his gaze firmly with my own. I felt a warmth creeping down my body, and by the time it had gone as far as it could go, I wanted to wag my tail myself, just to relieve the tension.

I thought of Bernice's hall pass and my Jimmy Stewart checklist. I figured Jimmy was gone and wouldn't mind if I took a vacation from my regard for him—I mean, he had millions of adoring fans when he was alive, right?—so I pictured my checklist in my mind and watched as the title did a slow dissolve from "James Stewart" to "Jackie Chan."

At that moment a voice from behind me interrupted our interchange with a faintly amused exclamation of, "Hey, John, does anybody else get service around here, or do we just have to listen to you mooning over your new girlfriend all night?"

John pulled himself up to his full height and wheeled around. In his very best John Cleese imitation, he said, "I'll thank you to keep a civil tongue in your head, sir. I still have those incriminating photographs of you with the milkmaid in the pantry." Then, wiggling his eyebrows, he said in a mock Chinese accent, "Vely foolish to make clazy Chinese waita' angry." Then suddenly he shifted into a third accent, this one clearly from movie Westerns and an imitation of John Wayne. "All right, podner," he drawled, "what would y'all an' the little lady like to have?"

Having taken their order for coffee, he sauntered away in a really good imitation of the John Wayne walk.

Clearly the fellow at the other table was a regular customer, well used to John's routines. He grinned over at us and said, "He's really on tonight, isn't he? But that's why I love coming here, because you can count on having the best dinner and show in town."

I looked at the liqueur glass and sighed contentedly. "Leesburg is certainly far away from this world," I mumbled. "And I'm really looking forward to moving in with you, Bernice. But, you know, I'm already feeling so mellow, I'm not sure I should have another drink if I'm going to drive out to Leesburg before bedtime."

Bernice shrugged away my objection. "No problem," she said, "you can stay overnight with me. The guest bed is made up. It's not in the rooms you'll be taking, but it will be fine for one night, and then you can actually see the apartment tomorrow and figure out what you'll need to do with it to make it home. In fact, why don't you stay the weekend, and go back to Leesburg on Sunday? That way, we can start moving my accumulated clutter into the garage. Michelle can lend you some clothes and a nightie, and I have a collection of brand new toothbrushes that I dole out to guests. And I can fill you in with more information about the restaurant for your web page write-up." Then, after a moment's thought, she added, "And, just maybe, you can get some more vibes on my ghost. We have a mystery to solve!"

Relieved of responsibility for being my own designated driver, I merely nodded and relaxed into my chair again. Then I got out my cell phone and punched in the automatic code for my sister Bibi.

Bibi answered right away, and I explained I'd be staying with a friend for a couple of nights, and that I was going to be moving to Alexandria the next week.

Bibi squeaked excitedly, "Is the friend male or female?"

"Whoa!" I said, "It's Bernice Wise, the psychotherapist I told you about from my poetry class." Then I added tantalizingly, "However, I do have a date for dinner Monday."

"No *way*! Who with?"

"Well, he jokingly called himself Chuck E. Cheese. I'll be back in Leesburg on Sunday and will give you all the details then."

"You'd *better*," said Bibi emphatically. "Humph! You drop two bombshells and then you make me wait two days for the details! Brat!"

"Love you, too," I said and hung up.

As I put the phone away, John reached from behind me unexpectedly, picking up my empty coffee cup, and when I turned to smile up at him, I saw he was wearing a Groucho Marx nose, glasses, and mustache.

"We must make arrangements for our Monday rendezvous," he said seductively in a Groucho voice. And then he added an enigmatic non sequitur, "Oriental art is very descriptive."

At that moment Penny walked up with a glass of iced tea in her hand.

"May I join you?" she asked and pulled up a chair without waiting for a response.

With a little wave to me, John took off his Groucho mask and mouthed silently, "I'll be back," as he walked away.

"I could kill that man," Penny said dramatically, though in a soft tone that only we could hear. Her polished veneer peeled a bit loose as she turned to Bernice and added through clenched teeth, "He's such an arrogant little prick."

"Ah, Penny," responded Bernice gently, "do I sense some anger from your choice of words? I assume you aren't referring to our waiter."

"No, it's our beloved *Daniel*," said Penny with irritation. "He thinks because he's a French chef, he doesn't have to behave civilly to people. I mean, he may feel he has a reason to be nasty to *me*, but lately he's been disagreeable to Reggie and John, too. And *we're* the owners of this place! Yet he acts as if he's the only one who knows how a restaurant should be run, and that if he were to leave, we'd immediately have to close down. And unfortunately, that might be true.

"We've just had an awful set-to in the kitchen, and he's barred me from ever coming in there again. I mean, he actually swore he'd leave—on the spot—if I ever again set foot in the kitchen. He can't mean it, but Reggie tells me I need to lie low for a while. I feel as if I want to bite somebody."

Penny closed her eyes and sighed audibly, still holding her glass tightly. Then she opened her eyes again and straightened up. "I have to get a grip." Turning to me, she said, "I apologize. You must think me very uncouth. We haven't really been introduced, and here I am throwing a tantrum in front of you. But Bernice is my therapist, so I bring her all my problems."

Bernice made the necessary introductions and explained I was going to be writing copy for the restaurant website and focusing particularly on Daniel's specialties.

"Oh, dear," said Penny to me, "I guess I haven't cast any of us in a very attractive light, have I?"

"Not to worry," said Bernice. "Running a restaurant isn't easy."

I added, "Hey—it's *your* website. And I agreed to write some copy because this is a great restaurant, and I want it to look good when it goes before the public. Although this is my first visit to this establishment, I'm already a big fan."

Bernice again looked as if a light bulb had gone on over her head. "Ariel is spending the weekend with me, Penny. She's about to become my new housemate. So why don't you come over tomorrow for lunch at about noon? We can gossip on everything about the restaurant, including Daniel's moods, the woes of restaurant ownership, and why Reggie wears argyle socks." Then she added conspiratorially, "And we'll fill you in on something that seems to be developing between Ariel and John."

At Bernice's final words, Penny looked at me in surprise. "Well!" she said. "Well, well, well!"

"Okay," said Bernice, "it's settled. We'll have tea and mixed grill. Ariel can grill you, we'll both grill her, and it'll be 'grill friend' time."

I laughed, and Penny's face relaxed.

"Oh, good," she said. "I have literally dozens of containers in my refrigerator from *every* deli in town containing *every* imaginable gourmet item necessary for elegant living—and I haven't a clue what half of them are. But I buy a lot of things just to sample them, because of the restaurant. Anyway, let me bring some of them."

"Wonderful," said Bernice. "I'm sure any of them will go with my patented crab meat and shrimp salad."

Penny leaned back, her mood obviously improved. "I accept," she said, and she pushed back her chair. "I'll see you tomorrow."

With all this talk of food, it occurred to me that the first things I'd need to move into Bernice's house would be my jogging shoes.

Reggie came over at that point. "Ladies," he said, "your chariot is at the door."

Bernice glanced at her watch. "Oh, it's eight-thirty—time to go."

I finished the last sip of liqueur and reached for my purse, then looked around for John. He was several tables away, so I decided to leave him a note. But I wanted it to be clever.

I checked Bernice's phone number in my cell address book, then I walked quickly to the bar and grabbed a restaurant matchbook. With a pen from my purse I wrote the number, adding under it, "Call this weekend. And use these to light my fire. Madam X." I knew I was being pretty bold, at least for me, but I figured it was long overdue.

By the time I'd finished writing it and had closed the matchbook, John had noticed we were leaving and hurried over to me.

"Sh-h-h," I said, putting the matchbook in his hand and closing his fingers around it, "don't say anything; spies are everywhere."

He quickly opened the matchbook and read the message, then grinned and pointed a finger at me.

I caught up with Bernice, who had just finished settling the bar bill. As we stepped out into the early autumn evening darkness, I looked up at the stars and sighed contentedly. When we were settled in the cab, I said to Bernice, "Thanks for the hall pass. I don't know what's going to come of this, but it feels good to be taking a chance!"

Bernice laughed. "I know you're referring to John, but the real chance you're about to take is moving in with an eccentric, middle-aged psychotherapist, her two whirling dervish offspring, and an obnoxious ghost!"

THE CHEF WHO DIED SAUTÉING

Chapter Four

Saturday, September 6th

THE TWINS JOINED us the next morning for a rich breakfast of spinach and feta crepes and fresh berries covered with whipped cream, after which Bernice placed a large cup of cappuccino in front of each of us.

"Mom bribes us into putting in an appearance on weekend mornings with menus like crepes or Belgian waffles or bagels and lox," said Mike as he scraped out the bowl of whipped cream.

Sitting back, Bernice sighed, "It's the only chance I have to schmooze with you two, what with school, your volunteer work at the TV studio, Michelle's theater rehearsals, and your job at the restaurant."

The cat had obviously forgiven me for stepping on her tail and had come to purr around my legs for a minute before deciding I had an available lap. When she jumped up, she immediately put her rear end toward me before settling down to receive some serious petting.

Michelle laughed. "That cat is such a slut. She'll make up to anyone, and the first thing she always does is show you her backside. That's why we named her Freud, because of her not-so-repressed sexual proclivities."

As fraternal twins often do, Michelle had quite different physical features from Mike. Where his face was long and thin, hers was rounder and softer. Mike had a fairly pronounced Semitic nose, obviously a gift from his father's side of the family. Michelle, on the other hand, had her mother's nose and lips. Yet there was something about the way they moved that showed they were indeed twins—a symmetry of sorts, as if they had choreographed all their moves, and often they were either totally synchronized or echoing each other.

Mike leaned back on two legs of his chair, gave an enormous burp, and said, "Par*done*."

"I'm glad you brought that up," said Bernice. Then eyeing him critically, she added, "I think that was a seven point two," and turning to me she explained, "We do Richter scale analyses around here."

"I fully understand," I said. "That was a delicious breakfast, and if I had my running shoes with me, I might go jog around the block a few times—especially after last night's dinner."

Michelle looked interested. "Do you jog?"

"I try to run every day."

"Maybe you can talk my mom into doing something physical," said Michelle, glancing sideways at Bernice.

"I do," sniffed Bernice. "I breathe! I take deep breaths whenever my children exasperate me!"

"Yeah," said Mike. He shifted his long legs to the side of the table, and slouching down in his chair, prodded his mother with his toe. "You also get lots of exercise *pitching* fits about my clothing and *running* the gamut of my faults."

Michelle joined in with, "And don't forget *jumping* to conclusions, *flying* off the handle, and *throwing* your weight around. All that mom stuff."

Bernice clasped her hands to her heart and said, "You malign me." Turning to me she added, "Sometimes I'm sorry I ever taught them to talk, much less to pun."

"But speaking of mom stuff," said Bernice, turning to Mike, "would you have time before work this coming week to help us move some of Ariel's stuff? The current plan, for what it's worth, is to bring her things from Leesburg on Thursday. If we rent a U-Haul, can you act as driver?"

Mike put on a devilish grin and asked, "What's it worth to you?"

Bernice said, "You can hit me up for a CD of one of those rock groups you like so much that bangs pots and pans around."

Michelle said with a mock whine, "You didn't bribe *me*! I'll help, too, if you bribe me," to which Mike replied in a sing-song voice, "Mom likes me be-est, Mom likes me be-est."

"Okay," said Bernice, "same deal for you, Michelle," after which Michelle stuck her tongue out at her brother.

"I warned you," Bernice said to me. "Dervishes!"

"I have three sisters," I laughed. "I'm used to it! Anyway, you two, how about I sweeten the deal and pay each of you ten dollars an hour for your time?"

Mike nodded with a big grin and two thumbs up. "You rock!" Then he leaned back in his chair and took a sip of his cappuccino. "But speaking of pots and pans," he added, "you should have hung around in the kitchen longer last night. It was really intense for a while."

Bernice turned to him with a serious look on her face. "Penny told us last night that Daniel had barred her from the kitchen. He must have been in quite a state."

"Oh, that's not the half of it," Mike responded. "Daniel was in a righteous rage after the encounter with Penny—a cold fury. During the second seating, John came into the kitchen with an order and then went to the cold room to get a bottle of vintage wine for a customer. Daniel started ragging on him, saying he couldn't possibly know anything about wine. He also called him a 'bourgeois little Chinaman' who should go and serve chow mein to tourists in Chinatown, and leave the serving of French cuisine to someone who had some taste. It was really rather nasty. Actually, I happen to know John is quite a wine connoisseur—he's from a restaurant family. You know, lately, Daniel hasn't been playing well with others—especially the owners."

Michelle added, "From what you've told me, I think he has some self esteem issues. Like maybe he should have a fine restaurant in Paris, because Americans don't fully appreciate his 'magnificent creations.'"

"Yeah, well, but I think it's more than that. He may be planning to leave when his contract's up in January. There's this tension between him and Penny that—hey, what do I know? I get along with him well enough, and my job *is* short term," said Mike. "I just keep out of the way and mind my own business. This is all about the paycheck until Michelle and I get our website business up and running."

"Well, I hope this doesn't spoil the interviews I'm doing, or cause problems for you with the website."

"Don't worry. We're not charging much, they'll all get their egos stroked, and if anything brings management of a company together, at least for a brief time, it's getting something cheap."

I thought about the various personalities that I had encountered the night before. There was a lot of talent there, and there definitely was also a lot of ego, which often led to jealousy and conflict. It was generally kept hidden from the customers, but my association with Bernice had allowed me to glimpse the turmoil beneath the surface. I wondered if it was possible to have a restaurant of the quality of the Riviera without the conflict.

"You know," I said, "I've been thinking of setting up a website for my courses at school. Is there a way I can trade some copy writing—like what I'm going to be doing for the restaurant—for some assistance with my site?"

"That'd be cool," said Michelle. "Something else to put in our portfolio."

Just at that moment, the doorbell rang and Michelle bounced up.

"I bet that's my delivery from Home Depot. I'll go show them where to unload everything." She ran out of the kitchen, and moments later came charging back to exit through to the back door. "I gotta unlock the gate so they can get into the backyard."

Mike looked at Bernice and said, "Mom, are you sure you know what you're doing, giving her *carte blanche* to tear up the backyard? It'll probably cost you more than the greenhouse you built for her last year when she turned the yard into a vegetable garden."

"Well, that was mostly a success, except for the mountain of okra nobody wanted to eat. And I don't mind the cost if it turns out to be pretty."

"What exactly is she doing, again?" I asked.

Bernice replied, "A Kabbalistic Tree of Life. And no matter what, it will be unusual."

"At least I won't have to mow it, weed it, sow it, reap it, or plow it," said Mike. "And the best part is there probably won't be any room for okra." He heaved himself out of his chair and added, "But I think I'll go give her some advice. I'm sure she'll appreciate that." And whistling, "Heigh-ho, heigh-ho, it's off to work we go," he followed his sister outside.

Bernice smiled indulgently after them. "Those two are so different," she sighed, "that Alan once asked if they were both his."

"Let me pitch in and do the dishes," I offered to Bernice after we'd finished our coffee. "I don't like cooking, but I do a great dishwashing meditation that helps me get in touch with my muse."

"You're on," said Bernice. "I love cooking, but dishwashing is a bane."

She cleared the table, and I started rinsing the dishes and putting them in the dishwasher. So when the phone rang at about thirty seconds after ten o'clock, I was up to my elbows in water.

Bernice picked up the phone, smiled when she heard the voice at the other end, and said, "It's for you."

I dried my hands and reached for the receiver. It could be only one person.

"Hello?" I said tentatively, and felt a stirring in my tummy and parts south even before I heard John's voice.

"Madam X? This is Monsieur Y. Have you a secure meeting place for Monday night? As you say, there are spies everywhere. Speak in code."

I laughed. "Hold on a minute." I grabbed a piece of paper and scribbled out a simple coded message. Then I asked John, "Do you have a pen and paper?"

"Yes."

"Okay, write this down. 'Kcolco xis ta secinreb ta em teem.' Got that?"

"Huh?"

"Let me spell it for you. K-c-o-l-c-o...x-i-s..." I finished spelling the coded message and said, "Now that I'm moving in with Bernice, I've been *looking backward* over my life. Do you get my drift?"

He was silent, so I added, "Do you *mirror* my mind?"

A moment later he shouted, "Aha! Madam X, I think we have a rendezvous. I'll see you at six on Monday at Bernice's. I'll get the address from Penny."

It was less than twenty-four hours since I'd gotten my new hall pass and I had a date. It had happened so quickly that it almost seemed unreal. Bernice had told me that the staff would bend over backwards for me, but this seemed to be a bit more than that—John did seem to be truly attracted to me. I knew almost nothing about him, but that was what first dates were for, wasn't it?

As I finished loading the dishwasher, Bernice bustled around putting away her kitchen paraphernalia. Jokingly, I said, "I do believe this kitchen is bigger than the one at the Riviera. In fact, the last time I saw a kitchen this size was on the ship that transported us to the Middle East. Do you, perchance, entertain a lot?"

She shrugged. "What can I say? I'm a tavern keeper at heart."

I nodded in the direction of an elegant old wood-burning iron stove, decorated with filigreed lacework. "Do you ever use this, or is it just a remnant of days gone by?"

"Oh, I use it in winter. Then it's good for heating the kitchen, and I can slow cook things like stews and soups. But for instant cooking gratification, I much prefer my gas stove."

I noticed the spice rack, which held at least fifty different spices and an assortment of items (eye of newt? toe of frog?) in apothecary jars.

"You mentioned that your ghost knocks spices out of your hand when you're cooking. Have you ever figured out why?"

"Actually, the encounters started right after I took a class in colonial cooking. I was in the middle of making peanut soup for the family when suddenly I felt the chili powder being yanked out of my hands. Now the ghost seems to show up if I'm cooking something that might have been a standard in colonial times. Listen, I don't have any peanuts right now, but I do have a lot of nice fall apples. Why don't I make a New England apple slump tonight, and we can see what happens? It's got cinnamon in it, and it's served with nutmeg sauce. Louisa May Alcott loved this recipe so much she named her house in Concord, Massachusetts for it—Apple Slump."

"But Alcott was Civil War vintage, not colonial."

"Oh, but the recipe is much older. It probably goes right back to Johnny Appleseed. It was one of the recipes I was taught in the cooking class."

"Why is it called a slump?" I asked.

"It has a lot of sugar in it," said Bernice, "so my suspicion is that first you get a wallop of a sugar high, and then you *slump!*"

"Just what I need this weekend," I muttered. "A few more calories."

WHEN OUR CHORES were finished, Bernice grabbed a set of keys from a rack near the telephone and said, "C'mon, let's go look at the apartment. The private entrance is out back, immediately to the right."

I nodded and followed her through the back porch into the yard. It was quite a deep piece of property, about one hundred fifty feet long, with a large shed in the back right corner. To the left was a three-car garage with an apartment above—it must originally have been the carriage house Bernice kept mentioning. It had fancy gabled windows and turrets.

"Wow," I said, "this property is quite a blend of architectural styles."

"Yeah, we have a little of everything from the past two centuries," agreed

Bernice.

Just then Mike yelled, "Mom—help!"

Bernice and I hurried toward the back of the yard and found both Mike and Michelle at ground level, Mike spread-eagled face down on a huge sheet of plastic, trying to keep it from flapping in the wind, and Michelle hunkering on her heels, hammering stakes into the edge of the plastic. Freud the Cat was sniffing at Mike and tentatively licking his eyebrows.

"So exactly what kind of help do you need?" asked Bernice.

"He needs a bigger audience," laughed Michelle.

"Not so!" yelled Mike, though his voice was a bit muffled because he was talking to the ground. He twisted his head a little, attempting to look at us, and said, "Michelle needs more stakes. And if more people would hold the edge of the plastic, I could get up."

Bernice knelt near Mike's left foot and said, "You can roll the other way now, if you like."

Mike grunted and oofed as he pushed himself away from Bernice and onto his right elbow.

"But I do need some more stakes," said Michelle. "Ariel, would you mind getting some? There's a basket of pegs in the garden shed over there," and she pointed to the little, low structure about thirty feet behind where I stood.

"Sure 'nuf," I responded and headed for the shed. I pushed open the door and stepped inside, but as I reached down for the basket of stakes, I felt a sudden thickening of air, as though I'd walked into some kind of force field. I straightened up and stepped out of the shed, putting down the basket outside. I could feel my heart beating from the surprise, so I took a few deep breaths and consciously tried to center myself.

Puzzled, I slowly stepped back into the shed. It was definitely there, what I could only describe as a thickening, though it didn't seem as startling this time, probably because I was expecting it. I carefully stepped further into the room with both hands out in front of me. It was like moving through something soft and cushy, less tactile than water, but definitely there. And then, a couple of feet into the room, it seemed to dissipate. I moved out of the shed again, and picked up the basket.

Bernice and the twins were looking my way when I came back to them, nobody moving. I set the basket of pegs on the plastic between the twins.

"Whazzup?" asked Mike, who was now sitting up.

"I know you have a ghost in the kitchen, Bernice," I said. "But you didn't tell me there's one in the garden shed."

She gave me a surprised look. "The shed? I don't know anything about the shed."

"Except," chimed in Michelle, "that it was the servants' quarters about a century ago."

"Yeah," added Mike, "and probably slave quarters before that."

"But none of you has ever felt anything weird about it?" I asked.

Mike looked at Michelle and said, "Maybe she means the Fog Lady," and Michelle nodded.

"The what?" demanded Bernice.

"The Fog Lady," said Mike again. "You want to tell, Michelle?"

"When Mike and I were little, maybe five or six years old, a couple of times just at dusk we saw a thing we thought was really strange. It seemed like it was a lady, but it was just a shape, and sort of misty."

"That's why we called it the Fog Lady," interjected Mike.

"Anyway, we used to like to play in the shed, because it was like a little play house, but after we'd seen the Fog Lady near it a couple of times, we decided we didn't want to play there any more."

"Why didn't you ever tell me about it?" asked Bernice.

"Well, Mom, you had us so busy when we were little telling you about our dreams and analyzing them every morning at breakfast, and having to 'share' our feelings," Mike said, "I thought it would be too much like homework to tell you about the Fog Lady."

Michelle put the back of her hand to her forehead, and leaning back theatrically, she sighed, "I repressed it."

"Oy, veh! What's a mother to do?" asked Bernice. "You try your best with your children, but do they ever appreciate it? No, they just give you grief."

Mike rolled his eyes and threw a plastic garden peg at his mother.

"You'd better watch it, Buster. There's zero tolerance in Virginia on acts of domestic violence," said Bernice.

"Oh, no," moaned Michelle, "I've got a whole garden full of domestic violets!"

"Enough already," grumbled Bernice, "I'm way too expensive to have to pay myself for therapy!"

Mike looked at Michelle and said, "Back to the stakeout," and they each grabbed a handful of garden pegs.

Bernice said, "Listen, you two, you could put bricks around the edge of the plastic to hold it in place while you're staking it. Then your dear old mother could get up off the ground. Besides which, I'd like to show Ariel her new digs before Penny gets here for lunch."

"Mom," said Mike in a mock whine, "you taught us to be sensitive, not sensible."

I looked around, saw a pile of bricks, and in less than two minutes had placed six of them around the edge of the plastic sheeting.

Once she was on her feet again, Bernice straightened her clothing and said, "Thank you for relieving me of my role as a garden ornament."

"My mom, the garden gnome," said Mike over his shoulder.

Chapter Five

BERNICE MADE A motion for me to follow her. Reaching into her pocket, she pulled out a set of keys and guided me toward a door at the left rear of the house. She unlocked it and ushered me into a small back hall that led to a narrow flight of stairs up to the second floor.

"This claustrophobic little space is really a private entrance to the apartment you'll be using," said Bernice. "However, you're always welcome to use the front door as well. There's access from the second floor landing inside the main house to the apartment living room—it may feel a little more pleasant to bring any guests in that way."

When we got to the landing at the top of the stairs, she handed me the keys.

"Red key is for this door and the one to the other landing, silver key is for downstairs, and gold is to the front door. Got that? There'll be a test later."

I unlocked the door, let is swing open, and went into a space I realized immediately was directly above and exactly the same size as the huge kitchen below.

"Oh, my gosh!" I exclaimed. "It's like walking into a cartoon sheik's tent, or Snoopy's doghouse. It's enormous!"

To the left of the door was a kitchenette, complete with an apartment washer-dryer combo, and a bathroom with tub and shower. The rest of the apartment had no dividing walls; instead, it was sectioned off by screens, allowing whoever might live there to divide it at will. It was light and airy, with the same nine-foot ceilings as downstairs, and several tall windows on two sides.

"It's about thirty feet on a side," said Bernice. "Do you think it will be big enough? You're more than welcome to use some of the den or living room or parlor or kitchen space as well, whenever you want to, as long as I don't have a client in whatever space you want to use. If you're planning a party for a hundred or more people, though, you need to give me some notice."

"It's great," I answered. "I love the idea of no walls. This new life I'm just embarking on should be free of restrictions of all kinds. After all, I do have a hall pass."

"There's work to be done before you can move in, though."

Looking at piles of clothing, books, board games, and patterns, a dressmaker's dummy, a couple of sewing machines, some cartons of Fisher Price toys, extraneous pieces of furniture, a stack of folding chairs, and many cardboard boxes of various sizes, some empty, and some already filled, I had to agree.

Catching my gaze, Bernice said, "Don't worry. We can get started now, and when Penny arrives, we'll throw some lunch together and recruit her into helping us pack while we talk. It'll be ship-shape in no time."

BY THE TIME the doorbell rang heralding Penny's arrival, we had already stacked and taped several boxes and piled them by the door, along with assorted pieces of excess furniture, where everything awaited the attention of additional bodies to help wrestle them downstairs.

On our way down the front stairs, Bernice mused, "I'll get Mike and maybe one of his buddies to move this stuff. Guys are great for doing things like moving furniture and attending to car maintenance and otherwise entertaining us with Alpha male pursuits. Testosterone is a wonderful thing—it's built empires, advanced science in countless ways, even given us hygienic civilization, and is always available for boy-toy and muscle-flexing activities.

"Men are awesome," she added as she opened the door, "and I think every woman should own one—as a pet."

This last comment was directed to both me and Penny, who stood on the doorstep looking chic and trim in designer jeans, a beige silk blouse, a matching cashmere sweater, a classy Fendi leather bag that I was reasonably sure wasn't a knockoff, and matching pumps with tiny heels. I didn't think she was suitably dressed for furniture packing and moving, but I hadn't rubbed too many wealthy shoulders yet in my lifetime, so what did I know?

She was also carrying a huge Barney's of New York bag bulging with what looked like foodstuffs.

As she glided in, Penny said with a slight lift to one corner of her mouth, "Ha! Discussing husbands, are we? Ariel, don't do it. Men are such high maintenance. Why get ensnared in a lifetime of subservience for a few moments of passion when these days you can have the passion and still maintain your independence? Men really only want your attention for about seven and a half minutes in any twenty-four hour period."

She walked ahead of us into the kitchen, and I heard her add softly, "And then you have to go douche!"

She carelessly tossed her handbag onto the table, went to the counter and set down the Barney's bag, then turned to the coffeemaker and poured herself a large cup of coffee.

"I brought goodies," she said, returning to the shopping bag, digging into it, and pulling out plastic bags and half a dozen containers from places like Bread and Chocolate and Marvelous Market.

"Is your crab meat and shrimp salad in the fridge, Bernice? I'll set it out with these other delicacies."

She handed a round loaf of olive bread to Bernice to slice and said, "Ariel, do you know the location of the plates and cutlery yet? Are the twins joining us? Service for five, please."

As she began slicing the loaf into generous portions, Bernice counseled, "Penny, you really must learn to be more assertive!" Then turning to me she added, "That's a psychotherapy joke."

"Oh, I'm learning, Bernice," said Penny. "I gave Reggie a *very* large piece of my mind this morning."

Just then, the backdoor opened, and Mike and Michelle entered, followed by Freud, who sported fragments of dead leaves and other garden debris attached to her coat.

"Hi, Aunt Penny," they said in unison, and Freud wandered over to nuzzle Penny and wipe some of the debris onto her slacks.

As Penny reached down to brush it off, Mike quipped, "That's Freud for you, just like her namesake, always into transference. What's lunch?"

THE LUNCH BUFFET was a gourmand's dream—and a dieter's nightmare. Temptation lay in every container, from the succulent shrimp salad to avocado and artichoke spreads, three kinds of humus, taramosalata, tiny spinach quiches, samosas, a couple of nut butters, and the delicious olive bread, which Bernice suggested we could enhance by dipping it in olive oil topped with freshly ground pepper.

Then Bernice asked if any of us would like to add a glass of wine to the meal.

"Good idea," said Mike, his mouth full of bread. "I'll get some."

He got up and headed to the pantry, returning in about five seconds with a bottle of Bordeaux and an opener.

Michelle piped up, "Oh, really, Mike, everybody knows you don't serve Bordeaux with peanut butter—it needs a *sweet* red."

Mike retorted, "You sound just like Daniel." Then turning to Penny, he added, "After you left last night, he actually called John a 'bourgeois little Chinaman' when he went to get a bottle of wine."

Penny's face took on a grim look, and she sighed in irritation. "He really is too much to tolerate sometimes. He doesn't believe anyone else in the restaurant has any purpose, other than to showcase his cuisine. Maybe he should do a culinary show on television instead of cooking for people who actually want to eat the food. He'd be happier just showing it off. I mean, basically, he's an egotist." She took a bite of shrimp salad and chewed it thoughtfully.

"Of course, Reggie isn't much better," she continued. "He's also an egotist. I, of course, am completely devoid of egotistical thoughts, being merely exceptionally talented and beautiful, rather than perfect.

"Reggie has a degree in hotel and restaurant management from the University of Houston, and *he* is incredibly good at public relations with the customers. But he's left *me* caught in a bind right now."

"How so?" I asked, amused that Penny was echoing my thoughts of earlier that day.

"Reggie got his reputation as an excellent *maître d'* by doing rescues. By that I mean if anything went wrong in the kitchen, he could pacify the customers—with free dessert, a bottle of wine, or even eating the bill when necessary. And the customers would go away feeling good in spite of whatever had gone wrong, and they'd pass the word to other people about how wonderful the restaurant was.

"When John joined the staff at the restaurant we were working at in Georgetown, he and Reggie would banter with each other, and they started doing comic routines with the customers. They enjoyed it so much, we all decided we should open our own restaurant. Reggie doesn't have a very good head for the business side—that's my expertise—but we thought that together we could make it work. And we have. But a lot of the credit for our success has to go to Daniel, who I'll grant you is a genius in the kitchen. And unfortunately for Reggie's ego, that means no more need for rescues."

Bernice said, "The poor man's suffering from a crisis deficiency."

I agreed. "He really *is* a great *maître d'*. The ambiance of the restaurant is wonderful. And I assume that means he gets on well with both staff and clientele."

"Yes," said Penny. "But it seems that the fewer the crises, the less satisfaction he gets out of running the restaurant, and the more energy he wants to put into his stock cars. And that in turn takes him away from a focus on the restaurant. So Daniel feels justified in trying to manage both the front and back ends of the business, and I get caught between the two of them."

She sighed again, and I saw a glance pass between her and Bernice. I got the feeling there was more she wasn't saying.

Mike, who was busy cleaning out one of the containers of artichoke dip, said, "Don't get me wrong—Daniel is as nice as he can be to those of us who work in the kitchen. I get along with him, and Peter practically worships him. But when it comes to any of you in management, John included, or any of the wait help like Jamal or Roy, Daniel doesn't seem to feel the need for courtesy. And I don't think it's just at this restaurant. Do you know he actually boasts about once having cold-cocked a waiter with a frozen halibut when the guy argued with him?"

Michelle said, "Wow! That's the perfect way to murder somebody. In one of my cinema classes, the instructor showed us an episode of an old Alfred Hitchcock film where a woman killed her husband with a frozen leg of lamb. Then she cooked it and served it to the cops when they came to investigate."

"Well, I have to tell you," Penny said grimly, "there are plenty of murderous thoughts being generated in that restaurant right now!"

"You know," I said, "guests generally don't care about what goes on in a restaurant kitchen as long as what comes out of it is satisfying."

"You don't have to worry about egos around here," said Mike, stacking up all the containers he had just emptied. "We're way too cool to be egotistical."

The twins went back out to the garden, and Bernice, Penny, and I spent a while sipping cappuccino and schmoozing about the restaurant while I took a few notes for use in my write-up for the website. Then Penny left, and Bernice and I went back to packing and cleaning the apartment for another few hours. At around six o'clock, Bernice called a halt to start dinner preparations.

While she was chopping apples for the slump, she asked me to fetch the cinnamon.

"There's none here," I said, after scrutinizing the spice rack.

"Then try the pantry. Turn right as you go through the door, and look for it on the wall ahead of you. I always store unopened spices on the second shelf."

I saw a large container of ground cinnamon just at eye level and moved toward it, but as I did so, I felt the same filmy thickness to the air that I'd felt out by the garden shed. I stepped back and carefully reached a hand into the "thick" place. It was a little bit cool and felt similar to the impression I'd had out in the shed. And I remembered the hand on my shoulder from yesterday afternoon.

"Hello," I said softly. "Somebody here want to play with me?"

I didn't seem to be getting a response, so I closed my eyes, centered myself, and tried to pick up an impression. And she came into focus in my mind's eye—and ear.

"I's Annie Grace," she said in a soft voice. *"He hadn't ought to have done it. There weren't no call for it. I wouldn't ha' told nobody nothin'."*

She was about five feet three inches tall and dressed in a blue cotton dress, with a white apron. She had a blue-checkered shawl around her shoulders and a matching head rag covering her hair. She had black shoes, and I visualized white cotton stockings that were held up at knee height by something resembling garters.

But what caught me most were her beautiful liquid brown eyes, which she locked onto my inner gaze—then, sure she had my attention, she slowly turned as I continued to watch, and I saw that the back of her head rag was bloody, and carried a severe indention. She'd clearly been clubbed with a very heavy object.

The image startled me, and I opened my eyes to the reality of the pantry. I reached a hand out to feel the air in front of me, but the thickness was gone. I grabbed the cinnamon from the shelf and took it to Bernice.

"Did you have any trouble finding it?" she asked, as if commenting on how long it had taken me to get the spice. She'd created a heaping pile of apple slices in the bowl and was washing her cutting board and knife.

"No," I said, "but I met your ghost again. Her name is Annie Grace, and she was apparently bludgeoned to death."

Bernice's eyes widened, "How...what? Did you actually see her, speak to her?"

"In my mind," I said. "However, once I'd picked up on her and saw the back of her head, I got startled, and she disappeared. But from her dress and her accent, I think maybe she was a slave on this property."

Bernice shook her head, obviously in amazement. "You say she was bludgeoned to death? By whom? Why? With what?"

I looked at Bernice and thought that even when she was being serious, she was funny. "Are you planning to do a newspaper article?" I asked.

"No," she said, flapping her hands. "But this is so exciting, and I want to know all about it. Besides which, I love a mystery, and as you said last night, now I have one right in my own kitchen. And moreover, I have a psychic here to help me solve it. So what do we do next?"

"I really don't know at this point. The sense I had that she was there disappeared when I got startled. I think maybe we should just leave it for the moment. Once I get settled in here, though, I might be able to establish a stronger connection."

"Well," said Bernice, who was obviously still quite excited that I'd seen the ghost, "after this, my glorious apple slump is going to be an anticlimax!"

Chapter Six

Sunday, September 7th

MICHELLE HAD LOANED me a pair of rubber-soled shoes the night before, so on Sunday morning I went out and power-walked my way around the neighborhood for about thirty minutes, hoping to ward off the effects of the last two days of sensual eating. Then I came back and showered and dressed in the borrowed jeans and George Mason sweatshirt she'd also loaned me.

Freud the Cat greeted me as soon as I walked into the kitchen that morning, escorting me to the table where the twins were reading assorted sections of the Sunday paper. Once I'd sat down, Freud curled around my ankles with her paws on my shoes.

"You really can't blame anybody else when you get stepped on," I said to her, reaching down to scratch her behind the ears.

"Listen to the lady, Freud," said Bernice, who was cooking something at the stove. "Taking responsibility for your actions is the first step to healing."

Mike mumbled, "The ongoing dialogue in modern psychology."

Sunday's breakfast was what Bernice and the twins referred to as "Wise Eggs," a version of Eggs Benedict, with Velveeta cheese sauce instead of Hollandaise, turkey ham instead of Canadian bacon, and an addition of fresh asparagus spears. So come to think of it, it really wasn't like Eggs Benedict at all, except for the eggs and the English muffin.

"I really do have to be thinking of getting home," I said when breakfast was over, the last of the food put away, and the dishes stacked in the dishwasher. "If I'm going to earn the money to pay the rent here, I need to go and grade some papers this weekend, and I should start packing up a few things from my room there."

"We're all on the run this morning," said Bernice.

"One more cappuccino for the road," said Mike, holding up a mug. "The milk's frothy and the coffee's fresh and strong!"

"Twist my arm!" I smiled, and took the brew to my corner of the table.

"Well, all right," said Bernice. "Ariel, while you're packing, don't forget to pack a little overnight bag for tomorrow night. You *are* staying, aren't you? You've already got a key to the front door, so you can just let yourself in. I won't change the linen in the guest bedroom until you've moved into the back apartment."

"Thanks," I said. "I did tell John to pick me up here, and it will make my date a little more relaxed if I don't have to think about driving back to Leesburg."

"Leesburg!" said Michelle, looking up from the Show section of the newspaper. "I used to go for horseback riding lessons near Leesburg. I love the old part of town—it's so quaint."

"But so is Old Town Alexandria," I said. "And you don't have to drive an hour to appreciate it."

"Spoken like someone who's had to make that drive on a regular basis," Bernice added. "I know what that drive is like—we did it every Tuesday and Saturday for nearly two years while Michelle was in her horsey phase."

"Didn't Mike learn horseback riding, too?" I asked.

"Naw," he answered. "Horseback riding is a girl thing. I wanted to do something more manly," he snickered.

"Yeah, right," said Michelle. "He took up tap dancing instead. Very macho."

"Hey, I quit when they wanted me to do ballet!"

To stem the tide that appeared to be rising, I interjected, "So what are you two doing now, besides the gardening project?"

"We're both seniors at George Mason University," said Michelle.

"Oh," I said, "that's where I teach!"

"Really? What do you teach?" asked Mike.

"Mostly freshman comp," I answered. "Plus I teach a creative writing class here in Alexandria that your mom keeps signing up for. She's my groupie."

"So, is she any good?" Michelle asked. "She won't let us read any of her stuff."

"Yes," I said, "she's very good. And very funny."

"Ya know," said Mike, with a faraway look, "I find it hard to picture Mom as a student. I can't visualize her 1960's retro-clothing fitting in with today's punk and hip-hop styles."

"You just don't understand class," said Bernice.

Before Mike could shoot another barb, I asked, "What are you studying?"

"Well," said Mike, "I'm in computer graphics, and Michelle is in theater arts. But what we really want to do is go into independent film making."

"Oh, wow," I said, "that sounds exciting!"

"Yeah, but it's not something we can study around here," said Mike. "And everybody keeps telling us it's really hard to break into film making and be a success, so we figured we'd better have a trade that can support us. That's why we're starting a little business building websites for people."

"In the meantime," added Michelle, "we're learning a lot working at the Fairfax County public access station. We do everything—camera work, lighting, sound, video editing, remote shoots, and production. We actually have our own series called *On the Edge*, for people our age who want to be cutting edge—like in music, art, the internet, stuff like that. That's what we're going over to work on today."

"That's Channel Ten, right? I used to pick up that channel when I lived in Reston. Some of their shows were pretty creative."

"Oh, it's lots of fun," said Mike. "Hey, maybe one of these days when we're there you can drop by and we'll give you a tour of the studio."

"I'd like that very much. I'm really interested in any form of communication."

"Who knows," said Bernice. "Maybe you'll wind up doing your own show. There are a lot of people in this area who are interested in things like ghosts, Tarot cards, and other psychic phenomena."

"You read Tarot cards?" asked Mike. "Would you read my fortune?"

I smiled. It happened all the time that when people learned this was a sideline of mine they immediately wanted a reading.

"Slow down, pardner," said Bernice to Mike.

"It's okay," I said. "I have a mini-deck with me in my purse." I did a little shrug for Bernice's benefit, and explained, "It's a great ice-breaker in social situations."

"I don't exactly read fortunes," I said to Mike. "I look at the cards to see what kinds of psychic energies might have caused a person to pick them. I don't have time to do a full reading right now, but we can do what I call a *carte du jour*. You pick a card at random with a focus or intention in mind. For example, if you want to know about your website business, you should hold that in mind while picking the card. Then I'll tell you what it might indicate concerning the focus you selected. Let me go get my purse, and I'll do a card for each of you before I leave."

I was back in a minute, my Waite-Ryder cards in hand. "Okay, Mike. What intention do you have? Is it your business, your education, or something else you want to focus on?"

"Let's go with the website business. Is it going to make us rich and famous?"

I grinned. "That's one of the two perennial questions. 'Does my lover love me?' and 'Will I be rich?'"

"Well, I don't have a lover—at the moment," Mike said. "So let's just go with the rich part."

"Okay," I said, fanning the deck. "Pick a card—any card."

Mike did so, while Bernice and Michelle watched quietly. The mood had changed subtly, as it does whenever people think they're about to receive a message from the oracle.

I took the card and looked at it. It was the Ace of Swords. "Aces always suggest a new beginning, but swords are air signs, suit of the mental plane. So, you're starting a new venture and doing it with logic and reason, and it also suggests you want to be your own boss."

"Right on!" Mike exclaimed.

"And it suggests you have incisive thinking ability."

"Incisive—that's me. Sharp as a tack in a box."

"Except," said Michelle, "you don't like to stay in the box much." Then she turned to me and said, "Oops, I didn't mean to interrupt. I'll be good!"

"That's okay," I said. "Mike's not wanting to stay in the box is clear from his having drawn the Ace of Swords, which shows he has an entrepreneurial drive.

"But," I continued, "because you're at the threshold of this new venture, I'm also getting that you need to find somebody who will mentor you. Because to succeed, you're going to need to stay focused and follow the rules. That's what the sword represents. So look for advice from people who've had success in this field.

"And for the moment, don't quit your day job. Or in your case, don't quit your night job as a dishwasher just yet. It's going to terminate all on its own, but in its own time frame. "

"That sounds good, but what about money? Will my business be lucrative?" Mike asked.

I looked at him. "It will probably make enough for you to feel satisfied. But money isn't the object here. It's about building a new business and learning how to focus."

"Good enough," he said, nodding. "It works for me. Michelle, you're next."

"What's your focus, Michelle?" I asked.

"Well, I've got a lot of projects going. No romance at the moment, though—but I'm really kind of interested in developing my spiritual philosophy. Can you tell me about that?" she asked.

"Certainly. Pick your card."

She closed her eyes and chose a card, and when she handed it to me, I had to laugh.

"You picked the Ten of Pentacles," I said, as I held it up for everyone to see. "Perfect for the girl who's building a Tree of Life in the back yard. The ten coins on the card form the shape of a Tree of Life."

"Oh, my gosh!" said Michelle softly. "That's spooky."

"Yes, drawing cards often is," I replied. "The ten of pentacles usually signifies wealth and abundance, sufficient to sustain you in anything you may want to accomplish in the future. The ten is a springboard into a new level of growth.

"But, it's about working in the physical plane, with physical issues, and I'd say that what's going to bring you the most spiritual satisfaction will be turning that abundance to humanitarian acts, doing something in the physical plane to contribute to other people in the community."

"We actually get letters from kids telling us we're making them think," Michelle added. "It really does give me a lot of satisfaction."

"In addition, you can provide a balancing influence for Mike's enthusiasms, and a spiritual focus he may not always stay in touch with."

She nodded. "I'm always telling him he's the 'thinker' and I'm the 'feeler' in our partnership."

"Well, more than that, this card is your support. You draw your strength from the love you express in community activities," I said. "And even if you don't yet know what you're going to do in terms of a career, everything you're doing now is leading you toward a favorable conclusion. All you need is the patience to let it manifest for you."

"Great," said Michelle. "That feels really good. *You're* really good. And it's almost like psychotherapy. Hey, Mom, are you sure you want her to move in? She might take over your practice."

"Unfortunately," I said, "Tarot reading isn't accepted by the American Psychological Association. And besides, I don't want to go into competition with your mom. I'd rather just stick to my teaching and writing."

Bernice said, "Maybe I'll have you do *my* cards every once in a while. Every therapist needs a therapist."

"Yeah," I added. "That's so true. I mean, I can do this for other people because I don't have any investment in what comes out. But I can't always do a reading for myself—because sometimes my own insecurities and desires get in the way."

"But you know," Bernice added thoughtfully, "maybe I should get a deck of Tarot cards to use in my practice—they seem to be a really good way to access the subconscious. Could you teach me how to read them?"

Michelle started rocking in her chair and saying in a soft sing-song voice, "I wanna learn, too—I wanna learn, too—I wanna learn, too…"

"Oh, great!" said Mike, throwing his hands up in the air. "Just what I need—three women psychoanalyzing everything that comes out of my mouth. If you guys—"

"Excuse me," said Michelle. "You mean *ladies*."

"—yeah, sure, whatever—if you—*ladies*—are going to bring Tarot cards to breakfast every day, I'm going to take a subscription to *Popular Mechanics*!"

"Ha!" countered Bernice. "The ultimate in the male withdrawal syndrome."

"Hey," quipped Michelle, "if you bring *Popular Mechanics* to breakfast, you can read about carbs while you eat your carbs."

"Oh, my, look at the time," said Bernice. "I'm going to have to postpone having you read for me because I have an appointment in about half an hour and I need to shower and dress. However, I don't have any burning issues at the moment, so I'll see you tomorrow when you drop your car off, or on Tuesday morning. Have fun with your paper grading."

Bernice was pushing herself up to her feet when the doorbell chimed. She glanced quizzically toward the living room, but Mike said, "That will probably be Peter," and he rolled to his feet. "He's going with us to the studio," he added, "'cause we need somebody to man one of the cameras for our taping today. We were one body short when I called around for crew, so I coerced Peter last night. I bribed him with a promise of free lunch."

Mike ambled out of the kitchen in one direction while Bernice headed toward her room, giving Michelle and me a little wave.

As Michelle rose to take the empty cups to the sink, I gathered my cards into a stack, and as I usually do, I pulled one for myself before putting them into their box, but I hadn't yet looked at it when Mike wandered back to the kitchen again with Peter, so I laid my napkin over the deck to avoid having to make any explanations about the cards.

Peter came in with a sketchbook under his arm. He gave a little smile as he glanced at Michelle and me.

"Hi," he said softly, nodding to Michelle. Then he turned to me. "Mike told me you might be here this morning. He opened the sketchbook he was carrying, tore out one of the pages, and handed it to me. "Here," he said. "I thought you might like this. "

It was a lovely geometric design—a nine-pointed star all done in shades of green and gold.

"It's beautiful! " I exclaimed, turning it in all directions before showing it to Mike and Michelle.

"Oh, pretty!" said Michelle.

"Just beautiful!" I added again.

"Well," he said shyly, "you seemed to like the one I did for Daniel, so I thought you might like one of your own."

"There you go again," said Mike in mock exasperation, "giving away your work when you could be earning money with it." Putting his hand on Peter's shoulder, he added, "Now repeat after me—I am a talented artist, and people want to pay me for my work."

Peter just shrugged and looked a bit embarrassed. "Right now I'm an apprentice chef, not an artist."

I smiled at him. "It's possible to be both," I said. "Thank you so much for the gift. It's very generous of you, and I'll honor it with a fine frame."

Something flashed in his eyes then, and I had a sense of connection with him that hadn't been there before.

"You're welcome," he said. "Maybe you could put it up outside your bedroom door. For protection."

"Maybe I can," I said smiling. "I'll be moving in here next week, but before I put it up, I'll have to see if the management has any objection. You know, Bernice will get the final say on decorating the outside of my door."

He nodded. Then without saying anything else, he turned to Mike and Michelle. "Uh, when do we have to go to the studio?"

Michelle glanced at her watch. "Oh, about two minutes ago. Hustle your bunnies, guys, it's nearly show time!"

She put a hand on the shoulder of each and herded them toward the door. "'Bye, Ariel! See ya later."

As the back door slammed behind them, I sat down again for a closer look at the design Peter had drawn. The multiple shades of green and gold gave it a glow like stained glass. And yet it had an almost three-dimensional quality, achieved through what seemed to me to be the slightest manipulation of perspective. The figure had a kind of life to it as if it were about to burst into flame. It didn't seem at all like the shy, reserved young man who had brought the design into being.

He appeared totally contained, but this design—this work that was truly art—showed a power, a force that gave the lie to that containment. I definitely wanted to show it to Bernice and get her take on the dual nature of Peter Smith.

Just as I was thinking that thought, Bernice came out, dressed to the nines in an Indian cotton blouse and wrap-around skirt in multiple shades of orange and brown.

"What? You're still here?"

"Yes, I've just been sitting here musing about Peter. Do you have a minute to look at this and give me an opinion?" I pushed the picture toward her.

"M-m-m," she purred, with a little frown. "He's going beyond the limits of Pennsylvania Dutch art, isn't he? This is very…"

"Dynamic?" I suggested.

"Yes! That's a good word. And it saves me from going all Freudian and making remarks about 'sexual tension' and 'libidinous energy.'" She smiled. "I think our shy little Peter likes you."

"Oh!" I said, a little stunned by her interpretation. "But I'm at least ten years older than he is."

"And?" she countered.

I looked at her, nonplussed.

"Don't worry about it," she said. "Just have a nice afternoon. And I'll see you tomorrow." And she hurried out the back door.

I shook my head, feeling less enlightened than I had before Bernice's comments. I wasn't convinced Bernice was right about the energy of the picture being sexual. Rather, it seemed to me there was something Peter was holding in that could only free itself in his art. And then I got an inner awareness that in Peter's family, feelings hadn't been allowed. He'd had to repress and deny his emotions. I didn't think he was attracted to me so much as he wanted to share with me that part of himself he'd had to deny because he saw me as empathetic. I made a mental note to engage him in further conversation when I went to the restaurant on Tuesday for the interview with Daniel.

I pushed myself out of my chair and picked up the napkin I'd used to cover my Tarot deck, flipping over the card I'd drawn for myself earlier. It was the Tower struck by lightning. As I stuffed the deck into its box, I wondered what the card might mean for me. I had thought the past forty-eight hours had brought some big changes, but this card indicated more change was on the way—enough that I'd have to learn to live in the moment. An unexpected event was coming.

THE FAT MAN in a tuxedo came pirouetting into my field of vision from the right, wearing a greatcoat over his tuxedo, looking like Dickens's Artful Dodger. He held his porkpie hat in place with the index finger of each hand, and as he twirled, the coat caught the air so that he looked like a giant, gyrating top.

Then he stopped abruptly, facing me, and smiled his enigmatic lopsided smirk with eyebrows raised, as if to say, "Can you figure this one out?" He opened his coat with the fingertips of his right hand, while with his left he plucked a sign from a voluminous inside pocket. As he turned it slowly in my direction, I could see the Latin message, IN VINO VERITAS.

I nodded to him, and watched as he did a slow-motion buck-and-wing off to stage right. Fadeout.

I WOKE WITH a start, filled with a sense of foreboding—I'd had one of my Fat Man dreams.

As I'd explained to Bernice—had it been just two days ago?—whenever the Fat Man appeared, either in dreams or in my conscious reality, he was usually bringing me a warning.

I reached over to the bedside table and fumbled for the lamp switch. As I clicked it on and light filled my corner of the dark bedroom, I pushed myself up to a sitting position, pulled the sheet up to cover my bare breasts and anchor it under my armpits, and reached for the notebook I always kept in my handbag.

"*In vino veritas,*" I said aloud. "In wine there is truth."

Chapter Seven

Monday, September 8th

On Monday afternoon I left campus at about four o'clock and drove directly to Bernice's. Traffic was pretty heavy, so it took nearly an hour to get there. In the driveway was a car I didn't recognize, but there was room for me to pull around it and park out of the way. I grabbed my school briefcase, my overnight bag, and all the clothes I'd brought for that night and the next day, including my jogging shoes and some sweats, and hurried around to the front door. I tested the latch with my elbow and was gratified that it opened, so I didn't have to dig for the key Bernice had given me.

Once inside, I pushed the door shut with my toe and ran for the stairs. Bernice appeared at the door to the kitchen, but I just nodded as I dashed upstairs and called, "Back in a minute."

I'd brought a stylish black silk dress with a filmy multicolored topper that had sparkly gold thread running through it, plus a black evening stole; I carefully laid them out on the bed. I stripped off the blazer and pants suit that I'd worn to school and dashed into the shower.

Realizing I didn't have any time to sing arias, I had the kind of three-minute shower my mother would have disparaged as "hitting only the strategic spots," dried quickly, and tried to decide what to do with my hair. I pulled it up, back, and sideways, and finally settled on a bit of a French twist with a little curl to the strands at the ears that escaped from the twist. I went light on the make-up—just a little brown liner and shadow, a hint of blush, and pale rose lipstick. Then I dabbed on some fresh scented perfume and went into the bedroom to dress.

I slid into the dress and felt a rush of pleasure at its silky sensuousness on my skin. I slipped into the little black pumps I'd brought—just one-inch heels, since I thought John was only about an inch taller than I was. I added gold hoop earrings. Then I put on the filmy topper and looked in the mirror.

"Very tasty, my dear," I thought as I looked at my reflection. "A nice mix of the young Joan Crawford with a touch of Alyson Hannigan!"

I'd stuck a black evening bag into my school briefcase, so I pulled it out and put lipstick, my driver's license, my cell phone, a little cash, and a toothbrush into it. While I was pawing through the briefcase, I noticed the digital camera and tape recorder that I'd brought for my interview with Daniel early the next morning. A practical thought nudged me, so I pulled out the two pieces of equipment and slipped them into the pocket of my trench coat, which I hung on a hook on the back of the door.

I wrapped the stole around my shoulders, went out into the hall, and headed downstairs for the kitchen to get Bernice's opinion on my choice of outfit.

As I made my entrance, I saw a good looking, rugged male slouched over a cup of coffee at the table. Since he *did* look somewhat like Omar Sharif, I realized this was probably Alan Wise. He looked me up and down appreciatively and whistled.

Bernice, who was standing at the preparation island with her back to me, said, "Alan, behave yourself."

"Give me a break," he said. "A *Vogue* model just appeared in your kitchen!"

Bernice turned and looked at me and raised her eyebrows with a smile. "Oh, wow, I understand! You do look scrumptious, Ariel."

I felt a shimmer of pleasure at the compliments. "Do you think this is appropriate for this evening, Bernice?"

The man said, "You're asking this from a woman who wears muumuus from the sixties?"

"As I said, behave yourself, Alan. Ariel, this is Alan Wise, my wiseacre ex-husband. Alan, this is Ariel, my new housemate, about whom I was just telling you."

I nodded and smiled, and Alan said, "Very nice to meet you, Ariel. And I repeat—" and he whistled again. "You need a male's opinion about your outfit, and I'd say it's perfect."

Bernice laughed. "Alan, you already have a date for tonight."

I caught a knowing look that passed between them and thought this must be one of their "encounter" evenings Bernice had mentioned.

Just at that moment the doorbell rang and Bernice said, "Ariel, that's probably John, so why don't you get it?"

I did, and it was indeed John, whose eyes widened when he saw me in my hot black outfit. I felt the tiniest little thrill at the obvious pleasure in his eyes.

He looked gorgeous in a dark wool suit with a matching vest and a maroon tie.

"*Carpe diem!*" shouted Bernice from the kitchen. "We won't wait up for you!"

John gave me his arm as I closed the door and escorted me to his car. He beeped the door unlocked and held it open for me, waiting so he could close it once I was settled. I realized a male hadn't been this gentlemanly to me since my high school prom.

As we headed down Duke Street for Old Town Alexandria, I asked, "Where's the concert?"

"Actually, it's in Chinatown in D.C." he said. "In addition to playing the viola in the Alexandria orchestra, my mother's part of a quintet. This is a Schubertiana evening that's a fundraiser for the Organization of Chinese American Women. It's an incredibly elegant and expensive dinner and concert combination, and I managed to wangle two tickets for free because I spent the afternoon chopping vegetables for the dinner. And it's at my uncle's restaurant—the cradle of my culinary training. In addition, everybody in my family is dying to meet you, because I told them you actually think I'm funny. Many of them speak Chinese better than they speak English, so a lot of my humor is lost on them. And I'm telling you this as a warning, because the dinner will be served at tables for ten, so you'll be in the thick of it."

"Wow," I said, "a new adventure."

He nodded with what I thought was a look of gratitude, and then continued, "Actually, my uncle owns two restaurants on the same site. The one downstairs is The Emperor's Palace, and it's what Americans would consider a typical, though high class, Chinese restaurant, with a full menu of the various Chinese styles Americans are used to—Hunan, Szechwan, Peking, Mandarin—and lots of seafood. The food is excellent, but it's more for the American palate.

"Upstairs is a second restaurant that most Americans would never realize is there. The name outside is in Chinese, but the menu isn't posted outside, and it isn't translated into English. The restaurant is extremely elegant, sort of the Chinese version of the Riviera Café, with upscale prices like you'd find in a five-star hotel in Hong Kong."

"And you say these restaurants were the cradle of your culinary training? That implies you're also a cook, as well as the best waiter-actor on the face of the planet."

He smiled at the compliment. By this time we had turned onto the Washington Street portion of George Washington Parkway and were now heading north toward D.C.

"Ye-es," he said, in what I realized was a Bela Lugosi imitation. "I have many hidden talents—I keep them in a coffin in my closet."

Then in a more normal voice, he continued, "I spent more time in my uncle's kitchen than I did at my own house when I was growing up. I've sometimes thought my parents must have sold me to him when I was a baby. Fortunately, I really liked the food industry, whereas I wasn't the least bit interested in my father's vocation, which is engineering. So it was my uncle who provided most of my pocket money, as well as paying for some of my education when the time came.

"I worked at everything—from dishwashing to stir-frying—activities that can sometimes become confused! But I've always liked the front-end work the best—waiting tables and entertaining the crowds. What can I say, I just like applause! My penchant for acting, though, comes from my mother's side of the family. All her brothers and sisters are performers—musicians, singers, dancers, actors—and this has been true for generations. But it's a bit of a trade secret that being a good waiter in a good restaurant can be a lucrative profession."

"Since you're the best," I said, "you must be very rich."

Without glancing at me, he simply nodded. "The family is pretty well off," he said. And then he added quietly, in what seemed an afterthought, "And I'm part owner of the Riviera Café."

"I've been told that," I said. "And Penny was saying the other day how the three of you were such a terrific team."

"Yes, I go way back with Penny and Reggie. I met them when we were all working at yet another restaurant in Georgetown, The Continental Club, which was a sort of dinner and theater place and which is now defunct. I'd decided when I finished college that I needed to branch out and get a little distance from my family. So I took my experience from the family business and my acting ability and hired on as a performing waiter.

"Reggie had visited Australia a year or so before—that's where he met Penny. She'd joined him at just about the same time I had, so they were working as *maître d'* and bookkeeper, and over time we became pretty good friends. He'd tried his hand at cooking, but, like me, he'd decided he liked working the front better.

"So when they decided to open the restaurant in Alexandria, they asked if I'd like to join them. I got a bit of help from my uncle, and they got an SBA loan, and *voilà*, we were in business! But I'm more a silent partner, although we've all become pretty loud lately, having to deal with Daniel's current obnoxiousness." He stopped talking and drove in silence for a few moments.

"How long has Daniel been with the restaurant?" I asked.

"Actually, since just about the time we opened. In fact, we built the reputation of the place on his ability to make food a love affair. But lately things have been very tense, and not at all loving."

"Why now? I mean, what's changed?"

"I'm still trying to sort it all out myself. Somehow the energy between Daniel and Penny and Reggie has shifted dramatically in the last few months." He shook his head but kept his eyes on the road.

"Daniel does have an eye for the ladies," I said. "Might that have anything to do with it?"

John sighed; he almost seemed relieved that I'd opened this avenue of thought. "The whole situation is very convoluted. Daniel's always flirted with Penny, telling her she'd be better off with him than with Reggie, that she needs to experience the passion of a Frenchman to know what true lovemaking is, and so on. But she'd wave him off with a shake of her head, and the three of them took it all in good humor.

"When Reggie started stock car racing a couple of years ago, they'd go out to the track in Maryland together on Saturday for the races. Daniel would fix them a lovely picnic lunch, and it was kind of their chance to have a date. And I got to play *maître d'* every Saturday night."

"That sounds really sweet," I said.

"It was, but it didn't last. Penny's mother became very ill last fall, and she took a few months off to visit her in Australia. Reggie kept racing, but he didn't talk about the races the way he had before, and he made a big show about working out a lot at his club. Then something seemed to shift after the closing banquet in October. Reggie's usually ebullient when he's out front in the restaurant, but he was pretty subdued for a few weeks.

"Penny was home in time for Christmas and Reggie seemed back to normal. But when racing season opened again in April, Reggie went into a depression, and it had nothing to do with the race because he came in closer to the lead than he'd ever been before. But after that first race, Penny didn't go back to the track with him for months. In fact, for a while, she seemed to be avoiding him altogether."

"Do you know why he was depressed?"

"No, I don't. But in June or July, the relationship between Daniel and Penny went all to hell. Daniel would snap at Penny over everything, and she started treating him like hired help—except it was in a way she wouldn't ever treat any of the rest of the staff. At about the same time, Penny started going to the races again.

"It doesn't take a genius to figure out that something had hurt Daniel's pride, and since the only two things important to him are his cooking and his flair with the ladies, it had to be the latter.

"I try to keep my nose out of this type of thing, but when it affects the restaurant, I get a bit stressed myself," he said, and his remark sounded somewhat grim.

"Anyway, we had a meeting yesterday where we were supposed to work out some of our grievances, but all it did was cause more friction. Daniel has a five-year contract to work for us, which he signed when he came, and the time is almost up. Now he's threatened to leave when that contract expires if Penny so much as sets foot in the kitchen ever again. Believe me when I say that working with those three hasn't been much fun lately. Not to mention that Daniel has affronted me personally, and I'm not even involved in any of these other issues. All I want is for my restaurant to succeed. As brilliant as Daniel is, I sometimes wish we had a different chef who was less intractable."

We were both quiet for a few moments, until John added, "But I'm tired of worrying about the business. Give me something else to think about, and tell me about you. What do you teach, what were you like as a little girl, how many siblings do you have, where did you get your gorgeous red hair, did you ever have any pets? All that sort of thing. I want to know all about you."

So I began blathering about myself, and filled up the empty airspace until we reached Interstate 395, crossed the Potomac, and headed in the direction of Chinatown. I had covered the general nature of my current coursework, the names and identifying marks of my three sisters, my family background, the genetics of my hair color, and the golden Lab dog named Arfer the family had owned once when we'd settled for five years in El Paso, Texas. I also explained why I'd joined the army a decade before. By the time I'd covered those topics in what seemed to me a torrent of verbiage, we were passing under the Dragon Gate in Chinatown. Moments later, John turned down an alley and pulled into a slot where all the parking spaces were marked *Emperor's Palace/Staff Only* and stopped the engine. He hurried to my side of the car to help me out and led me around to the front door of what I assumed was the family restaurant.

As we went upstairs he whispered, "I hope you're up for this. I'm about to put you on display."

Chapter Eight

THE RESTAURANT WAS absolutely gorgeous. The tables were laid with fine linen tablecloths and napkins, bone china, silver spoons, and little silver stands at each place to hold the chopsticks. That provided a much nicer place to rest them when they were not in use than in a tied paper wrapper. The walls were decorated with fine Chinese art and wall hangings, and the ceiling tiles were elaborately patterned and gilded squares.

And if it hadn't been for my dinner experience at the Riviera, I'd have been completely overwhelmed by the feast we were served.

John explained some of the main aspects of a Chinese banquet to me. "There are always ten to twelve courses, served to tables of ten to twelve people. In planning the meal, the chefs consider each course both as a dish in itself and as part of the banquet as a whole. They take the presentation, the smell, and the taste into account, with the key factor being balance.

"This balance appears in four ways. There's a balance of foods, with a selection of meats, seafood, and vegetables. There's a balance of color, with both light and dark colored dishes and dishes of green vegetables. There's a balance of taste, including hot, cold, sweet, sour, and salty. And there's a balance of textures, contrasting tough and soft, smooth and rough, crispy and sticky, juicy and dry."

The first course was a delightful lobster salad, followed by a "bird's nest" with scallops and Chinese vegetables. Then came a real delicacy—shark's fin soup.

"This soup is always served during the first half of the meal when one is not yet too full to appreciate it," John said. "Though you *will* be full soon, I guarantee."

Next came a few warm dishes—curry and black bean scallops followed by sweet and sour prawns, crispy skin chicken, and crab meat with mushrooms. I noticed John's relatives were all taking very small servings of each, and I followed suit, serving myself just enough for a taste.

Then came another soup—winter melon with mixed meat "to cleanse the palate," followed by steamed fish "for good luck," with hot tea "to wash down the grease," as John noted. The last course came on two plates: fried rice—white rather than the brown fried rice found in Chinese American takeout restaurants—and soft noodles with a delicate sauce.

And finally, we had a sweet dessert of iced mango pudding with lychees, and a plate of buns with a sweet sesame filling.

The dinner was truly a work of art, and the waiters were attentive yet unobtrusive, placing two of each new dish on the lazy Susan in the middle of the table and removing the dishes that had been finished. They exchanged our plates, spoons, and chopsticks regularly, whenever they were too messy or became too cluttered, and they cleaned up any spillage instantly. I could see how John's training in this restaurant was reflected in his manner at the Riviera.

Throughout the meal, John's relatives quizzed him both in English and Chinese about his relationship with me. In addition to his "aunties" who were seated with us, John's mother and father and other aunts, uncles, and cousins showed up at our table to be introduced. John's father got a waiter to bring him an extra chair so he could sit with us during the concert, but John's mother excused herself.

"I'm performing in just a few minutes," she explained in a beautifully modulated voice, "so I must not linger."

The Schubert concert was as rich as the banquet. The string quintet played for over an hour to an extremely appreciative audience, which forced the group to perform two encores.

After the applause had died down, people began to get up from the tables, gathering belongings and milling about. John's father took my hand to say goodbye. This gave me an opportunity to be effusive in my praise of John's mother's performance, at which he beamed.

The babble of conversation around us was mostly in Chinese, or more specifically, as John told me, in Cantonese. Other people to whom John had introduced me at our table took pains to speak to me, some saying goodbye in English, and others offering words of social pleasantry I didn't understand, though I certainly got their polite intention. So I simply answered each in turn with, "Many thanks. Very nice to meet you."

"Before we split," John said, "and I'm referring to leaving the premises, not separating into multiple personalities, let me take you downstairs to the kitchen, the true cradle of my culinary apprenticeship. You can meet my uncle and some of my cousins, whom he uses as slave labor. He thinks anybody with the Chan name should be working for him, and that encompasses about a fifth of the Chinese population worldwide!"

I grabbed my shawl and bag, dutifully following him through a pair of swinging doors set in a rounded Oriental archway and down a flight of stairs.

"There is a dumb waiter in the wall here for bringing the food up from downstairs." He glanced back at me and added, "And no comments about my chosen profession!"

When we got to the bottom of the stairs, he pushed through another set of swinging doors, then held one of them open for me to enter.

This kitchen was considerably different from that of the Riviera Café. It was much bigger, with several rows of preparation tables, baskets of vegetables and fruits, bowls of sauces, shakers of spices, and several woks. Some areas of the kitchen were empty of workers, but others were very active, with foods being chopped, steamed, or fried. There were many more people in this kitchen, some handling food and some washing dishes, and I realized that though the banquet was now complete, there was still food service going on in the restaurant on this floor, and it occurred to me that if the banquet hall seated a couple of hundred people, then the main restaurant must accommodate that many patrons, too.

John had a look on his face that reminded me of a little kid who had come home to Mom, his puppy, and apple pie. He grabbed my elbow and pulled me over to a stovetop area where a middle-aged man with a round Chinese face was watching a very attractive young woman prepare something that looked as if it contained chicken and mangoes. Both of them glanced up as we approached and gave us big smiles.

"Ariel," said John, "I'd like you to meet my uncle Jimmy and my cousin Lisa. Uncle Jimmy, I wanted Ariel to meet you and know where I spent most of my youth."

His uncle took my hand and made some pleasantries, and his cousin smiled and nodded, then went back to stirring the contents of her wok.

At that point a melodious female voice sounded from the other side of the kitchen. "John! I missed you this morning. Uncle Jimmy told me you were here helping out for a couple of hours while I was out."

We turned and looked at the woman who was hurrying toward us. Though she wasn't as young as his cousin Lisa, she was stunningly beautiful.

"Clarice!" said John, and he dropped my arm. "When did you get back from Hong Kong?" he asked as he enfolded this gorgeous woman, who gave him a warm embrace and a fervent kiss. When they broke the embrace, he kept his arm around her waist as he turned her in my direction.

Jimmy said, "Clarice learned so much in Hong Kong that I practically put her in charge after you left today. She had a lot to do with the fabulous banquet we just had."

"Ariel," said John, clearing his throat. "I'd like you to meet my cousin Clarice. I haven't seen her in a long while. Clarice, this is my friend Ariel."

I was a little nonplussed at the warmth of John's response to this young woman. Clearly they were "kissing cousins."

I made a sweeping gesture to the room with my hand. "Surely not *all* of these people are your cousins."

"Well, at some level I think we're all related. But only Lisa and her brother George are my first cousins. Clarice is a second cousin, I think, yes?" he asked, looking at Clarice, who nodded quietly.

"But it's a very big family, since Jimmy and my father also had many cousins. As the saying goes, by the dozens."

He still had his arm around Clarice's waist, and I suddenly wondered if he'd have invited me out had he known she was back from Hong Kong.

"I'm sorry," said Clarice, "but I have to get back to work." She tapped Jimmy on the shoulder. "This old slave driver will be reprimanding me in a minute if I don't."

Jimmy beamed at her. "You're a good worker," he said, "for a slave."

I murmured a polite goodbye to her, and we also made our goodbyes to Jimmy and Lisa. Then John guided me out the back door.

"Your cousins are lovely women," I said.

He looked surprised, as if I'd suggested something he'd never thought of. "Yes," he finally said, "I guess they are."

I was delightfully satiated. Along with the regular evening group of tourists and locals, we walked around Chinatown for about half an hour, looking at the Dragon Gate, the various stores and restaurants, and generally soaking up the atmosphere. Then we picked up the car and drove the few blocks to John's apartment, to end the evening with a nightcap.

JOHN'S APARTMENT WAS filled with movie memorabilia—pictures and posters, many of them autographed. A big comfy sofa, a couple of chairs covered in creamy leather, and a round glass coffee table made up the furniture in the living room. There was also one whole wall containing an enormous entertainment center with every imaginable video and audio player and a widescreen TV—plus floor to ceiling shelves of tapes, CDs, DVDs, and even vinyl records.

"Oh, my gosh!" I exclaimed, as I draped my shawl on the sofa. "I've never seen this many movies all in one place outside a rental store!"

John grinned as he took off his suit jacket and loosened his tie. "Yes, it's my own little movie mogul screening area. I use it to develop my acting personae—or at least that's my excuse."

He gestured toward the kitchen. "Have you had enough tea?" he asked.

"Possibly enough for the next week."

"Then how about a little brandy?"

I nodded.

"With a little jazz?"

"Sounds mellow."

He slipped a CD into the player, and soft mood music began to play from speakers in every corner of the room. Then he went to the kitchen and made clinking and puttering noises for a few minutes.

While he was busy in the kitchen, I took an opportunity to check out his collection of videos and DVDs, believing as I did that a modern guy's heart is often evident through his taste in entertainment. He had a full set of *Star Trek* videos, including all the movies and the original and *Next Generation* series episodes. Next to the television he had a complete set of Monty Python *Flying Circus* tapes, as well as John Cleese's *Fawlty Towers*, and of course *The Life of Brian* and *The Holy Grail*. All of these were for research purposes, I assumed. He also had a lot of old classics in all genres, including *Casablanca, Citizen Kane, The African Queen, High Noon*, and then separately such great comedies as *Harvey, Some Like It Hot, Fargo*, and all the Marx Brothers movies.

I heard John coming back in and turned to him.

"It looks as though you have all the American Film Institute top one hundred movies in every category."

He grinned and handed me my brandy. "I thought of calling AFI and suggesting they might want to confirm their choices with me first before they publish any more lists. Is there anything you'd like to watch? A western, a mystery, a comedy, a soppy romance?"

"Oh, do let's have a soppy romance!"

"How about *Sleepless in Seattle*? That's one of my favorites."

"Sounds good."

John had it on video, so he queued it up, turned off the jazz, and we settled on the couch together.

"Get comfy," he commanded, so I took off my shoes and pulled my feet up under me. I hoped I looked appropriately kittenish, and I must have because he gently put an arm around me and softly started stroking my shoulder. In a few moments I decided to take some initiative on my own and leaned my head against his arm. I had intended it as an enticement, but unfortunately before he had an opportunity to be enticed, I did the unthinkable—I fell asleep!

I don't know how far along the movie was when John said softly, "The title of the movie indicates it's supposed to keep you awake, not put you to sleep. So wake up, Sleeping Beauty." He clicked off the movie and the television with the remotes and carefully extracted his arm.

He leaned forward and gently touched my cheek, saying, "With all the gin joints in all the cities of the world, she had to walk into mine!"

"Oh, I'm so sorry!" I said.

"Hey, it's okay. You had a long day. I realize that teaching is no piece of cake, and then I turned a simple date into an encounter with the Chinese dynasties—that's enough to exhaust anybody. And you're interviewing the master of the chopping block tomorrow, so I'm going to give you a rain check for the movie. Maybe we can try this date thing again another time."

I gave him a grateful smile and nodded. "Maybe next weekend."

"Sounds good." He picked up his jacket and put it on, then straightened his tie.

"And," he added, "I really rather like it that you felt easy enough being with me to fall asleep."

He was draping my shawl around my shoulders when we heard a loud crash from the kitchen. We both jumped at the sound, and John rushed to see what had happened. I followed close behind, wondering if he had a cat I hadn't seen.

Just as I got to the door, I got a mental picture of two youths in the alley, running away. When I entered the kitchen, John was standing there with a confused look on his face, peering at his kitchen sink, which was on fire and full of glass.

Snapping out of his daze, he reached for a fire extinguisher that was attached to the wall near the stove. But before he could use it, the flames sizzled and went out.

"We'd better call 9-1-1," he said. "I think I've just been the victim of a Molotov cocktail attack, though a very ineffectual one, since whoever made it used a beer bottle. It looks as though it came through the window at an angle and hit the cupboard, then bounced into the sink. When it broke, all the beer went down the drain. But I don't think we should touch anything until somebody comes to look at it."

He called the police, and from his side of the conversation, I picked up that they'd be sending a car right away.

When John had clicked off his cell phone, he turned to me. "Even though nobody was hurt and there's no longer any fire, the duty officer told me they were taking any bomb threat incidents very seriously, particularly since it's just a couple of days until the anniversary of 9/11."

We walked back into the living room, but before we'd even had a chance to settle on the couch, the doorbell rang.

John clicked the intercom, and in answer to his query, a voice said, "D.C. Police, sir, Officers Webster and Copiah. Did you call 9-1-1?"

John said, "Yes, come on up, third floor, second apartment on the right." And he buzzed the front door open.

He waited for the officers at the door, then led them into the kitchen to survey the scene. I heard one of them burst out laughing and went to see why.

"Sorry, sir, but this sure is one for the books! There are a lot of stupid felons out there, and one of 'em musta had a grudge against you. But I can't imagine how on earth he thought he was gonna cause any damage by havin' beer catch fire."

Both of the cops stood looking at the sink, shaking their heads and grinning.

The cop turned around and addressed us both. "A couple a' detectives are on the way. I'm gonna head downstairs so I can let them in. They'll bag the glass for fingerprint analysis and check to see if there are any clues down in the street. We'll canvass the area, but I don't imagine anyone saw anything. For now, your kitchen's a crime scene, so you need to stay outta here for a little while. Officer Copiah here will wait with you."

"No problem," said John, as he guided me back into the living room.

The detectives arrived just a few minutes later with a couple of crime scene technicians. They sent Copiah down to join Webster in checking for evidence on the street and seeing if there were any witnesses. Then one of the detectives took statements from both of us, though I was dismissed in pretty short order when he determined this was my very first time in the apartment, and I didn't know anything about anybody. He spent a little more time with John, trying to establish whether he might know who would want to harm him or destroy his property.

Meanwhile, the crime scene technicians busied themselves in the kitchen, photographing the window, bagging the glass and the soggy cloth that had been stuffed in the neck of the bottle, and examining the trajectory of the missile to determine where on the street it had been thrown from. One of the detectives told John they could check any prints they might get from the bottle fragments against their print database the next day, but it might be a while before they had any solid information for us.

"If we can't establish any connection to you personally, and you can't come up with any suspects, it's possible it will just be considered an incident of random vandalism," said the detective who had taken our statements. "Certainly, if you think of anything that might be useful, please call me," he said, handing John one of his cards.

Then they all thanked us for our patience and left.

John looked at me a little ruefully. "I need to take you home, but I hope you won't mind waiting a few more minutes while I put something over the kitchen window to block it off."

"No problem. I'll help if you like."

All he had to cover the opening was a trash bag and duct tape, so I held the bag in place while he tore and affixed the tape.

It was nearly two a.m. by the time we were in the car and on our way back to Bernice's, and I was both wired and exhausted. I realized the combination of the drinks I'd had earlier, the shock of the attack, and the excitement connected with the police visit had left me nearly comatose.

John was silent most of the way, so I just leaned back, hypnotized by the headlights and dark tree shapes on the parkway return trip.

John was still silent as we pulled up into Bernice's driveway, but as he let me out of the car and escorted me to the front door, he finally spoke. "How are you doing?"

"I must admit I feel like one of the zombies from *Night of the Living Dead*."

"Well, then," he said chuckling, "let me get you inside so you can eat Bernice's brains instead of mine!"

"Bleugh! That's not something I want to add to this evening's events!"

"I guess it was a pretty unusual first date, huh?"

"Well," I said, "it's been right up there at the top in terms of giving me experiences I've never had before—a gourmet Chinese banquet with some lovely people whose language I didn't understand, a Molotov cocktail through the window, and being questioned by the cops. I really can't see anyone topping this experience in the foreseeable future!"

"You might not want to give me that kind of challenge. I have all the Monty Python tapes as research material, and next thing you know, you might find yourself in the middle of the Spanish Inquisition."

I laughed. "With you, it's more likely to be the Spinach Inquisition, and I'll find it on my plate!"

John smiled. "Ah, so, then we'll see what we can come up with for the future!" He leaned forward to give me a friendly kiss and added "I'll see you in the morning."

I watched him return to his car and start the engine. Then I gave a little wave and closed the door, sighing.

As I locked the door and turned to go upstairs, I felt a wave of exhaustion sweep over me. I'd held up pretty well through the events of the last couple of hours, but now I realized I must be experiencing the after effects of shock.

As I wearily climbed the stairs, I thought about my psychic hit of seeing the two boys running away from the scene. This, combined with watching the flaming beer bottle fizzle out in the sink, had allowed my mind to realize the danger was past. But the body doesn't always register what the rational mind knows to be true.

I had to acknowledge I knew almost nothing about John, except that he had a good sense of humor and a great collection of old movies. But he was currently having problems with Daniel at the Riviera, suggesting he wasn't universally easy to get along with. It crossed my mind the bomb might even be related to the strained relationships at the Riviera.

I unlocked my bedroom door, tossed my evening bag on a chair, stepped out of my shoes, and shimmied out of the little black dress.

I was tempted to skip the tooth brushing routine but decided I'd regret it in the morning, so I dragged myself into the bathroom for final ablutions. While I was brushing, my mind went back to scenes of the Chinese banquet. The world I'd experienced at John's uncle's restaurant was a different world from the one I was used to, and I didn't know a lot about the ethnic community he was part of. I'd heard there were Chinese gangs, and while it didn't seem likely this charming, playful waiter could be the target of a gangland hit, I'd been with him when a bomb had come sailing through his kitchen window. So was the bomb related to his being Chinese, to strained relationships in the Riviera, or to nothing at all?

My inner voice said it had to be the last of these options, but unfortunately, when I had a personal investment in the outcome, my psychic abilities generally turned off, and I was left to figure things out with my rational left brain, which at the moment was practically fried with exhaustion. So my impression that the bomb was a random, senseless act might just be wishful thinking.

As I crawled into bed, I solaced myself that I'd surely have more opportunities to figure out this situation. John had, after all, said we'd have to plan another date in the future. Then my right brain kicked in, and I flashed on an image of John with his arm around the waist of his delicious looking cousin, Clarice, giving her a very friendly hug. I sighed.

"And what about Clarice, John?" I thought. "How does she figure in your future?"

Chapter Nine

TUESDAY, SEPTEMBER 9TH

I HAD SET the clock radio in Bernice's guest room, but it went off far too early for my bleary eyes and fuzzy brain. I threw on sweats and jogging shoes and hurried out for a dash around the block, but all I could manage was about fifteen minutes before I said to my aching body, "Tomorrow is another day."

Back in my room, I showered quickly to straighten out my energy field, brushed my teeth vigorously to get rid of the fuzzy tongue feeling, then put on a fresh blouse with the pants and blazer I'd worn to class the day before. I dumped the contents of my evening bag back into my regular purse, double-checked that my camera and tape recorder were still in my trench coat pockets, got a notepad and pencil, and went downstairs to the kitchen.

Bernice was stirring a pot full of scrambled eggs, and Alan was sipping coffee in exactly the same position he'd been in the previous evening, with the addition of a furry Freud the Cat curled up in his lap.

"Hello again, folks," I said. "Did either of you move since I was here last?"

Bernice looked over at me quizzically. "I wasn't expecting you to be down so early. In fact, I wasn't expecting you to be here at all. So…how was the big date?"

"So big it required the police to monitor it. John was the victim of an abortive Molotov cocktail thrown through his kitchen window while we were in the living room."

Both Bernice and Alan chorused, "What?"

I gave them the details of the episode while I poured myself some coffee from the carafe and stirred some fancy coffee creamer into it.

"The police wanted a list of everybody John was connected with from both his uncle's restaurant in Chinatown and the Riviera. When they heard Jamal's name, one of them got excited—I guess because he's Muslim—and wanted to know if he's linked to any terrorist groups. John very calmly insisted he's just a student, trying to make his way in the world, and much too gentle to be a threat to anybody, especially John, who is his mentor."

"Well, the whole episode is an interesting turn of events," said Alan when I'd related all I knew. "I'll probably get information on it this morning—everything related to bomb threats automatically gets forwarded to my department."

"That's right," I said, "you're with the FBI, aren't you? What department are you in?"

"Anti-terrorism," he said with a smile. "I moved over to that division just after 9/11. To be on the safe side, I'll give a call over to one of my contacts in that precinct later and see if they have any clues."

"That would be good," said Bernice as she motioned me toward the table. "And please do let us know if you find out anything. We can't have the equanimity of our favorite restaurant disrupted."

Then she shifted gears to return to the still unanswered question she had started with. "But tell me, other than having your date interrupted by a potential bomb, how did the evening go? Is there fire? Is there smoke? I mean, other than from the bomb."

"I honestly don't know yet. It was a pleasant evening. The dinner and musicale were wonderful, and I met John's uncle who owns the restaurant and two of his gorgeous cousins who work there, as well as a whole crew of his relatives at the dinner. But when we got to his apartment and settled down for a romantic movie, I fell asleep. Since I'm interviewing Daniel this morning, John decided I needed to come back here to get some rest. We were just getting ready to leave his apartment when the bomb came through the window."

Then I added, "Just so I won't keep you on tenterhooks, I have to admit that though I like John a lot, I can't say yet whether there's a basis for anything long-term. I think I may have a rival in one of his cousins, who just got back from Hong Kong. She's a real knockout!"

"So," said Alan, "you mean there might be a place for me on your dance card?"

"Watch it, buster," said Bernice. "You're still supposed to be dancing attendance on me. At least you are if you want any breakfast."

I looked back and forth at the two of them. Theirs was a strange relationship—I'd heard of divorces where the non-custodial parent had visitation rights with the kids, but this was the first case I'd seen where the non-resident spouse had visitation rights with his former wife.

Alan surveyed me with a smile and said, "I know what you're thinking. The truth of our relationship is that I can't give up Bernice's cooking."

Bernice glared at him, but before she could say anything he added, "And she's still a pretty hot ticket. So, actually, our relationship works better as an affair than it did as a marriage."

I glanced at Bernice again, who now appeared mollified.

"All right, then," she said, "you may eat after all."
She seemed to have finally completed her scrambling and turned off the burner. She lifted two hefty serving plates and headed toward us with crispy bacon and the eggs. As we all served ourselves, I thought that what I probably wanted was a relationship with the comfort level of Bernice and Alan's, but, I decided, I *would* like it to be residential.

AN HOUR LATER I pulled up into the lot behind the Riviera, where John was standing beside the open door of his car. He waved to me, closed his car door, and came around to open mine.

"Have you been here long?" I asked.

"No, I just got here. Morning came way too early."

"Didn't your mother ever tell you not to stay up late on school nights?" I asked.

"She did, but she said it in Cantonese, and it just didn't have the same impact."

I laughed and headed toward the kitchen door for my meeting with Daniel. Then I felt John tap my shoulder, and I glanced around at him. He motioned with his head for me to follow him around to the front instead.

"I'd just as soon not have to confront Daniel this morning," he said. "I wouldn't want a murder on my hands this early in the day."

Then he suddenly slumped over into a crouch, looking like an aged man, and he began pushing an imaginary wheelbarrow and chanting, "Bring out yer dead! Bring out yer dead!"

A couple of passersby, with cameras and guidebooks in hand—obviously among the last of the summer's tourists—gave us a look of disapproval.

I whacked John playfully on the shoulder and whispered, "Maybe you should save it for inside. You're scaring the tourists."

"Never you mind, dearie," he called in his John Cleese voice over his shoulder to the woman, "It's only the plague, it is—nothin' to worry about."

Just as suddenly as he had dropped into his old man pantomime, he was up again, pulling me into a flower box alcove beside the front door.

"It's the water you know," he whispered conspiratorially. "They put fluoride in the water, and it causes people to go mad—MAD! It turns them into..." he paused dramatically, "...into senators and congressmen! Whatever you do, don't drink the water—only drink the wine!"

I started giggling almost hysterically, at which he grabbed me by the shoulders and said, "Sh-h-h, no hysterics! They'll incarcerate you!"

I reached into my purse and came out with my cell phone, whispering, "Car 54, where are you?"

John grinned, and I put the cell phone away, asking him with a smile of my own, "Who are you, really, under all these layers?"

He wrinkled his nose into a rat face and put his upper teeth over his lower lip. "I already told you," he answered. "I'm Chuck E. Cheese!"

"You dirty rat! You killed my brother!" I rasped at him, and stuck my cell phone in his ribs like a gun.

Laughing, he took my arm and guided me into the restaurant.

Once inside the Riviera, I took my camera and tape recorder out of my pockets and gave my coat to John, who hung it up with his jacket. Then he waved me to a table near the bar and went behind it to put on a pot of coffee. He must have flipped a switch somewhere also, because the soft sounds of jazz began to play through the dining room speakers.

I looked around the dining room. "It won't be difficult to write copy for the restaurant web page," I said. "The three selling points of any restaurant are the food, the service, and the ambiance, and this place certainly has all three."

I realized that just as Daniel carefully blended tastes to create sensual edible masterpieces, so someone had carefully blended colors and artwork for a visual feast.

"Who did the decorating?"

"It was Penny who suggested we go with 1930's Art Deco elegance with the basic color scheme of burgundy, red, and soft pinks. I'm partial to the high-backed banquette seating, and I felt that light oak and antique brass would go well with the lights."

I admired the deep burgundy of the carpet, upholstery, and wallpaper, offset with shades of pink from lily-shaped wall sconces and red, pink, and burgundy Tiffany-style light fixtures in the shapes of flowers.

"On the other hand, all the Erté prints and *Follies Bergère* paintings were Reggie's choices. He's very fond of delicate ladies in idealized *haute couture*. He designed the table settings, too," he said, gesturing to the room at large. "He's very insistent about perfection of form and detail."

"I noticed that on Friday night," I said. "He was scrutinizing the room when Bernice and I arrived for dinner."

I picked up my camera and began snapping pictures of the tables. They were laid with white cloths, topped diagonally with smaller pink cloths and rose-colored napkins, all folded in the shape of opened fans. The settings, too, were picture-perfect, with a water goblet and two wine glasses on the right, salad, fish, and main course cutlery set on either side of the cover plate, with the dessert fork and spoon set above, and a bread plate on the upper left crossed at the top with its own knife.

I looked back to John behind the bar and saw him reflected in the mirrored wall that ran its whole length. He seemed to be part of a Toulouse Lautrec-style oil painting that was on the wall behind the cash register counter opposite the bar. The painting was itself a bar scene, again of the French Follies, with a dissolute-looking man leaning on the bar and reflected in a mirror in the painting; the mirror also showed ladies on a stage doing the Can-Can. This painting—and the Erté prints—served to emphasize not only the French theme of the restaurant but the subtle humor one might expect from the service personnel.

"How do you like your coffee?" asked John.

Before I could formulate a clever answer, we heard the kitchen door bang open as Peter came stumbling in, ashen faced and wild-eyed, and leaned heavily against the bar. He looked back and forth from one to the other of us.

"What is it, man?" asked John.

"Daniel," Peter finally squeaked. "It's Daniel. I...I think he's dead!"

John ran to the kitchen door, and I followed closely behind him. Peter pointed to where Daniel lay, crumpled in front of the stove, his eyes starkly staring at nothing. There was clearly no life in them.

"My God," John murmured. "He looks like he's had a heart attack."

He knelt down to see if he could feel a pulse, first at Daniel's wrist, and then at his throat, but I was aware from the odor that his bowel had voided. He was definitely dead, and had been for a while.

John shook his head and stood up again. Turning to me he said, "Ariel, could you please go into the bar and call 9-1-1? Don't use your cell for the call, because they might want a landline confirmation. I'll see if I can get in touch with Reggie and Penny. They need to know what's happened."

Peter looked terribly shaken, and John took him by the elbow and directed him toward the door. "Peter, maybe you'd better go and sit in the dining room. I'll join you and Ariel there in a minute."

Then John pulled out his cell phone to call Reggie and Penny.

I went to the dining room with Peter and asked, "Where's the phone?"

"Over there at the entrance, near the cash register," he said softly, slumping into a chair at the table where I'd left all my things.

I put in the call to 9-1-1, giving the emergency dispatcher the name and address of the restaurant. I explained that Daniel showed no sign of life and had no discernable pulse, and that John Chan, one of the owners of the restaurant, thought it might be a heart attack. In response, the dispatcher asked me for my name and also whether anyone had been there when he collapsed. I told her that to the best of my knowledge, no one had been.

I hung up and joined Peter at the table. He was sitting with his head in his hands, crying.

"It's not fair," he said. "Daniel was helping me. He was teaching me. This shouldn't have happened. I gave him the artwork to protect him. This shouldn't have happened. It just shouldn't have happened." He went on and on and on, repeating the phrase.

I leaned forward and patted him on the shoulder, and he looked at me with red-rimmed eyes.

"I'm sorry," he whispered, visibly trying to get hold of himself. "I know I shouldn't be acting this way."

"It's okay, Peter," I said softly. "You were very close to Daniel, and he was your mentor. It's okay to grieve for him."

I watched him sympathetically while he continued to struggle with his feelings. But after a few moments, his face crumpled and he gave in to silent sobbing. He seemed so desperately lost in his grief, I almost wanted to take him in my arms and hold him and rock him, the way I would with one of my little nephews.

Then abruptly, he pulled himself up shook his head. "I've gotta stop this. It's not okay. I've gotta stop. My mother would never approve."

"Well, she's not here," I said, "and you have the right to your feelings."

He looked at me, as if weighing the truth of my words. Then he crossed his arms on the tabletop and put his head down again.

I sat watching him for a few seconds, trying to get in touch with my own feelings. This was the second traumatic event in less than twelve hours. I'd had an automatic adrenal rush when I realized Daniel was dead, and I was still a little bit spacey from it, but behind the physical sensations was something I finally recognized as uneasiness. Something wasn't right with the scene in the kitchen. Something I'd seen was bothering me, but I didn't know what it was.

I said, "Excuse me, Peter, I'll be right back," and I grabbed my camera and hurried into the kitchen. I photographed everything I could see from where I had been standing when we first found Daniel lying on the floor—the counter, the stove, the floor, and Daniel himself. I figured if I didn't move beyond where I'd been standing when we came in the first time, I wouldn't compromise the scene any further than I already had.

I didn't know where John had disappeared to, but I was alone for the moment in the kitchen, so I decided to center myself and see if I could tune in to what had happened to Daniel. As I did so, I seemed to move into Daniel's body, and I had a pleasurable sense of doing something creative that I loved to do—preparing another of my magnificent culinary specialties.

I began to visualize in front of me a heating sauté pan with a layer of oil in it on the stove top, and I felt my firm hand chopping the onions, then transferring the chopped onions into the pan and hearing them begin to sizzle.

I put down the knife and turned to look at a half-full bottle of wine. I saw the label on the bottle and felt Daniel's sense of pleasure, though the only thing that registered for me was the year, which was 1998. I sensed him smiling, and the pleasure he seemed to feel was almost gloating. I/he picked up a glass filled with the dark red liquid, and took a whiff of the aroma. *Umm*, I savored the odors of blackberry, chocolate, and vanilla—the smell was minty at first, but it also included licorice and something Daniel seemed to recognize but my own experience couldn't quite identify.

He raised the glass in his hand in a sort of toast, and looking intently at the shimmering ruby red liquid, he said, "Let's do it!"

I wasn't really sure *what* he was toasting—or agreeing to. I couldn't tell whether he was talking to himself or to someone else—I could only see what he was focusing on.

Then I/he took a sip of the wine, and though it was a vicarious experience, I could almost taste the sweetness of the vintage and feel the warmth as it flowed gently down my throat. Again, I sensed him gloating. Then he took another large mouthful and set the glass down.

For a moment, I/he concentrated on stirring the cooking onions. And then, suddenly, the pain began, starting in my belly and moving up into my chest. I bent forward, dropping the wooden spoon, and gripped my chest. I felt as if my heart was blowing up like a balloon, and the pain got worse and worse as I began to suffocate. Oh, God, oh, God!

I pulled myself out of Daniel's body to avoid the pain and saw him crumple to the floor, to the position he was actually in. For a moment, he was still with me. We seemed to have exited the body together. There was a sense of surprise, disbelief from Daniel. Then the essence of him was gone.

I leaned over, with my hands on my knees, trying to recover some equilibrium, trying to get some distance, and then I had a flash just for an instant of a woman standing at a stove, sautéing onions, being clobbered on the back of the head with a skillet. I actually saw the skillet come down and heard the crack of bone as it connected.

I gasped at the vision and staggered backward. This image wasn't from Daniel—it was Annie Grace!

For a few seconds I was utterly confused. I'd been trying to "feel" what had happened to Daniel, and I believed I had actually connected with his dying moments, but for some reason I'd also tuned in to Annie Grace, who, it seemed, had also died in the process of sautéing onions! I felt like a radio tuner that was picking up signals from two stations at the same time.

"Thank God I wasn't in *her* body when she got clobbered!" I whispered to Daniel's body. "I don't think I could have tolerated being killed twice in five minutes!"

Daniel didn't answer.

John appeared at the back door. "Who are you talking to?" he asked.

"Just myself," I said. "Where did you disappear to?"

"I had to go outside to get my cell phone to work," he said. Then, with one more glance to Daniel, he added, "We probably shouldn't be in here."

He took my arm and started to lead me out, but as we went, I glanced back over my shoulder at the bottle of wine and saw that the vintage was indeed 1998.

JOHN GUIDED ME back into the dining room, explaining as we went, "I reached Reggie, and he said he'd be here in about twenty minutes. I wasn't able to get any response from Penny."

I sat down at the table with Peter, but John continued to stand, looking as if he were thinking.

Finally he asked, "What were you doing back in the kitchen?"

I wasn't ready to talk about my experience viewing the deaths of Daniel and Annie Grace, so, with as much composure as I could muster, I said to the two of them, "Something about Daniel's death was really bothering me, but I couldn't put my finger on it, so I went back to take some pictures."

"There's one thing I noticed," Peter mumbled.

John turned on him. "What's that?" he demanded.

Peter looked up bleary eyed. "Daniel uses wine in his meat sauces, but the wine he had on the counter this morning is from Reggie's private stock."

"What do you mean, 'private stock'?" I asked.

It was John who answered my question. "Since Reggie started racing, he and Penny have performed a little ritual the night before a race. After the last seating is finished, they say goodnight to the staff, leave the restaurant, and then come right back in, just as if they were customers. They sit at the table beside the check-out, and he orders a glass of Cape Mantelle Cabernet Sauvignon, from Margaret River in Western Australia, and she orders a glass of DuBonnet."

The ritual confused me. "Why would they go out and come right back?"

"It's a requirement of Virginia liquor laws—an employee isn't allowed to drink on the job, and he can't just sit down and become a customer when he gets off work, he has to leave the premises. Reggie and Penny bought the Cape Mantelle as part of their regular order for the restaurant, but it never went on the wine list—it was strictly for Reggie's personal use—nobody else was ever served any."

I pictured Reggie swilling the expensive wine and asked, "Would he drink a whole bottle by himself the night before a race?"

"No," John smiled. "Usually he'd have just a couple of glasses, and we'd use a vacuum sealer and put the bottle back in the cooler for the next time. Penny says he gets a kick out of his little ritual. He says it's his reward to himself for going on another harrowing outing at the track. I think it's actually his way of justifying both the racing and regularly drinking a bottle of wine that costs more than fifty dollars wholesale!

"Anyway, Peter's right—the wine Daniel was drinking was Reggie's Cape Mantelle Cabernet Sauvignon."

What came into my head when he said this was the Fat Man of my dream, carrying the sign saying *In vino veritas*. I felt the prickly sensation of goose bumps on the back of my neck and down my arms, but something on the edge of my mind hinted it was more than what Peter had noticed. I hadn't known the wine was Reggie's private stock, but I did know something I'd seen wasn't right!

In vino veritas. In wine there is truth. So the truth was right here, in the wine. But what was the truth? Was there something in the wine that had caused Daniel's death? If the wine was from Reggie's private stock, had he doctored it and given it to Daniel? Or had someone else doctored it and given it to Daniel in an effort to frame Reggie? I wondered who among the staff had access to the wine. Probably everybody, but I made a mental note to check on this.

Chapter Ten

Two patrol officers arrived within a few minutes, followed within seconds by a police sergeant, who seemed to be their supervisor. As they walked into the restaurant, the sergeant asked, "Did someone call 9-1-1?"

John, who had been standing by the table where I sat with Peter, moved toward the kitchen at their appearance and said, "Yes! This way!"

John led them into the kitchen, but the sergeant immediately directed him to step out. John stood to one side, just outside the kitchen door, holding it open and staying close enough to watch the activity.

I watched from my seat as one of the policemen, a Hispanic man in his late forties, with curly brown hair and a bit of a midriff bulge, came out of the kitchen and asked John to help him prop open the kitchen doors with a couple of chairs. John continued to stand near the kitchen, watching quietly. The officer went back outside, and through the window I could see him stretching yellow police tape from one side of the front door around a couple of the parking signs on the street and back to the corner of the building, leaving the police a fairly large empty space to move around in. The officer stayed outside, I presumed to act as crowd control and to wait for the arrival of other emergency vehicles.

The sergeant was out of earshot but seemed to be giving directions. Shortly thereafter, the other officer, a pretty young woman in her late twenties, came out carrying a notebook, with a sheet of paper on top of it. She suggested John should come back and sit with us. John slowly wandered over and stood beside the table, looking a little dazed, as the officer went to the front door to lock it. Then she came toward us and asked our names, writing them down on the paper.

"Thank you, ma'am," she said courteously after I'd spelled my name for her. "I need to log everybody who comes and goes," she explained. Then she went back to the front door and took a position there as if she were standing sentry.

Within another minute we heard a siren draw close to the building; then it stopped, though we could still see the flashing of the strobe light on top of the emergency van. A few seconds later, the officer at the door let a team of four paramedics in. I could see they all had their names on their uniforms, and the officer duly noted the name of each on the log as they came in. She motioned them toward the kitchen doors, which had been propped open. I turned and watched them as they set about examining Daniel.

A few moments later, the sergeant stepped out of the kitchen. He reached up and toggled the microphone on his shoulder to call in to the dispatch officer, "We have what looks like a heart attack victim, white male, unattended, so we need an ME, a CIS team, and an ID tech on the premises."

The sergeant walked over to us and asked, "Which of you folks found the body?"

Peter looked up through bleary eyes. "I did."

"What time was that?"

"I guess it was a little before nine o'clock. I usually get here by eight-thirty, but I missed my bus this morning." Then he moaned a little. "I can't help feeling it's my fault," he said hoarsely. "If I'd been here on time...maybe I could have helped."

"Did *you* call 9-1-1?" asked the sergeant.

"No," I volunteered, "I did."

"Did all three of you go into the kitchen?" asked the sergeant.

"Yes," we all answered in unison.

"And then," offered John, "I asked Ariel here to call 9-1-1 while I tried to get hold of the other owners."

"And did any of you touch anything or move anything in the kitchen?"

Peter shook his head, while I answered, "No."

John said, "I did. I tried to take his pulse at his wrist, and then when I couldn't get anything, I tried again at his throat to see if he had any pulse. When I didn't get anything there, I had Ariel call 9-1-1 from out here instead of using the phone in the kitchen."

Then I remembered something. "Daniel told me he would be receiving a shipment of ducks at eight o'clock. I guess if they're here, then he must have been alive at that time, but I didn't think to check when I was in the kitchen."

"I *did* check that before I called Reggie," said John. "The ducks are here. So is the liquor shipment. Reggie handles that before he goes to the gym." Then he said to the sergeant, "I'm talking about Reggie Whitson, who's one of the other owners. He should be on his way here now."

The sergeant nodded. "If Mr. Whitson was here earlier this morning, we *will* need to talk to him." Then he said to John, "If you'll be seated, sir, investigators will be here shortly to ask all of you some questions. I'll just wait over here and jot a few notes down in my book."

John asked, "Is it okay if we drink our coffee? I had just poured some out here when Peter came out of the kitchen and told us about Daniel."

The sergeant nodded, so John sat down with us at the table. "There's plenty to go around if any of your crew would like some. Just help yourselves."

The sergeant said, "Thanks," and started to turn away, but on a whim I reached out and touched his sleeve to stop him. He looked at me with eyebrows raised.

I glanced at his nametag and saw that it read *Sgt. Greg Mason*. So I said, "Sergeant Mason, could I talk to you privately for a moment?"

He gave a little nod and motioned me over to the bar.

In a low voice, I said, "Sergeant, when we first found the body, I came out here and called 9-1-1, but then I realized something about the scene was bothering me, so I went back in and took some pictures with my digital camera. I just wanted to let you know I'd done that, and also that I think…I think there's something wrong with the wine."

The sergeant narrowed his eyes as I said this and asked, "What do you mean that something is wrong with the wine? What makes you say that?"

I grimaced a little apologetically, because I figured I might sound like a flake, but I answered, "I sometimes get little psychic hits."

He raised an eyebrow and looked at me dubiously.

"And I had a dream a couple of nights ago about wine, and it just seemed to me that it related to this situation."

"Okay," he said, though his face was inscrutable. "I think the detectives will definitely want to talk to you about this a bit more. But for the moment, do you mind just waiting with the others?"

I nodded and returned to the table.

Then the sergeant said, "Just sit tight for a little while, please."

He sat down at the next table and busied himself with his notepad, but I realized he was within earshot, and I knew not much would escape his notice.

At that moment, Reggie arrived. We could see through the windows that the patrolman on the street was holding him back.

John said to the sergeant, "That's Reggie Whitson," so the sergeant called out, "Okay, Baxter, tell Gomez to let him in."

Once he'd been let in and had given his name to Baxter, Reggie hurried over to the table and exclaimed, "What's going on? Is he really dead?"

The sergeant turned to him and said, "I'm going to ask you to sit down with the others, sir, and we'll let the investigative team sort things out when they get here."

Reggie sat at the table, as he'd been asked to do.

In answer to Reggie's question, John gave a little shrug and said, "We're pretty sure he is. It looks like a heart attack, but Ariel thinks something is fishy about it."

Then he turned to the sergeant and asked permission to get Reggie a cup of coffee. The sergeant nodded, and John went quickly to the bar and poured a cup.

"I couldn't reach Penny at all," he said when he sat back down. "Her cell phone must be turned off."

"This is her morning to see Bernice," Reggie explained. "Ariel, are you heading back over there? Will you tell her?"

I nodded. "I'll be happy to when I finally get there. But the sergeant said I'd need to talk to the CIS team when they get here, so I don't know when that will be. I mean, I guess we'll all be talking to the team. But I have a feeling somebody is going to grill me for my comment about the wine."

The three men looked at me quizzically.

"Why?" asked Reggie.

"Because I told the sergeant I had a dream the other night that suggested something was odd about wine. And there Daniel was, drinking wine that wasn't his early in the morning."

"What wine?" asked Reggie.

"Daniel seems to have been sampling some of your Cape Mantelle Cabernet Sauvignon this morning while preparing his soup stock," John said.

"Why, that bastard!" Reggie said loudly. "I *knew* he was nipping my wine! I bet he thought he was getting even with me for some imagined little grievance! The minute I left, he must have gone to the wine cooler and taken my bottle. That really ticks me off! If he weren't dead, I'd..." Reggie must have suddenly realized he was sounding threatening and finished with a little more control, "...I'd give him a piece of my mind. Not that that ever did much good. And to add insult to injury, he *is* dead, so now I can neither berate him nor run my restaurant."

I glanced up and noticed the sergeant, who was listening to this tirade.

The sergeant leaned over as Reggie subsided and directed a question to him. "Excuse me sir, did I hear you say you were here this morning with the deceased?"

"Yes, I was. On Tuesdays he takes his produce shipment at seven a.m. and a delivery of ducks at about eight. I also come in early to receive the alcohol delivery. This morning, he came in just about the time I was getting ready to leave. We had a few words with each other, and then I left."

It occurred to me there were a lot of comings and goings in the kitchen that morning, with lots of people who might have had a chance to poison Daniel—although it seemed unlikely a duck delivery guy would want to kill a chef!

"Where did you go from here?" asked the sergeant.

"I went to my club for a workout and massage. I was just finishing there when I got the call from John to come here."

Reggie looked a little nervous, probably about having spoken so loudly concerning Daniel, and perhaps also because he'd been at the restaurant with Daniel that morning.

With the suddenness of a flashbulb going off in my head, I realized one of the things that had struck me as odd this morning was that there were two wine glasses on the counter near Daniel's sauté pan. In my little vision, I hadn't been sure whether Daniel was alone in the kitchen when he drank the wine, but he'd given a toast and said, "Let's do it." Who would have been drinking with him that early in the day, and why? If Reggie was to be believed, it wasn't he. But it seemed there had been a veritable parade of people through the kitchen that morning.

While I was still wondering what was true, two more police cars pulled up outside, and three more people came in.

People on the street were beginning to gather outside the yellow tape and were peering in the windows, so Sergeant Mason went over to Baxter and gave her some instructions. Baxter finished writing in her notebook, then stepped outside to help Gomez disperse the crowd. Within a minute they had set up a barricade, and people were no longer able to get near the windows. Officer Gomez extended the range of the yellow tape to include the new vehicles and the barricades, and when Officer Baxter came back in she dropped the blinds for good measure.

The sergeant had a little discussion with the two detectives beyond earshot. The third person, whom I decided was probably the one Sergeant Mason had referred to as the ID tech, went into the kitchen and remained out of my line of vision. Then one of the detectives broke away from the huddle and came over to the table where we all sat.

"I'm Detective Flanagan. Before I get any other information from you folks, can you tell me the victim's name?"

"Daniel Lafayette," all three of the men said in chorus.

The detective wrote down the name and then asked, "And can you tell me if the victim had a medical doctor locally? And do you know how we might reach his next of kin?"

Reggie spoke first. "I don't think he had a local doctor. He never mentioned anyone to me."

John added, "I once heard him say he hated going to the doctor."

Peter nodded. "He said that more than once."

"How about you, ma'am? Do you know of any doctor he might have been seeing?"

"I'm afraid I'm going to be useless since I'd only met the man once before today."

The detective nodded, then asked, "How about next of kin?"

John volunteered, "He was from France, and I know he occasionally mentioned a sister in Paris, but he hadn't been home to see her, or anyone else, for that matter, for at least the five years he was working here."

Reggie agreed, "That's my take on the matter, too. Although I believe his sister's name was Elyse...spelled with a 'y' but pronounced 'Elise.'"

Peter said, "He had a CD of a Beethoven piece called *Für Elise* that he sometimes played in the kitchen while we were chopping vegetables. He said it reminded him of his sister."

"And would the sister's name also have been Lafayette?"

"To the best of my knowledge," John said, while the other two nodded.

"So he never mentioned a brother-in-law, or nieces or nephews?" Flanagan asked.

"No," said John, "but he sometimes referred to her as his 'sister, the sister,' so I think she was in a convent."

Reggie commented softly, with a little half sneer, "That's the French for you. The women go into convents, and the men jump anything in a skirt. Makes you wonder where the men find the women they jump."

While Flanagan was talking to us, yet another man had come in and gone into the kitchen. He now came back out and walked toward the table. Tapping Flanagan lightly on the shoulder he said, "He's dead, Jim."

John and I looked up, slightly startled, and Flanagan said softly to the fellow, "I wish you wouldn't do that." Then he looked at us sheepishly and explained, "This is our medical examiner. He and I go way back, and we were Trekkies together in our misspent youth."

The ME just smiled and said, "I've called Metropolitan to take the body to the morgue. We'll try to get the autopsy done this afternoon. Looks like natural causes, but I'll let all of you go through your paces."

"Thanks," said Flanagan. "Bones," he added softly.

Then he focused on those of us at the table again. "Ma'am, Sergeant Mason tells me you have some thoughts about the wine that he thinks we should pursue a little further, so if you wouldn't mind, we'd like you to come down to the station so we can get a more detailed statement. You can ride with the sergeant, and he'll be happy to drive you back here afterward to get your car.

"And gentlemen, we'd like to get complete statements from all of you. The two of you who were here when the body was found can go to the station with one of the patrol officers. Mr. Whitson, we still have a little bit more to do before we can clear the scene, and then I can interview you here."

We all nodded in agreement.

Then Reggie and John looked at each other, and I realized the same thought was going through both their minds, and that I was picking up on it. So I wasn't surprised when Reggie asked, "How long will the restaurant have to remain closed?" They seemed a little grim at the idea of being closed for any length of time.

"We need to be able to have the ID tech finish getting whatever evidence there may be of what went on in the kitchen this morning," Flanagan replied. "But a good guess is that you'll be back to business as usual by early this afternoon."

"Business as usual—ha!" Reggie exclaimed. "*If* we can find a chef, and *if* he can prepare French cuisine."

"Don't worry, Reggie," said John, "I have a cousin who trained at the Mandarin Hotel in Hong Kong that we can probably borrow from my uncle for a few weeks."

I looked at John and instantly knew where this was leading.

"I said we needed French cuisine," growled Reggie, "not Chinese."

"Have you ever heard of the Vong Restaurant in New York City? It's a top-flight place that features a blend of Thai and French cuisine. My cousin trained at the Vong Restaurant that's on the top floor of the Mandarin Hotel in Hong Kong," said John. "This cousin is a masterful French chef."

"What's his name?" asked Reggie, relenting.

With a big grin, John replied, "Clarice."

Reggie looked startled, and then he laughed. "Then call over there right now and see if you can arrange to steal her," Reggie said, looking toward the detective for approval.

Reggie must have thought my glance at John had been disapproving because he turned to me and said, "I know it seems a bit unfeeling, but we do have regulars who will show up for their meal tonight, and other customers who booked months ago. And if we want to stay in business, we'd better be able to feed them."

Then Reggie addressed Peter. "I assume you'll stay on?"

Peter glanced up and brightened a bit. I got the impression he'd been thinking his life was somehow over and his plans blighted. But he perked up at the question.

I thought how Peter's future had been tied to Daniel's mentoring, and how he must be feeling the loss of his hopes of becoming a chef himself. I wondered if he'd been privy to the meeting where Daniel had threatened to leave at the end of the year. His reaction seemed to indicate he hadn't had a clue. However, he appeared happy at being invited to stay on at the restaurant, even though he might not have the same status in a kitchen run by somebody other than Daniel.

"I guess I can stay, for a while," Peter said quietly.

"Good. Even if Clarice isn't available, there's enough kitchen expertise among the three of us that we can surely pull something together. We'll apologize to everybody for not providing them with Daniel's cuisine, we'll give them a free dessert and a ten percent discount, and they'll go away happy, believe me."

Reggie's excitement was obvious, and I realized from his last remark that he was back in rescue mode and that the restaurant could survive.

John had been jabbering into his cell phone in Chinese, but he now clicked it shut and turned back to us with a big grin. "Clarice is ours, my uncle said. But he warned me she's very strong-minded and will doubtless take ownership of the menu and is already gathering a carload of ingredients to bring with her. We probably will have no more say in how the meals are crafted than we did with Daniel."

Then he added, "I suspect that's why my uncle was so willing to let us shanghai her. He's a bit old-fashioned, and while he supports women in the kitchen, he's not likely to want to have one telling him what to do. Oh, but we do need to go and pick her up. She's only recently back from Hong Kong and doesn't have a driver's license yet—or a car."

I felt a pang while John was talking about Clarice. She sounded like a really strong-willed woman, and her entrance onto the stage of my life made me wonder if my hall pass was being revoked. Was it the psychic in me or the woman who felt John's eagerness to bring Clarice to the Riviera seemed suspicious?

Reggie was still consolidating his rescue plan. He said, "As soon as you get back from the police station with Peter, why don't you go give Clarice a hand as she raids your uncle's larder, and write up a receipt for everything she's bringing. And get her here as fast as you can." Then he added thoughtfully, "Does she have a sense of humor?"

John chuckled. "Yes, but not one you'd understand."

Reggie looked aghast. "What does that mean? She *can* speak English, can't she?"

"Oh, definitely. And she will, unless she wants to mystify you—or to insult you. Most people seem to think that Asians are very fun loving, because they laugh a lot. But Chinese humor is a little quirky—often based on our laughing at the oddities of life and other people's misfortunes. The Chinese loved Charlie Chaplin and Laurel and Hardy because of their slapstick visual comedy.

"And it may be best to continue keeping Penny out of the kitchen until they have a chance to get to know each other—just remember the Chinese ideogram for war is 'two women under one roof.' But you'll figure Clarice out, I'm sure."

I noticed Flanagan speaking to Officer Baxter, who had come back inside. She approached the table and spoke softly. "Gentlemen, I can drive two of you to the station now, if you're ready."

I looked at my watch for the first time since Peter had come out of the kitchen to tell us he'd just found Daniel, and I realized with astonishment the elapsed time had been only about an hour. It had seemed both very long and very short in duration—long because so much had occurred that would have long-term effects and because we would have to wait before learning any details about what had really happened to Daniel, but short because of the surrealistic quality of the experience and the extreme efficiency of the police. I thought how polite all these police people were, and how speedily they had accomplished their mission.

I watched as John and Peter went out. John gave me a rueful little wave as he exited through the front door. Then Detective Flanagan came over and took Reggie to a table in the far corner of the room, where he began asking him questions.

THE CHEF WHO DIED SAUTÉING

Sergeant Mason walked over and begged my pardon for not being quite ready to go, saying he needed to finish a couple of things in the kitchen. As I sat waiting for him, I had time to reflect for a few minutes.

I knew Reggie and John had the welfare of the restaurant uppermost in their minds, and Peter seemed to be thinking about his job and his future now that Daniel was gone. But nobody had mentioned what was usually most important when somebody dies—like where the deceased would be buried, or whether there would be some sort of memorial. Yes, there had been problems. But those problems were all over now, and it seemed to me some closure was needed before life should go on fully.

And so I was sitting alone with no one to talk to when a couple of paramedics came through wheeling a stretcher with a filled body bag on it.

I remembered John's earlier remarks about how the Chinese often laugh at people's misfortunes. And though I was sure his spirit had moved on, I thought how this morning Daniel had been the most unfortunate of us all.

Somehow, I couldn't think of a single funny line.

"Goodbye, Daniel," I said simply.

SERGEANT MASON HELPED me into his cruiser, and I affixed my seat belt as he climbed in on the driver's side.

As he pulled away from the curb, he said, "I want you to know I'm not prejudiced against psychics. I know of some police departments that have used them successfully, and there've been plenty of times when I've wished I had someone who could help me out in that way. The majority of the crimes in Alexandria are grand theft auto. So I'm looking at one or two or three of these in a given day, and I see how they disrupt the lives of the victims. And I wish there was some way I could just sense where the cars are and get them back for their owners."

I looked at him. He seemed like a really nice guy. He was about six feet tall, with sandy hair and gray eyes. He looked to be in his late thirties. And I couldn't help noticing he had a very attractive jaw line.

I thought to myself, "Get a grip!" I'd just had a date where a bomb came through the window, and there was a dead guy on his way to the morgue whose death might or might not be related to whoever threw the bomb. I needed to focus on the recent events and on my suspicions, not on how sexy the cop who was driving me to the station was.

"I'm pretty good at finding things," I said in reply to his comments. "But I've never had to go hunting for anything as big as a stolen car. However, it sounds like something a dowser might be able to do."

"What do you mean? I thought dowsers looked for water or oil or things like that."

"That's true, but the principle is the same for whatever you might want to find. A *good* dowser can find just about anything. Actually, I heard once that there's a dowser who used to live here in Alexandria who taught dowsing to the Marines. This was during the Vietnam conflict. He trained a group of them to dowse for land mines."

Sergeant Mason shook his head slightly. "Huh! It's hard to believe the Marines would use a psychic."

"Well, I went to a dowser's convention up in Vermont with a friend when I was a teen. We learned to dowse with L-rods, pendulums, and other tools. The guy who trained us said a lot of dowsers don't consider themselves to be psychic. They think of themselves as technicians. Of course," I added, "I think it's all the same thing."

Without taking his eyes off the road, he asked, "So tell me, then—how does this psychic stuff work?"

"That's a good question," I said. "I think it may be different for every psychic. I get hits in a lot of different ways. Like for instance, I have precognitive dreams sometimes, and that's why I think there's something wrong with the wine Daniel was drinking. In these dreams, I'm given some information to follow up on, even though I often can't interpret the clues right away. So what the dreams really do is put me on guard. Then if a situation comes up that seems to fit the warning, I'm more able to deal with it rationally.

"In this case, I had a dream last weekend that gave me the message '*In vino veritas*,' which translated from the Latin means, 'In wine there is truth.' So when I saw the wine bottle today, and the oddity of one dead body but two wine glasses, I realized this was the situation the dream was pointing to, and that there was something wrong with the wine."

"You seem pretty sure of yourself," he said with a grin. "Do you mostly get your information from dreams?"

I thought for a moment before answering him and decided this might not be the most appropriate time to tell him about my experiencing Daniel's dying moments. If things went smoothly, I'd pass that on later.

"Well, I also had an impression of two young people running away after the bomb came through John's window last night."

The sergeant did a double take and his face turned instantly serious. "What? What bomb?"

"Oh, gosh! I was so caught up in this morning's events that I forgot about it. I guess John did, too. It wasn't as serious as it sounds—a poorly constructed Molotov cocktail that came crashing through his kitchen window and fizzled out in the sink. The police in D.C. figured it was random vandalism, but now it occurs to me that somebody may be sabotaging the restaurant's personnel."

"That changes things a bit," said Mason. "I'm glad you thought of it. We aren't always able to connect events that happen here with things that occur in other jurisdictions. I'll pass this information on to Flanagan when we get together at the station. And don't forget to put it in your statement to him. We can put in a request to D.C. for the case file."

Then he added, "But couldn't that be the bottle your dream was referring to?"

"That was a beer bottle," I said. "And nobody was hurt. This was a wine bottle, and Daniel is dead. And usually, these kinds of dreams are warnings to me. Since I was supposed to be interviewing Daniel this morning, it's possible I might have gone in before he had any of the wine, and he might have offered me a glass. The dream would have stopped me from taking it."

"I see," he said. He was silent, paying attention to his driving for a few moments. Then he asked, "You also said you had a feeling something was wrong with the scene in the kitchen. What did you mean?"

"I guess...it's because I pay a lot of attention to my intuition. The sixth sense isn't something to be discounted. Whenever we do things on autopilot, we've actually turned ourselves over to our intuition. And I learned in the army to pay very close attention to any feelings I might have about things that aren't right with a situation. There are times when it could be a matter of life and death. I think the police probably use their intuition a lot—at least all the detective stories I've ever read would indicate you do. And that's being psychic."

"Well," he said, "we like to call that getting a gut feeling about something. But now that I think about it, you're absolutely right."

Before we reached the station, Sergeant Mason asked, "Have you ever been to the Alexandria police station before?"

I shook my head.

"Well, then, prepare yourself for a bit of a shock. The whole building is subsiding, and many of the halls look like an Escher print—rippled floors, lopsided doors, brick walls separating to the point that you can take some of the bricks out! It's a scandal," he said matter-of-factly. Then he added, "There are places where the skirting board is a good six to eight inches above the floor. There was somebody who did a story on the building for one of the newspapers, and ever since then we've had to put up with lots of jokes about the 'crooked police force.'"

When we reached the station, Sergeant Mason led me along one of the corridors with a rippled floor.

As I looked at the black and white checkerboard pattern I said, "This makes me think of *Alice in Wonderland*. I'd hate to be brought in on a drunk charge and have to try to navigate *this* hall!"

He smiled and led me to a common room where he asked if I wanted something to drink. I opted for a hot tea, which he prepared. Then he escorted me into an interrogation room where he pulled out a chair for me. He sat down across from me.

"You said while we were driving over that you'd been in the army. I was in the navy myself. Spent a couple of years as Shore Patrol. What was *your* billet?"

I laughed. It was one of those little inter-service quirks of jargon. "I realize that in the navy a billet's a job, but in the army it's a bed."

"Oh, right, I knew that," he said. "What was your assignment?"

"Most of the time I was a base guard. I manned a machine gun!"

He looked at me long and hard. "That's difficult for me to believe."

"Well, I was an army brat, so I'd grown up in service life. I have three younger sisters, and my family had limited resources for sending me to college, so I joined the army to 'be all I could be' right out of high school. My intention was to let my Uncle Sam support me for a few years and then pay for my college. But first I wound up being part of Operations Desert Shield and Desert Storm. That was an experience I hadn't expected."

"I was in before that happened, so my experience was less arduous."

"Well, except for a really brief period right at the end of the conflict, it wasn't all that hard. But that was the period where it became near to impossible to assign women to non-combat roles. There weren't any clear-cut front lines, and combat zones kept shifting, so more than once I found myself right in the middle of the action. And along with everything else that happened during that conflict, I learned about something called 'the desert experience.'"

"What do you mean?"

"Many spiritual texts talk about their leaders having to spend a period of time in the wilderness in order to reach enlightenment. As we sat waiting in the desert for something to happen, and with nothing to do but contemplate our own mortality, many of us had a subtle shift in consciousness and came to realize there are other dimensions beyond the one we call 'reality.'"

I gave a self-conscious smile. "I started writing about that experience, and when the conflict was over and I returned stateside, I put together a little book of my war poetry that actually got published and sometimes nets me a tiny royalty check."

"So you're a poet?"

"I said the royalty check is tiny. But, yes, I guess I am. But my real job is teaching. I used my GI Bill to get my education after I got out of the army."

"I did that, too. I really liked the shore patrol work, so I got my degree in criminology and joined the force. What do you teach?"

I smiled. "English."

"I guess I'd better watch my language," he said with a smile.

He glanced at his watch. "By the way, something you said on the way over here just registered," he said. "It's about the bomb. You said something about seeing two guys leaving the scene."

"I didn't actually see them. When we heard the crash, John rushed into the kitchen, and while I was following him, I had a mental impression—kind of a psychic hit—of two kids who were running away."

"Did you tell the D.C. police about that?"

"No, I didn't. It was just an impression. The police really focused their questioning on John since it was his apartment."

The sergeant was silent for a moment, looking at me seriously.

"So, is John your boyfriend?" he finally asked.

THE CHEF WHO DIED SAUTÉING

I looked at him quizzically. "Is that a cop question?"

He sat up a little straighter and said, "Sometimes it's important when we're putting a case together to know all the relationships among the people involved."

His answer sounded plausible, but my intuition told me he was fishing, and I had to remind myself again about my relationship with *him*. He was a cop, and if Daniel's death proved to be anything but natural, I could wind up as a suspect myself.

This thought caused me to do a little analysis of the situation. If Daniel's death wasn't a heart attack, but was as I thought the result of something in the wine, then who were the suspects? Reggie, Penny, and John, as the co-owners, appeared to have the most to gain from any positive change in the restaurant—but that didn't make any sense because they also stood to lose the most in losing their chef. On the other hand, Penny was having problems with Daniel, and Reggie might side with her in any major dispute. But after the altercation in the kitchen last Friday night, Reggie had actually appeared to side with Daniel. On the other hand, anybody who was watching would see that losing Daniel had effected a major change in Reggie's demeanor—he was acting as if he'd found his purpose again. And then there was John, whose enthusiasm at being able to bring his pretty cousin in to save the day was making my green eyes greener!

It was a paradox. Penny, Reggie, and John had the most to lose with the death of their chef. They each also stood to gain a small, personal victory. Penny would no longer be banned from the kitchen. Reggie could once again exercise his talent at rescuing the restaurant from any problems emanating from the kitchen. And John was excited, happy, and gaining some degree of power with the introduction of his cousin as chef.

It had been my personal observation that small victories—especially those based on motives of money, sex, and power—often played a more important role in people's lives than the big picture. And it seemed to me that all of the owners stood to gain some measure of increased power through small victories as a result of Daniel's death.

But maybe there were others whom I didn't yet know who'd stand to gain through Daniel's death. For instance, I didn't know the other waiters, but there had been mention that Daniel hadn't been getting along lately with anyone outside the kitchen staff.

And with duck, produce, and liquor deliverymen coming and going in the kitchen this morning, if Daniel truly hadn't died of natural causes, anybody could be a suspect! And because I was included in that suspect list, I was finding it hard just to sit back, relax, and scan the band for psychic hits.

WE'D BEEN CHATTING at the station for nearly an hour when Detective Flanagan showed up. "Sorry to keep you waiting. I've just finished with your friends from the restaurant."

Sergeant Mason got up to leave. He smiled at me and said, "Thanks for being so cooperative. I've enjoyed our little chat, but I need to go fill out some paperwork, so I'll let Detective Flanagan take it from here." Then turning to Flanagan, he said, "Ms. Quigley has some information that may be pertinent to the case regarding something that happened last night to one of the restaurant owners. I'll let her give you the details. But it does lend credence to the possibility that we might have a murder investigation here."

Flanagan looked as if his interest was suddenly aroused.

Mason reached for the door handle and said, "Let me know when you're done, and I'll drive Ms. Quigley back to the restaurant to get her car." Then he left.

Flanagan pulled out the chair Mason had vacated and sat down at the table across from me.

"I'm very interested in this new piece of information Sergeant Mason was referring to," he said, making a note in a little notebook. "But if you don't mind, I'd like to tape your testimony and get you to sign a transcript. It won't take long, but I like to have all the paperwork done while the case is fresh. That way, nothing will come back to bite me down the road."

He pulled out a tape recorder and set it on the table between us. When he turned it on, he recorded the date and time, his name and mine, and the case number and description.

"Okay, now, let's take it in order. First, please tell me everything you remember from the time you got to the restaurant this morning up until the police arrived on the scene."

I reiterated the events of the morning, and when I finished, he asked me to clarify why I thought the wine was poisoned. I told him what I had told Sergeant Mason about my dream.

Then he asked, "Do you personally know anything about how the staff at the restaurant got along with each other?"

"I'd only been to the restaurant once before today, and that was last Friday night," I said. "I did, however, see a disagreement between Penny Whitson and Chef Daniel while I was visiting the kitchen."

"Do you know what the disagreement was about?"

"Literally, it was about his not wanting to cook for an event she was involved with last Sunday. Later, Mrs. Whitson came out and said Daniel had barred her from the kitchen." I didn't feel right about passing on gossip about people I didn't know very well, so I stopped with that.

Detective Flanagan finally said, "Sergeant Mason indicated you had some other information that might be pertinent to our investigation. Something about an event that happened to one of the restaurant owners last night."

As I told him about the bomb incident, I watched his face. I could tell the story piqued his interest.

Finally, he clicked off the tape recorder. He asked me to wait a few minutes while he took it for transcription.

When he came back, I asked, "Where do you think the investigation will go from here?"

"We've bagged several items from the restaurant," he said, "including the wine bottle, the glasses, and the chef's wooden spoon. We're running fingerprint tests to see who might have been in the kitchen with the victim. The medical examiner has sent the body for an autopsy. Right now he thinks he may have just had a heart attack, but given your information about the bomb—and your sense of unease about the wine—we *will* send the wine and samples of blood, tissue, and stomach contents to the crime lab. However, their technicians are always backed up, and unless we get some corroboration from the autopsy, they aren't likely to put a rush on it."

I volunteered my digital photographs of the scene, but Flanagan said, "We took a lot of photos ourselves, so why don't you just download yours at home, and if you happen to note anything worth mentioning, give me a call." He handed me his card, and then he buzzed for Sergeant Mason to come back and drive me to my car. Five minutes later, I was out in the sunlight again.

On our drive back to the Riviera, I asked the sergeant, "Is being a policeman as exciting as movies and television make it out to be?"

He gave a little laugh. "It's a job," he said. Then he added, "We do have our share of both exciting and silly situations. You know about the Alexandria National Cemetery, don't you?"

I shook my head, so he continued, "It's connected to the main city cemetery, which is actually composed of several smaller cemeteries, some private and some church related. It's the responsibility of our officers to monitor the national cemetery, and it's an interesting place where interesting things sometimes happen.

"It's subject to the same subsidence that's taking place at the police station, and officers have sometimes felt their cars beginning to sink if they're parked there while on duty. And every now and then, a suspected felon thinks he can escape from us by running and hiding in the cemetery. Not long ago, I had to chase somebody on foot after I'd followed him in the cruiser to the end of the paved roadway."

He shook his head at the memory and continued, "I was talking about the cemetery just recently to a school group, so I've got a lot of facts about it in my head. It's one of the oldest cemeteries in the nation, dating back to 1862. There are about thirty-five hundred soldiers buried there, one hundred twenty-three of them unknown, and two hundred twenty-nine are African American.

"Anyway, the cemetery is full of Civil War dead. But strangely enough, since Virginia is a Southern state, there are no Rebel soldiers in the cemetery, only Union. There *were* thirty-nine Southerners at one time, but they were all moved. In earlier times this was a bit dismaying to Virginians, but even more so was that some of the soldiers who chased John Wilkes Booth were buried here."

He turned the cruiser onto King Street, and at that point he got a call from his dispatcher and had to chat with her for a couple of minutes about where he needed to go after dropping me off. When he finished with the call, he continued with his history of the cemetery and the city.

"Alexandria was an occupied city during the Civil War, and actually was occupied longer than any place else in the country. In fact, it was literally a 'reign of terror,' with a lot of crazies, drunks, and soldiers on the streets and murders occurring on an hourly basis. Even after order was restored, common citizens had to swear obedience to the U.S. government or face accusations of treason, arrest, and imprisonment. There was a curfew, people had their mail intercepted, and they couldn't go into Washington or the outlying areas without a pass.

"Nowadays, with the interest in Civil War memorabilia, some other places in the country have been experiencing grave robberies from people stealing medals and so forth from the soldiers. Anyway, most of the time we keep the cemetery under surveillance."

We were nearing the waterfront by this point, and as he pulled up behind the restaurant to let me out, Sergeant Mason said, "Thanks again for your cooperation."

"Thanks for the history lesson," I said and reached over to shake his hand. "Alexandria certainly has an interesting past," I added. I gave him a smile as I closed the cruiser door.

I got into my Jeep and started it. As I backed up and pulled away, I noticed the sergeant was still sitting in the lot, talking on his car phone again, so I gave him another little smile and wave as I went.

As I drove past the restaurant and considered everything that had happened to me since Friday afternoon when I first visited Bernice, I realized Alexandria had a pretty interesting "present," too.

Chapter Eleven

It was about two-thirty by the time I pulled into Bernice's driveway. Penny's car was still there, so I knew I was going to be interrogated and prepared myself for a talkathon.

I looked around as I walked into the kitchen, making sure Freud the Cat wasn't going to be under my feet, but she was snoozing in a dining chair. Penny and Bernice were both sitting there, too, looking relaxed and not in the least perturbed.

"That took a *long* time. How did the interview go?" Bernice asked. "Was Daniel appropriately behaved?"

I was stunned. "Haven't you two checked your messages?"

"No, this session was a *marathon*. And when we finished, we had lunch. So we haven't turned our phones back on yet. Why? What's up?"

I looked from one to the other, and finally I said, "John called hours ago to let you know. Daniel is dead."

I watched their faces change as the shock registered.

"What? What do you mean?" asked Penny. "How did he die?"

"The medical examiner says it looks like he had a heart attack."

Penny shook her head from side to side. "Oh, my God...what I said, what I said," she murmured.

Bernice reached to touch her hand. "You didn't do this, regardless of what you might have said."

I looked at them quizzically. "What are you two talking about?" I asked.

Penny glanced at Bernice with a question in her eyes, and Bernice said softly, "It's up to you."

Penny murmured in a small voice, "You know that I've been having trouble with Daniel?"

I nodded, and she continued.

"Well, this morning in my session with Bernice, I was saying that we all might be better off if Daniel were dead. I mean, he told us all on Sunday that he was planning to leave at the end of the year when his contract is up. But as owners, we'd be better off if he were dead, because we have him insured against death from accidents, natural causes, and so forth. We got a policy on him a while back because we realized we'd be in dire straits if anything were to happen to him.

"I mean, he's one of the reasons why the restaurant has its reputation. So if he were to die, we could at least collect on the policy. That way, we wouldn't have the debt of the building, and we might be able to salvage the business by finding someone else as a chef, but in any case, we wouldn't have to declare bankruptcy. But if he walks away, we're left holding the bag, and it's likely to be empty when we open it up. So I was saying it would be much better for all of us if he just died. And I'll admit I was feeling a little evil satisfaction in the thought!"

She looked at Bernice again, as if for encouragement, and then she added, "But that's a longer story."

She sipped her coffee and gazed thoughtfully into the distance for a few moments.

"Ariel," she said finally, "With everything that's happened, you've become very embroiled in the affairs of our restaurant in a short time, and I think you deserve to have the full background of what's been going on. So let me go back and fill in a few blanks."

"I'd appreciate that," I said. "John mentioned there had been a shift in the energy between you and Daniel over the last few months, but he didn't know any of the details."

"Ah, the details," Penny said with a dramatic roll of her eyes. Then she turned to face me directly. "As with many of our personal little dramas, I sometimes feel it is 'a tale told by an idiot, full of sound and fury, signifying nothing!'

"Last September, my mother, who was only in her mid-seventies, had a massive stroke, and I went back to my home in Perth to help out. She was very weak, and we knew she wouldn't last long, but I did what I could to make her remaining days comfortable and to help my father prepare for the change.

"As we had expected, she died within the month, and Dad took it really hard. Like many men, he'd never expected to outlive his wife, and he had no idea how he would cope on his own. So I stayed on through mid-November. My sister from Sydney had also come out, but she has a family, so she couldn't stay beyond the funeral.

"Well, we got through the funeral and moved my dad from the house into an apartment. We set him up with a service that would come in to assist him with housekeeping and food shopping.

"My parents had quite a few really good friends, and he still sails when he can, so Dad won't be without company, but he did have a period of adjustment. As I said, I stayed on until mid-November, but then I needed to come back here to pick up my life and do my own grieving.

"Reggie seemed to have lost a lot of weight while I was gone, and I attributed it to his having missed me. But he was also working out a lot at his club, and he looked very trim and fit. He was also wonderfully romantic when I got back, and we had a great Christmas, both personally and financially, with a full-blown New Year's Eve party at the restaurant that had been sold out by Halloween. And the new year started well, with more business than one might expect right after the holidays.

"Then the new racing season started in April. I couldn't make it up to Cumberland for the first race, and Reggie came home looking as though he'd been struck by lightning. I'd never seen him in such a deep depression, but he wouldn't talk about it.

"It took me several days and a couple of rounds of courage building with Bernice, but I finally got the story out of him.

"It seems that while I was off in Australia coping with the pain of losing my mother, he became 'lonely' and started flirting with one of the young women who worked in a concession stand at the track. She was cute, in her twenties, and I guess she had a thing for older men in racing suits.

"Well, as these things generally do, it went a bit further than flirting, and Reggie had weekend 'assignations' for the next few weeks. He'd stay up in Cumberland after the race and come home late Monday.

"Then, she got pregnant, though she never told him about it." Penny took a deep breath. "Stupid bloody fools! No protection, no nothing. I blame them both. I've been on the pill for five years, and Reggie hasn't needed to take any precautions with me since then, but what was he thinking? Did he expect her to be on the pill, just because *I* was? And why on earth didn't she insist on him wearing a condom? You'd think girls these days would have more sense!"

Penny paused to wipe her eyes. She took a big breath and blew it out slowly with a sigh.

"I guess it was his guilt at the affair that had him fawning all over me last winter. The thing is, though, the girl was in a car accident at the end of February. She hit a patch of ice and spun off the road, and both she and the baby died. Reggie didn't hear about it until he went back to Maryland for the opening of the racing season in April—obviously, nobody knew to tell him. And that was what had shaken him so badly. He hadn't known she was pregnant. And then she was dead, and so was the baby."

"If this is too hard for you…" I began, but Penny interrupted me.

"No, dear," she said. "I'm fine. I've been through it all time and again with Bernice, and you wouldn't want to miss the good part. I consider the confession he finally made to me and my consequent anger at him to be the 'sound and fury'—so this next bit is where the 'idiot' part comes in.

"I felt doubly screwed, pardon the phrase. He was cheating on me, and he was devastated that a child he'd never see anyway was lost—a child that wasn't mine. I refused to go to the track with him at all last spring, and I wallowed in my own self-pity. But I only wallowed for a few weeks, because I'm really rather more a bitch than I am a doormat. So I took revenge. Oh, yes! Sweet revenge!

"Why is it that revenge always seems to get us into a deeper mess than the mess we're avenging? What this idiot did for revenge," she said, tapping herself on the chest, "was to give in to the advances that had flowed freely from Daniel for over five years. I called him into the office one day and threw myself at him. The lovemaking was actually quite good—Daniel is...was...very passionate and very ingenious—but what I *really* wanted was just raw sex. I wanted to screw him the way I felt screwed, and I did—for about two months.

"Then I realized that *wasn't* what I wanted at all. I really love Reggie and I wanted us to be a couple again. We talked it all out—I told him about Daniel, and it hurt him, but he seemed to accept that he'd had it coming. We decided to pick up the pieces and rebuild our lives.

"I broke it off with Daniel, and started going to the races with Reggie again. But now I had a different problem. Evidently Daniel had taken the fling very seriously, and he was furious that I would consider breaking it off with him. He began to treat me like a nonentity, ignoring me when he could and being curt or rude when forced to talk to me. And he's been acting as if *Reggie* has been cuckolding *him.*

"So here we are. You saw what it was like last Friday, and I've been at my wit's end. Then, to put the frosting on the cake, he informed us at our meeting on Sunday he was leaving when his contract runs out in January, but just for good measure, he said he would leave immediately if I ever set foot in the kitchen again.

"And therein, my dear, hangs the tale, which may actually signify *more* than nothing. You now have an explanation for my lengthy session with Bernice this morning."

Penny leaned forward, elbows on the table, and dropped her head into her hands.

"So now Daniel's dead. Dear God, what a mess!"

Bernice and I sat quietly for a few moments, looking first at Penny and then at each other.

"On the practical side, did John and Reggie say anything about keeping the restaurant open?" Bernice asked.

"Actually, that was their first concern," I answered. "John's cousin Clarice will be coming over to the Riviera from Chinatown this afternoon to replace Daniel—from what John says, she's trained in French cuisine as well as Asian cooking. John was going to pick her up when he finished giving his statement to the police. I didn't see his car when I got back to the restaurant after giving my statement, so he's probably already on his way to Chinatown."

Bernice shot me a questioning look, and Penny raised her head.

"Why did *you* have to go to the police station?" asked Penny. "You're not involved with the restaurant."

"Well, I had a precognitive dream—or at least, I think it was precognitive. It was one of my Fat Man dreams, Bernice, and it fit the scene. I mentioned it to the police sergeant, and he said he treats that kind of thing as evidence. So the police asked me to go to the station and make a full statement for the record."

"I thought you said Daniel had a heart attack," said Bernice.

"I said the medical examiner in his preliminary exam told us it looked like a heart attack. But he said he'll do an autopsy."

"So you don't think it was a heart attack?" asked Penny.

I gave a little shrug.

My mind returned to the other aspect of that event, the feeling that I was actually in Daniel's body. I had tasted the wine, felt its pleasant burn, then felt the tightness in my chest as I began reacting to it. And I had been in his body as he crumpled to the floor. It had been an extremely powerful experience. But it had seemed prudent to not mention that to John and Peter, or to the police, so I had put it out of my mind. Now I realized it was one more thing that had convinced me Daniel had been poisoned.

So I recounted the events of the morning, including the details that Daniel seemed to have been drinking from a bottle of Reggie's private stock and that it appeared he might have been drinking with someone else.

"In addition to the dream I had directing my attention to the wine, I had an intuitive sense that something wasn't quite right with the scene in the kitchen—there were just too many anomalies. So I went back in to take some photos, and while I was there, I tuned in to Daniel. I experienced his dying moments almost as if I was in his body with him. I think his spirit left as soon as he died. But one thing I got was that he died very shortly after drinking some of the wine."

Bernice leaned toward me, her eyes wide. "Are you saying you think it was murder?" she asked. "You think somebody murdered Daniel?"

"Yes, I guess that's what I'm saying. But I honestly don't have any idea who it might be. He appeared to be toasting somebody, but while I was experiencing his last moments, he didn't look at anything except the wine."

Penny looked from me to Bernice and back again. "I bought Reggie that wine. Do you think the police suspect me? Or do they think Reggie might have poured the wine for Daniel? Do they suspect him?" She seemed really rattled. "Oh, my God, he might have, you know, he might have done it."

Bernice leaned over and put a hand on Penny's shoulder. "From what Ariel is saying, I don't think the police are suspecting anyone at the moment."

She looked at me for confirmation, and I nodded.

"But *you* think it was murder," Penny said, "and that means somebody at the restaurant might be a murderer."

"That may be true," I agreed, "but I can't get a sense of who it could be. Maybe I was just too close to the events to be objective yet."

Then I thought of something. "Bernice, maybe *you* can help us."

"What do you mean?" asked Bernice.

"Remember when you gave me the hall pass last week so I could pull myself out of the hole I was in and start dating again? What made you come up with that particular metaphor for my situation?"

"Well," said Bernice with a little self-conscious laugh, "I saw you as a little girl sitting in the schoolroom, all pent up and really needing to go to the bathroom but afraid to raise your hand and ask permission from a strict teacher who doesn't let anyone take a bathroom break. Then I heard you saying, 'I gotta go...I gotta go...I gotta go!' Then I saw you with a hall pass in your hand and a look of relief on your face. So I offered you a hall pass, and sure enough, a look of relief appeared on your face! So that's how it works—I trained as a Jungian therapist, so I deal with images and symbols."

"Bernice," I said, "you're psychic. I was locked in the pattern of waiting, and the hall pass concept was perfect because it instantly broke my pattern!"

"Oh, come on," she scoffed. "I'm not psychic. I'm just a good therapist."

"I beg to differ with you. Not about being a good therapist, but about not being psychic. When the symbols come into *your* head rather than coming from your clients, that's *tuning in*. And it *is* psychic. But don't be surprised—it's only another one of our senses. And I think everybody has the ability to tune in to some degree."

Penny said pensively, "Do you remember back when I first moved the office to the restaurant and had so much trouble getting settled in? During one of our sessions, I was complaining because I thought I wasn't doing things the way Reggie wanted them done, and I was into blaming and becoming very bitchy with everybody. I remember you suddenly became introspective for a minute, and then you told me to hang our Peter Max painting of *Angel with Heart* in the office. As soon as you said that, I felt a wave of relief and realized my problem didn't have anything to do with personalities—it had to do with my work environment and my need to make it fit my style."

Bernice agreed, "I do remember that. I got an image first of all of you at home at the dining room table with all the receipts and invoices arranged in front of you in colored plastic bins with the sunlight shining into the room. It was aesthetically pleasing to you. Then I saw you in the cramped little office at the restaurant, with no sunlight and no color. And your hands were manacled together. I asked myself how I could get the chains off your wrists and saw a painting on the wall full of rainbow colors. Then I remembered the Peter Max you had hanging in your living room."

"Bernice," I said with a little smile, "that's an awesome talent. And I call it psychic!"

"Well," said Bernice thoughtfully, "maybe it is. But I've only used it with clients, and I've only shared these two insights because you're here together asking me to do so. But how do you think it might help in finding a murderer?"

"I'm not really sure it would help us identify the murderer, but it might help us eliminate people whose pattern isn't congruent with poisoning someone."

"Do you think it would be okay for us to try tuning in to the restaurant staff and seeing what we can pick up?" Penny asked. "If you really think a crime has been committed in my restaurant—and don't forget that I *am* part owner—then shouldn't I be able to give you permission to 'question' the staff? I mean, if the police wanted to ask questions, I'd tell the staff to cooperate."

"Well," said Bernice, "it's not quite the same thing. I'd be very reluctant to try this with anyone who hasn't given me express permission."

"I understand," I said. "I won't draw a Tarot card for anyone but myself or someone who has given me permission to do a reading."

"However," Bernice added, "if you can get permission from everybody at the restaurant for me to do a little session with each of them, I'd be glad to see what I can come up with."

"Penny," I said, "I get the feeling you're more concerned about Reggie than anyone else at the moment, and probably more concerned with what *we* think than with what the police think."

She shook her head and grimaced. "You're absolutely right," she said with a little sigh. "He *does* have a motive, and it was *his* wine, so he's a logical suspect. But I really don't think he has it in him, and if you two could prove it, at least to my satisfaction, I'd feel a whole lot better."

"Well, we can't *prove* anything," I said, "But why don't I just phone? I told him I'd let you know about Daniel, so he'll be expecting my call. And if he says it's okay for Bernice to tune in on him, then she can let us know what she gets."

"Thanks," Penny said softly. "I'd really appreciate that."

When I got through to Reggie at the restaurant, I explained the situation to him.

He agreed immediately. "If you two want to run a psychic lie-detector test on me, go right ahead," he said. "I admit I sometimes didn't like Daniel, but we'd been friends a long time, and we'd made it through rough waters before. I really don't think he was going to leave the restaurant; I think that was a lot of bluff. And, you know, killing him would be a bit like cutting my nose off to spite my face! Hold on a minute."

I heard him talking to someone in the restaurant, and when he returned to the phone he said, "John's here with me. He and Peter just got here with Clarice and all the food she requisitioned from her uncle. I explained what you want to do, and he said you could give him the mental once-over, too. He claims he has nothing to hide, but I suspect there's *something* behind that inscrutable Chinese exterior—though I doubt it's murder."

"Thanks, Reggie," I said. "I know this will be a big relief to Penny."

"Unless your image shows me shooting, stabbing, poisoning, drowning, and garroting the pompous little...oh, listen to me. I still don't get it that he's dead!"

"That's all right," I said. "We're all still in a state of shock. Give it time. And that reminds me, while I have you on the phone, would you like us to see if we can contact his sister in France and get some idea of what she wants done about funeral arrangements? I have the rest of the day off, and I know you're up to your eyes at the moment."

"I'd be ever so grateful," he said. Then he added, "We're asking a lot of you."

"There's no problem. I'll do whatever I can." After saying good-bye, I hung up and turned to the others.

"It sounds as though he gave permission," said Penny. "I was sure he would."

"Yes, and so did John."

Penny turned to face Bernice. "Well, then, Bernice, are you ready? Is there anything special you have to do?"

"No," she said. "I just sort of ask myself a few questions and see what turns up. I usually get some kind of picture pretty quickly."

She closed her eyes for a second and drew a deep breath. As she exhaled, she lifted her head and looked out the window, but her gaze was still inward.

"The immediate image I get, Penny," she said, "is a picture of Reggie fencing, dressed up like a Shakespearean actor, twirling his sword and shouting, '*En garde!*' at his opponent." She was quiet again for a minute. "I think Reggie is an action-oriented sort of person. That ties in with his desire to be out racing at any opportunity. I think it probably also ties in with his getting caught up in an affair at the race track."

"He doesn't really plan ahead," agreed Penny.

"I get that," said Bernice. "If he were going to kill Daniel, it would make more sense for him to grab one of Daniel's large chef's knives and just put it through his heart with a single thrust. Then he'd tell the police he hadn't really meant to hurt him, just teach him a lesson."

"I think you're right," said Penny. "I realize this doesn't prove anything, but it does make me feel better."

"Do you get anything for John?" I asked.

"Not really," she answered. "I guess having him tell Reggie to tell you to tell me that I have permission is one step too far removed. I don't feel comfortable trying to get any images for him."

"What about me?" asked Penny. "I'd like to know what images you get for me in connection with Daniel's death."

"Well, I don't really need to *try* to get a mental picture of the scene. From everything you've told me about Daniel's reaction to your termination of the relationship, it's more likely he would try to kill *you* than visa versa. You were already 'killing him softly with your words,' as the song goes."

Bernice paused for a moment. Then she gave a little laugh and continued. "I do get a picture of you closing the gate on a bullpen, with the bull storming around inside. I think you were quite in control of the situation, Penny. *You* wouldn't have needed to kill him to keep him penned up."

Penny grinned. "Ha! The power of a woman! Yes, a raging bull was exactly what he'd become!"

I sat there quietly for a moment, thinking that Bernice's pictures were true to the personalities of both Reggie and Penny, but they didn't really exonerate either one of them. John had said Reggie's wine was kept in the cooler, so anybody connected with the restaurant could have doctored it, if that was indeed what had caused his death. And there was certainly motive enough going around. Each of the three owners had admitted to being at odds with Daniel, and their grievances were certainly enough to lead to murder if the conditions were right. Penny had been banned from the kitchen, John had been ridiculed, and Reggie had the oldest motive of all—Daniel had been sleeping with his wife. Peter was an unknown factor—if he had a motive to kill Daniel it was very well hidden.

Then Penny added, "I hope he's at peace now."

"That reminds me, Bernice, of something else I wanted to share. When I went back into the kitchen to take the pictures and relived Daniel's last moments, he *did* leave the body and disappear. I tried to reconnect but instead got a very strong image of Annie Grace, who seems to have been clobbered on the back of the head with a frying pan while she was cooking onions. I was struck by the similarity of the two deaths."

"If I were to read *that* experience as a symbol," said Bernice, "I'd have to say that Annie Grace was telling you Daniel's death wasn't natural!"

WE SPENT THE rest of Tuesday afternoon making arrangements for Daniel's funeral.

Penny said, "Daniel had a copy of his will in his personnel file, and there's also a copy of the insurance policy the restaurant has on him. I'll call Reggie and have him look for them. I'm pretty sure the will leaves his estate and personal effects to his sister Elyse, but when we took out the policy on him, he said if anything ever happened, he wanted us to bury him in the States, so as not to burden his sister with that responsibility. He signed a paper to that effect."

While Penny used her cell to call Reggie, I put in a call to Detective Flanagan.

When he answered, I asked, "Do you have any idea when Daniel's body might be released?"

"The autopsy is already complete," he said. "Although your chef showed enough arterial clogging that a heart attack by natural causes isn't out of the question, the medical examiner has ruled the death what we refer to as a

CUPPI, 'Case undetermined, pending police investigation.'"

"So, do you think it might have been murder?"

"Well, so far the only evidence we've found for foul play at the restaurant was the extra wine glass at the scene. But the fact that Mr. Chan's apartment was bombed less than twelve hours earlier has made us decide to keep the case open. The ME retained blood, tissue, and stomach-content samples, which will be sent to the toxicology lab for analysis. However, as I mentioned before, the lab's notoriously backed up, and since the ME hasn't officially ruled Mr. Lafayette's death a murder, it will probably take three to four weeks before we get any results."

"Well, then," I asked, "when might the body be released?" I told him Daniel's partners had a paper signed by Daniel giving them authority to dispose of the body.

"Then we can release it as soon as you determine how you want to deal with it," he said, "—burial, cremation, or shipping it to France."

When I hung up with the detective, I could hear Penny speaking French on the phone. After a short but animated discussion, she hung up and turned to us.

"That was Elyse's convent—Reggie found the phone number in Daniel's file. It's almost midnight there, and I was a little nervous about waking up the nuns, so I tried to be abjectly apologetic. That wasn't easy with my limited schoolgirl French, I can tell you! But it seems to have done the job.

"Elyse said she can't afford to have Daniel's body transported back to France, so she'd be very grateful if we'd bury him here in Virginia. I told her we'd let her know what arrangements we'll be making, but she said she wouldn't be able to attend, so we can use our best judgment. She'll be with us in spirit, and she said she'd have a novena said for his soul. Somehow, that comforts me."

"So what's the next step?" I asked.

"I'd like to have the interment on Sunday, if we can arrange it. That way, everyone from the restaurant can attend, and it will give me a few days to alert customers who knew Daniel. I'll print up some notices and pass them out at the restaurant."

Bernice volunteered to call St. Mary Catholic Church to ask about having a memorial service and burial. A few moments later she put her hand over the mouthpiece and turned to us.

"The priest said it won't be possible to bury Daniel at their cemetery on a Sunday, so he suggested we contact a funeral parlor. He said we could hold a memorial service at the church sometime after the burial, with an appropriate Catholic mass. What day might be good for that?"

Penny looked at the calendar. "How about Saturday, September 27?"

Bernice returned to her conversation with the priest, suggested that date, nodded, thanked him, and hung up.

"He said he'd put it in the church calendar for that Saturday."

We each called one of the many funeral parlors in the Alexandria area to check available services, costs, and connections with the different cemeteries in the area.

Finally, we settled on Greene Funeral Home and the nearby Bethel Cemetery since both were available for services the following Sunday.

"We can hold a little wake at the restaurant afterward," suggested Penny.

After we made the final calls to firm up arrangements and had made appointments to go by both the cemetery and the funeral home to sign all necessary papers and select a casket, Penny showed a moment of indecision.

"Do you think Daniel would prefer that we wait until we can have a Catholic funeral?" she asked. "He wasn't a good Catholic, but..."

"Many people do go back to the faith of their childhood at the end of their lives," said Bernice. "But he didn't have any choice in the matter."

Penny turned to me and asked, "What do you think, Ariel? Can you try to get in touch with him? To find out what *he* wants?"

"As I indicated earlier, Penny, I think he left this plane immediately. And my sense is his concern with his body is finished, so long as we dispose of it hygienically."

"You mean so long as we don't dump him on the street for the dingoes to eat, he won't care?" asked Penny wryly.

"Was that ever an Australian custom?" Bernice asked.

"Not so much a custom as a reason for deep burial."

The picture I got in my head wasn't pleasant, so I said, "Let's go pick out a casket and a burial site."

Chapter Twelve

Wednesday, September 10th

On Tuesday evening, supper had been very late. Bernice had suggested I stay on in Alexandria until my move on Thursday to save me two days of commuting to Leesburg. As soon as supper was over, Michelle took me by the hand and led me to the carriage house, where she allowed me to shop for clothing for the next two days, as it wouldn't do for a young English instructor to appear in front of her class in the same clothing two days in a row. She also handed me some work clothes I'd be able to use for moving day on Thursday.

When I'd called Bibi on Tuesday night to tell her I wasn't coming home and explained everything that had happened since I'd seen her on Monday morning, she said quite calmly, "Let me get this straight—since you started staying in Alexandria, you've encountered a bomb through the window and a dead chef. And you're still planning to move there? You're crazy! Mom is *not* gonna like this!"

"Then don't tell her," I countered.

"A story like this *cannot* be kept under wraps!"

I sighed. "I know you're right. But could we hold off until your birthday party on Saturday?"

"Oh, I'm sure we'll discuss it on Saturday, but don't expect me to keep something this juicy under my hat for four whole days. The family messaging system will not be idle!"

"All right, then, I'll tell Mom. In the next ten minutes, so don't call her for at least that long. I just don't want to have to explain everything to everybody right now. So wait until I'm at school tomorrow to call Cathy and Deirdre. Please?"

She's agreed reluctantly, and after I'd talked to my mom, I'd climbed into bed at Bernice's, emotionally and physically drained.

THE CHEF WHO DIED SAUTÉING

I was sitting in my office at George Mason, looking at a mountain of freshman comp papers I'd collected the previous Friday, which I'd ignored in the flurry of events. I was tired, but I knew the next few days were going to be full to overflowing—with the move to Bernice's, another day of teaching, Bibi's birthday party on Saturday, and Daniel's funeral on Sunday. As momentous as the events of the past couple of days still seemed, life goes on. I decided to grab a coffee and a chocolate bar from the machines in the hall and get the grading done.

I had assigned a five hundred word paper on the topic of popular sports, hoping everyone would have at least a passing knowledge of some sport and enough interest in one to write a decent essay. Most of them were the usual sort of thing I'd come to expect from first-year students who didn't really see why they should have to learn to write. Stuff along the lines of, "I went to the football game. I bought a hotdog. The game was exciting. I went home." But the sixth paper I picked up was from one of my more diligent students, and I was struck not only by the quality of the writing, but also by the immediacy of the topic.

> *Racing is a visceral sport.*
>
> *I started going to the racetrack when I was five years old. I loved to hang around in the pits watching my dad get ready for the race. To me, he was a superhero—in his neat racing suit with all the advertising slogans on it, his fancy helmet and his shiny racing car. When the race was over and he got out of the car, all the guys who were helping him would pat him on the back and tell him how great he was and how well he'd done on the track, and I figured they all knew he was a superhero, too. And, of course, I wanted to be just like him.*
>
> *As a kid, I raced all around the neighborhood on whatever wheeled conveyance I had—first on my tricycle, then on my bicycle. I loved the feeling of control over a machine and being able to move faster than my body was able to manage on its own.*
>
> *I continued going to all the races with my dad, working in the pits, tuning the car, and doing whatever I could to be part of the team. As soon as I learned to drive I began racing myself, starting with hotrods and progressing quickly to street stocks. For the last two seasons, I've been there with my dad in the pits as a racer, rather than as crew.*
>
> *It's hard to describe the thrill of the sport to someone who's never been in a racecar. There is power in speed—somehow the body knows that you're exceeding the normal boundaries, and it responds at the cellular level. Every nerve, every sense, every muscle works together to create something more than the whole. It's sexual in a*

> way that everything is sexual to the male of the species. Its part of the testosterone-driven need for a man to keep pushing outward into the world, making a place, defining himself and his territory.
>
> In racing the driver pushes himself to the edge, finding the point where he becomes one with the machine and knows exactly when to shift speed or direction slightly in order not to lose control. I imagine this is how early man felt when he was stalking prey—sensing the union between his body, the bow in his hand, and the deer or other animal in front of him. Knowing that the kill would be clean, that he would be able to feed his family, that his mate would come to him in the afterglow of victory, that he would produce fine young offspring that would perpetuate his line.
>
> Modern society provides us with food and shelter without our having to hunt, and modern man needs an outlet for his urges. Racing, like many other modern sports, meets this need, allowing us to feel like superheroes—fulfilled and energized, aware that we have what it takes to play our role in the human drama.

Because of yesterday's conversation with Penny about Reggie's racing and how it related to incidents at the restaurant, I paid special attention to this essay. It was so appropriate, and the writing was so much better than the rest of the students' work, that I caught myself looking around to see if someone had snuck it onto my desk when I wasn't watching. It was what Carl Jung would have called a synchronicity—one of those coincidences that have a powerful meaning in one's life.

I remembered Bernice's comments about how life presents us with symbols in order to get our attention.

"Well, then," I said to myself, "if this is a symbol, maybe it's also a clue."

There'd been times in my life when someone or other had told me to get a clue, but this week, I'd had way too many, and I wasn't sure what to do with them.

I did a mental inventory, and examined the similarities and synchronicities among the experiences I'd had recently. I'd felt a ghostly presence in Bernice's pantry and tool shed of a woman who appeared to have died from a blow to the head while cooking onions, and I had been about to interview a chef who had died just the day before, while cooking onions. I'd witnessed a fight in the kitchen of the Riviera involving the chef who was now dead, and one of the owners, and been given a lot of information from Mike, Penny and John concerning the strained relationships in the restaurant—enough information to implicate any one of them in connection with the death. I'd had a vision of two youths running away from John's apartment after the 'bomb,' and felt a bit of a 'bomb' when I realized that John seemed to be very involved with his cousin Clarice, who just happened to be available to take over the kitchen in the Riviera. I'd had a Fat Man dream telling me to pay attention to wine, then been confronted at the scene of the death with a bottle of wine belonging to Reggie, two wine glasses, and the very real image of Daniel drinking the wine shortly before collapsing.

And there were other things that might or might not be relevant—Peter's hex signs, one in Daniel's kitchen and one in my room, which were supposed to offer protection; Peter arriving late at the restaurant that morning; and now this essay, which gave me some insight into Reggie and why he liked racing.

I wanted to share the essay with Bernice, so I made a photocopy and tucked it into my briefcase.

I finished marking the last paper at seven o'clock, and with a sigh of relief, staggered out to my Jeep and aimed it toward Alexandria. Still pretty exhausted, I decided this wasn't an appropriate time to test the thrill of the race for myself, so I was especially cautious driving.

When I pulled into Bernice's driveway, I was still mulling over the insight I now had into Reggie's motivations. As I headed for the stairs, carrying my briefcase in one hand and pulling my rolling book-and-paper suitcase with the other, I heard Bernice calling me from down the hall.

"I saved you some gumbo," she said. "Dump your stuff and come eat!"

I put down my bags, pulled the essay out of my briefcase, and wandered into the kitchen, where Bernice was already microwaving a bowl of gumbo and cutting me a large chunk of sourdough bread.

"You look beat," she said, handing me a bread plate, knife, and butter. "Park yourself at the table and partake of this. I'm afraid you'll have to wait another forty seconds for the gumbo."

I smiled gratefully as I eased myself into one of the dining chairs. I was thoughtfully chewing on a mouthful of bread when she delivered the hot gumbo to the table.

"I want you to read this," I said, handing her the essay. "The universe seems to be telling me my involvement with Daniel's death isn't finished yet."

I watched her face as she read the paper and saw her raise her left eyebrow as she began to see the connection.

When she looked up, I said, "I know you see Reggie as action oriented and don't think he'd use poison as a means of disposing of a rival. But suppose he wanted to maintain his superhero status and had figured out a way to eliminate the rival without actually having to do it himself. It was *his* wine, and there *were* two glasses. And we know he was at the restaurant yesterday morning. If it does turn out that Daniel was poisoned and didn't die of a heart attack, I'm not sure we can rule out Reggie as a suspect just yet."

"I get your point. But the obvious question is why would he leave the evidence just sitting out? I mean, it draws attention directly to him, doesn't it?"

"Well, he might have just left the wine so that Daniel would drink enough for whatever he had in it to take effect. Or he might have left it to put everybody off track *because* it's so obvious."

Bernice smiled. "While we're puzzling out convoluted motivations," she said, "consider this: Mike, Jamal, and Roy had to go into the station yesterday afternoon to give statements and be fingerprinted, and Penny went in this morning.

"A few hours ago, I called Alan and asked him to check in with the police about what they might have found from fingerprints and so forth. Between them, the wine glasses and bottle had prints from nearly everybody who works at the restaurant—including Mike, which isn't surprising since he's the dishwasher. So if you're looking strictly at the physical evidence, it implicates everybody but thee and me. But Alan said they still haven't ruled out a heart attack. It's just all sort of up in the air."

I sighed. "There's a lot to think about, and I'm too tired to be able to put it all together right now."

"Then just sleep on it," she said. "I'll have breakfast for you and Mike at seven in the morning and you can have a nice, restful day carting big boxes here from Leesburg."

I gave a wan smile and got up from the table. "I'm reminded of the old Chinese curse that goes, 'May you live in interesting times.' And my life has certainly become interesting in the past few days."

Bernice chuckled. "Are you suggesting you were cursed by an old Chinese on Monday night?"

I went to bed laughing.

Chapter Thirteen

Thursday, September 11th

Moving day dawned with bleak skies and the threat of rain. I'd set the alarm for six, but when it went off, I had to hit the snooze button twice before I could force myself to actually get up. Once I was moving, I put my hair back with a rubber band, slithered into the grubby clothes I'd borrowed from Michelle the previous weekend that were still hanging over the back of a chair, and went out for a quick run around the block. As soon as my heart rate was up and I felt sufficiently virtuous, I dashed back to Bernice's, showered quickly, and donned the work clothes I'd borrowed from Michelle two evenings before—jeans, tee-shirt, and long-sleeve flannel shirt. I was beginning to feel like her sister, although as the eldest in my own family, I had usually been the one to pass along loans and hand-me-downs. Grabbing up jacket and purse, I went downstairs to the kitchen, where Bernice was creating a leaning tower of pancakes.

"I buzzed Mike just before you came down to let him know breakfast is just about ready," she said. "Michelle told me she'd be here about four this afternoon to help you unpack the U-Haul at this end."

At that moment the back door opened, and Mike came striding in, dressed in much the same fashion as I was, except that his flannel shirt had seen a bit more wear than mine. He grabbed a pancake, folded it in quarters, and stuffed it into his mouth. When he'd swallowed it, he said, "Hi, Mom. Hi, Ariel." He seemed a little more subdued than usual.

"How did things go the last couple of nights at the restaurant?" I asked.

He didn't meet my gaze but gave a little shrug. "I'll tell you all about it on the way to Leesburg."

He poured himself a coffee from the carafe into a forty-eight ounce insulated cup and stirred cream and a small mountain of sugar into it.

"When do we head out?" he asked as he picked up a pile of four pancakes.

"We can go just as soon as you're ready," I said. "The U-Haul place in Leesburg opened at seven."

I had barely backed my Jeep out of the driveway before Mike asked, "I understand you had a 'smashing' date with John last Monday night."

"Well, I guess you could say we had a bomb threat, but it kind of paled into nothing after Daniel's death on Tuesday."

"Mom mentioned the bomb to me, but she didn't really have any details. And things have been so hectic at the restaurant I haven't mentioned it to John. As a matter of fact, I've hardly talked to him at all. But tell me about the bomb. That's actually kind of exciting." Then he added hurriedly, "But it's good you weren't hurt or anything."

I got the sense Mike was avoiding talking about the restaurant. I wasn't sure why, but I was determined that once we'd finished talking about the bomb, I would be just as insistent on getting information from him about what was happening with all the staff at the Riviera.

"Well, actually," I said, "the bomb was just a bottle of beer *pretending* to be a bomb. Somebody thought he'd fashion a Molotov cocktail by stuffing a rag coated with candle wax into the neck of a beer bottle and hurling it through the kitchen window of John's apartment while we were in the living room. It broke the window and bounced off the side of a cupboard before it landed in his sink and fizzled out."

"Kickin'!" said Mike. "What'd you guys do?"

"Called the D.C. police and waited while they came and took statements and gathered the evidence."

"Were you scared?"

"No, I was startled but not really scared. In the army we had live-round training, and while there's always the tendency to be startled when you hear a loud noise or a crash, there's something else that kicks in and you take action to protect yourself."

I smiled at a memory. "During Desert Storm, whenever there was shelling, the routine was to shout, 'Incoming!' and drop and roll to any protected place. So when I returned stateside, the first night I was back home sleeping in my little bed, my Dad went outside to put out the trash, and he dropped a garbage can, making a lot of noise. I immediately hollered, 'Incoming!' and rolled off my bed and onto the floor. Scared my mom!

"Anyway," I continued, "it was clear even without having the police corroborate it that whoever threw the missile was inept. I mean, they used a beer bottle."

"Yeah," said Mike, "beer is pretty lame. Bet they even used light beer! Not really enough alcohol in beer to create any kind of effect, much less a bomb. Now, vodka or whiskey—that's different. Something with higher alcohol content that's got a real kick."

"Of course," I said, "the best explosive effect would have been with gasoline or kerosene, as John pointed out. Anyway, we figured that whoever threw it had no intention of confronting John face to face. But I'll admit that after the fact—after the police had come and gone—I think I did experience a kind of shock effect. I was really wired and wide awake but physically limp. And somehow, the date fizzled pretty much the way the bomb fizzled."

Mike seemed to be thinking for a few seconds before he asked, "Does John have any idea who might have tried to bomb him?"

"No, he doesn't. In fact, because whoever threw it used a beer bottle, he was inclined to think it was just an episode of random vandalism—maybe kids playing a prank. Or maybe a case of mistaken identity. The police said if he didn't come up with any possible suspects and if they didn't find any evidence as to who threw it or why, they'd probably rule it a random occurrence."

I glanced at Mike and saw he was nodding, but with a thoughtful look on his face. I still hadn't ruled out the possibility that there might be a connection between the bomb through John's window and Daniel's death, and I wanted to get Mike's perspective on the staff and all the interrelationships at the restaurant before I told him my suspicions about Daniel's having been murdered.

"So, tell me, what do you think? Does anybody at the restaurant have it in for John? Is he still in danger?"

"Well," said Mike, "I like John, and from what I pick up from the other waiters, so does everybody else at the restaurant. In fact, of all the owners John is just about everybody's favorite because he's the most laid back and easy to get along with. And he's a really good acting coach—Jamal has nothing but praise for him. Roy's a little less enthusiastic because his comedy comes from black culture, but I've heard him say how much he likes John, so you won't find anybody at the restaurant who's out to get him.

"In fact, the only person I can think of who hadn't been getting along with John lately was Daniel. And if *he* threw the bomb, then I guess John isn't still in danger, is he?

"But," he continued, "I can't see him following John home and hurling something through the window. He'd have been far more likely to throw flaming French epithets."

"But what about that time you mentioned where he cold cocked that guy he was mad at with a frozen fish?"

"Well, ya' know, Mom says *everybody* has the potential for violence. But I think Daniel would have had better taste than to use beer. I mean, I get this ridiculous visual of Daniel running down the street, wearing full chef regalia, and waving a flaming beer bottle. It just doesn't work."

I gave a little snort of laughter. "Yeah, it sounds like something out of a French farce. With Gérard Depardieu!"

Mike shook his head. "I'd heard a rumor Daniel was threatening to quit.

In fact, I thought that was why he wasn't getting along with John. But it's still hard to believe he's...gone."

"John told me on Monday night about a meeting all the owners had with Daniel on Sunday. Apparently he'd actually told them he was going to quit when his contract was up at the end of the year. Do you know anything about why he wanted to leave, Mike?"

He was silent for a moment. "You know, I keep my head down and don't get involved in any of the in-fighting that goes on. I figure I'm just the dishwasher, and my opinions wouldn't be appreciated, so I don't offer any. And everybody is nice to Peter and me no matter who else any of them might be mad at. Only once in a while does any flack fly in my direction, like that night you were in the kitchen and I was sort of split between Aunt Penny and Daniel.

"And because I'm not directly involved in any of the unpleasantness—and probably also because I'm usually up to my elbows in suds—I'm sort of like a 'silent butler.' Nobody pays any attention to me, and sometimes I hear things I think people might not want circulated if they realized I was listening. Also, Aunt Penny has sometimes let things slip around me that she might not say around other people—and I guess it's because I'm the son of her psychotherapist."

He paused again, then added, "All of this is my way of saying I've made some *assumptions* about what I think was going on."

"Well, if you're worried about betraying a trust..."

"It's not that so much," he countered. "But before I tell you what I think, I need to be sure you know I'm only going on what I've observed. I mean, I'm not betraying a confidence from anybody involved. Nobody has told me anything directly. All of this is just from my observations."

"Okay," I said. "The same is true for John, who told me some assumptions he'd made based on his observations. I'm trying to make some sense out of everything, and I'd just like to know if your assumptions coincide with John's." I decided not to tell him what Penny had shared with me on Tuesday. The whole situation was still very confusing to me, and I wanted to see if Mike's perspective might shed a new light on the events of the last few days.

"All right," said Mike, "then here's my view of what's gone on at the restaurant. I think Reggie had a fling with somebody he met at the racetrack while Penny was in Australia last fall. And he broke it off when she came back. But then, something happened that caused Penny to find out. I think the woman may have died. Anyway, in retribution, Penny had a fling with Daniel. And then she broke it off and went back to Reggie, causing Daniel to lose face. He retaliated by threatening to quit, and in the meantime he made everybody out front miserable. But I don't think he would have retaliated in a violent way. And I certainly don't think he would have done anything to John."

"Do you think it's possible Daniel might have paid somebody to do it?"

"I really don't think so. It's not in character. And I don't know anyone at the restaurant who might have those kinds of contacts."

"What about Roy or Jamal?"

Mike thought for a minute then said, "Well, as I indicated, both of them like John, so I can't see either one of them getting involved in a 'hit.' I mean, Jamal's talked about being the victim of some threats himself. Because he's Muslim, you know. He's from Egypt. But where you're from doesn't matter very much in a post-9/11 world."

"No," I said, "I guess it doesn't."

"Now, Roy does live in the projects north of Old Town, and once I heard him say his brother had been in some trouble with some of the gang types in that area. But Roy's married and works really hard to support his family, just like hundreds of other law-abiding citizens who live there. And you know," he added, "he seems to disapprove of people who make their living selling drugs or stealing or fencing stuff. I think he really wants to be a good role model for his kids. I like Roy. Did you know that African Americans are actually more law abiding than the average white citizen? I learned that in *Bowling for Columbine*."

"Yeah, that was a pretty educational flick. Makes you wonder whether you should ever bother watching the evening news, when so much of it is falsely negative. And I must admit I don't watch it very often."

I concentrated on driving for a couple of minutes as the traffic had become pretty heavy. When things lightened up again, I asked, "Well, then, what do you know about Peter? I haven't had much of a chance to talk to him about anything beyond his art."

"I don't really know very much. He was a quick-study last weekend for doing camera work—did a really good job for us at the studio. But if there's anybody at the restaurant who keeps more to himself than I do, it's Peter. Very quiet. Mentioned he has some family in Pennsylvania, I think, but I never hear him talk about them. He met Reggie up there at the races. I think Peter's dad owned a drug store and soda shop, like the kind you'd see on *Happy Days*, you know, and he wanted Peter to go into the business with him. But Peter didn't want to, so when Reggie offered him a job here in the big city, he jumped at it.

"I've heard him say he likes John—admires his sense of comedy. But, of course, he didn't say anything nice about any of the owners while Daniel was around. For that matter, neither did I. It wouldn't have been prudent.

"Last June, when Michelle and I celebrated our birthday by moving into the carriage house, we had a party to sort of warm our new digs. Not big—a few kids from school, a few from the studio, and I invited Jamal and Peter. Jamal wasn't able to come, but Peter showed up mid-way through the evening. And he brought each of us a small Pennsylvania Dutch design like the one he gave you last Sunday. Michelle tried to draw him out, and I think they talked for about an hour. Talk to her—she could probably tell you more about him."

"Thanks. I'll do that." I paused as I thought about what I wanted to ask next. "I don't suppose you'd know any reason why Reggie or Penny might have a grudge against John, do you?"

"Heck, no! From what I hear, if it weren't for John's willingness to go into business with them five years ago, they wouldn't have been able to buy the place. I mean, if anything, they're in his debt. And he is a pretty funny guy." Then he added, "I mean in terms of comedy—not, like, quirky. He's just plain funny, and always able to put people into a happy mood. Even the customers he insults keep laughing and coming back for more. So I wouldn't have a clue as to why anybody might want to blow him up."

"So, then," I asked, "who might have wanted to eliminate Daniel?"

Mike gave me a startled look, so I knew Bernice hadn't mentioned my suspicions to him yet. "*What?* What do you mean?" he asked. "John told us all Daniel had suffered a heart attack. And the police seemed to be going with that assumption when they took our statements. Are you suggesting somebody might have killed him?"

"Maybe." I filled Mike in on what had happened Tuesday morning, explaining what my perceptions had been after we'd found Daniel's body—my feeling something was out of place, my going back into the kitchen to snap a few pictures of the scene, and my psychic impressions of Daniel's last minutes before he died. I also told him about the appearance of Annie Grace, and Bernice's suggestion that she might have come to tell me Daniel's death wasn't natural.

"Too many things don't quite fit for me," I said. "And I won't be comfortable until I know there really wasn't anybody who might have wanted to get rid of Daniel."

Mike seemed thoughtful for a few moments. "That puts a new light on everything, doesn't it?"

"It does," I said. "We seem to have eliminated everybody at the restaurant as a suspect in the bombing, so it may have been just vandalism. But if Daniel's death wasn't a simple heart attack, then we need to take a look at all the staff again and see whether they might have had a reason to eliminate Daniel."

Mike nodded his head. "Okay," he said. "Let's take everybody one at a time." He held up his right hand and began to tick off suspects on his fingers. "My only grudge with Daniel was that he used too many pots. And Peter adored him—I mean, really put him on a pedestal. Both Jamal and Roy got in and out of the kitchen as quickly as they could and tried to have very little interaction with him. I think they admired his cuisine, and they bragged on him to the customers, of course, but they stayed out of the line of fire when he got his back up.

"I've already told you about Reggie and Penny," Mike said, holding up both his thumbs in his finger counting. "I guess either of them might have had a reason to do him in over the love triangle thing. I know that's often a big motive for murder."

He paused, and I glanced at him. He was still looking at his two thumbs.

"So...what about John?"

Mike seemed reluctant to answer. "Well," he said finally, "I dunno. One night a couple of weeks back, Daniel had dissed John, saying he didn't know the difference between fine French cooking and Chinese take-out. And John snapped back that he had a cousin apprenticing at a restaurant in Hong Kong, and one of these days she was going to replace Daniel."

I sat up straighter. "What did Daniel do?"

"He just laughed and said, 'What is *thees*? You think a woman could replace *me*?' Then John gave Daniel one of those enigmatic Asian smiles and went back into the dining room."

Mike paused again before adding thoughtfully, "I guess John's had the last laugh, hasn't he? His cousin *has* replaced Daniel."

"And how are things going in the kitchen now that Clarice has taken over?"

Once again, Mike seemed reluctant to answer. Finally, he said, "John and Clarice are kinda tight, if you know what I mean."

I could tell he was looking at me to get a reaction.

"I do know exactly what you mean," I said with a rueful little smile.

"I'm sorry. What with you guys starting to date and all."

"Never mind. I figured as much when I met Clarice on Monday night. I don't think he knew yet that she was back from Hong Kong when he invited me out. She's a real knockout, isn't she?"

Mike paused before answering. "Well," he said finally, "she's not hard on the eyes, but she's one tough cookie when it comes to laying down rules and having us do things her way."

Mike had given me something to think about.

I thought back to the day of Daniel's death, when John had been very quick—as well as happy and excited—to suggest his pretty cousin as Daniel's replacement. This brought up my first meeting with Clarice, the night before Daniel's death, at the banquet in Chinatown. John had seemed truly surprised to see Clarice back from Hong Kong that evening but not at all surprised at the major role she'd played in preparing the banquet. Could that—and his fear that Daniel might ruin the Riviera's business by leaving—have caused him to take action against Daniel that next morning?

And then I remembered John's jokingly dropping into a Monty Python character while we were out on the street that morning, as he chanted, "Bring out yer dead! Bring out yer dead!" And only later did we discover Daniel lying dead in the restaurant kitchen. Somehow, now, his clowning around seemed more than ironic—it was terribly macabre! And now that I knew of John's earlier threat to replace Daniel with Clarice, I wondered. Had his hiring Clarice for the Riviera really been a spur of the moment decision, or had it all been carefully planned?

When we got to Leesburg, we stopped at the U-Haul center and got the van I'd ordered, along with a few boxes, tape, and twine. Then we headed to the self-store center where most of my stuff had been in storage for the past several months. We filled the back of the van with the remnants of my life with Dennis—boxes, bookcases, a couch, and a small table and chairs. Then we drove in tandem to Bibi's farm. I showed Mike where to park to make loading the van easy, and we wandered into the house via the kitchen door carrying in the extra boxes.

Bibi wasn't in sight when we came in, but her four-year-old twins, Max and Alex, came running out immediately to take him over.

"Hey, coo'!" he said. "Twins! I'm a twin, too!"

Max eyed him in disbelief. "How can you be a twin?" he asked. "There's only one of you."

Alex wasn't put off by this discrepancy and said, "Do you want to come play? We have a new train set."

Not wanting to offend these two little people, Mike glanced at me for a cue, and I told Alex, "You can have him for five minutes. He's here to work with me moving stuff out of my bedroom."

"Well, come meet Irene, anyway," said Alex.

Again Mike glanced at me. "I thought your sister's name was Bibi," he said. Then to Alex and Max, "I'd like to meet your mom."

"Irene's not our mom," said Max in what sounded like disgust at Mike's lack of knowledge. "Irene's our ghost."

"You have a ghost?" exclaimed Mike. "Hey, we have a ghost at my house, too! You didn't tell me there was a ghost here, Ariel. Let's go, guys!"

And he trotted off to the playroom with the twins.

I found Bibi in the bedroom I'd been using. Practical as usual, she'd already stripped my bed and washed and folded the sheets and blankets.

"I thought since you were getting here so late you might want me to get started," she said.

"Thanks, sweetie."

"Before we're done, you're going to have to bring me up to date. Is there anything new with respect to the events you told me about?"

I was still mulling over my conversation in the car with Mike and didn't want to have to spend another hour explaining my suspicions and concerns, so I just said, "Not really. I spent yesterday catching up on all the papers that needed grading, and I'm here this morning in borrowed clothes. Pretty exciting, huh?"

"Well, while you box up the rest of your things, why don't I go make some cappuccino?"

"Sounds good. And if you meet a friendly young man down there, it's Mike. The twins took him to meet Irene, but I'd appreciate his help up here as soon as he can get free, 'cause I can't take the bed apart by myself."

THE CHEF WHO DIED SAUTÉING

Bibi went off to make caffeine-laced beverages for us, and she sent Mike up within a couple of minutes. We had boxed the contents of desk and bureau drawers in pretty short order, and by the time Bibi came up with cups of steamed and frothed milk and espresso, we were nearly through with the boxes of books, papers, and folded clothing that I'd kept with me when I'd moved in with Bibi's family.

When Bibi had handed the coffees around, I suggested we break for a few minutes before carting everything down to the van.

"So, how was the ghost?" I asked Mike.

"Very well behaved, from what I can tell," he said. "Alex had a one-sided conversation with her while Max tore around the room with the train engine making *choo-choo* noises. Alex kept shushing him and asking me if I'd heard what she'd said."

"And did you?"

"Fortunately for my credibility, he never actually waited for me to answer before he'd turn back to the conversation with her. So I just kept a polite look on my face, and when the five minutes you'd allotted were up, I said, 'Well, I've got to go now, Irene. Thanks, kids, for showing me your playroom. That's a great train, Max.' I can be really politic when I have to."

"Well," said Bibi, "you've made a great impression with the kids. They're already asking when you can come back and play and will you bring your twin. Alex said she could play with Harrison."

"Who's Harrison?" asked Mike.

"He's my five-year-old—he just went off to preschool a few minutes ago on the bus. It may seem hectic with the twins running around, but believe me it's blessedly quiet around here once Harrison leaves for school."

"Hard to believe," said Mike.

"Well, our mom used to say that when you have one child, you have one, and when you have two children, you have two, but when you add a third, you have six."

Mike looked confused. "Aren't there four of you?"

"She probably figured once she had six, she might as well *have* six. But she stopped at four."

Mike looked completely baffled and changed the subject. "So, about this ghost named Irene. Is she for real?"

"Oh, she's real. Although Alex seems to be the only one who can actually see her. Just after we moved here, I put a pot of beans on to cook for supper. I was using an old gas stove that had come with the house. Then I came upstairs to sort out some of our boxes. While I was busy organizing, I had the distinct impression of Cotillion perfume by Avon. I recognized it because someone had given me a bottle of that perfume for my birthday when I was eight years old.

"I knew the smell couldn't be coming from the bedroom where I was working, so I stepped out into the hall. Sure enough, the smell was stronger and seemed to be coming from downstairs. I ran down, wondering what was causing the smell, and when I went into the kitchen, I realized the fire had gone out on the stove, but the gas was still hissing. I turned it off and opened the windows to air out the kitchen. Once I'd taken care of the situation, the smell of Cotillion perfume immediately disappeared."

Mike said, "I never heard of smelling a ghost before. What's that called?"

"I call it clairolfaction," I smiled, "similar to clairvoyance and clairaudience."

Bibi continued, "Another time when I was particularly exasperated with the children, I had the hint of Cotillion and felt a hand on my shoulder. So I sat down and let myself get more centered, and pretty soon I felt better. And that's the first time I knew Alex was seeing her, because he came up and patted me, too, and he said, 'Irene doesn't want you to be mad, Mommy. So I told her we'd be good.'"

"Whoa!" said Mike. "A paranormal *au pair*."

"That's a good way of looking at it. But the really neat thing was that Alex had used her name. About a week later, I was telling a neighbor about the experiences we'd had of an unseen presence combined with the smell of the perfume, and my neighbor said, 'Oh, that was my mother-in-law, Irene. My husband's family used to own that property, and his mother died in your house. And she always wore Cotillion.' Anyway, her name really is Irene, and I smell her, Alex sees her, and occasionally one of the other boys or Victor hears her making noises around the house."

"So she's Irene, the friendly ghost!" said Mike.

Bibi smiled. "Yeah, for me ghosts are like cats. I don't mind them in the house so long as they're helpful and not harmful."

Listening to Mike and Bibi talk, mingled with the happy laughter from downstairs, I thought again about how nice it would be to have a family of my own. But I was also looking forward to being more on my own, making my own decisions again and not having the kids underfoot all the time. Everything in life is a dichotomy—a truth expressed so well by the Chinese yin-yang symbol.

I was reminded of a joke my dad used to tell about a teetotaler who checked into a fancy hotel room and was distressed to find a bottle of bitters on the bureau. He called down to the front desk and angrily demanded that someone come and remove the bottle of alcohol at once.

The desk clerk calmly replied, "I'm sorry, sir, but you have to take the bitters with the suite."

WE FINISHED BOXING all the miscellaneous minutiae and began carting it out to the van. The twins were eager to help, so I pointed to some small items they could easily carry.

Alex said, "Irene wants to help, too, but she's having trouble picking anything up."

As I put the box I was carrying down on the floor of the van, I said to

Bibi, "It's just occurred to me how unconcerned you are about the constant interaction of Alex with Irene. Doesn't it worry you that when he starts daycare if he talks about Irene he might get teased by some of the other kids about his 'invisible' friend?"

Bibi stopped in her tracks and just stared at me for a moment, looking bewildered. Then she started to laugh.

"Good golly, Miss Molly! This from someone who's been talking to an invisible fat man in a strange hat since she was five years old! As a matter of fact, I've been thinking for the last few weeks that you and I should start a little real estate sideline clearing psychic energies from people's houses so they'll sell more rapidly, and here you are afraid the kids will get teased because they have our abilities with the paranormal. Get a grip, girl!"

Bibi paused and then added, "Of course, that wouldn't work in Alexandria."

"Why not?"

"A friend of mine is an agent there, and strangely enough, when people buy houses in Old Town, they insist on having a ghost or two, and they want the ghostly presence documented. It's all about prestige and elitism. A hundred years ago, the houses were in pretty rough shape and were bought and sold for three or four hundred dollars. Now it's a couple of million."

"Really?" I thought about that for a few seconds. "Well, I guess I'm not surprised. Ghosts are becoming a big tourist attraction everywhere. Did you know the National Park Service used to hide the fact that many of their properties were haunted until they realized having ghosts on site improved tourism?"

Mike looked at the two of us. "If you two were to start a real estate ghost-busting service, you could be the stars of one of our shows!"

"See?" said Bibi. "There's gold in them thar haunted houses! If you want a ghost, we'll confirm you have one; if you don't want one, we'll help you get rid of it."

"Well, you may be right," I said. "One of the reasons Bernice is giving me such a break on the apartment is because of my ability to connect with Annie Grace."

"Yeah," said Mike, "that and the fact that mom's a soft touch. And I know she'd also like to have a normal adult to talk to—someone who isn't dysfunctional, depressive, or dependent."

I laughed and threw up my hands. "Well, I guess if someone as down to earth as Bernice thinks I'm normal, I shouldn't worry about the rest of the world."

"You think Mom's normal," Mike said with a wicked grin, "but I think she's paranormal. She reads minds, although she might not call it that."

"What do you mean?" asked Bibi.

"Well, you know she's a Jungian psychotherapist," Mike said. "I've heard her talk about people and the symbols or images she associates with them. I think she's 'seeing' the way people think. Not knowing *what* they think, but seeing *how* they think. And then she comes up with a metaphor or an analogy or some other kind of anchoring device she can give her clients so they can change patterns that don't work for them."

"Like she did for me," I said. "She gave me a symbolic hall pass, like in school, so I could change my pattern around relationships. And after Daniel's death, I mentioned Bernice's ability to scan people symbolically to Penny. So Penny had her do a scan on Reggie to see if she could tell whether he had anything to do with Daniel's death."

"And?"

"She said she thought he was too action oriented to get rid of somebody with poison. She saw him symbolically fencing—lunging, not skulking."

"Yeah," said Mike, "she's good at giving us symbols for good living. But also, she's really good at looking at things that happen to people and showing them how the external world is symbolizing what they're thinking or feeling. I remember we had a friend whose basement kept flooding. Mom suggested she was into some heavy sorrow, and she was going to need to deal with it."

"So," said Bibi thoughtfully, "if Bernice understands the importance of symbols in people's daily lives, maybe you should ask her what it means when on your first date with your new hall pass, someone throws a bomb through your new boyfriend's window? And what does it mean when the very next day his most significant employee dies while you're at the restaurant with him? What's the message for *you*?"

I stopped moving and just stood still thinking. The bomb in John's apartment had fizzled, and so had my relationship with John. And *that* was a symbol it was pretty hard to ignore, especially with what Mike had told me earlier that morning about Clarice. A chef had died, and I'd tuned into another cook who'd died, and the blow to the back of her head was like the one that had killed Dennis. And *that* had been a blow to *my* life. Was *that* the message for me? Maybe to sort out this death, I would need to deal with Dennis' death.

"Hey, sis, come back!" said Bibi. "You can munch on this food for thought later. Let's get your clothes from your closet and lay them in the back of my van—they'll be less likely to get crumpled there than in your Jeep. I'll come in with the kids this evening. We need to get your show on the road, or you'll still be up at midnight unpacking the U-Haul at the other end. So get a move on."

THE TRIP BACK to Alexandria was relatively uneventful. Mike drove the van, I drove my jeep, and Bibi promised to bring Victor with her later so he could drive the van back to Leesburg to turn it in for me. We were at Bernice's by two o'clock and spent the next couple of hours lugging boxes up the back stairs.

"I'm not good at carrying stuff," Bernice had said, "but I'll stuff a chicken and have a dinner ready for everybody by six. Michelle called and said she'll be a little late, but she'll help you unpack after dinner."

True to her word, she herded us into the dining room on schedule, and Michelle showed up a few minutes later. Just as we were finishing, Bibi and Victor arrived with all my clothing. They'd already taken the kids to Chuck E. Cheese, so they were happily playing in the back seat with the toys they'd won with their game coupons.

As I handed Victor the keys to the U-Haul, Bibi reminded me, "Don't forget my birthday party on Saturday. And prepare yourself, because Mom isn't happy you're flirting with danger these days."

"I'll take that under advisement," I said and gave her and Victor hugs and kisses.

Once I was back in the house, Michelle asked, "Shall we do it?" and we grabbed up armloads of my clothing and headed upstairs.

As I opened the door to my apartment, the stacks of boxes all around the walls loomed like a monolithic stone circle in the dim light. I flicked the wall switch and said, "Welcome to Stonehenge. Come on in."

We put all the clothes in the closet. Then we started in on the cartons with box cutters I'd picked up at the U-Haul rental center.

"Have a box cutter," I said.

Michelle began cutting open the boxes, and as she noted what each one contained, we made a decision as to where the contents of the box should go. Once we'd stored the contents away, we'd flattened the box and put it on a growing pile.

About half an hour into our efforts, Bernice knocked and poked her head into the room.

"Can I be of any assistance?" she asked.

Michelle looked at me and then said to Bernice, "Not unless you're really bored, Mom. We seem to have it under control, but you can come and play if you want to."

"Well, I don't want to get under foot, and I do have some client bills to get out."

"Then don't feel you have to pitch in," I said. "But maybe we can have a nightcap of hot chocolate with you when we're finished."

"Great idea. Just call down to me when you're ready and I'll stop and put the kettle on."

"Oh, Bernice, I wanted to get your okay before I put Peter's drawing up on my door. I have a frame I think it will fit into that isn't too heavy, so it should only need a small finishing nail to hold it."

"No problem. I think it would look lovely on the outside of your door."

Then she noticed Michelle was flattening a box, and she added, "Put all the boxes out on the landing at the top of the back stairs. I'll have Mike tie them up and store them in the garage for future use." She shut the door.

"Mom hates to throw out anything she might have to replace for cash sometime in the future," said Michelle. "These will probably end up as part of my dowry. Or, at least, I know she's hoping that one day we'll decide to move out on our own, and we won't have to be delayed by the need to go and purchase boxes."

We got into a rhythm, and things were moving along pretty well without my having to give her much direction. While we were working, she asked me about finding Daniel. I told her pretty much what I'd told Mike that morning on the way to Leesburg, including my suspicions that someone had tampered with the wine.

In discussing possible suspects with Mike, I'd received a lot of new information about John, Reggie, and Penny. But Peter was still a mystery to me. He was quiet and withdrawn, but he *was* the one who'd found Daniel's body. Was it possible his reaction to Daniel's death was an act? If so, he was a very good actor—but that wasn't really a novelty at the Riviera! Moreover, he blamed himself for Daniel's death because he'd been late to work. But was that really the reason? I decided to follow up on Mike's suggestion and ask Michelle for her take on Peter.

"Mike said Peter is really quiet and shy and that he's just devastated about Daniel's death, but he said he really doesn't know much about him. He mentioned you and he had a birthday party last June that Peter came to. Can you tell me anything about Peter?"

"Well, Mike had told me Peter was shy before the party, so I made a point of talking to him to draw him out. And what he told me was really pretty interesting. He's from a little town near Gettysburg, so he grew up with a lot of contact with the Amish. He said when he was a teenager he'd gotten a job painting hex signs like they make among the Pennsylvania Dutch for the tourist trade. He said he did that all through high school, so he must have been pretty good at it. And he went to a small junior college for a couple of years."

"Yeah, he told me he had a degree in graphic design," I said.

"That's right. So I told him I thought it was a little odd he's now working as a cook. I mean, it seems a far stretch. But he said he'd been working as a burger flipper at the racetrack in Cumberland where Reggie races, and Reggie offered him a job at the Riviera as a dishwasher and prep cook. He'd been to D.C. once on a school field trip, but it was just for a day. And he said he'd always wanted to come down and see more of it than just the White House, the Capitol Building, and the Mall monuments. So he took the job.

"Also, I got the impression from the way he talked that his relationship with his folks was strained at the time. I gather his mother's really strict, so he never feels he's living up to her expectations. He said her favorite saying was, 'Everything about this family is right as rain,' but nothing was really ever right. He said his dad was more laid back generally but wouldn't get in the way if his mom was on a tear."

This fit in with my impression of Peter, a young man who didn't think he had the right to feelings or ideas of his own.

Michelle continued, "Anyway, he got a place in a rooming house and started work at the Riviera. He told me he'd only been home to Pennsylvania three times after he started work here—once early on to move some of his things, once at Christmas, because the restaurant is dark for Christmas day, and then again last winter when one of his relatives died. In the spring, Daniel's sous-chef left, so Peter moved up to apprentice, and that's when Aunt Penny asked if Mike would like the job as dishwasher."

"What did you think of Peter personally?"

"If you mean would I date him, probably not. But he seems nice enough. Though I think he's maybe a little bit naïve, sort of average intelligence, not very sophisticated. I mean, it was interesting enough talking to him about his painting hex signs, but there wasn't much else we could talk about. And last Sunday, when he came to the studio with us, he mostly was asking questions on the way over about what was going to happen during the shooting, and what would be his responsibilities as a camera person, and technical stuff. And then when we got there, he sat down for a while behind the person who was doing the credits for the show, and I think he learned all about how to do the graphics. But I don't have a lot in common with him, and except for the art stuff, it's kind of hard to draw him out. Plus, I think maybe this thing with his family has given him some unresolved emotional baggage. And after twenty-one years of living with my mom, I know about the 'evils' of thinking I can rescue somebody—I don't go that route!"

As I was opening up the last box, Michelle said, "We're almost through, aren't we? I just got this awesome book this afternoon, and I wanted to ask you what you think about it. Let me go get it."

She returned in about five minutes with the book and turned it toward me so I could see its cover—*Star Maps* by Wm. R. Fix. The dust jacket showed an Egyptian figure standing in a starry boat and looking like part of a constellation.

"Neat cover!" I said. "What's the author's thesis?"

"Well, there are a couple of things that are important, I think," she said in a musing tone. "First, he uses the out-of-body and near-death experiences of people to show that we're all souls or consciousnesses first and bodies only secondarily. Then he gives evidence that our ancient ancestors, especially the Egyptians, knew about going 'back to the stars' at death. He says that's why there were what he calls 'star maps' painted on the walls of some of the Egyptian tombs, and why in some instances they were even painted inside mummy cases. They were guides for the consciousness of the dead to find their way back to the stars they came from!"

"Oh, my goodness!" I said. "I didn't know that!"

She beamed at me. "I *knew* you'd be interested. Of course, Mom will be interested, too, but I thought of you especially because Fix says all the pyramids were aimed at the circumpolar stars, and he shows how in many, many cultures, there's evidence in their artwork and symbolism that ancient people saw the universe as a kind of cosmic tree or pillar on a central axis. And I thought of the Tree of Life! Isn't that cool?"

"Wow!" I said. "Where'd you get the book? I'd love to read it when you're finished with it."

"I found it in a used book store in Old Town, and I couldn't resist buying it. So you can definitely read it when I'm finished."

"Here," I said, and went burrowing in the closet for a poster tube I'd already put away. "You'll want to look at this."

I uncapped the top of the tube and pulled out a mass of posters that I'd had on my wall in college. One of them was of the Kabbalistic Tree of Life, in color, with the Tarot cards of the Major Arcana superimposed over the paths between the circles on the tree.

Michelle's eyes lit up. "Oh, my," she murmured. "This is awesome, too. I mean, everything sort of fits together, doesn't it? All these different systems are just ways of looking at the same thing."

I smiled. "And what do you think that thing is?"

"Well, it's clear, isn't it? They're guides to helping us 'look up' and get back home again. You said on Sunday Tarot is actually a spiritual system developed to remind us we're souls, not just bodies, and that the pictures on the cards represent roles we have to play to learn the lessons we came here to learn. But ultimately, we're supposed to learn how to go home. Well, I think that's what Kabbalah is about, too. The ten Sephiroth represent the planets of the solar system. And each of them also compares to the energy centers in our bodies. So if we focus up instead of down, maybe we can have the kinds of enlightenment experiences Fix talks about in this book. And then maybe when we die, we won't get hung up in this plane, but we can just shoot right out of the solar system to wherever we're supposed to go. I mean, if we all went home when we finished up here, we wouldn't have to worry about ghosts, would we?"

"I think you're right," I agreed, "but I guarantee you there are so many of them hanging around on this plane that it'll be awhile before we talk them all into going home. But since you've brought that up, my sister Bibi is talking about starting a sort of ghost buster service to get rid of unwanted spirits in real estate properties. What do you think of that?"

"I think you should just go into ghost psychotherapy. Hang your shingle out right under Mom's!"

I chuckled. "I'm not quite ready to do that, but if you'll give me a hand, I *would* like to hang the beautiful hex sign Peter gave me on my door."

Chapter Fourteen

Friday, September 12th

WHEN I GOT home from teaching on Friday, Bernice was in session with a client. I went into the kitchen to grab a cup of tea, then climbed the stairs to my apartment. Taped to my door was a note from Bernice telling me Penny had reminded her of her standing Friday night reservation at the Riviera and had specifically asked her to bring me as well, so if I didn't have other plans, I should be ready to go at five forty-five when Rajneesh would arrive with his magic carpet.

That left me with a couple of hours, so I decided to shower and relax. When I came out of the shower, snug in my terry cloth robe and Bugs Bunny slippers, with a towel wrapped turban-style around my head, I thought about my digital camera, which was still in the pocket of my trench coat. I retrieved it and decided to download the pictures I'd taken in the restaurant kitchen following our discovery of Daniel's body.

I'd put my computer table in one corner of the sleeping area close to the phone line, so I unboxed the computer and all of the accessories, set it up, and turned it on. I had recently bought a new machine with one of those fancy five-way plugs on the front that allows you to plug in everything, including a whole range of options I didn't own yet. I realized that by the time I did own them, my computer would probably be out of date—heck, it was out of date already!—but I liked to be prepared for all contingencies. It did allow me to plug in my digital camera without having to climb around behind the table on hands and knees, and that was a blessing.

Within a couple of minutes, I had two new files, one containing a lot of pictures of the dining room, and another with a dozen shots of the kitchen. I labeled the first file "The Riviera," but I wasn't quite sure what to name the second file. I didn't want to be confronted with "Daniel's Death" every time I opened the "My Documents" file, so I settled on "Kitchen Anomalies." As I did so, I had the passing thought that the title might make a good website:

www.kitchen-anomalies.com, your source for all unexpected culinary items. The human mind is a really strange territory.

Despite the title, I still wasn't sure what I was looking for in the pictures, or what was really bothering me. But something still was. I looked at them again: Daniel on the floor from two directions; a close-up of the wooden spoon he'd been using to stir the sauté pan; a wide-angle view of the whole cooking area; a close-up of the wine bottle; a close-up of the glasses; a close-up of the sauté pan; a close-up of the preparation area showing the stove, cutting board, and blank wall behind it; a picture of the back door; a shot of the door to the freezer; one that showed the entry to the office, door slightly ajar; and one that showed the swinging door to the dining area.

I sat there feeling befuddled. Then I mentally slapped myself on the head.

"Duh!" I said out loud. "You're a Tarot reader. So treat these pictures like Tarot cards."

I turned on my printer, put some picture sized photographic paper in the tray, set the print layout specifications, highlighted all the pictures in the file, clicked print, and went away to dry my hair and get dressed while the printer did its job. When I came back, I gathered up the twelve images and laid them face down on the table. Then I mixed them up.

"No cheating," I said.

I closed my eyes and stated my intention—to choose the picture from the pile that could give me a clue as to why I was still uncomfortable with the scene in the kitchen. Then I reached into the pile with eyes still closed and chose one. Opening my eyes, I looked at it. It was the picture of the preparation area—stove, cutting board, and blank wall. Staring at it, I felt just as befuddled as I had before I started.

Then I realized that since I was going to the restaurant within the hour, I might as well take the picture with me. I could show it to John and see if he wanted to play a game of, "What's wrong with this picture?"

When we arrived at the restaurant, I noticed Reggie working the tables. He seemed to be everywhere at once, chatting pleasantly with everyone, offering them a free glass of wine and checking on their orders. He was obviously enjoying himself.

Penny gave us a big, warm smile; then in a low voice, she said, "I've been working for the past three days to get the word out about the service on Sunday."

She handed each of us a tasteful, printed card announcing the memorial service for Daniel, to be held at three p.m. on Sunday at the Greene Funeral Home, followed by a graveside interment afterward, with a gathering of friends at the restaurant to follow. There was a request that no flowers should be sent, but an address was given if anyone wanted to make a donation in Daniel's name to the Ursuline Sisters in Bordeaux.

There was also a mention of the requiem mass to be held at St. Mary's in two weeks.

"These announcements are lovely," I said.

"I just passed out a paper announcement Tuesday night at dinner," she said, "but I decided Daniel deserved better, so I got a classy print job done Wednesday morning, and since then all of our customers have gotten one of these. In addition, I've been calling all our once-a-month regulars and letting everyone know they're welcome to bring any friends they've fêted at the restaurant in the past. It would be nice to have a really good turnout for Daniel at the funeral." She looked at me as if she might be saying something heretical and added, "Just in case he decides to come after all."

I smiled but didn't say anything.

She looked soberly determined, and I had the distinct impression she wanted Bernice to tell her she was doing everything right.

Bernice reached for her hand and gave it a little squeeze. "I think this will be the perfect send-off for Daniel," she said.

"Well," sighed Penny, "after everything that transpired among all of us, I wouldn't want to do anything shabby."

Bernice added, "If you'd like some assistance tomorrow with calling people, you can email me a set of phone numbers. I'd be glad to help."

"No, dear," said Penny. "This is my penance, and frankly, I welcome it. Now go have a lovely dinner. I know Clarice has worked really hard to keep the restaurant's standards up, but do let us know how you critique everything, please. We really value the opinions of both of you."

I just nodded with a little smile and followed Jamal, who had come up and claimed a couple of menus before leading us to our table. Once he'd seated us and handed each of us a menu, he asked for drink orders.

Bernice ordered her usual Virgin Mary, but I realized I didn't really want a drink, so I said, "Just a cup of hot water with lemon, please, at least for the moment."

I looked around for John, but he didn't seem to be anywhere on the dining room floor. So I put my attention on the menu for a couple of minutes.

"Not surprisingly," murmured Bernice, as her eyes ran down the pages, "the selections have been a bit curtailed. No bouillabaisse, no chateaubriand, no salmon mousse. Oh, well. I'm sure Clarice will hit her stride and bring honor to herself and the restaurant in short order. She *is* offering steamed mussels in garlic butter sauce and salmon in puff pastry—new specialties."

Having given us a chance to review the altered menu, Jamal came back to take our orders. We both had a salad of field greens with the raspberry vinaigrette dressing. Bernice also ordered the mussels as a main course, and I decided to have a plain and simple London Broil.

John didn't show up in the dining room while we were making our way through the meal, so when Jamal came to clear the dinner plates and take our dessert orders, I asked, "Is John off tonight, Jamal?"

"No, Madam, I *think* he bathed," he replied.

We laughed at the incongruity, and he grinned. "Actually, he's been in the kitchen all week, helping to smooth the way for the new chef. I can get him for you, if you like."

"Well, do you think it would be all right for us to go into the kitchen?" asked Bernice. "I never used to worry about barging in on Daniel, particularly between sittings, but I haven't met the new chef yet, so I wouldn't want to disturb her."

"I'm not too sure of the protocol myself, yet," said Jamal softly, "but I can certainly ask Monsieur John. But can I get you something delectable for dessert this evening?"

Bernice just waved her hand and said, "Something with chocolate."

"We have nice chocolate crème," he said, "not quite a mousse. More...how should I describe it...a very elegant antelope."

We both grinned at the joke, and Bernice agreed to try it.

I was feeling like an overstuffed piece of furniture at the moment, so I asked, "Is there anything that's mostly fruit?"

"We have a nice blend of kiwi fruit, mango, and blackberries, if you like."

"That sounds lovely," I said, though the image of myself as an overstuffed chair covered in the colors of that dessert was making me ever so grateful I'd gone into a field other than interior design.

Before Jamal came back with the dessert course, John, dressed in a chef's apron and tall white hat, bustled out of the kitchen in our direction. As he moved through the room, he waved cheerfully to many of the regular customers and announced in a loud voice, "My relegation to the kitchen is only temporary, my friends. Rest assured I'll be back to comic servitude before you know it."

When he reached our table, he bowed and said, "My dears, you both look ravishing. Or should I say, from my temporarily elevated status as assistant chef, you look delicious?" And he reached for a hand from each of us and noisily kissed them in turn, first Bernice's, then mine, before he gently deposited them back on the tabletop.

Turning to me, he said, "Jamal indicated you were asking about me?" Then he leaned forward and whispered, somewhat conspiratorially, "For the moment, it may be politic not to visit in the kitchen. Our new chef is establishing her mastery over her domain, and she has requested that for the next few days we not bring anyone in to interrupt her."

"Well, we wanted primarily to acknowledge her mastery. The dinner was delicious."

"Yes, it was," I agreed enthusiastically, "and I hope you'll convey our esteem to her."

"I most certainly will," he said, beaming. "And in fact, if you like, I'll go and ask her to come out as well."

He turned to go, but I caught his hand and held him for a moment.

"I did have something else I wanted to ask you about, John," I said, reaching for my purse. "I downloaded my pictures from Tuesday morning, and for some reason, I'm sure this one has significance."

I held up the photo of the preparation area for him to look at. He frowned a little as he scrutinized it, as if he were thinking.

Then his eyes widened and he said, "Yes! It *is* important! It shows something—or perhaps I should say it shows an absence of something—that has been mystifying us."

"And that would be...?" I encouraged him.

"It's what it doesn't show that's important. You took this picture while you were by yourself in the kitchen before the police arrived on Tuesday, isn't that so? While I was outside trying to call Reggie and Penny, you came back into the kitchen, leaving Peter in the dining room. And you took pictures of the whole scene—Daniel and all the countertops, right?"

I nodded, so he continued.

"Okay, so in any of the pictures you took, was Daniel's knife roll present?"

I shook my head.

"Well," he said, almost triumphantly, as he put the photo on the table and tapped it with his finger, "this part of the preparation area is where Daniel always laid his knife roll. And it isn't in the picture. I noticed it was gone when I was helping Clarice set up the kitchen area for her needs Tuesday afternoon. It should have been there, but it wasn't. I thought perhaps the police had taken it away. But if it isn't in any of the other pictures, then it was missing from the kitchen when Peter found the body. Now that's very odd!"

Though he was keeping his voice to a whisper, he was clearly excited by this piece of information.

I finally got what he was saying, as well as what he was leaving out.

"What you mean then, is that Daniel, who was sautéing onions when he had his heart attack, must surely have had to chop them. So what's missing, at the very least, was the knife he used to chop the onions."

"Yes," he agreed, "and not just the knife he would have used to chop the onions he was cooking. His entire roll of knives is simply *gone*. And if it isn't in any of the pictures, then the police didn't take it, because it was missing before they arrived."

"Which implies," said Bernice, "that the person who was drinking with him took the knives."

"That's certainly what it suggests to me," he said. "And perhaps, since we didn't notice this discrepancy at the time, one of us should call the police and communicate this detail."

I'd been mulling over the bit of information I hadn't communicated to the police, namely my experiencing of Daniel's last moments. Clearly, he'd had his knife while I was experiencing his death. So John's suggestion that one of us should call the police struck me as being extremely important.

"I can call Detective Flanagan as soon as we get back home," I said. "I can email all my photos to him and point out the discrepancy."

"Good," he smiled. "Well, then, let me go and invite my cousin to come out so you can offer her your accolades in person."

As he started toward the kitchen, Bernice leaned toward me. "Could I see that picture, please?" she asked.

She examined it closely, then looked at me carefully.

"Ariel, this photo points out two discrepancies. If Daniel was alone, cooking onions, when he suddenly keeled over from a heart attack, then who turned off the gas on the stove? Whoever it was must have done it within minutes of Daniel's death, because the onions aren't burned."

I took the picture from her and examined it closely. There was definitely no flame under the sauté pan. I'd have to check the close-up of the sauté pan when I got home, but from looking at this picture, it was pretty obvious the onions weren't burned.

"You're absolutely right, Bernice. I'll note our observation of all of these items when I call the detective."

"Things get more and more curious, don't they?" said Bernice.

Within a couple of minutes, John returned to us with Clarice. The moment she came through the swinging kitchen door, nearly all the restaurant patrons turned to look at her. It was clear what the crowd was thinking in consonance: this stunning Asian woman was the new French chef. Daniel was gone, and that was a loss to be mourned, but they were sufficiently impressed by Clarice's looks—and by what they were eating tonight—that they were willing to give her a chance as his replacement.

Suddenly, Bernice called out, "Here's to our new chef!" And the room broke into applause.

Clarice was glowing as John brought her to our table and introduced her to Bernice, and he was clearly very proud of her and her culinary accomplishments. She said something in Chinese to him in a soft voice, and he answered her, again in Chinese. I realized their rapport was quite special—partly ethnic similarity, partly family connection, and clearly, whether he was aware of it or not, partly sexual attraction.

Bernice and I were effusive in our admiration for Clarice's skills and choices.

She seemed both grateful for the praise and humble. She said, "Ariel, it is so nice to meet you again. And Bernice, it is so nice to meet *you* for the *first* time! I thank you both. But this week I am merely getting my feet wet. Give me a month, and you will experience some truly remarkable meals."

John put a friendly arm around her shoulders and gave her a gentle hug. "She really is a wonder," he said. Then he turned her around and guided her back to the kitchen.

And *I* wondered with a little smile whether John's ingenuous response to the photograph I'd shown him was real—or a very good job of acting.

If he was acting, it would be because he had something to hide. He'd made a big production of noticing the missing knife roll. Could that be because he was the one who had moved it and wanted to divert suspicion from himself now that I had brought the picture to his attention? Could it be he was responsible for Daniel's death? And if so, what had been his motivation? Daniel had been rude to John and derogatory about his culinary knowledge, as well as about his race. That in itself—at least in some circles—could be motive enough for murder. And even though John had said he preferred working out front in the restaurant, he was obviously enjoying his role as sous chef with Clarice. For that matter, might he and Clarice have cooked up the scheme to get rid of Daniel? She was a terrifically strong-willed woman, and that kind of woman could get a man to do things for her that he might not do on his own.

I brought myself up short. Though I didn't think I was still jealous of Clarice, my willingness to construct a theory that implicated her and John certainly sounded like the fevered ramblings of a jealous mind—and a good plot for a daytime soap opera!

WHEN WE GOT home from dinner, Bernice asked if I'd like a nightcap of Bengal Tiger tea, hot milk, hot chocolate, chai tea, or anything else, but I begged off.

"I really want to make that phone call to the police and arrange to get these pictures to them."

"Well, then," said Bernice, "I'll say good night. I'm going to snuggle in with a good mystery and a large mug of tea. I'll let you catch me up on anything new in the morning."

I climbed the stairs thoughtfully, marveling at my own intuition. When I was a kid, my family had called me "the psychic detective." Once when I was eight, I'd found my father's wallet after my parents had turned the house upside down hunting for it. When they told me what was lost, I just walked right to it, brought it back to my dad, and said, "Is this what you're looking for?"

Somehow, my designation as a psychic detective was now expanding well beyond what it had meant then. Even though I wasn't terribly cognizant of the workings of a restaurant kitchen, I had sensed something was amiss, something none of the people who normally habituated the kitchen had noticed. I had taken a series of pictures that had captured important information and trusting the workings of my own subconscious, I had chosen the one picture from the twelve that pinpointed three discrepancies—the stove was turned off, the onions weren't burned, and the knife roll was missing.

I thought, *Ariel, you really are psychic*. And though I liked to say, and truly believed, that everybody has a sixth sense, I realized mine was more finely tuned than most.

"Daniel," I said, "I think you've gone beyond this plane, but I promise I *will* find out who poisoned you." Then a thought crossed my mind, and I added, "And Annie Grace, I promise to learn your story, too."

Once I got into my room, I changed into my sweats. Then I retrieved the picture I'd taken to the restaurant, got Detective Flanagan's and Sergeant Mason's cards from my purse, and sat down at my desk. I dialed Flanagan's number but was immediately routed to his voice mail. I didn't want to wait for him to call me back, so I decided to call Mason instead. He answered on the second ring.

He acknowledged remembering me as soon as I'd identified myself. "What can I do to help you?" he asked.

"This afternoon I downloaded the pictures I took at the restaurant on Tuesday morning before the police arrived," I said. "And I was puzzled by them, because I kept thinking there was something not quite right, though I couldn't identify what it was. So tonight when Mrs. Wise and I went to the restaurant, I had my friend John look at one of them in particular."

Then I explained to him what John had noticed about the missing knives and what Bernice had noticed about the unburned onions in the sauté pan and the turned off stove.

Mason listened quietly while I recounted all that we'd realized. Then he said, "I've been taking notes while you were talking, and I'll contact Flanagan. This business about the knife roll in particular is important information. I'm not sure whether the ID tech took note of the stove and the state of the onions, but it's good you and your friend noticed it. Flanagan will want to get in touch with you. If I can get hold of him, how late can he call you tonight?"

"I'll probably be up for a couple of hours," I said. "I want to journal everything I've seen, done, and sensed in relation to this situation to see if anything else comes up from my subconscious."

"You have an interesting way of talking," he said. "This is the first time I've worked with a psychic. But you seem to be right on the money."

"Aw, shucks," I said, and I could feel my cheeks getting red, "thanks. Oh, by the way, do you want me to email you these photos? I can do it right now, while we're talking."

"Yes, please, that's a good idea. I'll get them printed and labeled and put them in the case folder. And if you wouldn't mind, add any comments about them that you consider pertinent."

I thought for a moment about the sergeant's response to my psychic talent both Tuesday in his cruiser and tonight on this call, and I decided to put all my Tarot cards on the table.

"Sergeant Mason," I said, "I have something else I feel I should share. It's another psychic impression. And this one is probably the most over the edge of all of my impressions, so I hope it doesn't scare you off."

"Well," he replied, "as I said on Tuesday, we treat everything as evidence until it's either proved or disproved. I must say your work with the photographs gives you credibility. Generally, when we work with any informant, we take whatever they tell us at face value up to the point at which their information begins to prove false."

"I do understand," I said, "though I should probably note that no psychic can claim to be right more than eighty percent of the time. However, I'll always tell you if I'm getting an impression I'm not totally sure of."

"That's fine," he said. "Go ahead."

"Okay. Would I be right in assuming you've heard of out-of-body experiences?"

"Yes."

"Well, I had an in-body experience." And I told him about my projecting into Daniel's body while he was drinking the wine, sautéing the onions, and dying. "And that's why," I finished, "I'm so sure he was poisoned. But I'm not sure whether he was alone in the kitchen or not."

"Ms. Quigley," said the sergeant, "yesterday you accused me of being intuitive. And you may be right. I also think your participation in this mystery is at a very personal level. You're the only person whose comments about the decedent show any level of caring. Everyone else seemed interested only in getting the restaurant running again. And if this *is* a murder, then all of them are really suspects."

"I guess maybe they did seem a bit cold-hearted. But it's like theater people always say during a crisis, 'The show must go on.' If the restaurant were to founder because of the loss of the chef, many people would suffer. Each of them will grieve in his or her own way and time." Then as an afterthought, I added, "There's going to be a memorial service for Daniel on Sunday afternoon at three p.m. at Greene's Funeral Home, followed by a graveside ritual and a reception at the restaurant. You're welcome to come as my guest. Maybe you'll see another side of the staff."

There was a long silence at the other end, and I wasn't sure whether I'd offended him. Then he said, "I'm actually off on Sunday, and I'd be delighted to take you up on the offer."

We agreed to meet outside the funeral home at two forty-five on Sunday afternoon.

"Why don't I give you my cell phone number," he said. "That way, you can contact me in off hours if you need to."

We said our requisite polite goodbyes and hung up. I spent another fifteen minutes preparing the email and sending it to him. Finally, I turned off my computer and put on the kettle to make some tea, my first act of domesticity in my own little kitchenette.

As I waited for the kettle to boil, I got out my cell phone and keyed in Sgt. Mason's number on speed dial number seven. I realized I was feeling strangely buoyant after my conversation with him. He thought I was interesting!

And then I realized I'd just asked him on a date!

Chapter Fifteen

Saturday, September 13th

I was at a Halloween party in a big ballroom where there was singing, dancing, drinking, a huge buffet, and people playing all kinds of games on the sidelines. And everybody was in costume.

Bernice was dressed in a bright pink muumuu, but she was wearing a chef's hat and large white apron and waving a long wooden spoon as if she were directing an orchestra. Mike, Michelle, and Roy and Jamal, the two waiters at the Riviera, were all dressed in motley, like jesters, with caps and bells, and were juggling platters of food as she gave them directions. First one, then the other would fling a platter into the air and then catch it. Then they began tossing the platters back and forth to each other, but they never lost even a morsel of food from any of the platters.

Penny and Reggie were in domino masks and glittery black outfits that looked like they were from Vegas. She had on a green eyeshade and was holding a deck of cards with the Jack of Spades showing. He had one arm bare and the other in a black sleeve and glove and on his shirt was a row of pictures of cherries. It dawned on me that Penny was supposed to be a Black Jack dealer and Reggie was dressed as a slot machine.

"The house always wins," she cooed, and he replied in agreement, "The odds are in our favor!"

I was wearing a ball gown and a tiara and feeling very much like Cinderella, and I started looking around for John. Finally, I saw him in the crowd, dressed in a crown, doublet, hose, and cape, clearly a handsome Prince Charming type. How appropriate, I thought, I'm Cinderella, and he's Prince Charming! But he was dancing with another lovely woman, and as he turned her in my direction, I realized she was in a Walt Disney Snow White costume, blue and red and yellow, and she was John's cousin Clarice. I waved and tried to get their attention, but before either one of them looked my way, I heard a voice shout from above me, "Look, Ariel, no hands!" I looked up and saw two platforms for a high-wire act, but with no wire between them, and Dennis on a unicycle riding back and forth between the platforms. He was dressed like the god Hermes, with wings on his heels, a winged hat, and a winged staff *with serpents twined around it.*

Then the orchestra stopped the dance number and began playing a fanfare. Out from the kitchen came Daniel, Peter, Bernice, and Annie Grace, all of them together carrying a tray bearing a huge fancy cake that was shaped like a building in Old Town Alexandria. Then John and Clarice danced up, and they, too, took hold of the cake tray. Everybody applauded loudly. And Reggie, the one-armed bandit, went over to the cake tray and began bowing, as if he were taking credit for the cake.

Then I felt a tap on my shoulder, and the Fat Man appeared at my side, wearing his pork pie hat and Artful Dodger coat. He reached inside the coat and brought out a sign, but I could only read the first three words of the message, "Too many cooks..." before someone shouted, "The Queen of Spain will destroy us all!"

People began running in all directions as a rush of water came bursting through the kitchen doors and threatened to wash the cake and everything else away.

I found myself running, too, and a clock somewhere was striking midnight. I knew the witches and ghosts would come out at the stroke of twelve, and I ran down the stairs, like Cinderella running from the ball before her coach could turn into a pumpkin. The wind was howling, rain was falling, and like Cinderella, I lost my shoes in the mud just as the dead began to rise from their graves. Clattering down the stairs behind me was someone riding a donkey, but when I turned, I couldn't see who it was.

I woke with a sharp intake of breath in the cold room, heart pounding, and all in a sweat. The clock read 3:10, and it was still pitch dark outside. The dream I'd just come from had clearly held a message from the Fat Man, but there were also myriad dream images I'd need to sort out. And I was wide awake.

I switched on the light and reached for my notebook to write the dream down. It was a busy set of symbols, what with Cinderella's party at Halloween, and the sense that I'd left the ball and run into a graveyard.

As I pondered the Fat Man's message, I figured it had to be the old adage, "Too many cooks spoil the broth." I thought about how Daniel and Annie Grace were both in the dream, having baked a cake together that looked like the building that housed the Riviera Café. And I remembered how the image of Annie Grace's death had intruded while I was trying to tune in to Daniel just after his death.

For a minute I wondered if maybe the Fat Man's message was about "too many ghosts" of cooks. But Peter, Bernice, John, Clarice, and Reggie were all cooks, but they weren't ghosts. And Dennis, who was a ghost, was also in the dream, though he had nothing to do with the restaurant at all. Then I reminded myself that the Fat Man's message was always the most important part of any dream. And his message had distinctly said *Too many cooks...* So that was where I needed to focus my attention.

The cooks specifically related to the restaurant were Peter, John, and Clarice. And by a stretch, Reggie, who had experience as a chef, and who had included himself as a possible cook for the restaurant after Daniel's death but before the arrival of Clarice. The only person I'd excluded by this reasoning was Bernice, so there were still definitely too many cooks. All of my analysis to this point hadn't eliminated any of them as suspects. And narrowing the suspect field to just cooks only eliminated Penny. I wondered if I'd need four more Fat Man dreams before I'd finally determine the truth of the matter.

I put my journal aside and lay back on my pillows, thinking that maybe what I needed was to talk to Bernice to help me to sort out all these symbols. Then I dozed off again.

THE NEXT MORNING, I was down in the kitchen early waiting for Bernice to get up, and Freud the Cat and I had already made a pot of coffee by the time she came down to start breakfast.

"What are you doing up so early?" she asked as she sauntered in.

"I had one of my Fat Man dreams," I said, "and I think I need a therapist!"

She grinned. "You mean your dreams are driving you crazy?"

"No, but I know you're good at analyzing dream symbols, and I need some help sorting out this dream."

I related all the different symbols—the party, the costumes everyone was wearing, including Dennis as the Greek god of wisdom and healing, the Fat Man's message, the cake the two dead cooks had brought out with Peter's help, and the ending of the dream in the graveyard, as I lost my Cinderella shoes in the muck of a rainstorm.

When I got to the part about not being able to get John's attention on the dance floor, followed by Dennis and his high-wire act, Bernice nodded.

"Sounds like you've let go of John and just need to 'look up' to complete your healing regarding Dennis."

"Yes, I guess I *have* already given up on John's affections," I said, "but I don't know about Dennis. I feel there's still a lot of residual stuff I haven't dealt with yet. And you're probably right—I just need to look at the situation around Dennis' death more closely.

"But there's a lot more to this dream than that. Remember what I told you about what happened when I tried to get in touch with Daniel right after his death? How I was feeling his pain as he was dying and pulled away from his consciousness, only to have an image of Annie Grace's death bleed through?"

"Yes, you told us about that the afternoon of his death."

"And you said maybe Annie Grace was telling me Daniel's death wasn't natural," I said. "So, was the Fat Man trying to tell me something about the similarity between Annie Grace's and Daniel's deaths? Or was his message to me that I need to help solve Annie Grace's problem before I can figure out what happened to Daniel?"

"I guess it could be either, and maybe only Annie Grace can tell us."

"I haven't tried to get in touch with her again because I was hoping to have you as a sort of metaphysical ombudsman. She is, after all, your ghost."

Bernice smiled. "I've been wondering when I could tie you down and get you to do a little channeling about Annie Grace, to see just what she's still trying to tell us."

She looked at her watch. "Usually I like to sit and read the morning paper for an hour or so before Mike and Michelle wander in, but I can postpone my paper reading for a while if you'd like to tackle Annie Grace's problem."

"I really would," I said eagerly, "if only to get a little closure on what was apparently her murder. I have a couple of hours yet before I have to get ready to go to Leesburg for Bibi's birthday party."

Bernice said, "Okay, where would you like to work?"

"Right here is fine, if you think we can be undisturbed for an hour or so. You can ask the questions for both of us. Are you up for that? Maybe you could take notes—treat her like a psychotherapy client?"

She nodded. Then she poured herself some coffee, picked up a notebook she usually kept near the phone, and joined me at the table.

I centered myself, relaxing, and invited Annie Grace to come and join us. Within a few seconds, I got the impression of her standing near us. So I closed my eyes and said to Bernice, "Okay, ask away. She's here with us, and will speak through me."

Bernice said softly, "Annie Grace? Do you have something you want to tell us?"

I sensed a little irritation and heard Annie say in my mind, "What's *she* doin' askin' questions? She don' listen! I done try to talk to her, but she don' hear nuthin'!"

As I repeated these words to Bernice, she chuckled.

"I probably deserve that," she said. "But Annie, now I have someone to be your voice, so I'll do my best to hear what you have to say."

I felt the presence sort of settle in and realized my role was to get out of the way as much as possible while Annie talked to Bernice.

Again I heard Bernice say, "So, Annie Grace, what do you want to tell us?"

"It was de young massa kill me. He jus' pick up a fryin' pan and bam! He bang me on de head. An' I wouldna' tol' nuthin'. What I care what dey be doin'? Dey jus' careless white folk anyway."

"What was it they were doing, Annie Grace?"

"I seen de young one messin' wif his daddy's new wife. Dey was in my room! It was market day, an' I done gone to de market wif ol' Billy in de cart. An' de ol' massa had give me some money to buy me some calico for dressin' myself an' my little one. An' I bought me some dat day, along wif de supplies for de kitchen. Den while Billy took de green groceries to de kitchen, I took de cloth to my room. An' dere dey was, humpin' away on my bed!

"I knowed fo' sho' it wasn't sumpin' I need to see, so I turn right aroun' an' shut de door, an' I go to de kitchen like I weren't never in my room. An' I'm thinkin' to myself why dey be in my room anyway? Den I think it mus' be 'cause dey's nowhere else de ol' massa ain't likely to show up. 'Cause if dey be caught like dat, ol' massa gonna horsewhip dat boy to death! An' dey bof' be put in de stocks and whipped in public."

"So what happened next?" Bernice coaxed.

"Well, dat boy took his time finishin' what he was at, an' I thought maybe dey didn' even see me. But den while I was cookin' up some onions I had cut for de stew pot, I hear footsteps behin' me, an' nex' thing I know, I feels dis God Almighty pain on de back of my head an I's lyin' on de' floor, an' I cain't get up. Den jus' as sudden, I ain't in my body no mo', I's kinda standin' off to de side, an' dere's dis bright light, sorta drawin' me."

"Why didn't you go toward the light, Annie Grace?" Bernice asked.

"'Cause I see my body dere on de floor, and young massa standin' dere holdin' my big fryin' pan, an' my head's all mashed in an' bloody. An' den he put down de fryin' pan and started messin' up my kitchen! He's throwin' stuff aroun' like a crazy man, spillin' flour an' sugar an' dumpin' my soup pot an' turnin' the table upside down. An' den he run out.

"So I turn my back on dat light. I gotta know what he's doin', messin' up my kitchen like dat."

"And did you find out why he messed up the kitchen?"

"I sho' enuf did. He come back after some time wif his daddy, an' he's sayin' I musta let one too many tramps into my kitchen fo' a free meal. An' dey musta try to rob me. An' his daddy say, 'Dat's too bad. It gonna be hard to get another cook good as Annie Grace.' I try to tell him it was a lie, but I ain't got no voice. But I wants to tell someone. He ain't got no business messin' up my kitchen!"

"You're right, Annie Grace. He had no business messing up your kitchen," said Bernice. "I'm glad I've finally been able to hear your story."

I felt Annie Grace give an emphatic nod, and I'm sure my head bobbed for her.

"What year was it, Annie Grace?" asked Bernice.

In answer to this question, all I got was a sort of quizzical wondering as to why anyone would want to know that. And I said to Bernice, "I don't think the question makes sense to her. Try something else."

"What about your little one, Annie Grace?" asked Bernice. "Were you worried about your child?"

"I sho' enuf was, but only fo' a little bit, 'cause my sista' Mary Faith took care of her 'til she got growed up. An' dey was dere when de massa' buried me and tol' ever' body I'd let a tramp in my kitchen and de tramp done killed me, so dey all was thinkin' I got what I deserved, lettin' tramps on the property. So I gotta tell someone. An' I been tryin' jus' to do it—jus' to tell someone."

"Well, Annie Grace, you've succeeded. You've told us, and we'll see if we can set the record straight for you. What was your master's name?"

I didn't quite have the clarity with Annie's answer, but I got the "impression" of John Stewart, so I said that to Bernice.

Before Bernice could respond, I heard Annie Grace say, "I be goin' now."

And suddenly she was gone, the presence lifting like a veil from my consciousness, though I still seemed to have a full awareness of her memories. I opened my eyes and looked at Bernice.

"She was caught in a loop," I said.

"What do you mean?"

"She needed to tell someone the truth about what had happened. She was a slave, but with a position of responsibility. More than being killed, she was upset because she was being slandered. It seemed to me while she was here with me that she was proud of her position and kept her kitchen spotless. I got the impression she would occasionally provide a meal for passing strangers, white or black, if they looked like they were in need. But she never let anybody into her kitchen, except Billy, of course, when he was delivering supplies."

Bernice interjected, "Of course! And when the son desecrated her kitchen in his cover up of his crime, it made her so angry that she got caught in the need to tell someone what had really happened. It was a kind of vindication of her reputation. She's probably tried to get the attention of everyone who has cooked on these premises ever since.

"Also," she added smiling, "you dropped one other interesting little bombshell with the name of the master. I have copies of the ownership registry for the various owners of this property going back to 1763. And I'm pretty sure that for a period of about forty years, one of the families that owned it was named Seward. That's pretty close to Stewart. So I'll bet there are other records we can check to see what slaves he might have owned and even perhaps when she might have died."

"That's the kind of feedback that sooths my little psyche!" I said. "And by the way," I added, still with the images of having wandered the grounds in my mind with Annie Grace, "are you aware this wasn't the kitchen in that era? This was the family dining room. The kitchen where Annie Grace was killed is out where your garden is right now. And her quarters were indeed where the garden shed is now, as Michelle and Mike suggested. So I'm willing to bet the Fog Lady is gone, because I'm pretty sure that was Annie Grace, too. And what's more, Michelle has chosen the ideal spot in the garden to put a set of spiritual symbols."

"How so?" asked Bernice.

"Because," I said, "the Tree of Life she's built lies on what used to be the slave cemetery for this property. Annie Grace was buried there."

As I drove out to Leesburg, I was still on a high from the experience with Annie Grace. I could hardly wait to tell the rest of my family my newest ghost story.

We were the alphabetical Quigley sisters—Ariel, Beatrice, Catherine, and Deirdre. They called *me* the psychic detective and the ghost hunter, but *all* of my sisters had their own special psychic gifts, and all of us, including our mom, had had encounters with ghosts or other spirits.

My youngest sister Deirdre, who was still in school studying theater at High Point College in North Carolina, had brought a ghost home with her the previous Christmas. The school theater was supposed to be haunted by a ghost named Herschel, who would turn the lights on and off or play with the soundboard during performances and mess up people's cues.

Deirdre, though she was a student, sometimes appeared to run the theater department single-handedly. She acted, directed, built sets, sometimes ran the lights and the soundboard, and actually got paid to work as costume mistress. Because she was in the theater so much of the time, she'd had plenty of run-ins with Herschel. On nights when she was at the theater sewing costumes, he'd turn the lights on and off or play the practice organ in the rehearsal studio next door to the costume room.

She'd jokingly yelled out an invitation to him as she was locking up the theater to go home for Christmas, saying, "Hey, Herschel, you want to come home with me for the holidays?"

Sure enough, my parents had lights and radios going on and off at home for the next two weeks, until one day when my mom got caught by herself in the basement and the lights went out on *her*. She yelled out in irritation, "All right, Herschel, enough is enough! Stop messing with the lights! And when Deirdre goes back to school, you're going with her!"

The lights flicked back on immediately, and my mom said she heard an audible sigh. All was peaceful thereafter. Of course, when Deirdre got back to school, Herschel's antics started up again at the campus theater.

As a performer, Deirdre was a raconteur who could draw people in with her stories. She'd engage her audience so completely they'd literally hold their breath while she was talking. She once confided to me that while she was in conversation with people, she seemed to know what they were thinking, and she could charm them because she knew what they wanted to hear and what would entertain them.

"She's got the gift of the gab," my mom would say. "You'd think that child had kissed the Blarney Stone!"

When Deirdre was in her senior year in high school, there was a theater trip to Ireland. Deirdre always seemed to live on a shoestring in high school, but she made a deal with my parents that if they'd pay for half of the trip, she'd find a job and earn the other half. She sold burgers and fries at McDonald's for three months and earned enough to pay for her share of the trip and an optional add-on bus tour to Blarney Castle in County Cork.

THE CHEF WHO DIED SAUTÉING

"If I'm going to be accused of having kissed the Blarney Stone," she explained, "I guess I'd better do it."

She loved to tell the story of how tourists have to be willing to hang upside down in a shaft at the castle in order to kiss a particular stone, which the guides assure them is the Blarney Stone.

My sister Catherine had a green thumb and a knack for horticulture that seemed to go beyond the normal. She could grow bigger and more voluptuous roses, tastier tomatoes, and amazingly vital house plants. When she was a child, she'd asked to help my dad with a little garden plot he was growing one summer. He let her put in a row of beans, and oddly, her row had grown taller and produced more prolifically than his.

One day he said to her, "Are you doing anything special with your beans?"

"Not really," she answered. "I just go out every day and tell them they're beautiful and that I love them."

My dad loved to tell people, "Catherine knows beans about gardening!"

Catherine was an accountant and currently a manager at a savings and loan company in the Town Center in Reston, Virginia where she'd been given an opportunity to develop a botanical garden in the front entrance, complete with flowering plants, vines, bonsai trees, and a little waterfall. In an area where high-pressure businesses were the norm, she had managed to create an oasis of peace and harmony. Business was booming for her company because shoppers would come in to look at the garden, feel relaxed and safe, and somehow get the sense this was where they wanted to invest their savings.

Catherine's experiences with the paranormal ran to "hearing" nature spirits who, she said, would often tell her what and how to plant, and occasionally "seeing" the energies of the plants themselves. And once she saw a ghost cat walk across the living room carpet—I was there at the time, and I'd seen it, too, though not for the first time, since it would sometimes climb into bed with me.

"Whose cat is that?" she'd asked.

"It's a ghost cat, so it probably belonged to a previous owner," I said.

"Oh," she said, and that was that.

My sister Bibi, whose real name was Beatrice, was the one in the family who seemed able to make the universe work for her most effectively. She was a master of manifestation.

All her life Bibi had been able to get exactly what she wanted. But it wasn't the way most children did it, through whining, cajoling, nagging, and other forms of youthful extortion. She'd merely tell the universe what she wanted in a positive manner and very shortly, it would appear. It was one of the reasons why we labeled her "practical pig," because she never asked for more than she needed in any given transaction—no requests for the lottery. And that's probably why she was so successful.

Once when she was little, she walked up to my mom and said, "I want a copy of *The Little Mermaid* video!"

Mom said, "You'll have to wait for your birthday, dear."

"But I really want it now!" she said, and as she left the room, Mom saw her look up and say, "Please?" pause for a second, and then say very confidently, "Thank you!"

Two days later her friend Alex gave her a copy, having received two the previous weekend for *his* birthday.

Bibi was also very much a clothes horse.

"When I want something," she told me once, "I just visualize it hanging on a rack in a store with the price tag at what I can afford at the time. Then I go out and find it without fuss or bother."

I remember in high school she wanted a white linen suit, but all she had saved up was $35.00. Did that stop her? No way! She visualized exactly what she wanted and then went to K-Mart, of all places, and found a gorgeous, lined white linen suit—the only one on the rack and of course it was in her size. And the price tag was $35.00.

Shortly after marrying Victor, Bibi went into real estate. They were already in the Leesburg area, but after a couple of years she decided they should live on a farm. So, with an image of what she wanted in her head, she began looking for real estate locally and very shortly found exactly what she wanted.

Victor loved the farm, but he said to Bibi, "I'm not earning enough right now to buy that piece of property."

So Bibi sat down and figured out how much they would need and told the universe to give her more clients and to send Victor either a raise or a new job offer that would put their combined income up to the needed level. And within a couple of weeks her client base had increased and Victor was offered a job with a company that allowed him to travel from city to city trouble-shooting people's computer systems—and at exactly the income level Bibi had in mind. Then she made an offer for the farm property at the price she thought she should pay for it, though it was considerably less than the asking price, and sure enough the owners accepted the offer.

When the rest of us would ask her how she managed to make these things work, she'd shrug and say, "I guess the universe is Santa Claus!"

AS I DROVE up to the farmhouse, I saw the little fifteen-year-old Nissan that had been passed along from sister to sister since I was in high school and that now belonged to Deirdre. My dad, who had kept it running and viable all this time, called it "SLEAZE"—and that's what its license plate read. It carried the dents, scratches, and repairs reminiscent of all our automotive peccadilloes. It had become a family tradition that none of us could get another car until we'd shown ourselves to be roadworthy drivers in SLEAZE, which meant we had to have three accident-free years.

THE CHEF WHO DIED SAUTÉING

I also saw Catherine's silver Accord from her husband's Honda dealership with its license plate GRN THMB. It was parked next to Bibi's Grand Voyager labeled BIBI. I was amused at how we all seemed to show our personalities by the types of cars we drive and vanity plates we put on them. My Jeep sported the title PSI KICK, a name I'd chosen when I got out of the confinement of army life and felt it was time to kick up my heels a bit. When I moved from Maryland to Virginia, I applied for that license name again, and fortunately, it was available.

I stood there for a moment, looking at all the cars, and thinking about how much I currently enjoyed get-togethers with the family. With a good amount of steely control, the Quigley girls managed these days to overcome those 'family-of-origin' problems that most collections of siblings seem to face during reunion holidays: the kinds of disagreements that lead to arguments, confrontations, and even alienation.

We were probably no more or less dysfunctional than the average family, with problems arising seemingly out of thin air between any two of us. Shortly after I returned from my stint overseas, we'd had a truly horrific Christmas dinner. For some reason—maybe just that I'd been to war and thought I knew everything, and Catherine had just started college and thought she knew everything, and Bibi was a junior in college and *did* know everything—all three of us were sniping at each other with noses so far out of joint we could all have used plastic surgery. At one point Catherine stormed out of the dining room in a huff, saying she never wanted *anything* to do with *any* of us again, thank you very much.

My mother put her foot down. She said she would never be a party to the upsets of family gatherings again, and the next year, she, Dad, and Deirdre—the only one still living at home—spent Thanksgiving in Peru and Christmas in Cape Cod. So, the following year the four of us sibs made a pact to leave our personal problems on the porch for the duration of all family parties. And since then we'd held to the pact.

I wandered into Bibi's kitchen and was greeted with the smells of chili and cornbread, two foods that were her birthday specialties. Victor and Catherine's husband Mark were off in a corner at the bar Victor had built, drinking beer. My sisters were all busy at various counters, frosting cupcakes, making potato salad, and chopping raw veggies for dipping. My three nephews were on the floor in a den area beside the kitchen, occupied with a Veggie Tales video.

When the kids saw me, they all jumped up and ran in to fling their arms around my legs.

"You've been gone so long," said Harrison, who had a knack for making you feel wanted.

Alex and Max, who tended to talk at the same time, asked, "Did you bring a present for Mommy? It's her birthday today. We're having cupcakes!"

Harrison said with great seriousness, "Mommy said Irene could come for dinner if she wanted to, so we're going to set a place for her at the table. She says with everybody in the family being here all at once, it's going to be one of those dinners. She said Irene will help keep her sane."

Bibi laughed. "Never tell anything to your children that's not suitable for publication."

Catherine added, "I think inviting Irene is an excellent idea, although my inclination would be to put a couple of pots of geraniums on the table. They're a good calming influence, too."

Deirdre, who was now licking out the last of the chocolate frosting from the bowl and the beaters she'd used, said, "I never worry about anybody getting mad at me. You've gotta love me, 'cause…"

"You're the baby!" everybody shouted.

Our mom and dad arrived at that moment, with a shopping bag full of goodies—a present for Bibi and coloring books and crayons for the boys.

"Right on time," said Bibi. "Everything's ready, so let's put it all on the table."

"Who's the extra place setting for?" Mom asked.

"For Irene," said Bibi. "The boys wanted to invite her."

"Do I need to dish up a serving of chili for her?"

"Oh, no," said Harrison. "She only likes cupcakes. And if she gets too full, I'll help her."

During the year I'd been living at the farm, I'd come to realize that Irene was really accepted as a member of the household, though this was the first time she'd received the status of "invited guest" at a dinner party. I surmised Bibi might have been having a difficult day with the children. Sometimes in my musings, I wondered if Irene and the Fat Man knew each other.

My dad, who had retired the previous year from the army, had recently taken on a consulting job with a beltway bandit company that did military contracting.

"My job is all very hush-hush, of course," he said, "but after thirty-five years in military management, I can't help but compare these technological yuppies I'm working with now to the enlisted men I've seen over the years. These kids have degrees, but a lot of them are just as green as raw recruits. Except there's no way to tell them that. But I guess that's why they hired me, because I know my way around the Pentagon."

"I know what you're talking about," said Catherine. "I see some of them at the savings and loan during lunch hour, wearing their ID cards on chains around their necks. It's like they're all members of an elite club. But yesterday one of these bright young lights leaned over to get a cup of water at our cooler and got his chain caught on the tap without realizing it, and when he stood up, it jerked him back and he poured the water all down his front."

"There does seem to be something about living in the D.C. area that makes people full of themselves," I said. "But I'm not sure what that says for me, since I've now moved back into the thick of it myself." I paused for a second and added, "And I guess 'thick' really describes it, when you consider everything that's happened to me since I had dinner at the Riviera last Friday."

Catherine, who was knowledgeable about all the "in" places and activities in the D.C. area asked, "You ate *there*? On a *Friday*? Without a *reservation*? How did you get in? How could you afford it? And what do you mean by everything that's happened to you since last Friday?" She sounded a bit like the twins.

I looked at Bibi questioningly. "Didn't you tell everybody *everything*? What happened to your status as 'information-age diva'?"

"Catherine has been hard to get hold of this week," Bibi said with a shrug.

"I've been out of town since Tuesday at a conference," said Catherine. "I had my cell off while I was in session. I saw Bibi's number on my caller ID, but I figured since I was going to be here today, I'd hear everything worth the telling. What did I miss?"

I looked blank for a moment, trying to decide where to start, then began filling her in, finishing up by saying, "Chef Daniel's funeral will be tomorrow."

Catherine sat in sympathetic silence, taking it all in.

Mark, who had been listening and eating, but not talking, said, "The Riviera Café...I know one of the owners there. Reggie Whitson and I used to race together up at The Rock in Cumberland, Maryland. In fact, at the closing banquet last year, he invited me and Catherine down to the restaurant as his guests for dinner."

Catherine came out of her reverie then and added, "It was the most wonderful meal I ever experienced. Chef Daniel will be sorely missed."

"This must be hard on Reggie," Mark added. "I haven't seen him in months because they race at that speedway on Sundays this year, and I usually can't get away from the dealership. But I guess with this turn of events, he won't be racing this weekend."

Just at that moment, I smelled perfume. I looked at Bibi, whose eyes had widened.

"That's Irene's *Cotillion*," she said. "That's a warning for someone!"

But at that moment we didn't know who was being warned.

Chapter Sixteen

Sunday, September 14th

Sunday dawned pleasant and sunny—perfect weather for a late summer picnic. But we had a funeral to go to, and the normal high hilarity of Sunday breakfast with Bernice and the twins was missing. Even Freud the Cat seemed to sense a change in the energy and was curled on the doormat instead of all over us at the breakfast table.

Not that Mike didn't try to interject some macabre jokes about death. But Bernice insisted he curtail his black humor.

"Mom," he said, "in the wake of any death or disaster, humor is the first thing to surface. And everybody, including you, will tell you it's how people cope. It's what made *MASH* such a popular television series. And after 9/11, there was that joke that came out about…"

"That's enough, Mike," said Bernice.

"Geez, Mom, whose programming have you been listening to that tells you to be dour and somber for a funeral?"

"I'm sure you're absolutely, right, Mike, but allow me my little rituals, if you please. I'm not tearing my clothing or pulling out my hair, but I would like to handle my day of grieving without a comedy routine."

"Oh, my God, Mom!" erupted Mike. "Were you in love with Daniel?"

"No! I WAS *NOT!*" she said emphatically.

"Mike," said Michelle knowingly, "what Mom was in love with was the way Daniel treated her and flirted with her. Why do you think all women go ga-ga over Frenchmen? They know how to make women feel beautiful, sexually attractive, and good about themselves. And they can do it with a look, a kiss on the back of the hand, and half a dozen words."

Bernice looked at Michelle. "That also may be quite true, Michelle. I must admit I will miss Daniel's charm. But I have spent the last few hours mulling over Daniel's death, and in light of Ariel's psychic experience, it was not due to a simple heart attack. He was very likely poisoned with something designed to make his death look like a heart attack. And the person responsible is likely to be someone of our acquaintance."

"Oh, my gosh!" said Mike. "I hadn't thought about that. You know, Aunt Penny's asked everyone who works at the restaurant to speak at the service today. She says that in spite of the occasional unpleasantness, everyone on the staff admired Daniel's talents. So she wants us all to speak about him from our own perspectives."

"Well," said Michelle, "it seems likely, if what Mom says is right, one of them is going to be quite uncomfortable."

"And," I added, "maybe we should all agree to pay attention to who says what, and how they say it. And if anyone notices anything that seems odd or out of place, would you let me know afterward?"

They all looked at me and nodded solemnly.

Bernice then suggested, "Perhaps we should carpool to the funeral. There will probably be limited parking at the funeral home, and it's always hard to find parking near the restaurant."

"That's a good idea," I agreed. "But I'm meeting Sergeant Mason right before the funeral, so I'll sit with him while it's going on. And if he opts to go to the graveside and the restaurant afterward, I'll ride with him. But don't leave the funeral home without checking with me, in case he doesn't want to come and I need a ride."

Bernice asked, "Why is the sergeant coming to the funeral?"

"Well, actually, I invited him. He seemed to have the impression that Reggie and John were a little cold-hearted right after we found Daniel, and I wanted to show him they actually cared."

"And," she asked, "is that *all*?"

"Oh, I admit, I kind of like the curve of his jaw."

WHEN WE GOT to the funeral home, Sergeant Mason was already waiting outside. I was introducing him to Bernice and the twins when Penny came up and told us she had reserved seats in the second row for us all, so I introduced her, too. She hadn't met him when she'd gone to the police station on Wednesday.

In answer to her questioning look, the sergeant said, "I'm just here to pay my respects, ma'am. I'm not working this case."

Penny nodded and said, "Welcome, then." To Bernice she added, "I'm really gratified at the turnout. There are already nearly one hundred and fifty people inside, including many of our patrons and other restaurateurs and chefs from around the city who were acquainted with Daniel."

Turning to Mike, she asked, "Are you ready to say a few words?"

He glanced over at Bernice with a wicked smile, then straightened his look and said to Penny, "Yup."

We all went in and took our seats, with Mike opting to sit on the aisle because he said he'd need to go up to the podium at some point.

The coffin was closed and was sitting on a raised dais to the left of the podium. There were several sprays of flowers, all in muted tones of pink and purple. They matched the stained glass cross in the window at the back of the chapel, so I assumed Penny, with her flair for color, had arranged for them. I noticed the music being played was Beethoven's *Pastoral Symphony*, so again I assumed Penny had chosen that because of Daniel's love for Beethoven's *Für Elise*.

At three o'clock, the music faded, and Reggie stepped to the microphone to welcome everyone.

Then he began his eulogy. "We're here today to say goodbye to our friend and colleague, and the best damn chef I ever met, Daniel Lafayette.

"Chefs, like other artists, can be temperamental and pig-headed. And Daniel was no exception. But there wasn't any problem that arose in the nearly seven years we worked together that we couldn't solve by remembering we both had the same goal—to provide the best possible food and service to our customers. Each of us who worked closely with Daniel would like to take a few moments today to bid him *adieu* and to create the closure so necessary when a friend and colleague passes. And so, Daniel, for my part, I want to say I'll miss you. In fact, I already do."

Reggie stepped away from the podium, reached a hand to Penny, and guided her to the microphone.

Penny said, "Many of you may be aware that Daniel and I had experienced a bit of friction over the past few months. Reggie said Daniel could be pig-headed, and I must admit, I can be, too.

"Psychologists tell us," and as she said this line she looked at Bernice, "that if we have a fight with our life partner, we shouldn't go to bed until we've resolved the problem. Well, I think the advice is equally good for friends with whom we may have had a falling out. We should never let a day close on a relationship with anyone we value without dealing with our issues. So Daniel, I just want to say, I'm sorry I didn't make the effort to resolve our issues until it was too late."

Then Penny continued, "Several months ago, Daniel took a young man under his wing as an apprentice, Peter Smith." She gestured in the direction where Peter was sitting, face in his hands, shoulders hunched, clearly weeping. "Of all the staff at the restaurant, Peter was surely Daniel's favorite. He was gently teaching and guiding him. Peter? Would you like to say a few words?"

Peter stood and slowly made his way up to the microphone. Tears streaked his face, and his voice, when he finally spoke, was thick with emotion.

"Chef Daniel," he said, "was the only person in my life who ever treated me special. He gave me a chance at a real career. He said I could probably make it in a good hotel someday."

Gazing up and into the distance, with a kind of glassy look, Peter continued. "I think Daniel really cared about me, like a father should care about a son. I came from a family where none of us kids ever really knew where we stood. The doctors said my mother was schizophrenic, but all we knew in my house was that the rules for whatever we were supposed to do might change between breakfast and dinner. My own dad didn't have much time for us—he was too busy with his job and trying to keep my mom in some sort of balance."

He paused to wipe his face with his fingertips, then continued.

"In the kitchen with Daniel, there was a kind of order—a structure. There was artistry and order in the menu he prepared. And every day we did certain things the same way. There was nothing erratic, nothing to be afraid of. There was balance."

He stopped again and looked at the coffin. Then he made a little noise and cleared his throat, as he seemed to be addressing Daniel.

"Your death shouldn't have happened. It just shouldn't have happened. It wasn't part of the balance."

He stepped away from the microphone and went back to sit beside Reggie, and John got up to take his turn.

"Those of you who are in the restaurant business know there is often a rivalry between the front and the back of the house. And on a hot July night in a steamy kitchen, a waiter who's working in an air-conditioned dining room may sometimes find himself confronting the overheated temper of the chef. But I want it to be known how much I valued Daniel. He was a perfectionist, he never left any aspect of his job untended, and we all recognize it was his artistry in the kitchen that kept our customers coming back and gave the Riviera its reputation. So, Daniel, *mon frère*, I expect you're already stirring up a pot of bouillabaisse for an angelic banquet, and if so, I envy the angels."

John resumed his seat, and for the first time, I noticed Clarice was sitting by him. Then Roy got up and sauntered forward.

"Yo, brother," he said to the coffin. "It's time to break the code of silence. I never did tell anyone about that afternoon two years ago when I wandered into the kitchen early one afternoon as you were preppin' the night's meal. I don't even know if you saw me, as you were busy takin' a casserole dish outta the oven. As you turned to put it on the counter, your foot caught on somethin' and you lost your balance. The casserole dish slipped out of your hands, slid across the preparation area, and landed upside down on the floor.

"I learned a lot of 'pardon my French' words that evening, and I figured I'd be healthiest if I just backed my way outta the kitchen. I didn't know what you planned to do with the casserole, but I decided I wasn't gonna say anything, one way or another. Though I did notice scalloped potatoes weren't on the menu that night.

"Anyway, Daniel, *au revoir, mom ami*. And that's all the French I know."

Roy left the podium, and Jamal stepped up to the microphone.

"*Ah salaam aleichem,*" he began, "I welcome this opportunity to tell you about my experiences with our most illustrious chef. On the day I first started working at the elegant Riviera restaurant, it was explained to me that we of the wait staff are in servitude. And truly, I have experienced that this is the case.

"I understand the English have a quote that says, 'They also serve who only stand and wait,' and though we do not often simply stand, we do a great deal of serving and waiting. Just as many people have priests who stand as intermediaries between them and God, the Supreme One, and who are servants both to people and to God, so we on the wait staff function as intermediaries between our customers and the God who is in charge of the kitchen.

"Daniel Lafayette was indeed the Supreme One. And so he would tell us very often. And as I continued to work at the restaurant, I realized this must be true, because I have heard many of our customers say, 'Good God, this food is great!'"

There was a ripple of laughter through the audience. Then Jamal turned toward the coffin and added, "Goodbye, Daniel. You certainly made it easy for those of us who served and waited to please our customers."

As Jamal finished his remarks, Penny turned to nod at Mike, who lifted his lanky frame and walked up to the microphone.

I could sense Bernice was holding her breath, waiting to see what he might say.

"Like Peter and Jamal, I've been at the restaurant for only a short time," he began, "and not in the most illustrious position. I am, in fact, the low man on the totem pole, because I'm the dishwasher. However, there was a certain amount of equality between Daniel and me, with an equal division of labor—he dirtied pots, and I cleaned them.

"Daniel never had a harsh word for those of us in the kitchen—and where else in life might a person be constantly in hot water without getting yelled at?

"Another thing I always appreciated about Daniel was that he laughed at my jokes. Because of this, I made it a point always to come to work with a joke for him. And he always laughed. So in saying my goodbye to you, Daniel, I want to apologize. I'm sorry I don't have a joke for you today, but you've left me a grave man."

As Mike came back to his seat and slid in beside Michelle, I thought I noticed the glitter of a little moisture in his eyes.

Reggie then opened the floor to anyone else who might want to say a goodbye. A sprinkling of people stood in their places and commented on Daniel's talents, taste, and wit.

Finally, Bernice gathered herself and stood. Clearing her throat, she said, "I've heard many of you praise Daniel for his talents, his wit, his energy, and his attention to detail. But we're also all aware, I'm sure, of his eye for attractive females. Daniel, without question, loved the ladies. And what was unusual was he found *all* of us attractive. We didn't need to be young or even especially pretty. If we were female, he was attracted. And he flirted. And if we flirted back, then he treated us all as Goddesses. And so I want to say, Daniel, I know I speak for many, many, many women when I tell you we will miss your Gallic charm."

As Bernice sat down again, Reggie waited a few moments for any further comments. And at that point, I felt the urge to contribute a prayer I'd learned in my childhood when one of my grandparents had died. I stood and, turning toward Daniel, I said,

> *"Deep peace of the Running Wave to you.*
> *Deep peace of the Flowing Air to you.*
> *Deep peace of the Quiet Earth to you.*
> *Deep peace of the Shining Stars to you.*
> *Deep peace of the Son of Peace to you."*

When I had sat down again, Reggie announced that everyone was invited to the graveside interment, which he promised would be brief, to be followed immediately by a gathering at the restaurant. He asked the audience to remain seated for a few minutes while the pallbearers removed Daniel. Then as the music of Beethoven began again, the men of the Riviera all stood and went up to take their places on either side of the coffin—Reggie and John at the front, Peter and Mike in the middle, and Roy and Jamal at the back. They carried the coffin out the side door of the chapel to a waiting hearse, and Penny and Clarice led the rest of us out the front door.

Once we were outside, I turned to the sergeant and asked, "Are you going to be able to come to the cemetery and the restaurant, or do you need to get back to your family?"

He gave a tiny smile and said, "I don't have anything pressing I need to do. And I'd like very much to continue with the afternoon's activities."

"I...uh, carpooled here with Bernice," I blurted. "So I don't have my own transportation."

His smile widened a little. "Do you need to stay with them, or would you like to ride with me?"

"I'd very much like to ride with you. Just let me tell Bernice."

And I hurried to catch up with her and let her know I had another escort to the graveside at Bethel Cemetery.

The ritual at the cemetery was very brief, as Reggie had promised. As we arrived, a member of the funeral home staff handed each of us a flower. Penny had hired a violinist to play Dvorak's *Largo* from the *New World Symphony*, popularized as *Going Home*. And one of the funeral directors was in charge of guiding the pallbearers to deposit the coffin on the lowering equipment.

As soon as the coffin had been lowered into the grave, Reggie and Penny stepped forward and threw their flowers onto the top of the coffin—then the rest of us followed suit.

When this final ritual was over, Sergeant Mason silently offered me his arm to guide me back to his car. He helped me in and waited until I was settled and had put on my seat belt before securing the door. Then he went round to the driver's side, got in, buckled his own seatbelt, and started the engine, all in silence.

I looked at him, and he turned to look at me. He had put on his dark glasses as we left the funeral home and had worn them through the graveside ceremony. Now he took them off. I thought how incongruous it was that his eyes were very clear, though their color was a smoky gray.

He just sat there, one arm leaning against the steering wheel, his glasses dangling from that hand, scrutinizing me. It was as if he had something momentous to say but didn't know how to say it.

Finally, I broke the silence. "What?" I said, trying for a light inflection and managing to sound like a cartoon character.

He let out a breath and said, "All of the speeches at the memorial service were very moving. I was genuinely touched a couple of times, and I got the sense all the comments were heartfelt. Now, I need to remind you that I'm not on this case. But if I were, I'd have to say, if one of the restaurant staff were guilty of murdering Daniel Lafayette, he or she did an excellent job of feigning grief during the service."

"I have to agree with you, sergeant." I paused for a moment and then asked, "But have you by any chance heard anything about the case?"

"Well, Flanagan talked to the duck delivery person, who said your chef was alone, alive, and well when he delivered the ducks at eight o'clock that morning, so he didn't die any earlier than that. And it seems Mr. Whitson was at his health club from eight o'clock on, so at least he wasn't on the premises at the time of the death.

"The fingerprint analysis showed that in addition to the chef, three of the staff had handled the wine glasses, and three had handled the bottle. But they weren't exactly the same three."

"Who handled which?" I asked.

"The three who handled the glasses were Whitson, Chan, and Wise. The three who handled the bottle were both the Whitsons and Chan."

"Well," I said, "that makes sense. And it probably doesn't prove anything about anybody. Mike's the dishwasher, and Reggie and John are the two people who put the glasses away or tend bar. John would have served the bottle of wine to the Whitsons when Reggie had a glass on an earlier occasion and put it away again. Penny could easily have picked it up and poured a glass for Reggie on that occasion. And he could just as easily have handled the bottle himself."

"Too true," said the sergeant. "And please, since I'm not on this case, I'd like it if we could be on a first name basis, and if you'd call me Greg. Unless that makes you nervous. Some people get really nervous around cops."

I flashed him what I hoped was a million dollar smile and said, "Then call me Ariel."

"Also," he added, still giving me that deep scrutiny to see how I'd react, "I do have a family."

I tried hard not to react, but I wasn't sure I'd succeeded.

"I have a son," he said, "an eleven-year-old. He lives with my ex. I get to spend time with him on alternate weekends, if I'm not on shift. He's a great little guy."

I smiled again. "Sons are good," I said.

PARKING IN OLD Town on a Sunday is always problematic. We drove around a couple of blocks looking for an empty space on the street, until finally Greg suggested we use the underground lot on King Street under the Alexandria City Hall. We walked to the restaurant and saw a neatly lettered *Private Party* sign on the door. When we entered the dining room, we realized it *was* a party.

The tables had been pushed back to create a large open area, and there were several Chinese waiters in banquet uniforms walking around with trays of hot tea, wine, and non-alcoholic beverages, and pushing carts of dim sum. I saw John step out of the kitchen, and during the moment the door was open, I noticed three or four Chinese cooks working at the stove and preparation tables.

John came over to us and said, "Welcome to Daniel's wake." He took an appraising look at Greg, then shook hands with him. He gave me a kiss on the cheek.

"You may notice the restaurant has been taken over. My Uncle Jimmy had great respect for Daniel, and this," he said, waving a hand at the waiters with trays and carts laden with drink and food, "was his parting gift. Sunday is always dim sum day at his restaurant, so he had his staff make plenty of extra for us. He also sent along a full kitchen and service staff so that none of us would have to work today."

"How generous!" I said. "I knew I liked your uncle when I met him last week."

John gave a little nod. "A lot has happened in that week," he said, as Clarice came walking over, looking like a fashion model in her simple black dress.

He looked at her, then looked at Greg. Then he cocked his head to the side and said, "Many things have changed." He introduced the sergeant to Clarice, saying, "This is my cousin, who also happens to be the new chef of the Riviera. I hope you'll take the opportunity to come for dinner sometime soon as our guest."

"I certainly recommend it," I said to Greg, "if last Friday night's fare was any indication of what's to come. Why don't you bring your son the next time you have him with you?"

"Please," said John, "come in and have something to drink and eat. Enjoying fine food and drink is the best way we can imagine of honoring Daniel's memory."

We wandered among the guests, taking the opportunity to offer our condolences to all the staff. I noticed Bernice in deep conversation with Peter, who looked puffy-eyed and totally bereft, so I didn't intrude.

A few minutes later, however, she came up to us and said, "I do feel so sorry for Peter. That poor boy is just in agony! Poor Peter is feeling he might have let Daniel down by not getting to the restaurant on time on Tuesday. He was late because he overslept and missed his bus, but he keeps saying if he'd only been there when Daniel had his heart attack, maybe he could have done something to help. He's afraid Daniel won't forgive him. He just keeps saying he's a failure."

"What did you tell him?"

"Well, I don't like to do party psychology. But I did suggest he try to find a way to grieve and come to peace with Daniel. He just seems so miserable. So when he said he wanted to go home, I told him he really wasn't expected to stay, though I thought he should let John, Penny, and Reggie know he was leaving."

I glanced around and saw John patting Peter on the shoulder while Reggie hovered nearby. I felt sorry for Peter and hoped he'd be able to find some peace soon.

When I turned back, I realized Greg was watching me watch Peter.

"You really like people, don't you?" he asked.

"Yes, I do," I answered. "Whatever and whoever we are, we all have suffering. It affects us differently, and we show it differently. But I do believe Peter is really heartbroken about Daniel's death."

"Well, what strikes me at the moment is your degree of empathy. Not many people really notice other people the way you seem to." He eyed me appraisingly for a few moments. Then he smiled a little. "I wonder if that's what makes you psychic?"

I smiled at his remark and glanced back at Peter, who was still standing between John and Reggie. Reggie was saying something to him, and Peter was nodding, his eyes down. I sensed in him deep feelings of grief and despair, but in his hand I saw him holding a long chef's knife. I did a double take, blinking and shaking my head. There was no knife in his hand. And I watched as he turned away from John and Reggie and slowly made his way out the door.

"Okay," said Greg. "What was that all about?"

"Um-m," I mumbled. "Just a little psychic impression."

"Do you want to talk about it?"

"I think I do. But not here."

We made our goodbyes and headed up King Street to a coffee shop where we could sit and chat. I told him what I'd seen when I'd glanced back at Peter.

THE CHEF WHO DIED SAUTÉING

"I don't know what to make of this image. I don't think it's related to Daniel's death since he didn't die of a knife wound. Peter's a chef, and the knife appeared to be a chef's knife. Maybe it has to do with Peter having been the one to find Daniel's body. I mean, he's said over and over if he'd been on time to work the morning Daniel died, he would have been there when Daniel collapsed, and he might have saved him."

"Do you really think that's what the knife in his hand means?"

I shook my head. "I'm rationalizing. I sensed him feeling despair and grief, and it's possible he might be planning to hurt himself."

"Or could it mean he's going to hurt someone else?" Greg asked.

I sighed. "I don't know. I got a definite psychic image, and I feel I need to sort it out—but on the same level where it came from."

"What does that mean?" he asked.

"It's a form of dowsing. Except I don't use tools. It's inner dowsing."

He gave me one of those silent, raised eyebrow looks that said, "Un-huh. And I believe in the Tooth Fairy, too!"

"Humor me a minute, please. In dowsing, we're supposed to ask three questions before we start, just so we're not butting in where we don't belong. And the questions are: *'May* I dowse for this information? *Can* I dowse for this information? And *should* I dowse for this information?' And if we get an inner affirmation to all three questions, then we're permitted to go ahead. So I need to go inside for a minute, if you don't mind."

"I don't mind, as long as you come back out again."

I smiled and closed my eyes. I got the inner affirmations almost immediately and opened my eyes again.

"That was quick," said Greg. "I didn't even have time to sip my coffee. So what's next?"

"Well, in doing inner dowsing for information, it's important to separate each component and ask a specific question that has a 'yes' or 'no' answer. And it seems to me there are three possibilities for Peter having a chef's knife in his hand, other than the fact that he's a cook—one, he killed Daniel, two, he's going to kill himself, or three, he's going to kill someone else."

Greg nodded. "That about covers the field. In police work, we have to separate out all the components in order to determine what is and isn't a valid clue, and when you've gotten rid of everything that *isn't* truth, what you're left with *is* the truth."

"So I need to go inside again and ask those questions."

"Okay. I'll be here when you get back."

I closed my eyes, altered my state, and isolated the three components. Then I asked myself the questions one at a time.

"Does the vision of Peter with a knife mean that he killed Daniel?" The answer came back, "No."

"Does the vision of Peter with a knife mean that he's going to kill himself?" Again I got a, "No."

"Does the vision of Peter with a knife mean that he's going to stab somebody else?" And again I got, "No." But I realized all the "no" answers were foggy—nothing was clear-cut.

I opened my eyes again and shook my head. "Well, that didn't work."

I told Greg what I'd experienced and expressed my frustration. "I'm still bothered by the chef's knife. This could be important. So maybe I'm just not asking the right questions."

"Well," he said, "you can at least sleep well tonight. It seems that he didn't kill Daniel, and he's not going to kill himself—or you. So just set this piece to the puzzle aside for a little while. Maybe it'll make sense later."

"There are so many pieces to the puzzle," I countered. "I love jigsaws and usually work on the one thousand-piece ones, because they offer a challenge. But this situation reminds me of a puzzle I saw last summer in a gift shop in Williamsburg. It's a Ravensburger—they really are the best—with four ancient maps of the world. It takes up an area of sixty-three square feet and has eighteen thousand pieces."

Greg chuckled. "I imagine it does feel like that when you're looking at a possible crime scene from the perspective of someone who's never had to deal with crime. There's a technique you might want to consider that helps us sort things out a bit."

"Any technique for sorting out the myriad of details would be valuable. I'm used to dealing with the mundane, and my psychic hits have never before been related to something as important or as confusing as this."

"Well," he said, "At a trial, the jury wants a picture, one that makes sense and is supported by the evidence. The Commonwealth's Attorney will generally construct a scenario he or she can present in simple terms. The accused did this, in this manner, for this reason. Then the prosecution offers all the evidence that supports their case

"So, imagine a scene from your favorite cop show where the DA addresses the jury at the start of the trial. Now let's take everybody one at a time, and build the scenario that would fit into a one-minute opening argument."

"Okay. That sounds reasonable. The people who seem the most likely to be involved are Reggie, Penny, John, and Peter."

"Are you leaving out the other waiters and the dishwasher deliberately?" he asked.

"Well, the dishwasher is my friend Bernice's son, and I've gotten to know him pretty well in the last few days. He doesn't have any motive that I can see, and neither do Roy or Jamal."

"That's all right, then, but I have to tell you if I were a detective working this case, I'd examine them as closely as the others."

"Fair enough. Shall we start with Reggie?

"Ladies and gentlemen of the jury, it is the Commonwealth's intention to demonstrate that Reginald Whitson did murder Daniel Lafayette in cold blood. He coerced the victim, who was his friend and the chef at his restaurant, to drink some wine that he had laced with a poison. He did this for one of the oldest reasons that men give for committing murder—Daniel had been having an affair with his wife. Moreover, Daniel had threatened to leave the restaurant, a situation that would cause Mr. Whitson some difficulty. On the other hand, Mr. Whitson stood to gain considerable financial benefit from Daniel's death, since the owners of the restaurant had an insurance policy in his name. The evidence will lead you to one conclusion—Reginald Whitson killed Daniel Lafayette."

"Well done! "Greg clapped. "You've convinced me! But, we're not done yet. Who's next?"

"Penny, I guess. She said she had broken off the affair and Daniel had become enraged. But what if Daniel was the one who ended the affair? That, plus the other reasons that were given for Reggie could be motivation enough.

"For John the motivation could have been that he wanted to get his cousin a job as chef of one of the best restaurants in town. He said he didn't know she was back yet, but they could have set everything up by email.

"Peter doesn't really seem to have a motive, but he certainly had the opportunity. He said he'd arrived late and found Daniel dead, but that might have been a lie. He could have been there early enough to spike a glass of wine for Daniel."

"That's good work," said Greg. "Now you can try fitting your puzzle pieces into each of the scenarios."

"Well, it does make things a bit tidier—kind of like getting the frame for the jigsaw finished. After that, it's just a matter of fitting all the internal pieces together!"

"That's where the leg work of the detective's job comes in—finding the evidence and piecing it together to fit the possible scenarios."

"And I'm not a detective—not really. I *am* psychic. But I can't get a sense of who's the guilty person. I keep getting more clues, but they don't resolve anything. They just add to the confusion."

"That's often the case. Very few crimes are cut and dried. But why don't you put it out of your mind for a while? You may get more perspective on it if you don't focus on it quite so much. Come on, let me take you home."

Even though I hadn't achieved a resolution about the image I'd seen of Peter with the chef's knife, I felt better just having been able to talk the whole thing over with Greg. It was nice validation having a cop take me seriously.

And it didn't hurt that he was a seriously good looking guy!

Chapter Seventeen

Monday, September 15th

I first heard Hurricane Isabel was headed in our direction on Monday afternoon while I was driving home from school listening to National Public Radio. It was expected to make landfall in about seventy-two hours somewhere on the East Coast in the vicinity of the Carolinas, and if it did, it would also have an effect on Virginia, Maryland, Delaware, Pennsylvania, and possibly New Jersey. Nobody was sure what to expect at that point.

When I got to Bernice's and told her about the news report, she said, "Uh-oh. That could be really serious. We've been through a couple of big storms here in Alexandria, and something like that could come right up the river and bring a tide surge. We had some trouble with a big storm in 1996—widespread flooding, trees down everywhere, power outages. Maybe we'd better start battening the hatches. I'll put it on my 'To-Do' list to get the generator checked."

"You have a generator?"

"Yeah, I got one in preparation for Y2K. Haven't ever had to use it, thank the divinity, but it's good to be prepared. I also have half a dozen oil lamps that I'll get out and fill, just to be on the safe side."

"What about the Riviera?" I asked. "They're only a block from the water. Didn't I see a flood marker across the street on the side of the Torpedo Factory?"

"Yes, that was from the flood of thirty-three. But you're right—they could be in for trouble. There *was* serious flooding in Old Town in '96. As a matter of fact, I think they got a really good deal when they bought the property in '97 because it had been flooded just the year before. Since then, the City of Alexandria has done a lot to prevent flooding from the seasonal rise of the Potomac, but it's not likely to stand up to a hurricane coming for a visit up the river."

She paused as she considered what to do. "Maybe I should call Penny and offer to help batten their hatches, too."

She went to the phone, picked up the handset, and hit a button. Obviously, she had Penny's number programmed into the phone. She waited quietly for a few seconds as it rang, and I was expecting to hear her voice go into that mode we get when talking to an answer machine, but instead she suddenly said, "Oh...what? WHAT? Oh, my God, how awful for you! How is he?"

She turned away from the phone to let me in on the conversation and said, "Reggie was in a car accident and broke his arm. Penny's with him at the hospital!"

Turning back to the phone, she listened for another few seconds, then interjected. "Yes, yes, of course we will. Just let me change, and I'll be right over. But, Penny, the reason I called—oh, God, I hate to add anything else to your burdens at this point—but Ariel was listening to NPR, and it looks as though Hurricane Isabel is coming right to our doorstep. Once we get ready here, we would be more than happy to help you prepare for the blow at the restaurant. Let's talk about it when I get there. Yes, dear. Yes. Okay, I'll see you in a little bit."

As she cradled the phone, I shook my head in disbelief. "Geez, Louise," I said, "they've really been swamped with a run of bad luck lately! But perhaps 'swamped' isn't a positive word to use under the circumstances, given that a hurricane is on its way."

Then I remembered the smell of Irene's perfume at Bibi's party on Saturday while we were talking about Reggie and his racing. It now appeared Reggie was the person Irene had been giving us a warning for.

IT TOOK US longer to find parking than it did to drive to the hospital, but even with a stop to pick up some flowers and a silly card we were in Reggie's room within thirty minutes.

Reggie was sitting up in bed; his left arm was in a cast. He was poking at a little plate of hospital goulash on the dinner tray in front of him, examining it for foreign objects or buried treasure.

"Not a moment too soon," he said, pushing the tray away so he could accept a kiss on the cheek from Bernice. "Since you've obviously come to talk to me, and since it is extremely rude to eat while one is talking, I am forced to put this wonderful dinner aside."

"Really, Reggie," Penny said, "you *should* eat your dinner."

Reggie replied, "Oh, it's lovely! *You* should try it. Eat it right up. There's a troll in the kitchen that labored all day to make this *stee-euw*. Maybe we should hire him for the Riviera!"

Penny leaned over and gave him a gentle kiss. "I'm so glad to see you're chipper," she said softly, "for someone who might have been killed." And then she added, even more softly and tenderly, "I really don't want to lose you, you know."

When she stepped aside to sit down, I realized he'd been moved by her tenderness, and I thought perhaps, because of the accident, they really had got beyond the hurt of the last several months.

Reggie said, "I have been a bit of an ass, my dear."

"So have I," Penny responded.

"Mmm," he intoned, shifting the energy with a little grin, "but your ass is so much cuter than mine," at which we all laughed and Penny gave him a playful belt on his right arm.

"Ow! Behave yourself, and give me a chance to philosophize."

"Well, now," Bernice interjected. "You know the rules—if you want us to sign your cast, you have to tell us the whole story, and it has to be good!"

"Ah, yes, drama, pathos, lies! All in the name of art." Reggie cast his eyes toward the window, and peered thoughtfully into the distance for a moment. He obviously loved being the center of attention. "The question is how can I exact the greatest amount of sympathy from my dear friends and guests, without boring them beyond belief? And how do I turn an accident that developed in about five seconds into a three-act play worthy of the Great Bard?" Then he sang a few bars of, "Where do I begin, to tell the story of my love?"

"Oh, do get on with it, you ruddy great ham, you!" clucked Penny, and she poked him in the arm again with the fork from his dinner tray.

"Well," he began, "I keep my stock car on a trailer behind the house between races, but I have a reserved space in a garage away from the city center where I store it off-season. What with Daniel's sudden demise and all the changes at the restaurant, I realized I probably wouldn't have a chance to race again this season, so I decided to take the car over and bed it down for the winter.

"There's a large area where I can pull the truck in, set the ramp, and back my race car down before I drive it into the garage proper. However, I realized as soon as I started down the ramp that I had no brakes, and there was nothing I could do except control the steering to ensure I wouldn't drive off the ramp to the side. I just had to let the car keep going until it hit the wall. I wasn't doing much more than five or ten miles per hour, but the jolt first pushed me back in my seat, and then thrust me forward. Since I was watching behind me and my arm was across the steering wheel at the time, *it* decided to break under the forward momentum.

"I called Penny, who came to get me, and she called the body shop I deal with, who came to get the car. When I called John to let him know why I wasn't coming in tonight, he volunteered to retrieve my truck and trailer from the garage. And that's the whole of it!"

He sighed and said philosophically, "I'm sure there's a lesson to be learned here, somewhere."

"Well," said Penny softly, patting his hand, "you're going to be an invalid for the next few days."

"Yes," he agreed, looking deeply into her eyes, "and I plan to milk it for all it's worth!"

Wednesday, September 17th

When I got home from work on Wednesday night, I got a call from Bibi, who urged me to come to Leesburg and spend the next day and night with her family at the farm.

"You're liable to get the edge of Isabel there in Alexandria," said Bibi. "In fact, I just heard they're planning to close down the federal government offices tomorrow by about noon, and they expect everything to remain closed on Friday. And I'm worried. I was talking with a friend of mine about you being so close to Old Town and I smelled Irene's perfume. I think Irene may be warning us about you being in danger. So I'd really feel more comfortable if you'd come here."

"I hate to make you feel uncomfortable, Bibi," I answered, "but I've made a commitment to Bernice and Penny already to help batten the hatches at the restaurant and move some paintings and other stuff from there to Bernice's. Then Bernice is talking about hosting a dinner for everybody. So I probably wouldn't be able to come until late tomorrow evening, and then I'd be driving in the middle of the storm. But if it makes you feel any better, Bernice's house is actually a considerable distance from the waterfront, and it's made of stone block, so I think it will be pretty safe."

Bibi didn't want to take no for an answer. "But what about Irene's perfume? You can't discount it! It's definitely a warning about you and the hurricane. Something is going to be dangerous for you with respect to this hurricane."

"Listen, Sis," I said firmly, "I'm going to be fine. I promise to pay extra attention to everything around me. I won't stand under any trees with falling branches or go wind surfing on the river at the height of the water surge. And once the storm hits, I'll be inside, and I promise I'll stay there."

Bibi sighed and reluctantly let me have my own way. After she'd hung up, though, I sat for a few minutes, wondering just what Irene's warning might mean. Her signals were never spurious.

Last Sunday both Bibi and I had smelled Irene's perfume while the family was discussing Reggie. And sure enough, Reggie had broken his arm the next day in a car accident.

I felt a little shiver run up my back.

Chapter Eighteen
Thursday, September 18th

As arranged, we all met at the Riviera Café at nine o'clock Thursday morning, our cars filled with blankets and sheets to wrap paintings and other valuables from the restaurant that we'd be removing for safe keeping to Bernice's. I put my cell phone in the glove compartment of my Jeep, beeped the lock, stuffed my wallet and keys into my pockets, grabbed a pile of blankets, and pushed the car door shut with my rear end.

Everybody was there—John, Clarice, Bernice and the twins, Jamal, Roy, Peter, and of course, Penny and Reggie, the latter using his cast like an orchestra conductor, directing us with his elbow.

"I would have left him at home," Penny said, "but he didn't want to miss the party."

And it did feel festive—schools had announced closings, as had the federal government, and somehow the little kid had come out in all of us in spite of the gravity of the situation. We knew it was going to be bad, but we were able to take some action against the impending disaster, and somehow that made it less threatening—and heightened our spirits.

When we got to the restaurant, Bernice said, "Let's empty the walk-in refrigerator and freezer—just in case the power goes out. I have two freezers, two refrigerators, and a generator. Ariel has a third refrigerator upstairs, which she tells me is virtually empty, and the twins have a fourth in their apartment if it's needed."

Mike said, "I've been growing a science project in the back of our fridge for about two months. But in the interest of food salvage for the restaurant, I gave it a burial at sea this morning. Well, not really at sea."

"He flushed it," Michelle said, "and plugged the toilet. So I cleaned the fridge while he wielded the plumber's friend until everything went down."

We'd brought all the boxes I'd used in my move, which I'd broken down and flattened but hadn't yet stored in Bernice's garage, and I'd thrown in a couple of rolls of plastic packing tape that were left over. We would use the boxes to carry the fresh and frozen foods back to Bernice's and the tape to secure the wrappings on the paintings.

Once we had a load of boxes packed, the twins, assisted by Roy and Peter, acted as a shuttle crew, transporting them back to house, leaving the rest of us to continue with the packing.

Shortly after noon, we took a short break for lunch. Penny had made roast beef sandwiches for all of us and pulled a few sodas from the fridge. The twins and crew arrived just in time to join us. While the work was progressing quickly, we were afraid it might not be quick enough, and we returned to packing as soon as we had gobbled down our lunch.

As he grabbed another box of food and headed for the van, Mike said over his shoulder, "Hey, Mom. We won't have to go grocery shopping for months. It's really nice of the restaurant to give us all these leftovers!"

Penny laughed and threw a wet rag at him. "Brat!"

Mike turned around with a grin and the two of them went into a routine I assumed was a personal favorite.

"Pig!" he snapped with a toss of his head.

"Hog!"

"Warthog!"

"Baby!"

"Am not!"

"R2!"

"D2!"

"C3PO," Penny said smugly, and it was obvious she had won the exchange.

Michelle turned to Roy and said, "Let's get out of here before they start again."

When all the food had been boxed, the rest of us set about packing up the dining area. Clarice and John gathered the liquor from the bar area and put it in boxes. They secured everything else that was loose—the coffee maker and pots, the cappuccino machine, cups and saucers, bar paraphernalia, and the contents of the little refrigerator under the bar.

Penny moved right to the reservations desk and began packing up all the supplies and equipment from the counter—reservations book, cash register, swipe machine, paper rolls, and telephone. While Jamal gathered all the linen, Bernice and I took down the paintings and wrapped them in blankets for moving, securing their coverings with the plastic packing tape.

At one point as we were moving paintings out to the cars, Reggie commented, "I feel as if I'm orchestrating an elaborately conceived robbery where the perpetrators totally strip the premises they're raiding."

Bernice gave a little snort of laughter and said, "It reminds me of my days in residence at York University in Toronto. We had a quadrangle with a plinth—no statue, just a large concrete platform—four by eight and about two feet high. One evening a group of students decided to play a joke on one of the third floor residents and moved the entire contents of his room that was movable down to the plinth. They even set it up to look like a bedroom."

I paused in my packing and stretched my back as I asked, "May I assume, since your present activities have reminded you of that event, that you had a hand in the prank?"

Bernice smiled sweetly and didn't deny the allegation. "The fellow whose room had been stripped came by and laughed when he saw the set-up on the plinth, but I'm not sure what his reaction was when he got to his room and realized he was the butt of the joke." She gazed thoughtfully into the distance and said, "Plinth! I love that word. It's the word that taught me how to use a thesaurus properly."

"Bernice, that's a non sequitur worthy of this restaurant," said Reggie shaking his head. "Would you care to elaborate?"

"Well, when I was in tenth grade," she explained, "I had to write a composition about a rainstorm. I described water running down the hill and pooling at the bottom. But I wanted a different word than 'bottom,' which seemed common and rude to me at the time. So I checked the thesaurus that was in the classroom, and I found the word 'plinth,' which seemed to have elegance and class. So I used it in my paper. My teacher noted that he admired my creativity in using the thesaurus, but suggested in future perhaps I should combine it with use of a dictionary. I looked up the word 'plinth,' and to my embarrassment learned it meant the base of a statue. But I still love the word and was delighted to find we had one of them in the residence quadrangle."

"Pack!" ordered Penny in a louder than ordinary voice. "I'm going to go pack up the office, and when I come back, I fully expect you to have cleared this room!"

Once we'd finished getting the linens and paintings out to the cars, Bernice, Jamal, and I pushed all the tables together into one corner of the dining room, stacking chairs on them as we went. We realized if any flood waters got into the dining room, the carpets would be damaged and need replacing, but we hoped to protect the upholstery fabric on the chair seats. As it turned out, the seats of the banquettes were also removable, and we decided to take these with us to Bernice's.

"Maybe we should go into the moving business," I commented to Bernice. "We've certainly had enough practice this month."

"Oh, yes," she said with mock enthusiasm. "For my part we could call it 'Old Woman with Weak Back Moving and Storage.' My motto could be, 'No job too small.'"

Jamal laughed. Putting on his Peter Sellers accent, he said, "I like to watch."

Just at that point, Penny came into the dining room and said loudly, "Which one of you jokers stuffed Daniel's knife roll in my desk drawer?"

THE CHEF WHO DIED SAUTÉING

We all stopped in our tracks.

"What do you mean?" said John glancing at Clarice. "We've been looking for it for days."

"I just found it under some papers in the bottom drawer of my desk," said Penny. "So somebody had to have put it there on purpose."

"You know, there were a lot of things out of place in the kitchen on the day Daniel died. I knew something was wrong, but at the time I couldn't pinpoint it," I said. "I took a bunch of pictures before the police arrived, and last Friday I downloaded them. One of them seemed important to me, so I brought it to the restaurant for John to look at. When he saw it, the first thing he noticed was there were no knives on the counter. But Daniel had obviously just chopped up an onion. John and Clarice had been looking for the knife roll, and they thought perhaps the police had taken it. But my picture showed it was missing before the police arrived."

"Well," said Penny, "I guess we don't really have time at the moment to figure out who hid them. For now, I'm going to put them in the wine cooler along with these papers."

With a slightly impish look, John said, "I hope we don't find a body with one of these knives in it after the hurricane, as that would be a clear case of murder in cold blood."

Clarice looked at him as if he were an untrained puppy and she wanted to tug his leash. "John," she said, "sometimes your humor isn't appropriate."

He smiled at her. "Clarice, my dear, humor delights by surprise, which means most of it is inappropriate."

We got back to work and finished up in the dining room, then went out to the kitchen to see what help we could offer there. The food detail returned from Bernice's shortly thereafter to pick up their last load. Peter and Roy looked wet, bedraggled, and wind swept. Mike and Michelle had put on yellow rain slickers and appeared to be withstanding the worst of what the weather was bringing in. They shook the water droplets off, like dogs coming in from the rain.

"I didn't think the floods were supposed to be starting this soon," said Reggie wryly, looking at the puddles they left on the kitchen floor.

"Thanks for your support," said Mike. "I shall wear it always."

"The wind is *really* beginning to pick up," said Michelle as they loaded up for the final food run to Bernice's. As if in emphasis of this point, the kitchen door banged open as a gust of wind swept in, blowing some leaves and street debris onto the floor.

"I suggest you guys hurry up with whatever you're doing and get the heck home to higher ground. The radio says shelters have already been opened up, and the city's emergency operations center has started to coordinate response teams. They're announcing that everybody needs to get off the streets as soon as possible. And don't forget to shut off utilities when you're finished and unplug everything you can."

"In that case," said Bernice, "don't come back unless we call you. We'll all be heading in that direction as soon as we can."

Roy said to the group at large, "Just so you won't think I'm copping out, I'm going to follow them in my own car, but as soon as we have everything delivered, I'm heading home to my family. We'll need to make some preparations ourselves, and I don't want my kids to be scared if I'm not there."

Reggie motioned Roy and Mike to wait and called Jamal and Peter over. Though he wasn't talking loudly, I heard him say, "I just want you guys to know you don't need to worry about tips or your salaries for the next couple of weeks. Penny, John, and I have agreed that if the restaurant needs to be closed temporarily, we won't lay anybody off, and we'll try to compensate you for lost tips, at least until the beginning of the October." Then he sent them off on their last trip.

Turning our attention to the kitchen, we moved what electrical equipment we could into the wine cooler, which I realized was perfectly climate controlled because it was built like a huge, totally enclosed fiberglass shower stall, with a pressure-sealed, airtight door. The whole building could flood without a drop of water getting into this room. Penny had put some boxes from the office on the floor, but there was plenty of room left, so we began moving all loose items—dishes, glassware, cutlery trays, cutting boards, all comestibles from the dry pantry, and all the liquor from the bar area—into this room. When it was full, we used the shelves of the walk-in refrigerator and freezer, which the food brigade's last trip had left empty and available for storage.

Having secured the various items inside the restaurant, Jamal and John turned their attention to the outside, putting on their coats to brave the weather.

"Mike and Michelle were pretty smart to have put on slickers," John commented. "The rain is coming in fits and starts, but some of the fits are like the Tasmanian devil of cartoon fame."

Reggie said, "With what we're doing to this building today, it looks like we're fit to be tied."

Jamal asked, "Who's wearing a tie? I didn't know this was a formal affair."

Bernice laughed. "I like to keep my affairs informal," she said.

Penny yelled from inside the refrigerator, "Enough! Get back to work!"

John said, "Oh, my goodness, a voice from the refrigerator. Is that dinner calling?" But he motioned to Jamal to follow him outside.

The restaurant had a store of sandbags, which had been left behind by the previous owners and added to by Reggie and John, who had realized when they bought the site it was in a vulnerable position. Earlier that morning the guys had split the stack between the front and back doors, leaving more for the backside of the building, which was closer to the river. Now they taped Mylar across the back door, covering the entire frame, and stacked sandbags three feet high, hoping that would be enough.

Back in the main dining room, using the packing tape I'd brought, we began taping the inside of the windows with what Penny referred to as a Union Jack pattern—a huge cross and X on each pane. Then Reggie, John, and Penny went through the building one last time to see if there was anything they'd missed and to turn off the power at the main fuse box.

By five o'clock we were finished and ready to secure the front door and the French windows in the front with Mylar and the rest of the sandbags.

The rain was picking up again, but before we split off to our various vehicles, Reggie said, "Since all our food is now at your place, Bernice, and since we all have to make another trip there to deliver paintings and what not, why don't we have dinner *chez vous*, so to speak?"

"I had already suggested that to Penny," said Bernice, "and I can offer the use of my humble premises as our emergency operations center. In other words, let's have a party! We can sit out the storm in front of the fireplace, and if the lights go, I'll fire up the generator."

Then she added, "As a matter of fact, I anticipated this turn of affairs and started a large pot of stew simmering in my crock-pot this morning. It should be ready when we get there!"

Just at that point there was a blast of rain that seemed to be blowing upward rather than falling down, so we all scurried to our respective cars and began wending our way to Bernice's.

Chapter Nineteen

I WAS DRIVING in the rear of the caravan and got caught at a light for an extra couple of minutes, so I arrived at the house a bit after everyone else and wound up parked behind a long queue of other cars. I had a couple of the Erté prints in my back seat, but I couldn't quite decide what to do with them since I was parked at the tail end of the drive, far from the doors. The wind was blowing really hard by this time, so I knew I wouldn't be able to carry both of them, and even trying to carry one by myself might be a bit like raising a sail in this wind. In fact, I didn't even want to open my umbrella, for fear it might be blown inside out. I ran to the house to see if I could get some help bringing the prints inside safely.

The others had taken off their coats, which lay in a soggy pile in the foyer. I squelched my way into the kitchen, where everyone was gathered. People were toweling off, so I assumed Bernice had raided the linen closet.

"You look like a drowned rat, darling," said Penny.

"I won't take that personally," I responded, "since I see a whole room full of drowned rats."

John dropped into his Cagney voice and said to the room at large, "You dirty brother, you drowned my rat!"

Bernice looked my way. "I was just about to disrobe everybody and put all the wet clothes in the dryer, so when you've changed, bring your wet things down." Then turning to the group she said, "I need a count of who needs clothes. I'm putting you all in muumuus and caftans temporarily while your clothes dry. They're unisex, and one size fits all."

"Before you start with the strip show," I said, "I have two prints that need to come in from my car, but it's about a mile and a half down the driveway. Any volunteers to work on a rescue mission?"

John jumped up and said, "Come on, Peter, we'll get them."

Peter went with John to the foyer, and I followed them. John rummaged through the coats, grabbing the windbreaker he had been wearing. He hoisted a racing jacket from the pile and waved it like a flag.

"Poor Reggie's going to miss the Big Kahuna next weekend," he said as Peter went searching in the pile and found his own jacket. Then John shook Reggie's jacket to straighten it and laid it back on top of the heap. "You stay here and start getting dry, princess," he said to me. "Peter and I will make like knights and go save the pictures. Oh, do we need your keys?"

"Yes," I said. I took my room key off the ring and held the keys out. Peter took them, and I smiled gratefully as they went out into what was becoming a howling gale. The outside was a twilight world, with twigs blowing past and branches scraping against walls and windows. Even when the door was shut again, I could hear the wind squealing through the cracks. I shivered and muttered a little prayer that Bernice's trees would be strong enough to withstand the blast yet to come.

I took off my own jacket and slipped off my squishy shoes and socks, setting them in the line of footgear already against the wall in the foyer.

I was turning to go to my room when I noticed a piece of paper on the floor. When I picked it up, I realized it was a newspaper clipping, and I thought it must have fallen out of Reggie's jacket while John was shaking it. I went upstairs to get dry clothes, taking the article with me. I didn't want to put it into Reggie's damp coat—figuring I'd just give it to him directly once I was dry.

I left the article on my bed while I dried my hair and changed. As I sat down on the bed to put on dry socks and sneakers, I glanced at it for a few seconds. And then it struck me what the article was about, and I read the whole thing.

A twenty-two-year-old Cumberland, Maryland woman, Elizabeth Wright, the daughter of a local pharmacist, had died in an automobile accident the previous February, along with her unborn child. Her car had gone off a bridge, which had been particularly icy after a winter storm. The article said there had been some suggestion of suicide because of the lack of skid marks, but the incident had finally been judged an accident. Elizabeth was survived by her parents, Joel and Mary Wright and her older brother, Arthur Wright.

I realized this must be the woman Reggie had been involved with at the Allegheny County Fair Grounds racetrack. I was surprised and a little embarrassed that I'd found the article, since it suggested Reggie was still carrying a torch for the dead girl. However, I was glad I hadn't committed the gaffe of handing it to him in front of everybody in the kitchen. I stuffed it in my own pocket pending an appropriate moment when I could pass it off to him.

I grabbed my wet duds to throw them in the dryer downstairs and returned to the kitchen to be confronted by a motley crew. True to her word,

Bernice had provided muumuus and caftans, though she hadn't mentioned they were all in psychedelic colors, so the scene resembled a 1960s movie about Haight Asbury—all they needed were love beads and flowers. I couldn't help myself, and I burst into, "This is the dawning of the Age of Aquarius," and was joined by everybody but Peter, who looked a little uncomfortable and out of place in the baggy clothing, and Clarice, who appeared not to know the words but got into the spirit by drumming on the counter with a couple of wooden spoons.

When we stopped singing, I said to Mike and Michelle, "We're out of costume for this party," as the three of us were the only ones in jeans and shirts.

Mike said, "We stopped playing dress-up in Mom's clothes when we were five."

"Speak for yourself," said Michelle. "I never played at dress-up. And five was the age when I realized there was such a thing as fashion sense." And then she added, *sotto voce*, "And it wasn't to be found in Mom's closet."

Bernice rolled her eyes. Then she said to me, "Just throw your damp clothes in the laundry room. But be careful, as I think Freud the Cat is hiding from the crowd in there. We're going to have at least three loads, but with luck the electricity will hold out until all our clothes are finished in the dryer. But Mike and Michelle, since you've drawn my attention to yourselves, would you please grab the drying rack from the laundry room and set it up in the foyer with everybody's coats on it?"

Then Bernice took orders for cappuccino and hot chocolate and began bustling around setting out cups and spoons. I noticed Roy wasn't in evidence, so I assumed he'd already gone home to his family.

Once we had our drinks in hand, Jamal, Mike, Michelle, and Clarice sat down at the table and started playing a game of Yahtzee. A TV in the corner was tuned to the Weather Channel, and it was giving a running commentary on the hurricane, but in spite of the gale outside, a pleasant atmosphere settled over the kitchen.

Bernice and Penny began putting out bread and salads for dinner. The succulent aroma of the stew simmering in the crock-pot was filling the room.

Peter looked up and said, "Can I help with the vegetable chopping? That's one of *my* skills. The first thing Daniel taught me was how to chop a carrot properly."

Penny offered him a knife and cutting board, and in no time he'd amassed a mountain of chopped *crudités*.

Reggie, who was sitting on a stool at the center island, started philosophizing as Penny and Bernice laid out the plates.

"You know," he said, "with four disasters in only one week, I could almost think someone was trying to sabotage our restaurant. I mean, first there was the Molotov cocktail through John's window. Then Daniel dropped dead. Then my little accident. And now the hurricane, which could wreck unknown havoc on our little establishment. However, I'm not sure even a terrorist would be able to conjure up a hurricane on demand."

"Now, don't be paranoid, Reggie," said Bernice in a motherly tone.

"Hey," quipped John, "just because *you're* paranoid doesn't mean they're not out to get *us*."

"Thank you for sharing, one and all," said Reggie. "Anyway, maybe The Foot has decided to stomp us after all!"

"Don't be daft, Reggie," said Penny. "The Foot did not cut the brake lining on your car."

"What are you talking about?" asked Bernice. "Who cut your brakes?"

"Well, that's the question, isn't it?" said Reggie. "We got the word last evening from the body shop that my brakes failed because they'd been tampered with. Somebody had actually cut through the brake line."

Penny added, "We hadn't had a chance to tell anybody yet, because of the hurricane and everything else we had to take care of."

Reggie continued grimly, "I suspect whoever cut the line hoped I'd lose my brakes during a race and wind up as a part of the rock face that overlooks the track. But the person who did it was inept. What would have happened if I'd taken the car to the track was I'd have backed off the trailer exactly the way I did at the garage on Monday and wound up running into somebody's tent. However, I don't think I'm being paranoid when I say somebody *is* out to get us."

"But why would anybody want to sabotage the restaurant?" asked Bernice. "Who could possibly benefit from that?"

"As I said, that's the question, isn't it? However, the whole situation has made Penny and me start to reconsider our options. We've been talking and we're seriously considering going to Australia for an extended stay. So John, what would you think about buying us out?"

John raised his eyebrows and thought for a moment before asking, "Do I get flood sale prices?"

"Probably," said Penny, "though the place will be paid off by Daniel's insurance policy. But I imagine we can make you a deal you can't refuse. We really just need enough money to get us to Perth and get resettled." Then she added, "I imagine it will take Reggie two minutes to get a job there."

"Wouldn't you want your own place again there?" John asked.

"Well," said Reggie, "Perth isn't as expensive a place to live in as Alexandria. But we're not sure how long we'll want to stay. Maybe only a couple of years. Who knows? We might even buy a station in the Outback and go to sheep ranching."

Penny gave Reggie a withering look and said, "Surely you jest. Your scintillating humor would be lost on a herd of sheep."

I looked at John and could almost see his mental wheels turning. "Humor is important," he said. "The restaurant's reputation is based half on the funny business and half on the food. I like my role as a John Cleese head waiter, so I'll have to promote Jamal to manager and hire another waiter with similar comic flair."

"Me?" said Jamal from the table. "Oh, good, I'd get to watch," he said in his Peter Seller's voice. "I like to watch."

John continued, "Clarice's cuisine will be different from Daniel's..."

"Better!" she chimed in.

"Yes, right, better, that's what I meant," agreed John, turning to the table to point an affirmative finger at her, and I could see a partnership was continuing to develop between them. "But as long as we serve high quality food, I don't think we'll lose our regular clientele. And speaking of food, the veggies are chopped, the salad is tossed, the dressing has just the right piquancy, and we're ready to feed the five thousand."

"That's me," said Mike shoving away from the table. "And just in time, I might add, as I'm losing this game at the moment."

We all grabbed plates, loaded them with stew, rolls, and assorted salad goodies, took them to the table, and dug in.

"Good heavens!" exclaimed Penny. "This is awesome. What is your secret?"

"Sweet potatoes and a touch of cinnamon. You do know, don't you, that the real reason for the exploration of the New World was the hunt for spices such as cinnamon? The overland routes were long and dangerous, and the sea-faring explorers of the fifteenth and sixteenth centuries were looking for shorter, easier routes to India and the Spice Islands, because the spice trade could make them very wealthy indeed."

"If they lived through the perils of the voyage! Ah, yes, what we won't go through when we're motivated by enough money!"

Money, sex, and power, I thought. *The three driving forces of our lives. And any one of them could be a motive not just for exploration, but also for murder.*

Just as we finished dinner, the dryer buzzer rang, and Michelle took charge of disbursing the first round of dry clothing to Penny, Reggie, and Clarice and starting the second dryer load for Jamal, John, and Peter.

"Since you'll be staying the night," said Bernice, "you can just fold up the caftans on the table in the laundry room and use them for nighties later, if you like."

I thought it was my turn to be helpful, so I piled everybody's dishes on a large tray and headed for the sink. Bernice had started a fire in the wood stove. Setting a pot of water on to simmer, she turned to me as I was putting the dishes in the sink and asked, "Do you know how to lay a fire in a fireplace?"

"I do indeed."

"I think we need one in the living room fireplace, if you don't mind. Just leave the dishes for now. We'll have some dessert later, and we can take care of them then."

"I'm happy to show off my military wilderness training," I laughed and headed for the living room. The room would be perfect for our size party, with three beige leather sofas arranged in a U-shape around a large, square, glass-topped coffee table and an additional comfy chair at each corner of the U.

However, the wood basket there was empty, so I carried it back through the kitchen to the screened porch out back, where Bernice had a wood box. As I went through, I noticed Reggie was back on the stool at the center island.

It would seem his accident had put him out of the running as a suspect in Daniel's death, but I suddenly remembered my dream of him as a one-armed bandit and the comments he and Penny had made about the house always winning because the odds were in their favor. Now they were going to have John buy them out and they'd be leaving the country. I wondered if perhaps Reggie had staged his own accident.

Casually, I said, "There's no wood in the living room, so I need a macho man to carry some wood in this basket. How's your good right arm, Reggie?"

He looked surprised at being asked. "You mean my period of being coddled and catered to is over? Well, then, I guess I can help."

As we went out together, I saw that Bernice had several heavy-duty orange extension cords curled on the kitchen floor under a small window that looked onto the back porch. One end of each had already been fed through the window, and when we stepped onto the porch, I noticed an insulated slot in the end wall through which they were connected to the generator sitting outside, in anticipation of a possible power outage. Bernice had also put up storm windows for protection against the coming gale, so the porch was totally dry.

The light was an eerie shade of green, and I was both attracted and repelled by the forces of nature that had us all in thrall. I paused for a moment and watched the shadow play of the trees, which were already wildly waving their arms in the wind, looking like a troupe of ecstatic dancers. I was glad I was inside, safe and warm for the duration of whatever was to come.

"Only a madman would still be out in this blast," said Reggie.

"Or inveterate shoppers," I countered. "On the way back here from the restaurant I was listening to the radio and heard that the new mall was having its grand opening, and it seems there were plenty of people there for the bargains, in spite of warnings that they should get off the streets."

"You've made my point," said Reggie smiling.

I laughed and filled the basket with several logs. Then we trooped back through the kitchen to the living room, carrying the basket between us.

As we set the log basket on the floor, Reggie asked, "Do you need me to help with anything else? I've never laid a fire in my life, but I can hand you logs, if you like."

"Thank you, that would be a help," I said. Then in a soft voice I added,

"I also wanted to ask you if this is yours." I pulled out the newspaper clipping from my pocket and handed it to him.

He looked at it, and as comprehension dawned about its subject matter, his eyes widened, and he looked stricken. "Wha...where did you get this?" he asked.

"I found it on the floor earlier this afternoon. I assumed it had fallen out of your jacket pocket."

"Not *my* pocket," he said. "You know...what this is all about?"

I nodded. "That's why I thought it must be yours. I figured you were still...you know, carrying a torch. But if that's not the case, then someone else seems to be hanging on to the memory of this event."

"I hate to think it, but maybe it's Penny," he said. "I really...hurt her, you know."

"I know," I said. "She told me all about it. *And* she told me she really wants the two of you to stop beating up on yourselves and each other. But I *will* ask whether this is her clipping, though I doubt it. If it turns out it isn't, whose do you think it might be?"

He shook his head. "I don't know. But shall I call Penny?"

"Sure," I agreed.

He turned and chimed out, "Penn-nee!" and a couple of seconds later she came into the living room, with raised eyebrows and a smile.

"What's up?"

"I hate to bring up anything painful, but I found this little news item on the floor earlier, and I thought it might be Reggie's, but he says not. So I wondered if it was yours."

Penny read through the clipping, and her eyes misted up. "No, no." She shook her head. Then a questioning look crossed her face as she glanced from me to Reggie and back again. "But nobody else here knows about this episode in Reggie's life."

"Somebody does," I said. We all looked at each other quizzically and were silent for a moment, each of us caught in our own thoughts.

"But why would anybody care enough about my peccadillo to be carrying a reminder of it?" Reggie asked.

I reached for the newspaper clipping and folded it up again, slipping it back into my pocket. "I don't see the connection yet between your accident and the one this young woman had, but I have a feeling they're tied together, and so is Daniel's death. I need to ponder it for a little while yet, so you two go back to the kitchen and let me lay a fire here, and maybe I can confab with Bernice later. She has a good head for reasoning things out."

Reggie said, "Oh, didn't you want me to help hand logs to you?"

"No, that's okay. I'll just scoot the basket closer to the fireplace. I've had lots of practice laying fires." He nodded and was about to head for the kitchen when Penny reached for him, pulled him back, and turned to me.

"It's really strange, that article being here," she said. "Do you think there's a connection to all the episodes that have been happening to us—the attack on John, Daniel's death, and Reggie's brakes? I mean, it's just weird."

"I agree," Reggie commented. "Everything seems to be connected, with each of the principals in the restaurant being under attack this past week. Penny, I've been worried that you might be next."

"And you really have no idea who might be responsible?" I asked.

"No," he said. "Emphatically! The only people who could benefit, other than Daniel, of course, are the people who've been attacked. It would have to be someone who's utterly mad. And it's all quite puzzling."

"You're right, it's pretty weird," I said. "I *will* have a little *tête à tête* with Bernice later. And if someone really is out to sabotage the restaurant, everyone else who works there in any capacity will need to be warned—Mike, Peter, Jamal, Roy, and now even Clarice. But we don't want to shout 'Fire' until we've sorted out what's really going on."

"Okay," agreed Penny. "Just let us know if there's anything you want us to do." She paused, as if considering whether she should say anything else. Finally she did. "I think you ought to know this. While I was packing up at the restaurant, I discovered something else that's making me really uncomfortable. The gun we keep under the cash register is missing."

Reggie looked stricken. "Did you call the police and report it?"

"No, there was no opportunity, and I knew they had their hands full with real emergencies today. Also, with so many people packing different parts of the restaurant, it may just have been put away somewhere. I was planning to do a thorough check when we can get back into the building, then report it missing if it doesn't turn up."

He nodded. "Probably wise to do it that way," he said.

"It might be best to not mention this to anyone else tonight," I cautioned. "If we do have someone who is armed and dangerous in this group, we don't want to alarm that person unnecessarily."

As they left me alone again, I knelt down in front of the fireplace, began stacking kindling and small logs. I placed them so that air could circulate and stuffed a few twisted newspaper pages between layers for good measure. Then I pushed myself up from the hearth and dusted off my hands. I grabbed some fireplace matches off the mantle and set the paper twists on fire. The kindling caught rapidly, and within a few seconds the fire was under way.

I stood there alone, mulling over all that had happened in the two weeks since I'd first come to this house—from my encounters with Annie Grace, to my explosive date with John, to my involvement in Daniel's death, to Reggie's accident, to the hurricane we were currently experiencing. In addition to all the external events were my dreams and Irene's warnings, all of which I'd need to sort through again if I was to find a solution to this puzzle.

Though many aspects of the situation were quite serious—most notably Daniel's death—I couldn't help grinning wryly to myself as I thought of my present responsibility for building a fire to keep everyone warm and cozy during the hurricane.

"Ariel," I said to myself, "I think you've moved from the frying pan to the fire."

And suddenly in my mind's eye I saw the Fat Man doing a little pirouette, a smoking gun in his hand. I felt a shiver up my spine, and stopped grinning.

"Okay," I said to myself, "the Fat Man wants you to pay attention." So I leaned against the mantle, closed my eyes, took a deep breath to clear my mind, and let it out slowly. Then I focused on the image of the Fat Man with the smoking gun. It seemed obvious my vision of him was connected with the gun that was missing from the restaurant, and I got a little nod of affirmation even before I'd posed that as a question. But what did it mean for the case or for me personally? In my mind, I addressed the Fat Man, "Uh, could you give me a little more direction, please?" And again I saw him doing a little pirouette, only this time as he twirled, he pointed to a fireplace, over the mantle of which was a rifle. What popped into my head was a line by Chekhov, who once said that in writing fiction, you should never describe a gun over the fireplace unless you're going to have it go off by the end of the piece. I waited for more information, but nothing was forthcoming. Then I heard the dryer buzz from the other room and was brought back sharply to the present moment. I glanced up, but there was no rifle over Bernice's fireplace.

Part of me wished Greg was here to talk to so we could examine the image of the gun the way we had examined the image of the knife I'd flashed on the previous Sunday. His cop's eye view would be uncluttered with emotional baggage. But as Penny had noted, the police were sure to be busy today with emergencies, and I suspected he wouldn't have time for a speculative chat. So I filed away the information about the gun as one more thing to discuss later with Bernice.

As I wandered back into the kitchen, Michelle was handing out assorted clothing to Peter, John, and Jamal.

"Oh, thank you," said Jamal. "I don't think caftans are my style, even though in Egypt we often wear a body covering called a 'gallabaya,' which is very like a caftan."

"Oh, but you two guys are so cute in dresses," said John.

Peter blushed, ducked his head, and hurried for the bathroom to change, and I thought he really had been better off under Daniel's tutelage, safe in the kitchen and protected from the silly humor of the guys out in the front of the restaurant.

Shortly after the three of them were dressed again in their own clothes, the lights flickered several times and finally went out.

"It's a good thing we were prepared," said Bernice, who had spent some time while I was lighting the fire putting candles in holders. She lit two of the candles, then called Mike and Michelle over. Handing them the candles, she asked them to switch on the generator, unplug the major appliances that might be damaged by a power surge, and plug the refrigerators and freezers into the extension cords they'd laid out earlier.

Bernice lit an oil lamp in the kitchen area, then herded everybody into the living room where they settled into the sofas around the large coffee table. She put another oil lamp on the coffee table to give us a bit more light. Freud the Cat decided to accept the crowd and curled up on the mat in front of the hearth.

Shortly, Mike arrived with his arms full of board games and a couple of decks of cards.

"Okay," he said to all of us, "we have Balderdash, Trivial Pursuit, and Pictionary. Which game does everybody want to play? We'll go with whatever the largest number chooses."

"Pictionary would be too hard to play in this semi-darkness," said Bernice, "so how about Trivial Pursuit? That used to be one of my favorite games—we have just about every edition that's ever come out."

I raised my hand and said, "The only version of Trivial Pursuit I have a ghost of a chance of winning is the Silver Screen version, since that's the one I cut my teeth on as a kid. My siblings and I were all big movie fans."

John said, "I'd go along with that edition," at which everyone else groaned and moaned.

Penny put the damper on that suggestion. "If you're going to play Trivial Pursuit, I think I'll go do my nails. I have about as much chance of winning the game that way as by playing it!"

After a bit more good-natured wrangling, we settle on Balderdash. This had been a game my family had enjoyed, because we loved to make up creative definitions for funny-sounding words. As a poet, I particularly liked it—I'd often written Haiku verses for some of the words I encountered in it, though I'd never done anything with any of these little poems.

Playing Balderdash was fun and took up a couple of hours. Throughout the game, the comic waiters kept us in stitches with their insane definitions. My favorite round was for the word "pantler." The first definition was the little pocket in which the White Rabbit kept his watch—this caused Michelle to bounce up and down in her seat, chanting, "I'm late, I'm late, for a very important date!"

Mike, who was reading the definitions, threw a pillow at her and said, "I'm trying to be serious here," then nearly fell off his chair laughing as he read the next one. When he had wiped his hand down his face in an effort to make it straight and finally got calm, he read, "A pantler is a measuring device used by tailors to determine which leg of a gentleman's trousers needs extra material to accommodate the family jewels."

"That has to be Reggie," Penny choked out over her laughter. "He loves that phrase!"

Another definition was the little horns that are pictured on the head of the god Pan, and yet another was the nubs of horns that grow on the heads of baby deer before they reach maturity. Nearly everyone voted for this last definition, but Peter was the only one who voted for the real definition, which turned out to be "a butler for the pantry."

Jamal said, "You had an edge there, man, 'cause you're the keeper of the pantry!"

And Roy agreed with, "Peter, the pantler."

Peter seemed genuinely pleased at the acknowledgements and appeared relaxed and a little less shy than usual.

Playing games by candlelight had something of the energy of slumber parties I'd been to in my younger days. We'd all moved into a kind of blithe acceptance of whatever was to come with respect to the hurricane, especially since there didn't seem to be anything we could do about it.

After we finished with Balderdash, in which Bernice turned out to be the big winner, Mike suggested we might play cards.

Michelle countered with, "No, let's have Ariel *read* our cards—she does Tarot readings. She did this for us last week, and it was really interesting."

Bernice said, "Oh, yes, do go get your Tarot cards, Ariel. I really am interested in them." Then she added, "As a psychological tool, of course."

So I grabbed a candle and went upstairs for the cards, thinking as I came back down that this would be a parlor game to most of the group, but it might give *me* some insight into the unanswered questions I had over John's bomb, Daniel's death, and Reggie's accident.

When I got back to the living room, I put my deck in the middle of the table face down and stirred the cards into a pile, saying, "I usually ask people to pick with an intention, holding a question in mind that they want answered. But I think what I'd like to do is just tune in to what's most prominently on the mind of each of you, based on the card you choose, and you can tell me if I get it right. Will that be all right with everybody?"

They all seemed to agree, with nods and affirmative noises, so I continued, "Also, by the ethics of psychic operatives, I'm not permitted to read for anybody who doesn't give me permission. But I'm going to say that if you turn over a card, that constitutes your giving me permission, just so I don't have to ask everybody individually. Is that also all right with everybody?"

Again I heard the murmurs of agreement. "Okay, who's first?"

Everyone seemed a little reluctant, so I encouraged them. "Don't be nervous. All the cards can do is suggest states of mind and the energies you're harboring around things currently important to you. And if you don't think my reading is relevant, take it with a grain of salt!"

The room was pretty dim with only the candles and firelight, but I heard a couple of sighs and a bit of shuffling, and finally Mike said, "Well, I'm not a nervous Nellie—you read me last week, and it was fine." He reached into the pile for a card.

It was the Page of Wands. "Well, Mike, it looks to me as if you're still concerned with your learning process. The Page represents that part of you that knows you need to get more information and is willing to learn. Because the suit is Wands, it suggests it has to do with your true calling, your reason for working, so I'm betting it has to do with your computer/web/video training and the process you're in right now of learning all you can about these things. I think it's the video part you're most concerned with, but I'm getting also a computer and web connection."

"Sounds right to me," said Mike. "I'm in the middle of a computer graphics project at school right now, and it has to do with turning my creations into video suitable for putting on the web. So I'm spending a lot of my time thinking about that project, whenever I'm not doing anything else." He put his card back in the pile, to let me know he thought I was finished.

"Okay," I said, "who's next?"

There still seemed to be a little reluctance on the part of those who'd never before had a reading. "No need to hold back just to be polite. Bernice, how about you?"

Bernice half stood so she could reach the pile and picked out the Six of Pentacles.

"Good! The card of generosity. This is the One-Eyed Merchant T.S. Eliot talks about in his poem *The Waste Land*. It's about giving to others from your bountiful store."

"That's Mom," said Michelle. "She loves to throw parties, give people gifts, make big meals for everybody, and solve people's problems."

"Well, it's definitely what's on your mind right now, Bernice."

"I'd say that's accurate," she agreed. "I want to make sure everybody has a good time tonight."

I wondered whether she might have drawn a different card if I'd had a chance to talk to her about all my questions. But there'd be time to involve her when today's events were closer to conclusion. And I knew when I did ask her advice, she'd be like the picture on the card, of a man giving money to supplicants, and would willingly give me her two cents worth!

As Bernice put back her card, Michelle said, "I'll go next," and reaching into the pile, she turned over the card of The High Priestess.

"Have you started meditating, Michelle?"

"How did you know?" she asked.

"This card suggests a tapping into the subconscious side of the self, and I just got a hit that you have started doing some kind of meditation or other spiritual discipline."

"I don't think I'm very good at it yet," she said. "But somehow it makes me feel better when I do it."

"And it's a very appropriate card for another reason," I said, "because the curtain behind the priestess has what look like pomegranates, but if you were to reconstruct the tapestry without the woman sitting in front of it, you'd see it's the Tree of Life."

"Oh, wow!" said Michelle. "And last time, when I was building the Tree of Life in the backyard, I got another card that had a sort of Tree of Life on it. Like I said then, this is actually kind of spooky! But good spooky, not scary spooky." She had included the last remark so as not to put anybody else off, I thought.

Penny agreed to go next and leaned forward to pull out the Seven of Swords, which showed a boatman poling a little skiff with two travelers.

"Well, I guess what's on your mind today is the trip you're already planning back to Australia. This card is about travel and looking forward to new possibilities. Of course, it would hardly take a psychic to tell you that, since it's what you and Reggie were talking about earlier."

"Oh, don't worry. I can't be critical since this *is* the thing I'm most concerned about," she said, "though I guess I would like to know if we'd be doing the right thing by going to Perth."

I suddenly had a spontaneous picture of her with two small children in tow, walking down the street holding the hands of both of these little people, so I said, "I also see you with a couple of children. Are you thinking about finally having kids?"

"What?" squawked Reggie. "How did you know that? We hadn't mentioned that to anybody."

Penny sat there for a moment, shaking her head. "Well, we're still in the thinking stages, but Reggie's accident and everything else that's happened did cause us to consider our mortality."

"You know," added Bernice, "the thought of death often brings on the desire to procreate, as a defense against dying."

"Maybe that's it," said Penny. "I just thought it might be my biological clock suddenly setting off its alarm."

She put the card back in the pile, and I stirred the cards again.

"Since you seem to be on a roll," said Reggie, "I guess I'll let you read me next." He pulled out a card and took a look at it, then winced before turning it over to me. "Ouch!" he said, and I saw as I reached for it that he'd picked the Death card.

"Not to worry," I soothed, "the Death card doesn't mean death at all. It's the card that implies a major transformation, though, so it may feel as if all the old parts of you are dying. But it's really a card that means you're going through some big changes and shifts in your thinking, and when you come out the other side, you'll be totally transformed."

"So this doesn't mean I'm going to die?"

"Nope, not at all," I said. "But it means you're going to *change*...in a major way!"

"If the Death card isn't death," asked Mike, "then is there a card in the deck that *does* mean death?"

"Yes," I said.

Nobody said anything for a few seconds, waiting for me to tell them which card it was. When I didn't, Mike spoke again. "And? Which one is it?"

I just smiled and shook my head. "I'm not going to say, yet, because even *that* card can mean other things, depending on what's most important for the person at the moment. In fact, there are no absolutes with respect to the Tarot cards. There are hints we can take, and what I see them as doing is giving our intuition a direction to follow that will bring up other images and ideas for someone who's tuning in to intuition."

I didn't want to mystify anybody, but likewise I didn't want anyone who might turn up the card of death to be too spooked. The synchronicities between what people were concerned with and what they were turning up in the cards were already quite clear and might seem a little uncanny to the less sophisticated.

As dim as the light was in the room, I saw John exchange a look with Clarice, and then he said, "I'm getting the impression these cards are very similar, at least in purpose, to what we call the I-Ching in our Chinese culture, where we throw bones or stones or coins and get information from where they fall with respect to each other."

"I haven't studied the I-Ching," I said, "but from what I've read about it, I'm aware the results are very similar. But that's true of casting the Runes of the Scandinavians as well, or any of a number of other ways of accessing the unconscious and learning to use our intuition."

"Well," said John, "I was making the connection as a means of talking myself into participating in the readings you're doing. So I guess it's my turn, although I have to tell you, you've exposed a side of yourself that's a little bit scary." He said this last very lightly, almost jokingly, but I thought there was a lot of truth to the remark.

So I said, "Okay, then, pick a card—any card."

And he did, turning over the Ace of Cups.

Though the light was dim, I tried to look directly at his eyes as I said, "You're starting a new relationship, John, a new love relationship." I smiled. "The potential is there for you to find exactly what you want in a woman. Good luck!"

"And you're saying this is what I'm thinking about?" he asked.

I grinned. "If it isn't, it should be."

Everybody laughed, and looking a little sheepish, he put the card back in the pile. Then he glanced at Clarice and nudged her slightly, so she said, "I'll go now."

She pulled a card and looked at it questioningly before handing it to me. It was the Queen of Cups.

"Well, my dear, Cups represent our heart energy, so you are the Queen of Hearts, the beautiful, desirable woman who is the ideal of most men. Goddess of love and beauty, dreamy, romantic, gentle hearted, and loving. And that's who you most desire to be at the moment. I hope you don't mind my telling this in the company of so many men. You may discover yourself getting lots of offers, at least from the unattached members of *this* group!"

I think Clarice was both pleased and embarrassed by this reading, which she clearly hadn't expected.

She said simply, "Thank you," and put the card back.

"Okay, Peter and Jamal, are you guys going to play, too?"

Jamal, who was sitting next to Bernice at the far end of the sofa, pushed himself up and leaned toward the pile. He reached for a card, then stopped, dug down under, and finally came up with one that seemed to satisfy him. He looked at it quizzically, then handed it to me.

"Seems appropriate," he muttered.

He had drawn the card of the Fool, which shows a young man walking along with his eyes on the heavens above and a little bag on a stick over his shoulder. A dog is yapping around his feet. And he's just about to step off a precipice.

"I think it really is perfect for you," I said, "especially since you love to imitate Peter Sellers in *Being There*. This is the card of unlimited potential. It's who we are before we've manifested all our talents. You're still connected to your divine origins, the holy part of yourself, and you have loads of untapped potential. Who knows, perhaps like the character in *Being There*, you, too, can walk on water."

Jamal grinned. "I like that!" he said emphatically, and leaned back in his seat.

"So, Peter," I said, "do you want to play?"

"Come on, Peter," said Mike encouragingly, "let's see what you *really* think."

"I'm not sure I want to," said Peter. "I'm sorry, but the church I was raised in sort of frowns on psychic stuff. I hope you don't mind."

To emphasize his rejection of having a reading, he pushed the whole pile of cards in my direction, but as he did so, the Nine of Swords flipped over, showing a woman sitting on a bed, her face buried in her hands in deep depression, with nine swords hanging in the air over her head.

I turned it back face down and gave Peter a big smile.

"I don't mind at all," I said. "And you don't have to worry about rejecting me—when it comes to other people's belief in my psychic ability, I have the hide of an elephant."

It didn't matter to me how anybody in the group might take what I'd just said, since I truly didn't want to say anything else—I just wanted to think. The card Peter had inadvertently drawn could represent his depression over the death of Daniel and his concern for his job now that Reggie and Penny were asking John to buy them out. But I wasn't convinced that was all it meant.

Before I put the cards away, I pulled one out for myself, though I didn't share it with anybody else. And it didn't surprise me when I pulled the Justice card, which shows a woman with a pair of balance scales and the sword of justice, for at the moment, all I wanted to do was weigh things. I wanted a chance to think through all the pieces to what I saw as the puzzle of John's bomb, Daniel's death, and Reggie's accident.

And now Peter had given me one more thing to ponder, for without consciously meaning to do so, he had just turned up the true death card in the deck.

Chapter Twenty

IT WAS NEARING ten o'clock by the time we'd finished the readings, and Bernice said it was definitely time for dessert. She dragged Penny with her into the kitchen, and they returned with a raspberry cheesecake and a large bowl of chocolate mousse, plus napkins, dessert plates, spoons, and forks.

When we were finished, I gathered all the plates, napkins, and utensils together and drew John into helping tidy the kitchen. I hadn't had a chance to talk to him privately since the morning of Daniel's death, and I wanted to be sure the air between us was clear.

As we walked into the kitchen together, he said in a conspiratorial voice, "The encounters between Madam X and Monsieur Y always seem overly melodramatic. Somehow, back when I met you, I pictured us in a black and white 1940s movie in exotic Paris, exchanging notes in the shadow of the *Arch of Triumph*."

"Another underrated movie! I think you're a little tall for Charles Boyer," I said, "though I appreciate being cast as Ingrid Bergman. Again!"

"And here we are again, Madam X, in the middle of a hurricane. How will we carry out our mission?"

"Well, since the generator is only connected to the refrigerators and freezers, I guess we can't run the dishwasher until the electricity comes back on. So how about I wash and you dry?"

"Sounds like a plan," he agreed.

As I began running water in the sink, I said, "The cards you and Clarice drew tonight echoed a dream I had a few days ago."

"Oh?" he said softly.

"You were Prince Charming, and she was Snow White—which seems appropriate, since she is truly the fairest of us all."

He was silent for a few moments. Then he said, "I've been a little embarrassed. And I was finding it hard to figure out what to say to you. I mean, you're the one who pointed out to me that I have beautiful cousins. I sort of...hadn't noticed. Clarice had been away for three years. We'd been friends before she went to Hong Kong, and we'd exchanged emails discussing cuisine while she was away. But working so closely with her this past week..." He left the rest of the explanation hanging.

"It's okay, you know. As you said, the relationship between us was melodramatic from the start. I think both of us may need something a little less tumultuous."

He looked at me gratefully, cuffed me gently on the arm, and dropped into his British accent. "Ah, my dear, you really are a *peach*!"

Less than a week ago, I'd seriously suspected John and Clarice of conspiring to murder Daniel and take over the Riviera kitchen. Their behavior today certainly hadn't seemed suspicious. On the other hand, nobody's behavior had seemed suspicious. In fact, in all my mulling over clues and contemplating elaborate scenarios, only one thing had really made sense—people usually take action for small, personal gains. And their motives are usually based on money, sex, or power. With John now in relationship with Clarice, and with the two of them currently running the Riviera and John about to become the sole owner there, all three motives still made John a possible suspect. I decided to keep an open mind—and to continue to suspect everybody!

While we were out of the living room, Penny started playing Bernice's piano, rendering what my dad would have called "honky-tonk tunes," though I got the impression her particular style was influenced by her Australian background. By the time John and I were finished in the kitchen, Bernice and Michelle were clamoring for some Broadway musical numbers, so we ran through a whole repertoire of show tunes.

The wind was keening furiously and rain was smashing against the windows. I was thinking it might be getting on toward time for bedding down this crowd, or at least assigning them some sleeping places, when Reggie said, "This reminds me of summer camp in my youth. Camp stew for supper, songs around the fire—the only thing missing is the ghost stories before bedtime, to scare the wits out of all the little campers!"

"How appropriate you should bring that up," said Bernice. "Just this week, Ariel got rid of my ghost for me. How about telling everybody about Annie Grace, Ariel?"

"Oh, this is rich," said Michelle, "Mom told us this story."

I smiled and began to relate the story of Annie Grace's murder by her master's son, concluding with the detail that her body had been buried in the back yard, where the Tree of Life now lay.

Michelle said, "I think this is so cool! But Mike and I have been talking about Annie Grace and wondering if there might be any records locally to confirm that she died and when it might have happened."

"Well, Bernice said she has records of the ownership papers going back to 1763, and that one of the owners had a similar sounding surname to the one Annie Grace told us."

Bernice added, "I haven't had a chance to look anything up yet, but Annie Grace was a slave, so her master may not have been subject at the time to reporting her death. She *was* property."

"However," Penny said, "it occurs to me you might find some record for the purchase of a replacement for her. That could perhaps give you the year the murder took place."

"Well," I said, "that would probably be the best way to proceed. Since Annie Grace has gone on, I'm pretty sure we won't get any more information from her."

"Do you really talk to ghosts?" asked Clarice. "I mean, *really*? How does the information come to you?"

"I think of it as talking, because sometimes I ask questions in my mind, and I immediately get answers. But in the case of Annie Grace, I wanted Bernice involved. Annie Grace had been trying unsuccessfully to talk to Bernice, so I had Bernice ask the questions, and the answers came *from* Annie Grace *through* me. I could hear the voice, but it felt as if I, Ariel, were sitting a little way off, out of the way and not in control, just watching it happen."

"That sounds uncomfortable," said Clarice. "I wouldn't want somebody else invading *my* mind."

"The important thing," I answered, "is not to judge what you're seeing or hearing while it's going on. That would be a sure way to cut off the flow of information. It's not easy, but being nonjudgmental with a spirit entity allows me to be more understanding of all people, whether they're in bodies or disincarnate. Because if judging cuts off the flow when one is talking to spirits, then it must also cut off the spiritual connection when one is talking face to face with a real, live person."

"That sounds deep," said Mike.

"But Ariel is right," agreed Bernice. "It's the way I work as a psychologist. I can't afford to judge any of my clients, or I won't be able to give them any help."

"The reason I was asking about talking to ghosts," said Clarice, "is that in Chinese culture, there's an annual celebration called the Festival of the Hungry Ghosts. People put out cakes and other things to placate the dead, who come from the underworld on that day. The Chinese people always honor the dead, but the ghosts who come for this celebration haven't been properly buried. And nobody wants to talk to them—we do all these elaborate things to make them go away!"

"That's really interesting!" I said. "I guess all cultures have their own versions of ghost stories, based pretty much on how they view the afterlife and what they think happens to consciousness after death. I know part of my belief comes from the fact that my own family has had so many experiences with what seem to be nonphysical entities, and we all wanted to know how and why we were experiencing things that so many other people discredit."

"I know the Aussies are big on ghosts," said Penny. "There's a paranormal sleuth organization that looks for all sorts of weird phenomena, and there are supposed to be many haunted places in Australia."

I looked around the group and saw that Jamal was smiling, so I asked, "What's your experience with the realm of ghosts, Jamal?"

"I am Egyptian, as most of you know," he said, "and though I've not had any experiences myself, my culture does have a long tradition going back to the time of the pharaohs about what happens to the spirit after the body dies. I am sure you all know of the *Egyptian Book of the Dead*. In ancient times, of course, the rich could have themselves mummified, and that was supposed to assist in moving them to an afterlife experience in which they would be judged by the Gods to determine if they would be allowed to live eternally in happiness. There was only one form of the spirit that went to the afterlife. It was called the *akh*.

"But there is also evidence the people believed in a ghost-like form of the dead person that hung around the tomb after death. It was called the *ka,* and people who tended the tomb would put out food for it near the embalmed body of the dead person, in case the *ka* got hungry. And then finally, there was a form of the spirit that could project out of the body and fly anywhere on the earth. And that form of spirit the ancient peoples called the *ba*. So, depending on the times, the writers, and perhaps what those around experienced, it would seem that various 'parts' of the dead person's spirit were thought to survive physical death."

"So," asked Penny, "you mean the writers from different periods may have believed different things about the spirit of the dead person?"

"Yes," said Jamal, "though there was never a time that I'm aware of when the ancient Egyptians didn't believe 'something,' call it soul or spirit, survived physical death."

"I studied some of this in my lit classes," I said. "Shakespeare loved to use the supernatural in his plays, you know, what with the witches and fairies and so forth. But several times he wrote plays where ghosts appear as characters. Anyway, I remember my professor saying that in Shakespeare's time, there were three ways of looking at a ghost: the Catholic view, the Protestant view, and the scientific view. And all these views are hinted at in *Hamlet* where the ghost of Hamlet's father appears in the first scene of the play."

"What were the differences between the three views?" Bernice asked.

"Well, as I recall, the Catholic view saw ghosts as tormented spirits who are in Purgatory, and who need to get some unfinished business taken care of before they can go on to their eternal rest. And usually they were believed to come back to impart information to the living, like how and why they were suffering, or where treasure or property was buried, or, as in the case of

Hamlet's father, who had killed them.

"But the Protestant view didn't allow for Purgatory, so Protestants saw ghosts as demons from hell, come back to seduce the living into committing sin. And they could use the likeness of the dead to work that seduction."

"Oh, wow," said Mike, "kind of like the First Evil on *Buffy, the Vampire Slayer*, where he could shape-shift into anybody who had died—including Buffy herself, because she had died twice, but been brought back to life!"

"Yes, it does sound something like that, doesn't it?" said Penny, though from her tone of voice, I was pretty sure she'd never seen an episode of *Buffy* and was just being agreeable.

"Anyway, in *Hamlet*, one of the reasons Hamlet finds it so hard to revenge his father's murder is that an 'honest' ghost wasn't supposed to want revenge. So there's always the lurking fear on Hamlet's part that the ghost may be a hell-spawned demon sent to lure him to his destruction.

"I also remember my professor saying that ghosts couldn't speak unless spoken to, and that to keep them under control, you had to talk to them in Latin or in palindromes."

"That sounds like an effort on the part of the Catholic Church to keep a finger on the pulse of the masses, who would need to call in the clergy if they had any encounters with ghosts!" said Bernice.

"Well, they would need to call either the clergy or scientists or scholars. In fact, one of the soldiers asks Horatio to speak to the ghost of Hamlet's father in the first scene of the play, because he's been studying in Wittenberg and knows Latin."

"So," Penny asked, "if the Catholics said a ghost was a spirit from Purgatory, and the Protestants said a ghost was a demon from Hell, what did the scientific view say?"

"Oh," I laughed, "the scientists said, '*What* ghost'?"

Everyone else laughed, too, after which Bernice added, "Rather like today, where it's still hard to get anyone in the scientific community to admit to out-of-body or near-death experiences, regardless of the evidence. For some reason, scientists would rather think the end is the end because they can't prove one way or the other in the laboratory that it isn't."

"And yet," I interjected, "there's a huge amount of evidence from ordinary people that consciousness continues. And those who attest to having had near death experiences come back to their conscious life changed."

"Yes, well," said Bernice, "the Catholic and Protestant Churches and the scientific community all wanted to control people's minds in Shakespeare's day, and it seems to me that part hasn't changed."

"You're probably right," I agreed. "In many circles, stories about ghosts might be met with disbelief and even downright anger. And yet, in any group in which I share my experiences, there are always those who have their own stories of strange things they've experienced, but they just don't feel secure enough to share them with other people, for fear of being ostracized."

"So you really believe the dead survive?" asked Peter, who had been silent to this point.

"I more than believe it," I assured him. "I trust my own senses—all six of them!—and for my part, I know consciousness continues. But not all of us become ghosts. Maybe what happens after death is that there are options, like with Jamal's three forms of spirit. Maybe some of us go straight to the afterworld, whatever that is, the Light, the Love, the Oneness, the Peace, or whatever it is people call what they experience in those near-death encounters. That would be like Jamal's Egyptian *akh*. And maybe some of us after death just hang around the place where we've been buried—a sort of ectoplasmic residue near the gravesite. There've been plenty of sightings of such visions over the centuries since people developed writing systems and started recording their experiences.

"In fact, the ancient Greeks believed there were four reasons why people might come back as ghosts rather than go on to the afterlife. First were those who'd died violently—battle dead, executed criminals, and the like, plus suicides and murder victims, who were the bitterest ghosts of this lot. Second were those who'd died before marrying—these ghosts could be either men or women, but women were thought to be particularly angry if they'd missed out on marriage and family—these were what defined women in that culture. The third group of ghosts was those who didn't get a proper burial and were therefore doomed to wander the earth for a hundred years. Finally, there were those who'd died an untimely death, who'd hang around because they didn't feel they'd finished what they came for.

"Maybe some of us don't linger near our burial site or go to the other side, but instead we hang around and strive for encounters with the living, where we can still interact and have an influence on those who are embodied. So maybe that's what the *ba* is. But now that Jamal and Penny have brought up so much interesting information about what people believed in other cultures and timeframes, I promise you I'm going to do some more research into these subjects!"

"Ghost stories told around the fire should be spo-o-o-oky and sca-a-a-ry!" said Mike in a quivering voice. "Haven't you ever had an experience with ghosts that scared you?"

"Mike's a horror freak," Michelle said by way of explanation for his question. "He wrote a vampire screenplay last year in his writing class."

I paused for a couple of seconds thinking about whether I wanted to share the one experience I'd had that had really scared me. For the most part, my encounters with those who had passed over but not necessarily on to another level had suggested they had unfinished business and wanted a flesh-and-bones person to take care of it. But I *had* had one very uncomfortable experience with a haunt that wanted to mess with my mind. After brief consideration, I decided to plunge ahead with that story. Maybe it would give a fuller view of ghosts and their capabilities.

"I did have one experience where I was initially scared," I said. "I don't know what the 'thing' was that scared me, but my sisters and I took to calling it 'the Dark Man.'" I gave a slight shudder. I decided if I was going to tell this story, I might as well make it good, so I changed my voice a little, as if I were telling a ghost story at a Girl Scout campfire.

"At the end of the summer when I enlisted in the army, on leave just after basic training, my sisters and I went on a trip with our grandparents up to Maine to a quiet, remote fishing village, where they'd rented a cottage for a couple of weeks. There were four bedrooms in the place, and because Bibi and I were the oldest, we had rooms to ourselves, while Catherine and Deirdre had to share a room. My room was in the back on the west side of the house.

"The first night we were there, I didn't sleep very well—all sorts of nightmares, which I'm not often given to. And the second night I was in a sort of hypnogogic state—lucid dreaming, I guess you'd say—when I began to have the impression there were *snakes* in my bed, writhing under and over and around me!"

"Yug!" exclaimed Michelle. "That would freak me out!"

"It was a nasty experience, but I knew it was a dream, and that I could put a stop to it. So I pulled myself together—sort of climbing back into three-dimensional consciousness, though it was a little like swimming through glue—and I sat up in bed. And then I had the distinct impression there was somebody else in the room with me."

I shuddered again, involuntarily. The experience really had frightened me.

"I hadn't turned on the lights yet, but when I opened my eyes, there was plenty of ambient light in the room—enough for me to see there was a dark figure sitting in the little rocking chair, rocking back and forth. I couldn't see any features, mind you, but I had the distinct impression of a smiling, gloating, toad of a man. And I *knew* he was the source of the nightmares and the snaky-things I'd just experienced."

"Ee-uww!" Michelle said. "What did you do?"

"Well, at first my stomach was in a knot, and I didn't seem to be able to move because I was tied down by the writhing snakes. And I couldn't speak at first because of the fear. But then the lack of power made me shift from fear to frustration, and suddenly my army training kicked in and I went from a desire for *flight* to a willingness to *fight*. I was in battle mode, really angry, and I said to him, 'You're not welcome here!' and I flipped on the light. Once the light was on, I couldn't see him anymore, but I decided not to stay in that room, so I went down the hall and made Bibi shove over in her bed. I don't know why, but for some reason I didn't think he'd come after me. And he didn't.

"The next day, I told my sisters all about the experience, and we did a little research on the house, the owners, and the 'Dark Man' in the west back bedroom.

"Though we never established who he might have been, we did collect another six stories from local residents, neighbors, and the daughters of the owners of the house, all documenting his habits. He tended to appear only to women, and usually he liked to mess with their minds and their dreams. In one instance, he lay down with a girl and tried to fondle her. In another episode, he lay down *on top* of a girl. All very dramatic and scary, and usually sexual. The scare tactics seemed to be his whole purpose—he liked to scare young women. I think that may have been what energized him—other people's fear!"

"Did you sleep in that room again?" asked Clarice.

"Actually, I did, but not before I got some help I thought I could trust. While we were asking around the town about the Dark Man, I got sent to a Native American woman—I don't know which tribe she was from, but I remember her name was Berta Whiterabbit. She told me how to clear a house of unwanted spirits. So I did what she suggested, and to test out whether it had worked, I tried sleeping in that room again. And I guess it must have worked; I didn't have any more nightmares or any more encounters with the Dark Man, and he didn't bother anybody else in the house while we were there."

"What did you have to do?" asked Michelle.

John intoned, "Enquiring minds want to know!" and the rest of the listeners also chimed in with, "Yeah, tell us!" and other murmurs of interest.

"I had to get the owners involved because Berta said the owner of a space has the right to rid it of unwanted guests. This seems to me to be a little bit like the idea that vampires can't come in unless you invite them, because it says a ghost has to go if you '*un*-invite' it.

"Anyway, the owner's wife was receptive to the idea of getting rid of the Dark Man—he'd bothered her and her girls and other guests for a long time, so don't ask me why she hadn't ever taken action on her own. But the key to the house clearing was to change the energy in the house, so the whole place had to be smudged with sage. And then we had to block all entrances and exits to keep the ghost from hiding in the house or from coming back in after we'd forced it out. We did the blocking by taping juniper branches over all the windows and doors and on all the mirrors."

"Why the mirrors?" asked Bernice.

"It seems to be a part of Native American tradition that ghosts can hide in mirrors. Frankly, I didn't ask, I just took it for granted that if this was a Native American ritual, and the mirror thing was part of Native American lore, we should do it.

"Anyway, two days after I'd had my experience with the Dark Man, the owner's wife, my grandmother, and all my sisters and I put up little snips of juniper everywhere in the house it seemed warranted, including the mail box in the front hall, the coal chute to the basement, and the doggie door in the kitchen.

"Then we started in the attic, burning sage smudges and sweeping all corners of the room with juniper branches, as Berta had told us to do, and saying, 'Shoo! Shoo! Shoo!' to tell any unwanted energies to go.

"And the final step, in case you ever want to do a house clearing yourself, is to sweep all these invisible energies to the front door, where the owner has to say, 'As owner of this house, I command all spirits, ghosts, and unwanted energies to go from this space and never return.' And then the participants sweep the energies out and put some juniper on the front door frame above the door, and close it.

"And just to be on the safe side, I visualized the Dark Man wrapped up in chains of light as we went, and in my mind I pictured him being marched down the stairs and out the front door like a prisoner, and while my sisters and the owner's wife were taping juniper over the front door, I saw the Dark Man being enveloped in a cloud of light and swirled away to another dimension, where he can clean up his act and stop having a desire to torment the living."

"But you didn't have to do anything like that with Annie Grace," said Bernice.

"No," I said, "but I think that's because she was trying to tell us something specific. Once she got our attention, I was able to communicate with her fairly easily—with your help, Bernice. Sometimes ghosts only haunt a person or place because they want to clear the record, or get an apology for what was done to them, or say goodbye. The extent of their haunting seems to range from little gentle nudges to full blown ectoplasmic manifestations, depending on their level of angst."

Peter leaned forward and asked intently, "What do you mean?"

"Well, from what I've read and experienced, some spirits, like Annie Grace, try to get your attention in a non-frightening manner. They don't have a harmful intention—they just want to communicate information. Others might want revenge of some sort and could create some very scary manifestations in the process. For instance, there's supposed to be a ghost in a house in D.C. that's a misogynist—he likes to push ladies downstairs. This is a house that's run by the National Park Service, but because of some actual incidents that have happened in that house, they don't allow women to go upstairs anymore."

"Good Lord," said Penny, "that's a rather drastic way of excluding women from your club!"

Reggie laughed. "You really don't like any form of chauvinism, do you, darling?"

"Definitely not, but I imagine it's rather hard to call a ghost to task."

"Exactly!" I said. "That's why I'm more interested in finding ways to help these disembodied spirits move on than in keeping them around as tourist attractions.

"Another case I heard of concerned a ghost that appeared to want revenge. Two partners out in California during the Gold Rush had a claim together, but when they struck gold, one of them killed the other with his shovel.

"It seems the murdered partner didn't take kindly to this and followed his killer around twenty-four seven tormenting him. He'd do simple things like whistling in his ear, poking him, tripping him up, things designed to annoy and frustrate. But occasionally the annoyances would be more intense, and the survivor would feel his face being slapped, or kicks or pricks, blows to his back, and other physical manifestations.

"The next level was when the survivor started experiencing poltergeist activity, with knives and other objects flying past him. When his panning equipment at the mine fell over on him, crushing his leg, he broke down and turned himself in to the local sheriff. According to the story, he said he'd rather be hanged than driven mad. And after he was hanged, the claim they'd discovered was turned over to the family of the murdered man and nobody ever heard of the ghost again."

"This story smacks of *The Treasure of Sierra Madre*," said John with a little smirk.

"I guess it does, at that," I said, "though in *The Treasure of Sierra Madre*, which is a retelling of *The Pardoner's Tale* out of Chaucer, there's no ghost. Death itself is the specter, and the guys kill each other off out of greed. But," I said smiling at him, "the idea I'm trying to get across is that revenge *can* be a motive among the dead just as it can motivate the living."

At just this point, the wind began to howl like a wounded animal, echoing through the fireplace, where the pile of burning logs sank in on itself with a spray of sparks and cinders. Almost instinctively we all glanced nervously at each other and huddled closer together.

Jamal said with a little shudder, "Woo-o-o, I've been thinking for the past hour that this is what it must have been like to be a cave man. Scary stories around the fire about saber-tooth tigers and giant lizards, and the wind howling mercilessly outside the cave entrance. Of course, my ancestors would have been experiencing sandstorms and flooding of the Nile, and jabbering about crocodiles and sand fleas. But the idea's the same. All of which is to say, I'm nervous!"

Bernice said wryly, "You may be right about our similarity tonight to cave dwellers, but I'd just as soon you didn't start painting pictures on the walls."

Mike turned to me with his eyes wide and a big grin on his face. "Do you remember, Ariel, when Mom suggested you might want to do your own show over at the Fairfax cable station? With your knowledge of ghosts, you really *should* become a producer. You could do interviews with people who have ghosts in their houses and maybe even with the ghosts themselves. It wouldn't be hard to get crew for a show like that."

I smiled at his enthusiasm. "But what if my guests don't show up on camera?"

He frowned and bit his upper lip. "We'll have to work on that," he said finally.

Michelle was nodding at the idea of a show, but unexpectedly she gave a broad yawn. "I'm tired," she announced. "I don't know about any of you, but Mom has a big kettle of water simmering on the wood stove, and I'm going to get some more hot chocolate. Then I'm going to find an unoccupied couch in this cave of ours and flake out for a few hours. I don't even want to think about the clean-up job we'll have to face in the yard once all this is over, much less how we're going to live without electricity. I expect there are lots of lines down, and as good as the power company is at keeping up with repairs, this isn't gonna be any small job. We're such soft creatures."

There were general murmurs of assent from the rest of the group, and Bernice, ever the consummate hostess, got up and addressed us all. "Mike and Michelle, dig out sleeping bags, pillows, and pillowcases for yourselves and the guys who'll be sleeping down here. Penny and Reggie, you take the master bedroom upstairs—you know which one it is, Penny, to the immediate right when you get upstairs, and it's already been freshly made up. Clarice, you can have the room two doors to the right of that. Mike and Michelle, you two use the front parlor, and the rest of you can bed down in here."

Then she billowed her way out to the kitchen, calling over her shoulder, "Hot chocolate and cookies in the kitchen for everyone in five minutes. You're all welcome to put your caftans back on as nighties if you like."

"Mom! Nobody would want to do that!" huffed Mike, rolling his eyes and stomping out of the room after Michelle.

In less than a minute Mike and Michelle came in again with pillows and sleeping bags for John, Peter, and Jamal and handed them around.

John turned with a bemused look and inquired, "Do you have any teddy bears?"

Once he'd gotten a grin from me, he playfully cuffed Peter and Jamal and motioned them over to the couches, indicating they should each take one of the two closest to the fire, while he selected the one furthest from the hearth. I watched as Peter sat down on the couch he'd been directed to—he seemed reluctant and somehow sad.

"Do you guys want the cookies and bedtime hot chocolate?" I asked, hoping to cheer him up a bit.

John and Jamal, who had been making up their beds, immediately headed for the offered goodies, but Peter shook his head.

"I think I'll just sack out now," he said and put his head on his pillow.

I thought again about the Tarot card he'd accidentally drawn—the Nine of Swords, a card showing a woman sitting on a bed, hands covering her face as if weeping. Over the grief-stricken person's head are nine swords, suspended horizontally, seemingly in thin air. It was a card of foreboding, suggesting deep depression and possibly death. Thinking about the swords spread out at the top of the card reminded me again of Daniel's knife roll, missing from the kitchen since before we had found Daniel's body, but discovered again today, hidden in Penny's desk.

Peter had found Daniel's body. Certainly he had seemed since that morning to be suffering grievously over Daniel's death. But I couldn't help wondering if he was responsible for the missing knife roll. And if he had moved it, was he also Daniel's poisoner?

I remembered, too, the vision I'd had at the wake, of Peter with a chef's knife in his hand. We now knew someone had cut Reggie's brake lines. Could that have been Peter?

On the other hand, the Nine of Swords was often a warning of one's own death or that of someone dear and the grieving that would follow such a loss. Was Reggie correct in his concern that someone was out to sabotage the restaurant? And if so, was Peter the next victim on the list? I couldn't get a clear impression, but I was more determined than ever to work through the clues with Bernice.

Chapter Twenty-One

AFTER ALL THE crew had retired to their respective nests, Bernice put the leftovers away and I washed up all the cups and cookie plates. As I hung the dishtowel up, I said to Bernice, "I'd really like to try putting everything that's been going on into perspective. So can I run a few ideas by you before we go to bed?"

"Certainly, my dear. Why don't you join me in my boudoir? Do you want more hot chocolate?"

"Maybe a cup of hot tea instead. Some of that Bengal Tiger stuff that tastes so spicy but won't add any more calories."

Bernice quickly made two cups of the chosen brew and dug two more cookies out of the jar, offering one to me. I waved it away, so she put them in the pocket of her caftan. Then handing me my own candle in a holder, she led me to the bedroom next to her downstairs office. It was a room I hadn't been in before, and it was as magnificent as the rest of the house. It had a king size bed with an Art Nouveau gilt headboard—it looked as though it should be titled *Peacock Fan Meets Rising Sun*. The rest of the furniture was also gilded, but looked French provincial in style.

She had five fairy tale prints on her walls, a couple of them by Arthur Rackham, and I couldn't resist wandering around the room and looking at them more closely by candlelight. I noticed they included the stories of *Cinderella, Sleeping Beauty, Beauty and the Beast, The Little Mermaid*, and one I didn't recognize.

"What's this story?" I asked.

"It's a Russian tale, called *Vasalisa, the Wise*. It's about a little girl whose mother has died, but whose spirit goes into a little doll she gives to Vasalisa, who carries it in her pocket. Whenever Vasalisa needs to get the point, or is about to make the wrong decision, the pocket doll will jump up and down in her pocket to get her attention and help her with the decision."

"That's a little like my Fat Man dreams, except I usually have to be asleep to get one of them, and I usually have to ponder what the message is. Sounds like Vasalisa has a pretty good deal with the pocket doll!"

"Yeah, we should all be so lucky as to have someone tap us on the shoulder when we're about to make the wrong decision! More often, it seems like it takes a two-by-four across the side of the head to get our attention! Anyway, the story is all about transformation through courage, and through listening to the wisdom of our intuition, which I think is the mothers and grandmothers within us. Vasalisa's wicked stepmother and stepsisters contrive to put out the fire in the hearth, and they send Vasalisa into the woods to the house of Baba Yaga, the witch, to get a new fire. Baba Yaga is a famous Russian witch, who lives in a house on chicken legs."

"Oh, I remember seeing a picture of it. It's one of the subjects of Mussorgsky's composition, *Pictures at an Exhibition*."

"That's right. Anyway, they're hoping the witch will eat the girl, but the doll in her pocket—her intuition—is her protection. And Baba Yaga tests her with all sorts of tasks, which the pocket doll helps her accomplish, and when she's ready the witch sends her back to her stepmother's cottage with the hearth fire in a skull on the top of a stick—which makes for a most unusual and scary lighting device. The stepmother and sisters see the skull coming, and it burns them to cinders, so Vasalisa is now the mistress of her own fate. It's a very powerful role model for women!"

"Wow! I'd guess so."

"I like Russian fairy tales—they don't end 'And they all lived happily ever after,' but rather, 'They all lived as happily as they could, until they died.' So they don't set you up for impossible expectations."

Bernice plumped up the vast array of pillows on her bed, then put three of them at the foot of the bed and patted them, inviting me to join her as she snuggled into those against the headboard.

I put my candle down next to hers on the bedside table, then climbed up and draped myself over the pillows she'd put down for me.

"Okay," I said softly, "it's time for some rational thinking, and I'd like your opinion on my deductions."

"Fire away."

"First of all, I think you should read this," I said. Reaching into my pocket, I pulled out the article I'd found earlier that day and handed it to Bernice. "I found it on the floor of the foyer near the coat pile this afternoon."

She read it and looked up at me.

"Reggie acknowledged that it's about the girl he was involved with. But he and Penny both told me it didn't belong to them. However, it's another piece of the puzzle, and I think it would be good if we tried to figure out how the pieces we have fit together.

"So," I said, "we now have four discrepancies, three incidents, two prophetic dreams—"

"—and a partridge in a pear tree?" finished Bernice with a glint in her eye.

I laughed. "Actually, it's 'one newspaper article.' But what I really want to focus on is Daniel's death. Even though neither John nor Reggie was seriously injured, all the incidents may well be connected. So if we focus on the death, and who might have caused it, we may solve *all* the mysteries."

"Okay," said Bernice. "Well, first of all, we both believe Daniel didn't die of natural causes."

"Yes," I mused, "and there are so many things I'm not comfortable with about the restaurant scene that morning. In addition, there are my Fat Man dreams about the truth being in the wine and there being too many cooks, not to mention all the other symbols in the second dream. I've had so many Fat Man encounters and dreams in my life that I have to trust my intuition—I know I'm not mistaken about this. Something was wrong with the wine at the scene of the crime. I think somebody had doctored it, but I don't have any sense of who or when."

Bernice nodded. "Go on."

"But there were other things about the scene that still bother me. Why was Daniel drinking Reggie's private stock? And there were two wine glasses at the scene. So who, if anybody, was drinking with Daniel? And who, or what, was Daniel drinking a toast to?

"Also, the fire was off under the sauté pan when we found the body. Who turned it off? Certainly not Daniel.

"Then Daniel's knives went missing before anybody found the body, and they turned up just this morning in a drawer in Penny's office. Who would have hidden them there? And was the person who had the second wine glass, who turned off the fire, and who hid the knives the same person who doctored the wine?"

"Maybe we're looking at several people," said Bernice. "All these oddities you've mentioned don't necessarily have to be the work of one person."

"I agree with that, but I'm trying to reduce the number of suspects logically to the most likely candidate. I did an exercise with Greg—Sergeant Mason—last Sunday. We looked at the key suspects from the perspective of a courtroom scenario. But too many people have a motive, and I still can't make all the clues fit in with any particular suspect.

"I think Daniel was poisoned by someone who wanted it to look like a heart attack. And I think whoever was responsible was in the kitchen sometime that morning. I'm just not sure that it was the same person who turned off the stove and hid the knives."

"Okay," said Bernice, "who do you see as possible suspects?"

"I guess everybody associated with the restaurant except maybe me," I smiled. "And thee, of course. And I guess I'd better include Mike, or his mom will beat me up."

"Well, then, let's make a list." She reached for a tablet and pen from her bedside table. "Let's take it from the top and just list everybody." And she started writing and slowly naming the possibilities: "Daniel...Reggie...Penny...John...Jamal...Roy...Peter...anybody else?"

"I can't think of anyone."

"Okay, let's consider each component in relation to each of these people." She carefully drew a grid on the page, with columns for the four discrepancies and John and Reggie's accidents, again naming them as she wrote: "Reggie's private stock...two glasses...stove turned off...knives hidden...Molotov cocktail...cut brakes...and...oh, yes, the newspaper article."

She turned the page in my direction for approval.

"Looks good," I said. "Oh, and we can add the onions not being burned, because that means somebody either was with Daniel or came in and found him shortly after he collapsed."

She dutifully added the onions.

"Okay, we can start with the Molotov cocktail, since that was the first incident, and it could have been heaved through the window by anybody except John, including Daniel."

"That's true," Bernice agreed. "And anybody could have cut Reggie's brakes, except Daniel."

This remark took me by surprise. "That may not be true," I said. "Reggie's car was on his trailer and had been there since his previous race, which occurred the weekend before you first took me to the restaurant. So Daniel might have cut the brakes, if he'd been so inclined and actually knew anything about cars."

"Oh, my God!" I exclaimed suddenly. "With everything that's happened this week, I totally forgot to mention a vision I had last Sunday at the end of the wake." I told Bernice about my image of Peter with a chef's knife. "And he left the party early. He just might be the one who cut the brakes."

"You're absolutely right," she said. "I'll change both these Xs to check marks." She did so with a flourish.

I said, "You realize we're no further ahead than when we started."

Bernice agreed, "True. But if you've ever done the kind of puzzle that involves using a grid, you know that if you follow the clues properly and logically, by the end you'll have eliminated all the suspects but one." She paused for a moment, then added, "Either that, or you know which person from which color house was wearing which color hat."

I looked at her and blinked.

"I like puzzle books," she said, by way of explanation.

"Okay, back to the restaurant kitchen," I said. "Let's go through the suspects and see who might have done what on the morning of Daniel's death."

Bernice hesitated for a moment. "Since Daniel was in the kitchen cooking and there were several deliveries that morning, the back door to the restaurant was open, and virtually anyone could have come in—even a total stranger."

"True," I said, "but why would a total stranger want to poison Daniel? If a street person came in looking for money, he'd be more likely to clobber him. And it just doesn't feel right."

"All right, then, let's start with Daniel," she said. "He could have gotten a bottle of Reggie's wine and two glasses. But he's not likely to have hidden his own knives or turned the stove off as he collapsed to the floor."

"Right," I said. "And that wasn't one of the things I saw him do while I was sharing his body. So who's next? John said there was a half bottle of wine left in the cooler from the last time Reggie'd had a race. So anybody could easily have tampered with it. Reggie could have brought it out, having poisoned it in order to get rid of Daniel. And he could have set up two glasses. And he could have turned off the stove, since he wouldn't want his restaurant to burn down. However, there'd have been no reason for him to hide the knives. So put a big question mark there."

She did, and then looked at me quizzically. "I can't think of anybody who'd have a reason to hide the knives."

I agreed, and she put question marks beside everybody's names in that column.

"As for turning off the stove, probably anyone who might have been a witness to the scene would have done that. So I'd better put a check mark by everybody's name in that column."

And again I nodded. Then I said, "However, it's unlikely that Jamal, Peter, or Roy would have brought out a bottle of Reggie's wine to have a drink with Daniel. So put an X by their names in that column; and put check marks for Reggie and Penny," and then I added, "and John."

She did as I suggested, but then she commented, "That doesn't, however, eliminate Jamal, Peter, or Roy from having put out two glasses, so everyone gets a check there. And actually, nobody can be eliminated as possible suspects for having poisoned the wine, so I'd better add a column for potential poisoners, and put a check mark beside everybody for that column. I mean, even Daniel could have poisoned the wine and done himself in." Then she said, "You know, maybe we should put in another column for who might want to get rid of Daniel."

"Okay," I agreed. "Motive should be a part of this. On all the TV shows the police look for motive, means, and opportunity. And our list at the moment is mostly opportunity."

"Well, then, I'll add *two* more columns," she said. "First, 'motive for killing Daniel.' Then, I guess if he was poisoned, somebody needed to have access to whatever the poison was, so we need the heading, 'access to poison.'"

"But without a lab report," I said, "it's going to be hard to figure out who that might be, and the police have said it'll be a while before they have any lab results."

I sighed. "Oh, gosh, it seems to me everybody had the opportunity, as we've already decided, since the back door was open. And who knows who might have had a motive to kill him? Except for Peter, who worshipped him. But at the memorial service, I really got the impression that everybody was sorry he was dead."

Then something clicked in my head. "You know, it occurred to me earlier this evening that Peter might be the one who hid the knives. He found Daniel, and he might have thought that Daniel's knives could have been stolen, or taken as evidence by the police, or some such thing. So he might have hidden them out of deference to Daniel. So put a circle around the question mark in his column, to indicate he might have hidden the knives."

Then I had another thought. "But that would mean he didn't come to tell us about Daniel's death right away."

"If that's true," said Bernice, "then consider this scenario. Suppose Daniel died, from either poison or natural causes, and Peter came in and found him lying on the floor. He'd know better than to touch anything, but he'd probably turn off the stove automatically. Then, if, as you suggested, he wanted to protect the knives, he could easily have rolled the case up and gone and hidden it in Penny's office before coming into the dining room."

"There's a time discrepancy, I think. Daniel had been dead about an hour, according to Greg Mason. And the onions in the sauté pan weren't burned, as they would have been if they'd been cooking for an hour. In fact, if they'd been cooking that long, the kitchen might have been full of smoke. So this would mean Peter had been there an hour before I came in with John. If he did what you suggested, he found Daniel, turned off the stove and hid the knives, and then left. Why would he do that?"

"Peter's very shy," said Bernice, "and a bit withdrawn. He knew you were coming in, so maybe he hoped you would find the body, and he wouldn't have to deal with the police."

"That's possible," I said. "You know, I met John at the restaurant that morning. He said he had driven up just before I did, and he came over and suggested we go in the front door, because he didn't want to encounter Daniel immediately, having had an unpleasant scene with him on Sunday night, according to his story to me."

"Well," said Bernice, "do you think John could have been there earlier than you thought? Could *he* be the one who set out the glasses and maybe tried to poison Daniel? Could John be the one who set everything up? Maybe the Molotov cocktail is totally unrelated and really was just an act of vandalism, as the police suggested. Or...could he have hired someone to throw the bottle through his kitchen window, so that you'd be there to witness it, and thereby make Daniel's death seem like the second in a series of attacks against the Riviera's owners? After all, John did stand to benefit from Daniel's death." She shook her head. "It's really unfortunate that *all* the restaurant owners stood to benefit from Daniel's death."

"You're right," I agreed, again pondering the possibility of John's culpability. "Well, I don't know if the attack with the Molotov cocktail was a set-up for my benefit. After all, I might *not* have gone to John's apartment with him after the banquet. But...I guess it's a possibility, isn't it?" Then I considered Bernice's other question about whether John might have been at the restaurant earlier than I thought. "And...when I pulled up in the parking lot for my interview with Daniel on Tuesday morning, John seemed to be getting out of his car. But maybe he wasn't getting out. Maybe he was getting back in. But remember his Tarot card from earlier tonight? He had the Ace of Cups, so he's a lover, just getting started on a new level of knowing how to love. And in his talks with me, he's shown a lot of understanding for Daniel's position and *seems* to have been able to take Daniel's comments as part of the comedy routine of the restaurant."

"Are you sure," asked Bernice pensively, "that the Ace of Cups doesn't suggest he's the one who doctored the wine?"

I was drawn up short by her question. "Well, I don't usually interpret the aces with any negativity. If he'd drawn the five, I'd have clearly thought it possible, because the fives generally suggest some unpleasantness. But the Ace is a card of new beginnings."

But Bernice had stirred my suspicions about John and Clarice again. And I wasn't entirely sure they were clear of blame. "I suppose you could be right. And the symbol could mean both things, I guess. He is beginning fresh, taking over the restaurant with his pretty cousin. To whom he is now clearly attracted. But people are paradoxical, aren't they? He could be a lover on the one hand, and a poisoner on the other. And Mike says John threatened Daniel with Clarice some weeks back, saying she could take Daniel's place. Hm-m-m." I shifted uncomfortably on the bed.

"If he is guilty, he's amazingly ingenuous. It's hard for me to see him chatting in the restaurant with me the way he did that morning if he'd known Daniel was lying dead on the floor behind us."

"You're right," Bernice agreed. "But we very often hear friends and neighbors say of serial killers or people who commit horrendous crimes that they were so well behaved and nice to everybody."

"And the problem is I like everybody at the restaurant. But in all likelihood, one of them is a killer."

"That *is* the problem, isn't it? So besides John, then, have we totally eliminated the other owners? What would you say about Reggie?"

"He was at his club from eight o'clock until John called him, which means he wasn't there when the ducks were delivered or when Daniel died. Greg Mason told me this last Sunday. He *had* been there earlier, though, so he could have put out the glasses, but he wasn't the one who turned off the stove or hid the knife roll. However, he could have cut his own brakes to make it look as if somebody was out to get him. And he could have hired someone to throw the Molotov cocktail, though heaven knows why he'd have done that."

"Okay," asked Bernice, "how does Penny look as a suspect?"

"Well, Penny was with you that morning. What time did she get here?"

"Actually, the detective who's on the case talked to me about the time she spent with me that morning. We started our session at eight thirty, but she had arrived at eight o'clock looking incredibly stylish and carrying a bag of baklava to go with our coffee." She sighed. "I remember this because I told her I tend to beware of clothes horses bearing Greek food."

I laughed, and it felt good to relieve a bit of the tension that was building as we reviewed all the aspects of the case.

"So that would seem to eliminate her from being the one who put out the two glasses and turned off the stove." I said. "And when I came in and told you about Daniel that afternoon, she really seemed shocked. However, that doesn't mean she didn't poison the wine. And if she had poisoned the wine, it would mean she intended it for Reggie. But the two of them seem pretty tight these days. I mean, that's why Daniel was threatening to leave, wasn't it, because she'd gone back to Reggie?"

Bernice sighed again. "I think we're running out of suspects. And this chart—and I hate to admit this because I love charts—has been absolutely no help at all. The only column left on the chart is the one about the article, and I don't see how it fits. I mean, who besides Penny, Reggie, and Daniel would have cared about Reggie's affair enough to be carrying around a newspaper article about the girl? And how could it relate to Daniel's death?"

I grimaced and shook my head wearily. "You know, maybe we *should* examine the possibility that somebody has been trying to sabotage the restaurant. In that case Reggie, Daniel, and John could *all* have been legitimate targets."

"Oh, no! Four more columns? I guess I could adjust the motive column on the chart to consider the possibility of sabotage. Even though I can't imagine who would want to do that, it *is* a distinct possibility. But adding more possible victims just confuses things further."

"Yes, it does. But Penny told Reggie and me something troubling while I was laying the fire. She said she discovered the gun they keep under the cash register at the restaurant was missing when she was packing up."

"That is troubling," Bernice agreed.

"And in thinking about sabotage of people who work at the restaurant, I meant to mention to you that Peter actually drew the true death card tonight, even though he did it involuntarily while pushing the deck away."

"Are you serious?"

"I am. And I've been debating warning him. He seemed spooked enough over the whole idea of Tarot cards and all the stories about ghosts tonight. I figured I could sleep on it and maybe talk to him tomorrow morning."

We sat quietly for a moment, finishing our tea. I gazed at the candles, letting the hypnotic effect of the flickering light help me empty my mind. Bernice was right, there were too many variables that either fit all the suspects or didn't fit any of them.

"Somehow, I feel we've got all the pieces," I said finally, as I got up from the bed. "But I don't think we've yet put them all together the right way."

"Probably not," she said. "Maybe we *should* sleep on it."

I nodded. "G'night."

Candle in one hand and cup in the other, I wandered back toward the kitchen. I could hear stentorian snores coming from the living room, so the still raging storm didn't seem to be keeping anybody awake. I put my candle down on the counter, rinsed out my cup in the sink, and on a whim, I stepped out onto the back porch.

The storm was coming from the south, so the north of the house was slightly sheltered and seemed almost calm, but the tops of the trees were flailing about. I could hear the wind, but everything was in darkness, though there still seemed to be some ambient light at a distance. Then suddenly, a flash of blue light lit up the horizon. I was quite startled, but when my eyes adjusted again, I realized the ambient light was gone. I had to assume the flash was a transformer exploding, and I realized how insignificant human technology was when it came up against the forces of nature.

Dennis and I used to watch thunderstorms together because it gave us a sense of being part of something more than ourselves. Whenever there was an exceedingly brilliant flash of lightning, Dennis would pull his fist down in a gesture of triumph and shout out, "Yea, God!"

And then, as always happened when I thought of Dennis, I thought of the flasher who'd been responsible for his death. I knew the guy hadn't intended to kill Dennis; he'd just been reacting to being cornered. But what made him want to flash women in the first place? What had pushed him over the edge into that kind of antisocial dysfunction? For the first time since Dennis died, I suddenly felt sorry for the flasher and whatever it was in his life that had distorted him.

Though I'd never gone to the prison where he was locked away, I saw him in my mind sitting in a cell, and I said, "I hope there's some way you can put the pieces of *your* life together and find some peace."

And again, I saw a blue flash of light as another transformer exploded.

In literature, authors often show nature mirroring the lives and emotions of their human characters, and critics say it's trite. But here I stood, watching the storm outside mirroring my own inner turmoil. So what was the message for me?

To nobody in particular, I said, "Nature has no conscience. But people are supposed to. So what makes somebody do crazy things, like the things that have been happening lately?"

I shivered involuntarily and slipped my hands into my pockets. That's when I felt the folded newspaper article I'd put back into my pocket after Bernice had read it. I went back into the kitchen, picked up my candle, and headed for the stairs, thinking about the article as I went, repeating the name "Elizabeth Wright" over and over in my mind.

When I got to my door, I reached for my keys to let myself in and only then remembered I'd given my key ring to John and Peter so they could go out to my car and get the paintings. All I had in my pocket was my room key. I'd have to remember to get the rest of the keys back tomorrow.

My eyes rested momentarily on the beautiful hex sign on my door as I slid the door key into the lock. Then as I turned it and heard the tumblers click, something clicked in my head as well. I felt as if I had a doll in my pocket, and it was jumping up and down. The name "Elizabeth Wright" fell into place with all the other clues I'd discussed with Bernice, and everything Michelle, Mike, and John had told me about the restaurant, as well as something Peter had said. "Elizabeth Wright," I whispered. "Right as rain."

I opened the door to my apartment and walked in, still pondering the inevitable conclusions to which I was now driven. But before I could turn and close the door, I felt myself being shoved further into the room, and the door was slammed shut and locked behind me.

Oh, you fool! I thought to myself.

Chapter Twenty-Two

I FELT POWERFUL emotions—fear, anger, frustration, guilt, despair. And none of these emotions were mine.

In the split second before I turned around, I realized that once again my army training was kicking in automatically, making me alert and prepared to deal with whatever contingency might occur. And I knew who was in the room with me.

Turning, I said, "Hello, Peter. Or should I call you Arthur?"

He stepped closer to me until I could see his face in the candlelight. He was holding a large chef's knife, which he raised and pointed at me as he walked forward.

"You have to take me to see him. I have to go see him. I have to find out if he knows. You have to take me. You talk to ghosts. You can talk to him."

Peter's eyes were focused somewhere beyond me, and I realized the topic of the evening had pushed him over some line known only to him.

"Are you talking about Daniel?"

"Yes, yes, Daniel." He seemed dissociated, almost as if he were a ghost himself. "I have to talk to him. I have to ask him about the poison."

"There's a hurricane going on out there, Peter. We can't go out now."

"We *have* to go now. Don't you see? If I wait, it might be too late. You have to go with me. You can talk to him."

I thought about my attempt to contact Daniel in the restaurant kitchen, and my not sensing him at the funeral. He simply wasn't lingering on this plane, but I weighed the advisability of saying this to a slightly deranged man with a large knife in his hand.

I thought it might actually be safer to play along with him until I could disarm him or otherwise change my disadvantage. I also thought it would be easier to learn the full story from him if I acted as though he were totally in charge.

"I don't know that I can find him in this weather, Peter. Spirits aren't that easy to detect even when the atmosphere is quiet and peaceful."

"But you know how to find ghosts. You found that Annie Grace. And the Dark Man. You can do it. And then I'll be able to tell him I didn't mean for it to harm him. He doesn't need to be stuck here on earth."

He gestured at me with the knife and said, "We've got to go. Now!"

"Let me get a coat," I said. "And you'd better have one, too. I have a spare one you can wear."

Without waiting for an answer, I put the candle down on the service bar in the kitchenette and turned to my coat closet. He followed close behind, and I had a moment of fear when I felt the point of the knife pushing into my back.

"Don't try anything," he said.

I took a deep breath, let it out slowly, and said, without moving, "You don't want to hurt me, Peter. You gave me the hex sign for protection."

"My hex signs don't work. Daniel is dead. I didn't protect him, did I?"

"I know you didn't want to hurt Daniel, and you don't want to hurt me, either. I know it was an accident with Daniel, and you don't want to have an accident with me. That would just make things worse. That would just leave you with another ghost to deal with."

He stepped back quickly and said, "No, no. I don't. No. Not that."

I pulled out the trench coat I had worn the day I'd gone to the restaurant to interview Daniel and carefully put it on. Then I reached back into the closet and found a windbreaker I thought would be big enough for Peter. Without turning around, I reached behind me, not wanting to startle him.

"Here," I said. "Put this on."

"Don't turn around until I tell you to," he warned. "I don't want to hurt you. I really don't want to hurt you. But you have to do this."

He rustled behind me for a few seconds as he put on the windbreaker. Then he said, "All right, you can turn around now."

"I need my car keys if you want me to drive you to the graveyard," I said.

He reached into his jeans pocket and pulled out my keys. He dropped them on the counter and backed away. I guess he thought if I got too close, I'd jump him. I picked up the keys and took a step toward the door to the hall. I hoped I might be able to get somebody's attention as we went out of the house, but he stopped me and gestured to the back staircase door.

"We'll go out this way," he said. Then he added, "Mike brought me up this staircase this morning when we put food in your refrigerator. Nobody will see us leave if we go out this way."

And I was sure he was right.

"May I blow out the candle before we leave? I don't want to start a fire."

"No, take it with you. We can use it to light the way downstairs. Then you can blow it out when we get outside."

"Okay," I said. I picked up the candle and went through the door to the narrow staircase, leading to the back yard.

I could hear the wind rattling the door at the foot of the stairs, and I knew this was an insane outing. But then, the person in charge wasn't totally sane at that moment, and I didn't have any choice but to go along.

The full blast of the storm hit as I opened the door, and the candle went out instantly. I dropped it on the grass, pulled the collar of my coat up, and plunged my hands into my pockets—and then I realized I had something better than a pocket doll in my right hand pocket.

Peter was still directly behind me, with the knife pointed at me as he pulled the door shut, and I was careful not to give away my excitement. For in my pocket was the little tape recorder I had taken to the restaurant to use in my interview with Daniel, which I had never taken out and put away. I had put fresh batteries in it the morning Daniel had died, and I was sure they were still good. I also had a one hundred twenty minute tape in it. As we walked through the rain down the driveway to my car, I switched it on. I was sure I could get Peter to talk to me about why and how he had poisoned the wine, and I knew it was probably my only chance to get all the information from him about this crime.

As we came up to the car, he pulled me up short.

"Get in on the passenger side," he said.

I did as he told me, still not wanting to argue with his knife. I opened the door and slid across into the driver's seat. He was right behind me and put the knife against my ribs.

"Just drive to the cemetery," he said.

I started the engine and began backing out of the driveway, turning the car in the direction of Old Town. We drove in silence for a while, then I thought of the tape recorder with its wheels turning in my pocket, and I decided to try to get Peter talking.

"I found the article about Elizabeth Wright this afternoon," I said. "She was your sister, wasn't she?"

"He ruined her. He ruined her life."

"Who did, Peter? Who ruined her?" I knew the answer, but I wanted him to say it for the record.

"Reggie. Reggie did. He didn't care about her. And he didn't care about me. He hired me for the restaurant, so I thought he was my friend. He told me I could change my name and get away from my parents. But he just wanted to get me out of the way because he knew I was protective of my little sister. He didn't care that she got pregnant. She was just a toy to him, like his stupid racecar. He just used her when Penny was away, and then when his wife came back, he threw Elizabeth away."

"Did he know she was pregnant?" I asked.

"She called him. But he never called back. She couldn't take that. So she told me everything when I was home at Christmas. She just didn't know what to do."

"Did she tell your parents? Wouldn't they help?"

"Our religion was very strict. My mother never would have forgiven her. She would have been thrown out of the house. Now my mother knows, because of the autopsy after she drowned, and she won't ever forgive her, even though Elizabeth is dead. So, no, she didn't tell. She couldn't."

"That's very sad," I said.

"It wasn't an accident, you know. Her death. She called me and told me she was going to do it."

"So you blame Reggie for her death?"

"Yes. He's responsible. He should have called her. He should have helped her. I wanted to make him pay. The Bible says, 'An eye for an eye.'"

"So what did you do?" I asked.

"All sorts of ideas went through my head. I even thought of burning the restaurant down. But then Daniel took me on as an apprentice and was really nice to me. And I knew I couldn't do anything to hurt *him*. So I really didn't know what to do. Then I think Penny and Daniel started an affair, and I figured it served Reggie right! But I also knew if Reggie ever found out, Daniel could be in trouble. So that's when I painted the hex sign for Daniel—so he could put it up in the kitchen for protection."

"You got something from your father's pharmacy, didn't you?"

"Yes," he said softly.

"What was it?"

"Ephedrine."

"You got it for Reggie, didn't you?"

"Yes."

And there it was, I thought, *the answer to the mystery*. It seemed that Peter had planned to kill Reggie by poisoning his wine, and Daniel had been the unintended victim.

"So," I said, finishing getting the details, "when you found him that morning, you realized right away what had happened."

"Yes." His voice was subdued, now that the truth was finally out to someone who was listening.

"When did you find him?"

Very softly, he said, "About an hour before you and John got to the restaurant. I think he'd just died a few minutes before."

"Are you the one who turned off the stove?" I asked.

"Yes."

"Did you hide Daniel's knives?"

"Yes," he said. "I didn't want anybody else to take them. I guess I wanted to protect them. I didn't want anybody to use his knives after he was dead."

"Did you want them?"

He seemed nonplussed by the idea. "NO!" he whined, "I didn't want them for myself. I just didn't want anybody to...use them. They were his."

"So, after you turned the stove off and hid the knives, where did you go?"

"I just took a walk through the park and along the water. I knew you and John were coming in soon, and I wanted John to find the body. I knew he'd take care of everything. When I got back, you and John were in the front of the restaurant, and I could tell you hadn't found him. There was music playing, and I could hear your voices, and they weren't upset. So I knew I had to tell you."

I'd been driving very slowly. The wind and rain made the going difficult, and a couple of times we hit patches of deep water that I thought might drown out the engine or cause us to lose braking power, but my dear old Jeep just kept chugging along. There were no lights on, and only one or two other cars were on the road. It really was spooky—a very wet city of the dead.

We were driving east on King Street toward the waterfront as I headed toward Bethel Cemetery. I turned south on Henry Street, then west on Gibbon until we reached the cemetery itself. There were no gates, and we were able to drive right in.

"He's in the Catholic part, isn't he?" asked Peter. "Go to the Catholic part."

"I'm...a little disoriented," I said. "I didn't drive here for Daniel's funeral, so I'm confused about where to go."

"You can find him," Peter said. "Use that psychic stuff."

I really couldn't remember where Daniel was in the cemetery. Greg had been driving, and we had been following a procession of cars, and there were so many small cemeteries within the larger one. I couldn't get a sense of anything, so I just stayed on the road and went as far as we could go. I knew I could be in trouble unless I helped Peter, but I had no clue as to where I might find Daniel's grave. So I hatched a creative plan.

I noticed a shed a little way down the road, and I pulled up beside it, leaving my headlights shining down the path. "There!" I said. "I think his grave is over there."

Peter peered out the window, but the rain was blowing really hard. "Where?" he said. "I don't see anything."

"I can feel Daniel. I'm sure he's over there!"

I opened my door and started to get out, but Peter grabbed my arm and held on tight.

"Come out this way," he said, "and stay close to me. I don't want to hurt you, but you have to help me talk to Daniel."

"I won't leave you," I said, sliding across to the passenger door as he tugged on my arm.

"No, I guess you won't."

The rain was beating on us horizontally, and the wind came close to knocking me over, so I headed to the side of the shed, where we could be somewhat sheltered by the overhang, and looked out into the cluster of gravestones to the right of the car.

"I'm really sorry, Peter," I said in a loud voice so he could hear me above the wind.

"Yeah," he said. "I think you are. Somehow, I don't think you're judging me, even though I've made lots of mistakes."

"I don't think you're a bad person, Peter. We all make mistakes."

This time he laughed a short, self-deprecatory snort. "Yeah! And I just can't get it right. I cut Reggie's brakes so he'd have an accident, and all he did was break his arm. And now he's leaving the country, and I'll probably never have another chance."

I thought for a moment, then asked, "What about John? How does he fit into all of this?"

"What do you mean?" He sounded genuinely puzzled.

"Why did you throw the Molotov cocktail into his kitchen?"

"No! *I* didn't do that! I don't have anything against John. Why would I want to hurt John?"

He was quiet for a few moments as we stood watching the wind blow the branches of the trees, then he added, "But I guess I can understand why you might think I did it. I just can't seem to do anything right. I couldn't protect Elizabeth, and I'm responsible for the death of the only person who ever took me seriously. But take me to Daniel so I can find out what I need to know."

I glanced at Peter and said, "It's hard to pick out Daniel. There are so many ghosts here. I think the storm has disturbed them. But try calling him."

He still held my arm tightly. "There are lots of ghosts?" he asked in a quavering voice. "How many ghosts are there?"

I looked out at the headstones and said, "We're in a graveyard, Peter. They're *everywhere*."

"I...didn't...I didn't...realize."

And then we heard a laugh. Not a ghostly laugh, but a definitely human laugh.

I turned, and in the lights from the car I saw Reggie stepping out of the darkness, a gun in his hand.

"Drop the knife, Peter," he ordered. Peter did as he was told.

"Well, aren't we a happy little group?" Reggie chuckled. "A sniveling little nobody and a busybody psychic who just couldn't keep her nose out of other people's business."

He walked up to Peter and poked him with the gun. "I should just shoot you right now," he said. "You cut the brake lining on my car, you little prick."

"You poisoned Daniel!" said Peter. "And you were responsible for my sister's death!"

I was confused. "Peter, didn't you tell me you got the ephedrine to poison Reggie? And that Daniel accidentally drank it?"

"No!" he yelled, still looking at Reggie. "I told you I got it *for* Reggie. He said he needed to lose weight. I *told* him to be careful, that too much might cause a heart attack. And he used the information I gave him to kill Daniel!"

"But you wouldn't have figured it out, would you, if Miss Busybody here hadn't thought there was something wrong with the wine? I figured I was home free when everybody thought he was sampling my private stock and had had a heart attack. But you had to make everybody suspicious. And you couldn't leave it alone. So I knew it was only a matter of time before Peter would figure it out."

I looked at Reggie. "I don't understand. Why did you kill Daniel?"

"He slept with my wife. And he was planning to ruin me. He was going to leave the restaurant. He knew we'd never be able to keep our customers without him, and he didn't care."

I realized that this was the first time I'd seen the real Reggie—every other time I'd talked to him he had been playing a role, and he was an excellent actor.

"But I have to thank you both. It was very convenient of the two people who might eventually finger me to leave the house together and come to a nice, secluded place."

"How did you know we were coming here?"

"The inside doors in the house aren't really very thick. It's quite easy to overhear a conversation if you're close enough—and listening. And Peter wasn't being very quiet in his demands. The rest is just like the story of *Little Red Riding Hood*—I took a shortcut and beat you to the shed."

He waved the gun dramatically. "And now comes the good part. A murder-suicide. Peter, you've realized that Ariel has found you out. You wanted to kill me, from a far-fetched belief that I had something to do with your sister's death, but you accidentally poisoned Daniel instead."

I winced as I realized that was exactly what I had thought. Some psychic I was!

Reggie continued. "You couldn't let Ariel expose you to the police, so you dragged her out here and shot her—with the gun you took from the restaurant when we were packing up. Then, filled with remorse, you shot yourself. That's what the police will say tomorrow—after I tell them that your father is a pharmacist, and the circumstances of your sister's death."

I had a sudden vision of Reggie as the one-armed bandit in my dream, claiming, "The odds are in our favor." And at that moment he was right.

In an attempt to distract him, I said, "You may not want to do that here, Reggie. We're surrounded by ghosts."

He snorted. "Don't give me any of that ghost crap. It's all right for parlor games, and for this wimp here, but I don't believe it!"

Suddenly a huge branch cracked right behind him and fell to the ground, causing him to jump and look around.

I kicked out toward the most visible target, his cast. He screamed in pain and grabbed his arm, and fell forward. I moved in and elbowed him on the side of his neck, grabbed the gun and knocked him down. I sat on his back, pinning him to the ground with one knee on the cast, and holding his other arm behind his back in a hammerlock.

"You bitch! You broke my arm again!" He continued to writhe in pain, but I had the advantage—and the gun.

"Peter," I ordered, "get my cell phone out of my glove compartment and speed-dial seven. That should connect you to Sergeant Mason. Tell him we need a police car out here right away. We have the person who murdered Daniel Lafayette."

A patrol car arrived within minutes, and the officers took custody of Reggie. They asked us to follow them to the station where we could give our statements.

Peter looked at me as we climbed into my jeep. "I would have turned myself in, you know, as soon as Reggie was dead. I wanted to come here tonight to get proof from Daniel that it was Reggie who had killed him. And then I was going to go back to the house and kill Reggie. I figured it was my last chance. I wanted Reggie to die to balance my sister's death.

"Peter," I said, "I really understand the need for balance. When you go to war, you have to believe that what you are doing is justified. And justification is the balance beam of the law. But now you don't have to kill Reggie. The law will deal with him and correct the balance."

Peter looked at me questioningly. "But how can we prove anything? The evidence does kind of point to me, doesn't it? Even you thought it did. It's our word against his."

I smiled, reached into my pocked and pulled out the tape recorder. "I think our word will be the one that's listened to. But I still have one more question. Did you put out the second wine glass?"

"Yes. I saw that Daniel had been drinking out of Reggie's bottle. I didn't want anybody to think, you know, that he was a thief or anything."

I nodded.

"Will you let me confess to cutting Reggie's brake line before you give them the tape? I think I'd better accept responsibility for that."

And I nodded again.

We followed the patrol car to the police station, which was very near, though it took us nearly twenty minutes to get there in the howling wind and rain. As I drove up to the parking lot, I saw the sheriff's deputy in his hut at the gate and rolled down my window to talk to him.

"What are you doing out in this storm, lady?"

"We're following them," I said, pointing to the two officers who were escorting Reggie into the station.

"And I have somebody here who wants to turn himself in for an attempted murder. I understand Sergeant Greg Mason is on duty tonight, so could you please tell him Ariel Quigley is here? And tell him I'm with Peter Smith, also known as Arthur Wright, who wants to confess to trying to kill Reggie Whitson, the man who has just been arrested for the murder of Daniel Lafayette."

GREG SHOWED UP with another officer, who accompanied Peter into the building. Then Greg waited for me while I parked my car and escorted me into an interrogation room, where he relieved me of my rain soaked coat and got me a blanket to wrap up in and a cup of coffee.

"Peter is with Flanagan right now," he said. "But I can take a preliminary statement from you."

I gave him my tape recorder, which we listened to together, and then I related an accounting of all the details of the evening, from my discussion with Bernice about all the clues in the case and our conclusions, to Peter's insistence that I take him to the cemetery to talk to Daniel, to the sudden appearance of Reggie and how I was able to disarm him.

Greg sat across the table from me as I gave my statement, shaking his head several times during my narrative.

"You've really got some moxie, girl," he said grinning. "And I guess you were right about the wine, right from the start. We'll be able to get that lab test done now—when the lab reopens. But tell me," he asked, "did you really see a lot of ghosts?"

"Oh, heavens, no," I said. "Only about four."

His eyes widened, and then he just laughed. His laugh was really nice, I thought, and sort of therapeutic.

"We could use you on the force," he said. "Your procedure was pretty nearly impeccable, considering you were being held at gun point." He shook his head again. "You got both Peter and Reggie to confess all the details, and you even got them to name their poison. That was cool thinking."

"Thanks," I said, smiling into those smoky gray eyes. "It all seemed to come together. I mean, I noticed all the discrepancies right at the start, and I did have the dream about the wine. So it was like something inside me was insisting I solve the puzzle. And I kept having clues given to me, like the newspaper clipping. Also, I was really fortunate the tape recorder was still in my pocket. But my thinking wasn't as cool as you might imagine. Reason told me it was Peter who had accidentally murdered Daniel. So I was surprised when Reggie turned up, prepared to kill us both." I gave a little self-deprecatory laugh. "I told you psychics were only right about eighty percent of the time."

"Well, that eighty percent is what solved this crime, and I have to tell you I'm impressed, particularly with the way you disarmed a dangerous felon in the middle of a tense situation."

"The army training kicks in when it's needed. And I had an advantage—he really was a one-armed bandit. I just aimed at the cast—it was definitely a more visible target than—well, you know what!"

Greg chuckled. "Go for the soft tissue—it'll put them down every time."

He got up from his chair and helped me out of mine. "Do you want me to drive you home in a cruiser?"

"No, I'll be okay. My Jeep's pretty reliable." I said.

"Then let me get someone to escort you," he insisted.

"That would be nice." I smiled again, and felt a warm and fuzzy feeling. Greg was a really nice guy. And for some reason, he was beginning to remind me of Jimmy Stewart.

I WAS EXHAUSTED. I really didn't want to talk to anybody, but when I got back to the house, everybody was in the living room waiting for me. In their varied night gear, with their wide eyes peering at me from the darkness of the candlelit room, they reminded me of the innocent audience on "The Muppet Show" from my childhood, totally unaware of what was coming next.

A barrage of questions greeted me.

"Where have you been?"

"Where's Reggie?"

"Where's Peter?"

"What happened?"

"What on earth were you doing out in this storm?"

Bernice finally stood up, held her hands up in front of her, and called a halt. "I called the police, because you were missing, and they said you were at the station house. Would you care to fill us in?"

"Hold your horses! Let me put on some dry clothes, and make me something hot to drink, please. I'll be with you in about five minutes."

I started up the stairs, and then my good sense kicked in. So I called back over my shoulder, "Bernice, would you mind coming up with me? I need some advice."

As soon as Bernice joined me on the stairs, I whispered, "If you wouldn't mind, whip up a quick cup of hot chocolate, and then get Penny. I need to talk to the two of you alone."

As soon as I got to my room, I stripped off all my damp clothing and grabbed a dry sweat suit. By the time Penny and Bernice arrived at the door with a cup of hot cocoa, I was dressed and ready to explain all the evening's events.

I asked them to sit down. "Penny," I began, "The only way to deliver bad news is straight out. Reggie has been arrested for the murder of Daniel. His jealousy of your relationship with Daniel, his insecurity over Daniel's expertise in the kitchen, and his anger at Daniel's threat of leaving pushed him over the edge. He had some ephedrine he'd been using to lose weight, and he overdosed a bottle of his wine, knowing that Daniel occasionally stole a glass, as a sort of revenge whenever Reggie irritated him. Then he must have said something to set Daniel off that morning before he went to the gym. I expect he'll be in prison for quite some time."

Penny's eyes filled with tears, and she looked from Bernice to me in shock. She stood up and slowly left the room.

Bernice jumped up, too. "I'm going to go with her."

"Before you go, there are a few more things you need to know to sort out all the twists and tangles. Peter did cut Reggie's brake line, and he's confessed to that. He's Elizabeth Wright's brother, and Reggie was the father of her unborn child. But Reggie tried to kill the two of us tonight because he thought we had stumbled onto the truth. Fortunately, his broken arm made him less of a threat than he might have been otherwise, and I was able to disarm him. I'll explain everything later, but you go now and be with Penny, and I'll go give everyone else the news."

Two hours later I finally climbed into my bed. I remembered Irene's warning on Wednesday night and the promise I'd made to Bibi to stay inside during the hurricane. I was pretty sure everybody in my family was going to be mad at me for my not heeding her warning.

"Oh, well," I said softly.

I crawled under my comforter and realized that in spite of the hurricane still blowing outside, I was more peaceful than I'd been since the Fat Man dream ten days earlier had signaled a coming crisis. I felt warm, cozy, and safe.

In seconds I was sound asleep.

The Chef Who Died Sautéing

Epilogue

Saturday, September 27th

On Saturday a week after Isabel's departure, I went with Bernice, the twins, and Alan, who had stayed the night with Bernice, to St. Mary's for the requiem mass for Daniel. Penny had left for Australia three days earlier, leaving Bernice in charge of the final arrangements with the priest for the mass. Many of the people who had been at the funeral and wake were also in attendance, along with others who had been unable to attend the burial. It wasn't so much a memorial for Daniel as it was an acknowledgement of his religious background and a ritual to mark his passing and to show deference to his sister Elyse.

As we came out of the church afterward, we paused to speak to John. Because Reggie was responsible for Daniel's death, there would be no insurance payment, and Penny had signed off on the restaurant in return for John assuming the mortgage. Old Town had been especially hard hit by the tide surge that followed Isabel, and the water level had reached the height of nearly five feet at the corner where the Riviera stood. John showed us pictures of the flood, including people canoeing on the streets.

Our sandbagging had helped quite a bit, and the Riviera had fared better than some of the other businesses in the area, but there had still been water damage to the carpet and some of the upholstery inside the building.

"We've already managed to replace the upholstery, and when we took up the waterlogged carpet, we discovered the floors underneath were hardwood and in pretty good shape. I've decided, as the soon-to-be-sole-owner, to sand and polish the floors rather than re-carpeting. But I still think I'll be ready to open again by next week—some of my uncle's contacts from Chinatown will be working with me over the weekend, and I expect they'll be wanting to come sometime Monday to get the art work and empty your freezers, Bernice."

"You are aware, aren't you," added Clarice, "that there's a jazz concert—'A Farewell to Isabel'—being hosted by the City of Alexandria. If you're planning to go to the concert, then come over to the restaurant afterward. We're working twenty-four seven to get things up to standard again. We've brought some goodies from Chinatown and the espresso machine is working, so we'll stop for a break when you get there."

Mike grinned and said, "Hey, Chinese take-out! You can count *me* in!"

WHEN BERNICE, ALAN, and the twins and I arrived at the Riviera after the concert, we found the French windows open, presumably to continue airing out the restaurant. John had set up a couple of tables in front of the windows, and he seated us there and started making the cappuccino. Clarice appeared with plates heaped with several varieties of Chinese delicacies, and we enjoyed a veritable feast.

Through a mouthful of oyster stew, Mike said to John, "Hey, boss, can I consider this my going away party?"

"Sure," said John, "except I hope you'll work another couple of weeks after we reopen. And even then, you aren't going very far away."

"What's this?" asked Alan. "What are you talking about?"

"John's been doing a lot of negotiating, Dad," said Mike. "In addition to buying the Riviera, he's starting a fulltime nepotism system here. The kid who came in to do the dishes during the reception after Daniel's funeral is another one of John's younger cousins, and he wants to give him a job. So he's going to pay me for the website I'm building, and he's also talked his Uncle Jimmy into having a website built. If word of this gets around, and they think I'm any good, which I am, we could be huge!

"Anyway, I'll get enough money from these two contracts to more than make up for not having to wash dishes anymore. And Ariel, I found that mentor you told me to look for. One of my graphic arts teachers this term has a website business, and he's agreed to mentor me and critique our work."

"That's great!" said Bernice. "Sounds like Ariel was right on the money with your reading, Mike. And I wanted to mention to you, Ariel, that what you saw for Penny was accurate as well. She called me last night to say she's staying with a cousin who has two little children, and she adores them. So those must have been the two children you saw with her in your reading for her." She paused and gave a little shake of her head. "I guess the only person who was wrong about psychic stuff was me—I totally misread Reggie when I saw him fencing and thought he wouldn't be devious enough to poison Daniel."

"Actually, that's not true, Bernice. You saw him fencing in a costume like a Shakespearean actor. And this morning I woke up thinking of *Hamlet*. In that play, there's a fencing match at the end of Act V where Laertes has poisoned the tip of his sword—and King Claudius has poisoned a cup of wine! You actually had the answer to the whole puzzle then, but we didn't see it because we were looking for a way to exonerate Reggie to make Penny feel better."

"Oh, my goodness!" said Bernice. "What I saw was another clue and we just misread it."

"I told Ariel you were psychic, Mom," said Mike.

Clarice smiled. "I think it was Lao Tse who said, 'The family that reads minds together stays together'—it rhymes in Chinese."

Everybody laughed, and John said grinning, "Wait a minute! *You're* the chef and *I'm* the comic. Let's keep lines of demarcation clean here."

I took a sip of my tea and realized that even without Reggie and Penny, the camaraderie of the restaurant would continue. Then it occurred to me that with Penny gone, Bernice's barter arrangement of "psychotherapy for food" would come to an end. But as if he were reading *my* thoughts, John said, "Listen, Bernice, Friday night wouldn't be the same without you at that table in the corner. Maybe we could make arrangements for you to work with various members of my family as a trade for dinners here."

He glanced over at Clarice, who nodded and added, "A lot of them are crazy."

John continued, "Seriously, though, we owe both of you so much for having solved the mystery of Daniel's death. That table is there for the two of you any Friday night you show up."

Clarice looked at me with a little frown and asked, "Ariel, I've been wondering since the night of the hurricane. I know you're psychic, and that you had a lot of dreams and insights that helped to solve the murder. How does that work? How did you finally put all the pieces together?"

"I didn't, really. I examined all the possibilities again and again, trying to make some rational sense of it all. But murder isn't rational. Bernice and I discussed all the clues the night of the hurricane party, but all we came up with was the realization that anyone could have done anything. I got another hit on the way to my room and knew there was danger. But before I could fully consider what it involved, Peter had me at knifepoint. Odd as it may seem, I was forced to be rational while I was doing something most people wouldn't think was a rational act at all—taking Peter to the cemetery to talk to Daniel's ghost, So I misunderstood everything Peter was saying to me, and this put us both in danger because I had missed the real threat—the missing gun." I shrugged. "I never did sort out all the tangles before Reggie showed up."

I paused for a moment, collecting my thoughts. "You know, my Fat Man dreams are often quite complex, and every Tarot card has layers and layers of meaning. I've come to the realization that if I'm going to use my psychic ability to any great extent in the real world, I need to look at those layers of complexity more fully. I don't mean through analyzing them rationally because that may lead me down the wrong path. I mean that I have to allow my intuition time to sort out all the pieces and then be very attentive to the answers I receive."

"It's pretty awesome," said Michelle, "being part of something like this. You never think of things like this happening to you. And Ariel, you're pretty awesome. It's so cool having our very own psychic detective in the family now."

And I realized these people—all of them—really *were* my extended family, and I got a little misty.

John said, "There's just one more thing. I guess there was no connection between Peter and Reggie and the bomb through the window at my place, was there?"

"No, there wasn't. But, you know, with everything else that's happened since, I totally forgot to mention to you that I did have an image at the time of two youths running away."

Alan raised his eyebrows and was about to speak when one of the serendipitous events that seem to run my life occurred. Greg Mason, in uniform, walked past the restaurant, saw us all sitting at the tables, and sauntered in. He nodded to Alan, and Alan nodded back, indicating to me they already knew each other.

"I hope I'm not disturbing you folks," said the sergeant, "but Detective Flanagan happened to mention to me just this morning that the lab has tested the wine and your chef's stomach contents for ephedrine with positive results. Detective Flanagan told me if I happened to encounter Ms. Quigley this afternoon at the jazz concert, I could pass the information along to her. He will be calling those of you who were involved in the investigation himself within the next couple of days, and I'm sure you'll be hearing from the Commonwealth's Attorney's office as well."

Alan glanced at me, then leaned forward and said, "I'm glad you stopped by, sergeant. I had been meaning to mention to you and Flanagan that I heard via the grapevine the D.C. police had two more complaints of beer bottle bombs in the last couple of weeks similar to the one Mr. Chan and Ms. Quigley experienced. They've picked up a couple of kids from a local gang, and their vandalism seems to have been racially motivated, with random bombings in Chinatown. It appears they chose you as a victim, John, just because your light was on. I'm sure you'll be hearing from the D.C. police any time now about their resolution of the case."

"Was there any damage in the other bombings?" asked John, who had shot me a strange look when Alan mentioned the two kids.

"No," said Alan, "the kids really didn't know what they were doing. They just got it into their heads to see how much mayhem they could cause."

"Kid stuff," said Greg, who shook his head and sighed. Then he turned to me.

"And Ms. Quigley—Ariel—you'll also be hearing from Detective Flanagan, with thanks for having helped close the books on the cases of Mr. Whitson's automobile accident and Mr. Lafayette's murder. The police had found out from the body shop on the Wednesday following the accident that the brake line had been cut, but in the preparations for the hurricane, nobody was available to follow up. You saved them a lot of leg work by bringing in Mr. Wright."

With that he excused himself again for interrupting us, and amidst all our statements of thanks for the information, he turned and left.

He'd been gone about five seconds when I suddenly remembered I'd left my tape recorder at the police station on the night of the hurricane.

"Excuse me," I said hurriedly to everyone at the table. "I just remembered something I need to ask the sergeant." And I ran out after him.

I called his name, and he stopped and turned.

"I left my tape recorder at the station last week."

He gave me a nice smile. "I've been meaning to call you and let you know we still have it, but this week has been pretty busy. If you'd like to come by tomorrow, I can have it ready for you."

"I have some plans tomorrow," I said, thinking about the stacks of student papers I had in my briefcase, "but I could probably come over in the late afternoon."

"I'm on duty until six p.m.," he said. "If you come by then, I could give it to you in person." Then he added, "If you're free, I'd be willing to change into some street clothes and take you out for a pizza."

"I'd like that," I said. "I'll see you at six o'clock."

As he turned and headed for his cruiser, I found myself watching him with interest and faint stirrings. I continued watching until he climbed into his police car and pulled away from the curb.

I thought to myself, *I'm more in touch with my abilities than I've ever been, I've just heard some great jazz and had some excellent Chinese food, and I have a new extended family.*

Then I smiled and added, *And I still have a hall pass.*

Honora Finkelstein has been an intelligence officer with the U. S. Navy, a small-press publisher, a technical writer, and a prize-winning features editor for Arundel Communications in Northern Virginia. She has been widely published in newspapers, magazines, and journals, has co-authored two nonfiction books, and has taught futurist and self-development workshops across the United States, in Canada, and in Europe. She is a member of Sisters in Crime, Romance Writers of America, Kiss of Death Chapter, and the International Women's Writing Guild; she was a workshop director for the latter organization for 15 years. She has a Ph.D. in English and is an adjunct associate professor in Western culture, literature, and writing at the University of Southern Indiana and the University of Evansville in Evansville, Indiana and the Union Institute & University in Cincinnati, Ohio.

Her interest in metaphysical subjects goes back to childhood when she had her first out-of-body experience while learning to tie her shoes. In the 1990s she produced and hosted a talk show on self-development and futurist topics called *Kaleidoscope for Tomorrow* on community cable television in Fairfax, Virginia, an experience that qualified her as an "agent provocateur." To the embarrassment of some of her more traditional friends and academic colleagues, she also does past life and Tarot card readings and occasionally talks to ghosts.

Susan Smily, during her 25 years in the classroom, was an author, publisher, and workshop leader in elementary science education in Canada, Australia, and the United States (acquiring a gray hair for every student she taught). She created her own business for the development and production of a wide range of elementary education materials, worked as a writer, editor, and consultant with several educational programs, and made presentations at over 40 school and district professional development days. She was also once the Science Teacher of the Year (cover girl) for Boreal Science Supply Catalogue and as a result had coffee stains on her face in every high school in Canada.

She is the author of "Pianissimo," a one-act play that was presented off Broadway on April 13-15, 1998, at the Festival of Collective Voices, at the Harold Clurman Theatre in New York.

She has traveled extensively in North America, Europe, Australia, and the Far East. She developed an interest in metaphysical studies in the early 1990s and has since become involved in studying many areas of spirituality, including Native American, Vedanta, and Kabbalah. She is also an energy reader and "psychic diagnostician."

Both Finkelstein and Smily are Reiki teacher-masters, interfaith ministers, certified hypnotherapists, and Hemi-Sync® outreach instructors for the Monroe Institute in Faber, Virginia. Referring to themselves as the "Jewish-Irish comedy team" (Smily is Jewish and Finkelstein is Irish), they are currently at work on their second Ariel Quigley mystery novel and a nonfiction book on ghosts.

Sources Consulted

Books:

American Heritage Cookbook & Illustrated History of American Eating and Drinking. American Heritage Publishing Co., Inc., 1964, for information about "Louisa May Alcott's Apple Slump," 568.

Fix, Wm. R. *Star Maps.* London: Octopus Book Ltd., 1979, for information on the star maps in Egyptian tombs.

Geberth, Vernon. *Practical Homicide Investigation: Tactics, Procedures, and Forensic Techniques,* Boca Raton: CRC Press, 1996.

Ions, Veronica. *Egyptian Mythology.* London: The Hamlyn Publishing Group Ltd., 1965, for information on the Egyptian afterlife.

Matacia, Louis J., Rev., B.S.T., L.S., and Ginette Matacia, P.I. Reg. VA, "Matacia's Treasure Soldiers," self-published monograph, for information on dowsing.

Miller, T. Michael. *Murder & Mayhem: Criminal Conduct in Old Alexandria, Virginia, 1749-1900.* Bowie, Maryland: Heritage Books, Inc., 1998, for information about Alexandria during the Civil War.

Ogden, Daniel. *Magic, Witchcraft, and Ghosts in the Greek and Roman Worlds.* New York: Oxford University Press, 2002, for information on categories of the restless dead in the ancient world, 148-151.

Web sites:

Cape Mentelle Winery, Western Australia, for descriptions of Cape Mentelle wines: http://www.capementelle.com.au/home_fr.html

Chinese Banquets, for information on balance in a Chinese banquet: www.welcome-to-china.com/china/cult/69p.htm

Virginia Department of Criminal Justice Services, for information on The Division of Forensic Science: www.dcjs.org

"Festival of the Hungry Ghosts," for information on Chinese ghosts and protection rituals: www.hostelscentral.com/hostels-article-100.html

Hsai, C.T. "The Chinese Sense of Humor." *Renditions,* from the Chinese University of Hong Kong: www.renditions.org/renditions/sps/s_9.html

Intercontinental Grand Stanford, Hong Kong, for Chinese menus: http://hongkong.meetings.intercontinental.com/ kowgra/weddings.html

Virginia General Assembly, Legislative Information System, for the Code of Virginia: http://legl.state.va.us

Vongerichten, Jean George, for information on Vong restaurants and the Mandarin Oriental Hotel, Hong Kong: http://www.starchefs.com/JGVong/html/index.shtml

Printed in the United States
59152LVS00003B/25-72